"I MUST WARN YOU . . ."

"Warn me! You dare to warn me? You popinjay—bastard son of an unknown father—you are less than nothing! Keep quiet while you still live!"

Chikara's words cut like a whiplash. Yoshi would not accept these insults without responding. He slapped Chikara across the face.

"Striking a warrior cannot be forgiven. I cannot allow this insult to go unpunished!" shouted Chikara.

"Consider the consequences!" answered Yoshi.

"Quiet, fool!" Chikara hissed.

"Are you ready? . . ."

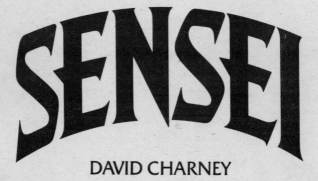

SENSEI

DAVID CHARNEY

ACE CHARTER BOOKS, NEW YORK

An Ace Charter Original

Published by arrangement with the author

ISBN: 0-441-75887-8

First Ace Charter Printing: January 1983

Published simultaneously in Canada

Manufactured in the United States of America

Ace Books, 200 Madison Avenue, New York, New York 10016

TO LOUISE
WHO SHOWED ME THE WAY

SENSEI

Preface

At the hour of the hare—six A.M.—on the tenth day in the fourth month of 1149, a palanquin borne on the shoulders of four bearers reached the base of the mountain behind the temple of Seiken-ji at the seaside town of Okitsu.

The morning light brought hazy definition to the tall pine trees that rimmed the road. A steady rain made the road mud-slippery. The bone-hard feet of the bearers splashed water with each step. Wet loin cloths slapped against the ridges of muscle that banded their thighs. The sound of their breathing blended with the drumming of rain and pounding of feet.

A muffled moan escaped from the palanquin and the bearers rolled their eyes and tried for more speed. The sky flickered with lightning followed by a bass rumble that rang across the valley to their left echoing back from Satta Mountain. The moans in the palanquin sharpened to screams of pain and exhortations to go faster.

One bearer stumbled, but quickly regained his footing. Lightning and thunder intensified, the rain beat flesh, trees, road, and palanquin equally.

An iron-bound gate loomed in the half-light. Its wooden side-supports rose to an ornately carved crosspiece. On each side, a rough stone and plaster wall disappeared into the darkness of the forest. The carving over the doorway announced the entrance to Okitsu Castle, home of the Tadamori clan.

A bearer grunted a signal; it was too much effort to talk. The sentry opened the gate and ran out, hand on sword. He peered into the palanquin. Color drained from his cheeks. "Hurry," he shouted. "Bring them to the house."

He ran awkwardly ahead of the bearers to warn the household. His robe was held in one hand to keep it from dragging in the mud. He would have been comical if it were not for the expression on his face. The woman in the palanquin! It could mean the sentry's life if anything happened to her while the palanquin was in his jurisdiction. He stumbled up the stairs to the main entrance of the castle and frantically unlatched the bolts that barred the way.

"Lord Fumio!" His voice was an almost feminine shriek. "Lord Fumio, it is Lady Masaka." The thunder outside and the steady screaming from the palanquin almost drowned him out.

In seconds, the castle was awake with figures scurrying from room to room. Doors slid open before the bearers.

"In here, quickly." The voice was one accustomed to command. Lord Tadamori-no-Fumio motioned to the bearers from the doorway.

They gently laid the palanquin down. Fumio opened the hangings, exposing his cousin who writhed in agony while her maid held her hand and tried to calm her with murmurs of sympathy. Without looking away Fumio motioned over his shoulder to an aide. "Pay the bearers. Pay them well," he said, and signaled the bearers and aides to leave with his cousin's maid.

Lady Masaka was half-hidden by a quilt that covered her swollen abdomen. In spite of the labor pains that distorted her features, she was obviously a beautiful woman. The wide sleeves of her plum-colored kimono accentuated slim arms, and though most of her makeup was gone, the softly painted brows over her almond eyes, the tiny nose, and soft chin would have placed her in the forefront of any group of noble ladies. Her hair was loose from where it had been combed in a straight waterfall of black; yet even with unkempt hair her appearance was regal.

Lord Fumio had felt it a mistake to send one so young and inexperienced to the court in Kyoto but she had overruled his wise counsel. Now he saw the result. Undoubtedly the goodness and trust that so often motivated her had brought her to this unfortunate moment.

"Why did you wait so long, dear cousin?" he whispered as he rolled her onto a clean pallet.

She grimaced in pain, turning her features ugly. "Let me die. I was mad to come here."

"No, no." He patted damp strands of hair from her face. "You were right to come. I'm glad."

Her body tensed and sweat dewed her ashen skin. It was coming! Coming after all these months of stress. How many times had she wished she were dead, dreading the birth of this unwanted child? Thank Buddha for this last place of sanctuary. Fumio was right—she should not have gone to the capital. She sobbed with more than the physical pain of the approaching birth.

Lord Fumio held her hand firmly. He called for the peasant midwife. She was already prepared, waiting behind a screen with soft cotton cloths in one hand and a bucket of hot water in the other.

"Who was the father, Masaka? Tell me and I'll kill him."

"No, Fumio, please." She bit her lip. "There was no one. The baby came from a dream. It is supernatural, a gift from Amaterasu!"

Fumio was incredulous. He released Masaka's hand and rose to his feet. The midwife took his place while Fumio walked to the other side of the screen. He bowed his head thinking over what Masaka had said. He was a man of the world, but . . . He listened to the thunder and felt the rain shake the walls of the castle. Could such things be? Impossible! She must think him a fool to expect him to believe such peasant nonsense. Still . . . they had grown up together. She was the daughter of his father's brother and entitled to the protection of the castle. True or not, he would have to believe her story. Nothing else was acceptable, though he couldn't imagine why she refused to name the father. Could he have been a commoner whom she wanted to protect? On the whole, Fumio preferred the supernatural version. His hand sought the hilt of his sword. Woe to anyone who questioned Lady Masaka or Lord Fumio in this castle.

At that moment, the cry of a newborn baby cut through the rumble of thunder. The midwife called, "It's a boy! An angel. Look at him."

Fumio turned. He saw Masaka stretched out still and pale, a smile of relief and pride touching the corners of her mouth. The midwife held the baby up for him to see. Thunder roared, and lightning flared through the wood-lattice walls. The baby wailed like an ancestral spirit.

PART ONE

One

===

Isao frowned unhappily at his meager bowl of gruel. "We can wait no longer," he said, putting the bowl on the dirt floor of his hut. "Dress the children. It is time to leave."

Shinobu fluttered her hands. "What is to become of us?" she cried putting her own bowl aside. "Is there no way we can settle our debts and not have to leave our home? Poor as it is, it is all we have."

Isao was already busy wrapping his thin body in a threadbare robe. "We've talked about it long enough. Foolish woman. If you want to live to greet tomorrow's dawn, hurry and get the children ready."

The couple's two children huddled in one corner of the strawroofed hut on a bed of worn matting. Tears tracked their doll-like faces. The boy, Mutsu, was only four years old, the girl, Akika, was five. They did not understand why they were being bundled out of bed with hardly any breakfast.

Isao and Shinobu were little more than children themselves. They had married at fifteen and had struggled for the past six years to make their plot of ground support themselves, their children, and the tax collectors of Lord Chikara, their master. For farmers like Isao, the mountainous land and the climate left much to be desired; the warm season was short, and at various times throughout the year the land was subject to rain storms, typhoons, and earthquakes. In the spring, small streams turned into raging torrents that washed out crops and destroyed delicate seedlings. Summer often brought drought to burn the crops that survived the rain.

The rice and grain had sufficed until last year when Shinobu's father fell sick and Isao used the grain to pay a local healer. Despite every effort, the old man died, but not before the grain store was depleted and nothing was left for the tax collectors.

Tomorrow, Lord Chikara's bailiff would come for his share of the crop. There was no excuse for nonpayment!

Shinobu's hands trembled as she tied the children's robes in place. Her round face was set in a tragic mask.

"I'm still hungry," wailed Mutsu.

"Me, too," echoed Akika.

Shinobu gave them each a half of her own scanty bowl and watched tearfully as their chopsticks flew to their mouths. They gulped the gruel hungrily.

"Hurry, or we'll never eat another meal in this world," said Isao. His pinched face with its gaunt cheekbones and deep-set eyes could have been any age; the work and worry of the last few years had left him an old man at twenty-one. His sleeveless robe exposed arms roped with blue veins and wiry muscles. The easy smile of youth was gone, leaving a perpetual frown of discontent, weariness, and strain.

"Come, children," said Shinobu. "We leave at once."

"Can I take my doll, mama?" asked Akika.

"Yes, but hurry child," she answered. She turned to Isao who was anxiously looking out from under the cloth hanging that served as a door. "We're coming. We're coming," she said placatingly.

Isao held the cloth to one side and half pushed Shinobu and the children out.

"We should have left yesterday," he said, nervously sucking in his breath. "I was mad to let you talk me into waiting."

"It was an inauspicious day. We could not leave when the signs were wrong."

"I hope you are right. If your priest cannot help us now, we are truly lost, auspicious day or not."

Shinobu hurried down the dirt road to the edge of the forest. She was confident that she had decided wisely. To have started their journey on an inauspicious day would have doomed the family to failure. "The priest will help us," she said over her shoulder. "He is a good man. A thousand times he has told us he hates the landowners who use us so badly. He will help. I am sure of it."

In spite of the morning sun that shone on their one *cho*—three acres—of cultivated land, the forest was dark and cool. Only specks of sunlight filtered through the trees. Gnarled roots and dense thicket made the route difficult, and time after time Isao had to back away from an obstacle and go around it, often carrying the children on his back.

"Are you sure we are going in the right direction?" asked Shinobu hesitantly as they made a wide detour around a fallen tree.

"Leave that to me. We will cut across to the road from Okitsu Castle, then follow it down the mountain to the temple. If you are right and the priest is waiting, we will be safe there."

"Amida Buddha will protect us," said Shinobu as she herded the children ahead of her.

It was late in the afternoon before the family broke out of the woods near the south gate of the castle. They hid along the edges of the road as they worked their way down the mountain, covering the two miles from the castle gate to the sanctuary of the Seiken-ji temple. As they drew closer they could see its red-tiled roofs above the pine forest; the front yard was overgrown with vegetation, its walls dark and weathered with age, yet it looked like the Western Paradise to the frightened, hungry family. When work parties passed them on the road, Isao pressed his wife and children back into the forest and waited for the passersby to disappear from sight.

At the hour of the bird—six P.M.—they were in sight of the temple gate.

"We will wait till nightfall," said Isao, a dark vein throbbing in his forehead.

"The children are hungry," wailed Shinobu. "We have to bring them in and feed them."

"We are all hungry. But if we are to see tomorrow, we must overcome our weakness. When we are far from here, when Lord Chikara's men can no longer reach us, then we will eat and sleep and laugh. Till then we must be strong."

He picked up the children, hugged them to his ragged cloak, and rubbed his gaunt cheeks against theirs. "They understand, Shinobu. They understand we love them and it is for their sake we suffer now."

"Isao, you are wise. We listen bravely and try to follow your example. If only I had not given all our crop to the healers. How different it would have been. This is all my fault."

"Never, dear wife. Together we made the decision to help your father. We cannot regret it now. What is done is done. We will wait for the night." He looked away so Shinobu could not see his expression. It was easy to talk of no regrets but he felt a cold presence deep in his stomach, a foreboding. Would any of them see another day?

Two

==

As Isao, Shinobu, and their children trembled in the woods an oxcart lumbered past on its way up the mountain. The highbacked cart was decorated with gold leaf over a bamboo latticework body. Its single passenger stared languidly at the forest through blinds that covered the back. The scenery bored him.

Tadamori-no-Yoshi patted his top-knot and made himself lean back and relax as he cooled himself with a scented fan. He was almost home after a bone-rattling trip from the Imperial capital of Kyoto, over two hundred miles of rutted, stone-filled roads. It would have been more comfortable traveling by horse or carried by bearers, but that would have been beneath the dignity of a young nobleman returning from the capital for the unwelcome wedding of his favorite cousin. Thinking of the wedding, his brow creased slightly in displeasure and he made a conscious effort to smooth it. It would not do to mar his white makeup. He shifted to avoid wrinkling his over-robe of magenta with dusty rose flower patterns and his soft pink under-robe. Carefully brushing the cloak where it had rested on the side of the cart, he reminisced about a more pleasant subject, his last visit to Okitsu, three years ago, and the days he had spent with cousin Nami.

An idyllic period! Sixteen-year-old Yoshi fresh from three years in Kyoto and fourteen-year-old Nami just coming into her own. The two of them had been thrown together for an entire summer, left to themselves while Yoshi's older cousins and the adults were busy with their own affairs. The summer had been spent in lazy talk. They had both been embarrassed and formal at first, but as time passed they opened to each other like wisteria blossoms after a spring rain. From stories of Yoshi's adventures in the Confucian school and Nami's readings from popular romances, they progressed to writing each other subtle poems mixing naïveté and budding sensuality. From Yoshi's self-conscious braggadocio about minor triumphs in perfume-smelling and poetry-reading competitions, he went on to confess his private doubts and insecurities while Nami left behind her romances and poetry to tell him of the writings in her pillow-book—the most intimate diary a girl could have.

Neither Yoshi's nor Nami's confessions contained much of substance. Yoshi's first three years in Kyoto had been devoted to studying and trying to gain acceptance from the courtiers around him. As he had told Nami: "I am in agony when the other courtiers make fun of me. Is it my fault I arrived at the court so late? Buddha! I was already thirteen the first time I saw Kyoto. Most of the other boys were born there. I am the only one who arrived later than the age of ten or eleven. If only—"

"Dear Yoshi, you must not be upset. I find you extremely sophisticated and knowledgeable. You speak with the accent of the court. No one would guess you had only been there three years." Nami had put a tiny hand on Yoshi's sleeve to reassure him. He had tingled at the touch but would not allow himself to be placated.

"No," he had said. "To them I am a country bumpkin. I try so hard, yet they do not accept me. Winning court competitions is not enough, wearing the latest fashions is not enough. I do everything expected of me, but nothing satisfies them. Why could not uncle have had more power in the court? Why did I have to be the oldest student to enroll at the Confucian school?''

"But, Yoshi, you are sixteen. Surely someone as old and as sophisticated as you should not feel rejected. You must give the courtiers more time. Before you realize it, you will be one of them." Another touch, another tingle.

"I wish it were so. Anyway, I am pleased we are able to speak to each other so freely. I have never confessed these secrets to anyone and I feel relieved to be able to tell you about them." And, in truth, Yoshi had not felt so at ease since he originally left Okitsu. He was able to relax and put aside the facade of weary worldliness he usually wore.

"Yoshi, do you like the way my hair falls?" Nami had changed the subject, ready for her own confession.

"It is exquisite. I cannot imagine hair of finer texture."

"But don't you think Yuriko, the cook's daughter, has longer hair?"

"Perhaps longer, but not as shiny . . . not as fine."

"Oh, Yoshi. I am torn by the most painful spasms of jealousy when I see her hair. It *is* longer than mine and I hate myself for being jealous and I hate her for having longer hair. Do you think me despicable for being jealous?"

"How could I ever think that?"

"Oh, Yoshi, you are teasing me. I have just confessed to a heinous sin. Jealousy! And you make fun. You are not being very nice." Nami had stamped her foot and looked at Yoshi crossly.

"Forgive me, Nami. I did not mean to make fun of you. I understand the secret you confided in me and I admire the honesty that let you bring it in the open. You have no cause for jealousy. Your hair is much more beautiful than Yuriko's." And Yoshi had reached out tentatively to touch her arm.

Nami's confessions would have caused excruciating boredom to an outsider, but to Yoshi they had been revelations of her inner self and they had made him ache to hold her in his arms and declare his love.

Nami, without friends her age, had taken full advantage of her effect on Yoshi, focusing all her charms and venting all her frustrations on him. In short, she had used him shamefully.

It had been the most satisfying summer of love-struck Yoshi's life and he told himself he would love Nami forever.

Yoshi's fan waved indolently as he savored the memory of her slim, young arms and her smooth ivory skin. Lovely! Dainty!

How surprised she would be to see how worldly he had become. Three additional years of refinement and of style. She would surely be impressed when she saw his costly clothing, and not just for the cost, but for the sensitivity of the colors and patterns. And how she would also be impressed by his speech, his manner, and his heightened command of poetry. Despite his sophisticated life in Kyoto, Yoshi had not given up his simple youthful infatuation. He had taken it for granted that someday he would. . . . No, he had not declared himself, but he had always expected Nami to wait for him. Now, when Nami saw him, she would love him as much as he loved her. They would exchange poems, confidences, and finally vows of love. The corner of his mouth twitched in a smile that quickly faded . . . of course it would be impossible. He was daydreaming again. Nami would soon be married and would be surrounded by family and friends.

The crushing weight of reality after his high-flown fantasy was almost as distressing as the shock he had received on reading the announcement of Nami's impending wedding to a powerful neighbor. Jealousy and disappointment had almost made him lose the control he had spent so much time and effort developing. A total of six years at the Confucian school and the court of the Taira rulers. If the court had taught Yoshi nothing else, it had taught him the importance of maintaining a cool exterior. When he had received the wedding announcement, he had decided he would put a good face on it and conceal his feelings. Now, he waved his scented fan lethargically and made himself forget the coming ceremony.

Yoshi's thoughts turned to the unpleasant encounter that

would soon face him. Nami's brother, Ietaka, would undoubtedly be at the castle. How to handle his relationship
with Ietaka? Ietaka was a boor and Yoshi had never understood why so many people liked him. All he cared about was
politics, peasants, and all manner of things no loyal member
of the court should be involved with. Ietaka lived in Kyoto,
not far from Yoshi, but they avoided each other. Where
Yoshi was eager to embrace the world of the court, Ietaka
was—by Yoshi's lights—twisted and antisocial, refusing to
recognize the importance of proper court behavior; Yoshi
was convinced that his distressing attitude was due to an
unfortunate childhood experience. At the age of eleven,
Ietaka had been kidnapped by bandits and sold into slavery to
a Taira bailiff. For six years, from the age of eleven to
seventeen, he had been a slave on an island plantation. The
family had given him up for lost, but, as if by a miracle, he
escaped and found his way back to Okitsu in the year before
Yoshi's last visit. While Yoshi and Nami were exploring
their "eternal love," Ietaka had been making a nuisance of
himself with Uncle Fumio.

Ietaka had developed a profound hatred for the court of the
ruling Taira family and a distrust for anyone who accepted
them. He considered Yoshi an irresponsible gadfly and Yoshi
knew it. "Poof," thought Yoshi. He might be a gadfly but he
was a loyal supporter of his divine majesty, the Emperor of
Japan, and that was what really mattered.

Yoshi put Ietaka out of his mind. There would be others
waiting: his mother, Lady Masaka, and his uncle, Lord
Fumio, both of whom he loved and respected. His cousin,
Sanemoto, who had been like an older brother to him. And
also their neighbor, Lord Chikara, the prospective groom.
What of him? wondered Yoshi. He was an older man with a
reputation for strong-mindedness and discipline, a samurai to
be respected. . . . But Yoshi's insides churned at the
thought of this country samurai touching his precious Nami.

"Yoshi-san," called the driver, breaking in on Yoshi's
reverie with a shout meant to be heard over the rattle of the
two iron-bound wheels. "We will reach the castle within the

hour." His head bobbed up and down from the roughness of the road; his mouth was open exposing a gap-toothed smile.

Yoshi was too wrapped up in his own thoughts to marvel at how the driver was able to smile after three miserable weeks of travel. Discomfort and boredom made him want to shout with irritation. He restrained himself; pride would allow him to give no less than he received. He regarded the driver through the front opening of the cart. "Yes, thank you for such a comfortable and pleasant journey," he said wryly. Even seeing the loincloth-clad driver on his bare wooden seat, it did not occur to Yoshi that in comparison his own trip had not been too uncomfortable: the inside of the carriage had seat pads, straw mats, and a roof to protect him from the hot spring sun and the rain that had added to the unpleasantness of the long trip.

Yoshi prepared himself for his homecoming. He reapplied white face powder and a touch of rouge, brushed his overlong hair, and checked the black dye on his teeth to be sure no white showed. Uncle Fumio's *shoen*—estate farm—was only minutes away. He twisted impatiently trying to see some part of the ten thousand-*cho* estate where he had been raised. The forest at the sides of the road was too thick. Sometimes he thought he spied a terraced rice paddy through the trees but it was always just a trick of the light. He would have to enter the *shoen* before he would see the result of the years of labor that had turned the land into an imitation of China's rice fields.

The oxcart stopped at the gate while the sentry checked the driver and passenger. Yoshi took a last look behind him to where, over a mile down the mountain, Seiken-ji temple was visible above the pine forest. Beyond the temple, he could see the pale yellow beaches and blue water of Suruga Bay framing the town of Okitsu. Despite an effort to remain blasé, Yoshi found the familiar scene thrilling after a three-year absence.

At last, the sentry was satisfied and the cart was allowed to bump over the great beam that stretched along the ground between the gate supports. Okitsu Castle was as substantial as any in Japan. Yoshi's uncle had spared no expense in its construction. The main building soared three stories above a stone base and had only one—easily defensible—entrance. Round red-lacquered pillars supported deep-eaved roofs with corners turned up in the Chinese fashion. Each story was set back from the one below it. Carved and painted wood beams rose in a series of red and gold peaks to give an air of lightness to the entire structure, an air belied by heavy shutters which covered the upper two stories. The shutters formed defensive positions capable of protecting two hundred bowmen in case of attack. Yoshi knew that in warm weather the shutters would be replaced with light bamboo blinds or removed entirely to bring the inside rooms in harmony with the outside gardens.

The castle was on a flat area near the mountaintop. Behind the main building were smaller buildings connected by covered passages. One passage led to the building where Yoshi's mother, Lady Masaka, ruled, and where the cooks, gardeners, servants, and maids lived. Kitchens and storerooms were connected by short corridors.

The fortress sprawled comfortably behind its enclosing walls, an impressive structure, well-built and well-protected by the thousand samurai in Lord Fumio's employ.

The cart stopped at the south entrance. The driver scrambled from his seat like a mountain monkey and unhitched the dusty ox. He opened the front of the cart and dropped a ladder so Yoshi could descend in a dignified manner.

At the head of the stairs, Lord Fumio waited; his long, powerful legs set wide apart in a *hakama*—pants-skirt—one arm akimbo, the other raised in greeting. Tall and square built with a rugged face lined by experience, he was a plain man, attractive in a no-nonsense way. His thinning hair was pulled back tightly in a high bun that rose from the back of his head. He was dressed simply to match his tastes and appearance. Fumio was obviously happy to welcome his nephew back from the court.

Cousin Ietaka was at his side. Almost as tall as his uncle, Ietaka was heavier, without the sharpness of feature that the years had given his uncle. His round face, with its button nose and wide mouth, looked as though it was meant to smile, but, at Okitsu, Ietaka's mouth was usually turned down at the corners expressing his dissatisfaction with his surroundings. Only his wide, heavy jaw suggested his strength of character.

For a moment, Yoshi's face clouded, but for each curse there is a corresponding blessing and directly behind Ietaka was his sister, Nami, and beside her stood Yoshi's mother. Yoshi's irritation at being greeted by Ietaka melted and he smiled with pleasure. It was good to see his mother, but Nami was a special treat. She had grown from a thin, wistful child to a beautiful seventeen-year-old woman. She was tiny, with small hands and feet, her skin like porcelain, fragile but firm. Her small nose with its seashell nostrils smoothly divided her high-cheekboned face in perfect symmetry over a painted rosebud mouth. Her long almond-shaped eyes smiled uncertainly at Yoshi.

Yoshi's smile froze in place as he was overcome by a sense of loss. With disconcerting suddenness the joy of seeing Nami changed to a feeling of aching emptiness. She was a vision infinitely more beautiful than he remembered her. His knees turned weak and his hands trembled as he stared at her perfect features. He knew he should be happy for her good fortune—a rich and powerful husband—but the thought of her married to another proved almost too much to bear. It took a major effort to conceal the wave of jealousy that shook him when he realized she was lost to him forever. Well, *shigata ga nai*—what would be, would be.

As darkness settled over the castle grounds, Yoshi swallowed his distress. His white face was smooth and properly withdrawn as he waved his fan and mounted the steps to greet his family.

Three

===

"Now," said Isao. "Quickly! Cross the road before we are discovered!"

The pine forest darkened as the sun sank behind the mountain. As Yoshi walked up the steps of Okitsu Castle, Isao led Shinobu and the children across the road and helped them climb over the white stone and plaster wall that surrounded Seiken-ji. They hurried through a gravel courtyard to the base of the temple. Isao motioned them to stay silently under the veranda while he went ahead to find Genkai, the priest.

He knocked softly on the weathered door of the priest's quarters.

No answer.

He knocked again. Time froze as he crouched waiting for a response. Just when he was sure no one was there, the bolts were released. In spite of his own fear, Isao thought how sad that even in temples it was necessary to lock entrances against the highwaymen who infested the province.

The door opened. Isao saw the priest by the light of a small oil lamp. Genkai wore a coarse-woven yellow robe. He was very tall, lean and wiry. His brow was broad with small blue veins showing at the temples. A bold nose jutted from between sunken cheeks leading the eye down past a full-lipped sensitive mouth to a square chin. Though he seemed much older than Isao, they were actually almost of an age. The oil lamp cast a weak circle of light and filled his eye sockets with deep shadows. Even in the semidark he radiated tranquility and brought courage to the farmer's heart. His voice was deep and soft. "How may I serve thee?" he asked with simple dignity.

Isao fell to the floor, pressing his forehead to the timbers. "We are in fear for our lives," he said brokenly. "My family is waiting outside. May I bring them in? They are frightened in the dark."

"*Isogi*—hurry! Come in! Let Buddha light thy path."

Isao scuttled to the door on his knees. He whispered Shinobu's name calling her inside with the children.

"Shinobu?" The priest recognized her as one of the women who came to the temple regularly. He loved the devout laborers, farmers, and wives who, in spite of the hardship of their lives, managed to maintain their religious principles. His face suffused with warmth. This was why he had joined the priesthood: the chance to help others find the safety and peace he had discovered under the protection of Buddha.

Genkai had found religion only a few years earlier. His unswerving devotion had advanced him quickly in the heirarchy of the priests of Seiken-ji. Despite his youth, he lived in a state of constant grace, always aware of the eye of god upon him. He spoke in the orotund tones of the true believer, not to make an impression on his listeners but because it helped him feel spiritual connections to a world of peace and gentility that was missing in the reality around him. His voice with its rising and falling intonations expressed his conviction that he spoke the true words of the Amida Buddha.

As a child of the aristocracy, surrounded by servants and workers, he had learned to love the people who labored for little reward and no appreciation. This love had developed despite the disapproval and even ridicule of his peers. The idea that a member of the country aristocracy should unselfishly love lowly peasants was anathema to his friends and

family. But Genkai had inherited a stubborn streak that gave
him the strength to give up secular pleasures and to accept the
rigors of the priestly life.

Genkai spoke tenderly, reassuring the fugitives with his
quiet voice. "Why have you come to the house of god at this
strange hour and in this strange manner?"

Shinobu fell to her knees beside Isao. "Please help us,"
she cried. "We have no place else to turn. You have always
spoken against the harshness of the *daimyo*. It is the *daimyo's*
wrath that drives us from our home. We need help . . . a
place to hide . . . I told my husband we would be safe here."

"Amida Buddha provides refuge for all who call his name.
But tell me, what have you done to make you fugitives?"
Genkai's voice rose and fell in a soft chanting cadence.

"We used our rice to pay the healers for treating Shinobu's
father," said Isao, without lifting his face from the floor.
Then he looked up and moaned, "There is none left to pay
our taxes. Our lives will be forfeit if Lord Chikara's samurai
find us."

"Lord Chikara again," said the priest, his voice rising.
"He has no respect for god or man." He signaled the family
to rise. "How did you get to god's house?" he asked. "Did
anyone see you on the way?"

"We walked. Since early this morning, we have walked
across the mountain. No one saw us. The children, Mutsu
and Akika, can go no farther. We beg for help. Can we stay
until they stop searching for us?"

"You are under the protection of Amida Nyorai, standing
in the light of god's infinite mercy. You have only to ask his
help and pray for salvation and he will gather you to his
shining heaven. I can see you are poor people, filled with
pain and suffering from the world of men. Here you will find
the peace and security which only the gods can offer."
Genkai's voice rose and fell, rose and fell, bathing the fugitives in hypnotic calm. "Come with me. You will be safe
from the world's troubles at Seiken-ji temple." Genkai
raised his hand reassuringly, palm outward in a motion that
promised the blessing and protection of Buddha. The oil

lamp behind him reflected from his shaven head, creating a halo of light, and assuring the fugitives of the all-powerful protection of the gods.

Genkai detached the lamp from its pedestal and held it high to light the way down a long corridor from his quarters to the main temple. Thirty paces ahead they came to an apparently solid wall. Genkai removed a panel to reveal a secret room.

"You can stay here in darkness until it is safe to leave. The children must be silent. I will bring food and water when I can," he said gravely.

"Amida Buddha, bless you forever," said Isao helping Shinobu and the children into the dark space.

As the panel closed, Akika wailed, "I lost my doll."

"Don't cry. We will make another when we are safe once more," said Shinobu, wrapping her arms around the child to comfort her.

Four

==

Outside Chikara's fortress, birds sang and a cool breeze stirred the foliage. Inside, the main room was dark and still. Surrounded by Chinese hangings and priceless vases, Chikara sat on a dais listening to a report from one of his samurai captains.

"They were gone when we got there, sire."

"Well, where did they go? A farmer and his family can't disappear without a trace. Send more men. Question the peasants in the area. If we don't punish these people there will be no law in our lands." Chikara was contemptuous of the farmers who served as the basis for his wealth. He was one of the many cousins of Taira Kiyomori, newly declared supreme chancellor of Japan, and was typical of the local lords who had grown rich by developing their holdings with a strong hand. The government had given him a grant of land and a title as a reward for heroism during his military service. Sent to the provinces to administer his lands, Chikara was determined to return to the capital with great wealth. His would become the most powerful *shoen* in the eastern provinces! His reputation as a ruthless warrior and his actions as an efficient administrator had drawn thousands of free farmers into his domain. He had turned a small country estate into a fortress with an army capable of enforcing his law without fear of reprisal.

He stared at the samurai who knelt with his head near the floor unable to look higher than the feet of his master.

"Lord Chikara," the samurai said in a low voice. "We think we know where they are hidden, but we don't dare break in to search."

Lord Chikara leaned against his embroidered elbow rest. His hawklike nose and opaque black eyes gave him the look of a predatory bird. And like a bird, he hissed, "You speak to me of not daring to search! There is no place on these lands where my men cannot march freely to uphold the law. I will deal with you later, Shigeru. Now, tell me where they are."

Shigeru pressed his forehead to the polished wood floor, his voice an inaudible murmur.

"Speak louder," snapped Chikara angrily.

"We think they are hiding in the Seiken-ji temple," murmured the abject samurai.

"The monks have meddled in my affairs once too often. This time I will not sit back. I said an example would be made and I mean to see that promise fulfilled. Take a handful of my guards. Go to the temple and bring those people out. Justice must be done."

"Yes, sire."

"We'll see about your punishment later," Chikara glared at Shigeru.

"Yes, sire," said the samurai scuttling out backwards.

Chikara, alone in the large room, took a deep breath and closed his eyes to calm himself. The lives of a family of farmers should not be important enough to upset him.

After a minute, he turned to study his latest acquisition, a hand-painted screen. Like many Heian lords, Chikara collected Chinese art and admired the culture of China. The farmers were quickly forgotten as he lost himself in admiration of the screen painter's intricate brushwork.

Five

On the morning after his arrival at Okitsu Castle, Yoshi sat cross-legged on the porch facing Mount Satta. He was a handsome young man by court standards, slim and above average height. This morning, he wore light green over a peach-colored shift, soft colors for a man of Okitsu. The lack of musculature in his soft arms, and his long, delicate fingers accentuated the androgynous appearance that was the height of twelfth century court fashion. Like others of his class, he blackened his teeth to cover the unsightly "gravestones of the mouth," and used liberal applications of white face powder to help him affect a habitually masklike, bored expression. Unfortunately, youth made him subject to strong emotional tides that often defeated his attempts at diffidence. His ubiquitous fan and mincing manner were in slavish imitation of the courtiers he admired at the court. Despite his appearance, he was completely masculine and had already been intimate with several court ladies. He never confused the casual sex of the court with his intense passion for Nami. In his view, sex and romantic love did not necessarily have anything in common.

As Yoshi inhaled the scents of pine and new spring blossoms, he decided to create a poem to celebrate the moment.

He poured a tiny pool of water on a flat stone and rubbed his inkstick through it until it thickened and turned black. Dipping his brush lightly into the ink he started to compose his poem:

The pine branch trembles . . .

The brush hesitated; he found his mind wandering. Perhaps it was the air, perhaps it was being home again. His hand remained poised over the paper as he reflected on his position as the illegitimate son of Lady Masaka.

Uncle Fumio was kind and generous, but though there was no stigma attached to illegitimacy, Yoshi missed the assurance of knowing his father. Often he daydreamed of an imaginary father, creating a heroic figure, larger than life, a samurai lord of great sensitivity, great charm, and great strength. Perhaps Yoshi's daydreams resulted from a lack of parental affection. Fumio had tried to take the place of Yoshi's father; he gave generously of himself. Yoshi accepted the proffered love and guidance, but it was not the same as having a real father. Knowing his mother was in residence at the castle was a help but he had grown up seeing little of her. She spent most of her time secluded in the north wing. Because Fumio was a widower, she had taken over the duties of principal wife. She was the ruler of the northern or service wing, and as "Northern Person," she kept occupied managing the castle affairs through her entourage of ladies-in-waiting, butlers, cooks, and overseers. Except for an occasional visit to a local shrine, she stayed out of sight in her private quarters—as was usual for a woman in her position.

Yoshi had heard of the supposedly miraculous events of his birth. Though Uncle Fumio professed to believe the story, the local people whispered that Fumio, himself, was Yoshi's father. Yoshi sighed. Whenever he thought of his uncle, he thought of the undeserved tragedies that had befallen him. How, soon after he returned from the campaigns that won him his estate and his title, his life was marked by a series of disasters. First, his wife died along with her stillborn child.

Then, six months later, his house was destroyed and his favorite consort killed in one of the minor earthquakes that regularly rocked the countryside.

Since that day, Fumio had avoided entanglements with women. He rebuilt his castle to its present size and contented himself with playing rich uncle to the nieces and nephews that his more fortunate relatives brought forth.

Before Yoshi had left for Kyoto, Fumio had trained him in the manly pursuits—hunting, swordplay, and archery—and had taught him to believe unquestioningly in the social structure of which he was a part. All power came from the Emperor. Certain classes were inherently superior to others. Yoshi was the nephew of a *daimyo*—a man who had absolute power over ten thousand *cho* of land, the undisputed baronial head of his estates. Whatever the questions about his birth, Yoshi was, in every respect, a nobleman and tried to live up to his own impression of what was expected of a nobleman.

Yoshi brought the back of the brush to his mouth as he gazed out over the gardens and mused on his six years in the Imperial city, wonderful years spent mainly studying calligraphy, poetry, art, and dance.

His reverie was broken by a discreet cough. Ietaka and Nami were behind him. "What beautiful calligraphy," said Nami, craning her neck to peer over Yoshi's shoulder. A peace offering.

Yoshi lowered the brush, picked up his perennial fan and motioned them to join him. Nami wore a sky blue patterned robe over plum-colored silk. Her waist length hair was adorned with jewelry and clasped with a stiff white silk bow halfway down her back. Yoshi's heart raced at the sight of her. "Thank you, Nami, it is kind of you to say so," he said formally, suppressing the swell of emotion that threatened to betray him. His cheeks reddened through their layer of powder and rouge. He had to conceal his feelings. Too late to change Nami's destiny, he would only cause pain if he confessed to his unattainable love. "I am sorry I was too fatigued to discuss your wedding last night. Now that we have the entire morning, Nami, you can tell me all about your future husband and the coming celebration," he said with forced warmth.

Aristocratic marriages followed a set tradition. The prospective groom "secretly" visited his intended wife and stayed until dawn. If all went well, a messenger delivered a love poem on the following morning. The messenger was deluged with gifts from the family to demonstrate the happiness of the bride-to-be.

On the second night, the groom again spent the night "secretly." Though the family was aware of his return, his presence was still unacknowledged.

Soon thereafter, the bride's family prepared rice cakes for the groom in the bride's quarters and the marriage was considered consummated. A letter of commitment from the bride's father or guardian followed, and a celebration feast was held a few days later. Here a priest performed a purification ritual and the couple exchanged winecups in a toast. The wedding was now complete in every respect.

Nami was already two thirds of the way through the ceremony and she glowed with happiness as she exclaimed, "Oh, Yoshi, I am so happy at my good fortune. Lord Chikara is a kind and patient suitor. He has already visited me twice this week. He sent the most beautiful next-morning poem after our first night. He is strong and virile . . . everything I could desire. We shall complete the formal ceremony in the next few days."

Nami's enthusiasm was a stab at Yoshi's vitals. In distress, he looked to Ietaka and saw that the big man was also unhappy at his sister's coming marriage. Yoshi found the strength to compose himself. His face became bland and expressionless behind its mask. "I am glad I could come in time. I am only sorry I shall not be able to see you once you are married," he said patting his hair in an effort at nonchalance.

"Have no fear, Yoshi. I do not intend to become a slave to Chikara's castle. I am not an old-fashioned woman. I will never disappear into the household as your mother did."

Ietaka smiled for the first time. "Trust my sister," he said. "She will never succumb to the pressures of the reactionary Taira society."

Yoshi was annoyed at the gratuitous political comment, but he said, "I hope you are right. I would be distraught if our longtime friendship were to end." He adjusted his pale green robe, indolently waved his fan, and changed the painful subject. "One of us is missing," he said. "Where is cousin Sanemoto? I did not see him last night, and when I asked for him Uncle Fumio avoided my question. Is something wrong?"

Ietaka shifted uncomfortably and turned to his sister. "You tell him," he said. "If I give my view he will think me prejudiced."

Nami sighed. "Uncle Fumio does not wish to discuss Sanemoto because he was terribly hurt by his actions. You see, over two years ago, despite uncle's objections, our cousin took the name Genkai, and became one of the priests at Seiken-ji."

"Sanemoto? Genkai . . . a priest?" Yoshi waved his fan agitatedly. "I cannot believe it!" Yoshi's disorientation was understandable. His earliest memories were of Sanemoto; they had been closer than brothers for many years.

Sanemoto had been orphaned shortly after birth. His mother—the oldest sister of Lord Fumio—and his father—a minor Imperial functionary—were murdered by roving bandits while on their way to a government posting in Kai province. Only the baby and an old, half-blind nursemaid were spared when the bandits robbed and slaughtered the rest of the party.

The nursemaid, loyal to the last, staggered with the baby in her arms for almost forty miles before collapsing at the gates of Okitsu Castle.

The episode occurred in the fall of 1147, two years before Yoshi's birth. Lord Fumio adopted the baby, loving him from the start, and considering him his own son. Hence, from the day Yoshi came screaming into the world, he and the slightly older Sanemoto were together. They were as different as two children could be, but, even so, they were closer than brothers.

Because he had no parents to control him, Sanemoto was restless, always questioning authority. Yoshi, on the other hand, would, chameleonlike, fall into whatever pattern was expected of him. Yoshi had always been obedient, striving to please his mother and his uncle; Sanemoto had been a rebel, seeking something more to believe in than his uncle and the Emperor.

Yoshi looked up to Sanemoto. He was annoyed and jealous that, as Sanemoto grew older, he chose to spend more time with the teenage children of the castle help. However, Sanemoto's friendship with the children did not prevent him from leading the younger Yoshi in campaigns of mischief; they were constantly confusing the serving staff, and confounding the samurai guards. The restlessness and mischief-making were a screen for insecurity, and Yoshi had never been able to see beyond Sanemoto's laughing mouth and deep sparkling eyes. Yoshi's childhood had been spent living up to the social demands of his environment. He was not introspective and was easily taken in by appearances. His mental activity was given over to daydreams of his missing father, and to selfish fantasies of his coming place in the court. How could he understand that Sanemoto's rebellion was a search for deeper meaning and higher authority?

Lacking this understanding, Yoshi was surprised that Sanemoto had shaved his head and taken the name Genkai.

Yoshi shook his head in wonder. "He had no interest in religion," he said. "A priest! What possessed him?"

"His attitudes changed," said Nami. "After your last visit Sanemoto became more restless than before. He seemed a lost soul until he discovered the monks of Seiken-ji. Once he found Buddha he underwent a metamorphosis. He became calm and at peace with himself. Soon he renounced the world and used his energies to speak against the landowners. He told the peasants that all men were equal in the sight of Buddha."

"Surely Sanemoto does not believe such nonsense!" Yoshi was genuinely shocked. His fan waved energetically. No one of his social class ever contemplated equality for peasants.

"I believe there is much of value in his views," interrupted Ietaka testily. "Do not dismiss them lightly!"

"I cannot believe he would turn against our teachings. What you suggest is treason against the Emperor. He cannot believe those lies—not as Sanemoto and not as Genkai." Yoshi shook his head in disbelief and added, "What a strange unpredictable world we live in."

Ietaka was cool in the face of Yoshi's bewilderment. "The world is more predictable than the people in it," he said. "True, as a child, Genkai showed no interest in religion but he did love the people around him. Even the *esemono*—the lowest of the laborers—were not beneath his regard. Unlike you, he had an inquiring mind that kept him from accepting everything bad he was told. The change in Sanemoto began shortly after your last visit when one of his pranks backfired. He had led the gardener's son on a night foray into the kitchen. Sanemoto thought it would be a lark to switch spices into the wrong containers." Ietaka paused and smiled wryly. "Unfortunately for the jokers a samurai guard heard them. He challenged them, and in the excitement of the escape attempt, the gardener's son burst through a paper screen and fell from the second story balcony. He broke his leg in two places.

"As punishment for his part in the affair, Sanemoto was ordered to spend his time with the invalid until he was completely recovered. Uncle thought he was teaching Sanemoto a lesson in humility and responsibility. He succeeded far beyond his expectations. You know that Sanemoto was already sympathetic to the problems of the castle staff. The time he spent in close contact with the gardener and his family made him love them and identify with them more than with his own family." Ietaka regarded Yoshi and Nami sadly. He, too, had missed the warmth of his own family. He sighed and continued. "He saw a closeness that he had missed in his relationship with Uncle Fumio. As hard as Uncle tried—and he loved Sanemoto more than he loved any of us—he could not give our cousin the close-knit family his nature cried for. At that time, Sanemoto had not yet discovered religion, he was distressed, unable to come to grips with his turbulent thoughts. He wondered why good people were forced into subservient labor while others— often less deserving—lived lives of ease. Sanemoto had developed an awareness of others seldom seen in people of our class.''

Yoshi bristled at this statement, so typical of Ietaka, and opened his mouth to interrupt. Ietaka gestured him to silence. When he continued his tone was thoughtful. ''Perhaps it was my influence that sent him to seek counsel. Whatever the cause, he began to visit the temple daily searching for truth and a meaning to life. When the priests discovered his natural affinity for the poor farmers and merchants they taught him his mission was to help them to a better life. I understand his feelings and sympathize with the difficult path he has chosen. I love him and my heart breaks at the thought of all he will suffer if he continues to oppose the Imperial powers. He is naïve in that he thinks goodness should accompany power.''

Yoshi was ready to argue that goodness did indeed accompany power, but before he could speak, Nami said softly, ''It was the search for goodness that made Sanemoto turn to the priesthood. . . . Now, whatever we say or do, nothing will dissuade him from his chosen course.''

Yoshi clicked his tongue. ''Madness,'' he said. ''Madness!'' And he shook his head for emphasis.

Six

At the same moment, Genkai was also shaking his head. "No," he said calmly, "there is no farmer here. I demand that you leave at once. We are a temple of Buddha. You and your soldiers have no right on our property."

"I am sorry, priest. My lord has ordered me to search the temple, and search it I shall." The samurai's lips were set in a hard line and his voice was cold.

"Not as long as I can defy you." Genkai raised his chin. He focused on a point beyond the samurai's head concealing growing anger.

"Take him!" Shigeru motioned to two of his guards. They leaped forward. One pulled Genkai's arm up behind his back forcing him to his knees while the other tied his ankles. Genkai's shaven head glistened with sweat and a small angry pulse popped up in his temples. "You mustn't," he said at last. "This is a house of Buddha. It is forbidden. . . ."

"Gag him," ordered the samurai.

Shigeru had his men search the temple's living quarters. They walked down the corridors, checking each room, driving the priest ahead of them. They passed the secret panel without a glance, continuing into the temple's main room where three great bronze statues of the Buddha stood on a dais. They searched behind the statues, under the dais, and through the halls, growing angrier with each passing minute.

A valuable screen was broken, a scroll torn from the wall, a shutter splintered. They found no sign of the refugees.

Shigeru was furious. With Chikara's threats and orders ringing in his ears, he didn't dare return without the farmer's head.

"It does not matter anymore what we do here," he rasped to Genkai. "If the gods are angry, they will not grow more so. I want the farmer and I will use any means to find him. An informer told us his wife brought him here so you will talk or you will die."

He took the screen from the oil lamp and heated the point of his dagger in the flame. "Where are they hidden?" he asked, bringing the red-hot tip close to Genkai's eyes.

Genkai sputtered and choked around his gag.

Shigeru lowered the blade. He turned to one of his men. "Take it off!" he ordered. When the gag was removed he pressed his face close to Genkai's. "What can you tell us?" he demanded.

"That you will be damned for a thousand generations. You, your Lord Chikara, and all your helpers. Damned, damned, damned!" shouted Genkai, his face purple with emotion.

"Gag him again. This time we will use the hot blade before we take off the gag." He placed the dagger's tip in the flame once more.

"Shigeru! I found something," called one of the samurai from the corridor.

"What is it?" asked Shigeru.

"A child's toy, a doll, here in the corner."

"Quickly! Tear the corner apart. Take out the panels. They are hidden there somewhere."

The samurai began a systematic search, tearing down screens and shutters, banging on the wooden walls. In a matter of minutes they found the secret room and pulled out the four fugitives.

Isao was easily overpowered by two of the burly warriors.

They dragged him to Shigeru. Another samurai led the unre-
sisting Shinobu who clutched Mutsu and Akika to her breast,
trying to quiet their sobbing. A warrior pulled the children
from her arms and the parents were forced to their knees
before Shigeru.

"Take the gag off the priest," he ordered.

"By all rights, you should be joining these criminals," he
told Genkai. "However, I have no orders where you are
concerned. You will witness Lord Chikara's justice and
perhaps it will be a lesson to you. Even priests are not above
the law."

Genkai was once more in control of his emotions. He
asked Shigeru to let him speak to the captives. Shigeru
nodded coldly. Genkai led the family in a recital of the
Amidist prayer which guaranteed them a space in the Western Paradise. Then they bowed in resignation and, while
Genkai watched in horror, Shigeru drew his long sword and
with two lightning sweeps cut through their neck muscles.
Shinobu's head hit the wooden floor even before Isao's head
stopped rolling. A gush of blood, black in the lamplight,
poured from the arteries of the victims.

Genkai was stunned for a moment. He quickly recovered,
and shook his head sadly, knowing his next request was
useless.

"Leave the children," he begged. "I will take care of
them. They are no business of yours. They are only babies,
innocent of wrong. Leave them to the protection of
Buddha."

"A lesson has to be made, priest. Bring them here."
Shigeru's face was impassive. No plea could reach him. His
duty was clear.

The screaming children were held in place and the sword
made a shining arc in the lamplight. Once . . . and again.
The pitiful little bodies collapsed to the floor next to their
parents.

"Heed the lesson well, priest," said Shigeru, wiping his
blade on the robe of the headless girl child.

"I pity you and your lord!" boomed Genkai. "You will

suffer on the wheel of eternity for this desecration of the temple and for the murder of these innocents. Before you die, you will pay dearly for what you have done.'' The echo of Genkai's curse rang from the temple walls. Genkai glared at the samurai. These man-beasts had undermined the very foundations of his belief. The temple was sacred and the priests of Seiken-ji had always been free to offer sanctuary to the poor and homeless. Further, Genkai had personally promised a safe haven to the farmer's family and the Buddha had been powerless to honor his promise.

He turned his anger on the hapless samurai, knowing in his heart it served no purpose. The samurai were as much victims as the farmer; they, too, were powerless to alter the course of events. Only their master could be held accour͏able. Chikara! The abominable Chikara!

"Leave him tied,'' said Shigeru, shaken by the slim priest's intensity. "His fellow priests will release him. Take the heads to show as examples to the others.'' He turned to Genkai. "Count yourself lucky to have kept your own head.''

The heads were wrapped in the robe stripped from Shinobu's body, and the samurai left without a backward glance at Genkai who, with no one to see, twisted his bound body back and forth in a paroxysm of misery and helpless anger.

Seven

Shortly after Yoshi finished his afternoon tea on the veranda, Fumio came bustling out, obviously distraught. He was followed by an angry Ietaka.

"Damn the man, why does he make problems for us?" Fumio blew his lips in exasperation.

Ietaka said thickly, "Chikara must be spoken to."

Yoshi looked at them curiously. "What is the matter?" he asked with an indolent wave of his fan.

"Nami's prospective husband," exclaimed Fumio. "His samurai beheaded a family of his peasants for nonpayment of taxes."

"His peasants? Then, Uncle, what is the problem?" Yoshi's slim, dark eyes opened wide in affected surprise.

"The deaths occurred in Genkai's temple after he was held prisoner. Though I do not agree with Genkai's beliefs, he is my adopted son and deserves better treatment. The farmer was hiding in Seiken-ji with his children. Can you imagine . . . hiding on sacred ground! Genkai should never have allowed them to enter and Chikara's men should never have followed without permission of the monks. They exceeded their authority. The temple is on my lands and I, too, should have been consulted before they acted." Fumio shrugged and rolled his eyes upward as though supplicating the gods. "What can I do about it now?"

Yoshi's heart leaped. Here was a chance to subvert Nami's marriage. A few subtle words could turn Fumio against Chikara. But no. Manipulation for personal gain was an art he had seen in the court, but it was not Yoshi's way. Diffident, withdrawn, effete, all these things he might be, but he would not lie or act against his beliefs for personal gain and he believed that Chikara had acted correctly. "Forget the entire affair," he advised. "It was Chikara's right to execute them and their fault for hiding in the temple." Yoshi rose and arranged his robe, brushing out an imaginary wrinkle with one delicate hand.

"Yes, I suppose you are right." Fumio's tension eased.

"No! Yoshi is wrong." Ietaka's voice quivered. "The samurai had no right to invade the temple. Chikara ordered them there. No wonder his peasants hate and fear him. This was a political action by one of the worst Taira despots. If even the temples are not safe from his depradations, our country is doomed." He turned to Yoshi. "You are Genkai's cousin and friend. Can't you imagine how he felt? I cry for him as much as for the victims of this heinous crime. A priest must be respected in the house of god."

"Ietaka, you are misled by your hatred and suspicion of the Taira family. Just remember that Uncle Fumio cannot afford to offend Lord Chikara. He is a neighbor who will soon have strong ties with our family." Yoshi's white face was impassive as he spoke in support of a man who had earned his jealous resentment. "Chikara committed no serious wrong. His samurai were overzealous. That is not a crime."

Yoshi like most of his peers in Kyoto, had had no contact with the peasant class. Though he thought of himself as openminded and fair in his dealings with people, he scarcely considered the majority of peasants as human. The court thought of the lowest classes as *esemono*—people of doubtful quality—when they thought of them at all. Ietaka had known the *esemono* during his slavery, and Genkai had come to know them on the *shoen*, but six years of conditioning in the court of Kyoto had left Yoshi unsympathetic to their plight; he did not understand them. On the other hand, though he hated Chikara for taking Nami from him, he was a neighbor and a samurai who had achieved fame as a soldier and former member of the court.

Fumio said, "Yoshi speaks with wisdom beyond his years. I think he gives good counsel."

Ietaka was about to respond when a servant announced a visitor. Genkai swept into the room, yellow robes rustling, his eyes fixed straight ahead, his bald head shining with sweat; he noticed neither Yoshi nor Ietaka as he spoke to Fumio. "Have you heard?" he demanded. "A foul, inhuman act. The entire family murdered! They tied me and made me watch while they beheaded them. And for what? A bit of rice!" He glanced past the two cousins still blind to their presence. "This bestial behavior is an affront to Buddha. It must stop. You will have to take action against Chikara," he said.

Fumio again rolled his eyes upward. "What would you have me do? I am sorry you were involved, but Lord Chikara acted correctly. We are agreed: maintain the law or fall to anarchy."

"Yoshi! Ietaka!" Genkai acknowledged them. "Forgive my preoccupation. You've heard the news. Do you see the importance of confronting Chikara immediately? Our Nami is to marry this man within the week. He is a devil from the underworld of Yomi and we must band together in the name of Buddha to stop him from further evil. If Uncle Fumio will not act, will you join me in demanding at least an apology and a promise to control his samurai in the future?" said Genkai fervently.

"Genkai, please . . . Uncle is right. Chikara was only upholding the law." Yoshi's tone was placating though his fan waved in agitation.

"I do not agree," snapped Ietaka. "There are considerations more important than the government's laws. Chikara owes a measure of respect to the temple of Buddha and to the family of the woman he is to marry. He had no right to act without our permission.''

"You forget, Cousin: Chikara earned his right to enforce the Imperial laws on his *shoen* before we were born." Yoshi was growing annoyed. He should have known Ietaka would side with Genkai. It was to be expected from one who saw everything as a political plot against the people of Japan; but why was Genkai being so difficult? Though he was a priest he should have understood that religion could not be allowed to interfere with the important structures of society. And why did Genkai's righteous air make Yoshi—his dearest friend—feel guilty? Suddenly he saw why Fumio had difficulty with Genkai. In the face of such religious zeal any proper person would have difficulty.

"His men acted inhumanly, and I will tell him so," intoned Genkai with infuriating calm while Ietaka nodded encouragement.

"Genkai, even though you are a priest, you speak like a fool. You will tell him nothing—for Nami's sake and your own." Yoshi's mouth pursed with irritation and the fan waved too quickly. He paused for breath then added soothingly, "Listen to me for the sake of our childhood friendship. Only a madman insults a samurai lord to his face."

Ietaka grudgingly agreed that caution was required. He joined Yoshi and Fumio in trying to convince Genkai that a conflict must be avoided. They finally extracted a promise that Genkai would take no action until he had had time to think of the consequences; they were certain that on reflection, Genkai would realize the foolishness of a confrontation.

Inwardly, however, Genkai was determined to face Chikara. Right and the Buddha were on his side, but he would conceal his true feelings to avoid friction.

He spent so little time with his family. He had seen Ietaka during the past week, but Yoshi . . . was it three years? So much had happened to him, it seemed a lifetime since Yoshi's last visit. And Yoshi, too! How different he appeared—a schoolboy then, a handsome young courtier now. Genkai noted the oversoft colors of Yoshi's clothing and the omnipresent fan. A surface change, yet Genkai was sure that underneath he was the same malleable Yoshi. How unfair to visit his problems on his cousin. He would try to make up for causing him discomfort. Genkai dropped the priestly air that had become so much a part of him and reverted to his boyhood manner. Yoshi folded his fan, and even big, serious Ietaka relaxed. Soon they were all laughing as they reminisced about their childhood; it was as if they had never left Okitsu Castle. The court, the Buddha, and Lord Chikara were forgotten as they relived their childish escapades.

Lord Fumio looked proudly from one to the other. These were the boys he remembered, full of good spirits, manly, and fun-loving. Not the courtier, the troublemaker, and the Amidist priest.

After an hour, Fumio politely left the cousins to their memories.

On the surface, Yoshi was happy—it was good to be with his cousins again—but a sweet pang shadowed his heart. Nostalgia, a longing for innocence, or the tenderness of his now hopeless love for Nami . . . whatever it was, it filled him with a sense of impermanence and a dread of the future.

Eight

The next day, Lord Fumio rose early and went riding. He had to think and he thought best on a horse. The earthy smell of droppings on the riding path satisfied him as much as flowers and pine had satisfied Yoshi the day before. A sturdy, honest man, made noble by the accidents of battle, Fumio did not delude himself about his abilities. At forty-seven, he was as strong as any of his samurai and as brave, but he was not equipped to solve questions of tact and diplomacy. How to deal with the problem of Genkai? His adopted son was wasting what should have been an honorable career in the service of the Emperor . . . and for what? A holy man's dream of a world to come.

Fumio found it impossible to accept the sincerity of Genkai's change. While the air of religious strength might convince others, Fumio thought he could still see the lighthearted boy behind those priestly robes.

Fumio had little interest in religion. Man was here to serve the Emperor and to fight, eat, and love women, in that order. But when Genkai took his vows in the spreading Amida Buddha sect, Fumio was disturbed more by his choice of Amida than by his becoming a priest. Why—if he must be a priest—couldn't he have joined the Tendai sect? The Tendai were warriors and had political, military, and economic power. This earned them respect from the aristocracy and the military. Fumio could have accepted Genkai as one of the Tendai; it was the growing popularity of the Amidists among the lower classes that made Fumio uncomfortable. He was suspicious of the Amidist movement and he thought Genkai, as an Amidist priest, was preaching little less than revolution, wasting his energies bringing religion to the lower classes, telling them they could spend their next life in Paradise merely by reciting a simple formula: *Namu Amida Butsu*—I call on thee, Amida Buddha. This was another example of the dissolution of law and the coming end of the world, the kind of doctrine that created unrest and dissatisfaction among the farmers and laborers and broke down the bonds of discipline that made society function. One day, the promise of Nirvana to the farmers; the next day, a refusal to pay taxes. This was the inexorable path that led to the killing of Isao and his family.

Now the problem had been thrust into Fumio's hands. What could he do? Soon Chikara would be a member of the family. Fumio and Chikara had campaigned together in their youth and Fumio remembered many of their experiences with pleasure. Chikara had been open and straightforward until some twenty years ago when he spent a year at court. The palace intrigues had fascinated him and taught him the means to gain power. He had grown stronger and, in Fumio's opinion, more devious.

Fumio had to decide how to deal with the insult to Genkai and the death of the peasants on his lands. Here, Yoshi had shown good sense and even Ietaka had agreed that caution was required. How unfortunate that these problems came at such an inauspicious time.

During the course of these meditations Fumio had circled the mountain and returned to the castle gates. Up ahead he saw Chikara and his younger brother, Kagesuke, dismounting.

Fumio made his decision. Chikara would be treated as an honored guest. What was done was done! He rode toward his guests suppressing a premonition of disaster. Where was Genkai?

Chikara was resplendent in blue and gold formal dress. His tall slim figure and hawklike face were enhanced by thick hair combed back tightly under a black *eboshi*. The deep blue overcloak was drawn into a skirtlike *hakama* which covered it to the waist. A loose jacket could not hide his powerful appearance. His brother, Kagasuke, not much older than Yoshi, was muscular and thick-waisted, with a sullen face and puffy eyes. He always followed Chikara. Chikara waved a negligent hand at Fumio. "Lord Fumio, I hope we are not too early. I was impatient to see you and your niece," he said.

Fumio dismounted and handed the reins to a groom. "Lord Chikara," he said with a bow, "please come in." Acting the host made Fumio feel like an innkeeper; he did not like the feeling. He bowed again and asked his guests, "Would you like to wash after your ride?"

"Yes, perhaps hot towels and a cup of sake before we discuss the coming ceremonies."

He motioned to Kagasuke to see that the horses were cared for and arrogantly entered the castle ahead of his host.

As Fumio and Chikara disappeared inside, they did not notice Yoshi, Ietaka, and Genkai sitting on a side porch under the gabled eaves.

Yoshi asked Ietaka, "Why are they here today?"

"They are discussing the wedding arrangements. There is always business involved in a marriage between two *shoen*."

"I hoped it was to apologize for his samurai's behavior at the temple," said Genkai stiffly.

"I am younger than you, cousin, yet I have experience in these matters from the court and I will give you advice," said Yoshi pompously. "Forget the incident entirely! If you search for revenge you will be disappointed. Chikara is too powerful." His slim wrist snapped the scented fan to emphasize his point.

Genkai regarded Yoshi intently. "Forget the incident? Never! Chikara was wrong; he must apologize to me and swear to the everlasting Buddha it will never recur. I realize nothing can bring back the farmer's family in this cycle.'' He lifted his face heavenward as though in communion with higher powers. "They are in a safer, happier place far from the problems of this life. I think of the future . . .'' He lowered his gaze and leaned toward his cousins. "I think of the fate of other peasants who make one minor mistake . . . and I think of Chikara and his hope of salvation and eternal life."

Even Ietaka drew back as Genkai spoke. "Salvation!" he blurted. "Even if he were already my brother-in-law, I would damn him to the underworld of Yomi. The man deserves no salvation. Though I warned you to move carefully, I did not mean that Chikara should be let off with only an apology and a promise. He deserves punishment. He is typical of the brutal thoughtless Taira lords who rule our lives."

"Shh!" Yoshi bristled indignantly. "You speak treason. It is dangerous enough for Genkai to ask for an apology without searching for more trouble."

Ietaka lost his temper. He towered over Yoshi and snarled, "You are a thoughtless, shallow nonentity, not as good as the *esemono* you despise. Someday you will discover what a fool you are."

"Fool?" Yoshi's voice rose and Genkai had to step between the cousins to prevent them from fighting. The situation was saved and the conversation stopped short as the side wall slid open. Lord Chikara and Lord Fumio strode onto the porch followed by Kagasuke.

Angry as he was, Yoshi recognized that Chikara made an impressive figure. Chikara was the same height and approximate build as Yoshi, but he had an air of confidence, power, security, and a certain arrogance. Yoshi suddenly felt foolish and weak in his soft colors and heavy makeup. His skin tightened on the back of his neck, a primitive reaction, a touch of fear.

Chikara bowed politely to the group. "We are leaving. I hope to see you all at the rice-cake ceremony later this week."

Yoshi and Ietaka returned the bow; Genkai remained erect, his square chin raised slightly. "May I have a word with you alone?" he asked coolly.

"I will soon be a member of your family. Surely there is nothing we cannot say in front of each other." Chikara's lips drew back in a tight smile that sent chills up the backs of everyone in the room except Genkai.

"I do not wish to embarrass my uncle," said Genkai.

Chikara glanced at Fumio with one eyebrow raised in question. "Shall we speak here or in private?" he asked.

Tiny beads of perspiration appeared on Fumio's lip; he nodded for the conversation to continue. Careful nephew, careful, his eyes pleaded.

Chikara, despite his menacing expression, did not wish to jeopardize his relationship with Nami. The marriage had to be completed! He could not bear losing her. She had become an obsession with him since the day he had noticed her as a fourteen-year-old running free on the Tadamori *shoen*. In this respect he was no different from Yoshi but, unlike Yoshi, he was a mature man, accustomed to imposing his decisions on those around him. The courtship of a young girl by an older man was not unusual. Chikara did not consider age difference an obstacle, but as attractive as he found Nami, he was not one to make hasty decisions where his future was concerned. He had not taken Nami lightly and had spent two years observing her and considering the possibilities before he spoke to Fumio about the marriage and the merger of their *shoen* that would result. At first, he had thought only of the political advantage of joining his *shoen* to Fumio's. As Nami matured, he began to see qualities in her even more valuable than merely a connection to Fumio's land. She had intelligence and social finesse—the way she manipulated Fumio! It was a priceless talent. He dreamt she would help him in his rise to power. She would be the woman he needed when he returned to the capital. And the passage of time gave her another quality; she became a transcendentally beautiful woman. His passion for collecting objects of art focused on Nami; she would be his finest acquisition. He had become obsessed by a woman who was little more than a child and he would settle for no other.

Chikara hoped that by speaking in front of Fumio and the others, Genkai would have to exercise restraint. "What you have to say may embarrass your uncle; it will not, however, embarrass me. I am ready to listen," said Chikara.

Genkai hesitated, collecting his thoughts. "How can I make you aware of the consequences of your actions?" he asked solemnly. "Men, acting under your orders, committed a crime against Buddha when they broke into our temple and slaughtered the farmer and his family. Though the acts were theirs, the ultimate responsibility was yours. I ask you to pray for forgiveness, apologize to me, promise that these crimes will never recur, and prove your sincerity by making reparations to the temple your men defiled. There is no excuse in the eyes of Buddha for treating human beings in this fashion."

As Genkai spoke, any sympathy Chikara might have had for the priest disappeared like foam on water. The man was a dangerous fanatic. To speak of farmers as human beings was to shake the foundations of society, and to say that Lord Chikara must answer for his supposed crimes was to suggest revolution. Whatever pain a rift with the Tadamori family would cause, no honorable man could ignore this diatribe.

Chikara glared at Genkai, furious at the way the priest's beatific smile mocked him. "Enough," he said grimly. "When you ask me to pay . . . that is extortion and I grow angry. I will make no apology. I will make no promises for the future. And I will pay no reparations. My men acted on my orders; they were within the law. Should I have consulted your uncle and given the criminals time to flee? No! Despite Fumio, my power extends to wherever my people may hide. The farmer and his family accepted my protection and understood its conditions. They suffered as a result of their own misconduct."

Yoshi winced at Chikara's scornful dismissal of his uncle's prerogatives, and his imperious rejection of Genkai's requests. Genkai was wrong. But he deserved better than a supercilious adult-to-child lecture. Was this how it would be when the two *shoen* were united?

Yoshi's shoulders tensed. In Kyoto, Chikara's boorish behavior would have been reprimanded, but Yoshi held himself in check; it was not his place to interfere.

"Priest," Chikara continued scornfully, "you have insulted me. I care nothing for you or your temple, but for your uncle's sake I will accept your apology if you apologize at once!"

Chikara was angry. The damnable priest and his infuriating righteousness! Chikara felt that Genkai—too mad to understand the consequences of his beliefs—was a threat to his world. And he was being driven to an action he would surely regret. How to avoid it without losing face?

The tension grew. It was as if lightning was building between mountain and cloud. The air crackled with the intensity of Chikara, rooted in earth, and Genkai, floating in the heavens. Suddenly, Yoshi could not bear to see his beloved cousin insulted, and his uncle forced to stand by, helpless and silent. Before Genkai could answer Chikara's arrogant demand, Yoshi spoke impulsively, "One moment, Lord Chikara!" The fan flicked agitatedly. "You are not yet a member of the family. While you are in Tadamori Castle, we expect you to respect our sovereignty. Your attitude is an affront to my family. We are not accustomed to being insulted in this crude fashion. I must warn you that—"

Chikara interrupted with a snarl. Yoshi had given him the excuse he needed to save face. "Warn me! You dare to warn me?" He glared contemptuously at Yoshi. "Genkai is a priest and gains some measure of protection from his robes. You popinjay—bastard son of an unknown father—you are less than nothing! Keep quiet while you still live!"

The words cut like a whiplash. Blood drained from behind Yoshi's makeup. His face became even whiter than before. No one had ever spoken to him that way. He felt a hot rush of uncontrollable anger. Earlier, he had supported this hateful man against his own interests, and this was his reward! Not only to lose Nami but to be denigrated before his family. Popinjay! Bastard! He would not accept these insults without responding. He stepped forward and slapped his fan across Chikara's face. The sound of the slap echoed in the silence that fell on the room. The calling of the birds, the strident rasp of a cicada, and the distant swell and ebb of the ocean suddenly rang in Yoshi's ears.

The side of Chikara's face turned red; Genkai's beatific smile faded, Fumio stiffened to his full height, and Ietaka's mouth hung open in horror. Kagasuke's sword was halfway out of its scabbard before Chikara's raised hand stopped him in place.

Chikara's hands made white-knuckled fists; his eyes were opaque onyx jewels, his lips a pale thin slash. Red slowly faded from his discolored cheek. When he spoke his voice was soft, more menacing than if it had been loud or angry. "You are less than a man, but you are the nephew of a friend and neighbor, almost my relative by marriage. As the latter, I could have forgiven anything you might have said to me. When you interrupted, the provocation was great, yet I did not act. Even when the priest accused me of bestial crimes, I bowed my head and tried to accept his insults." He turned to Yoshi. "Striking a warrior cannot be forgiven. I would be justified if I cut you down without another word."

Genkai, Ietaka, and Fumio were frozen in place.

Chikara continued, "I have always lived by the principles of duty, loyalty, integrity, and honor. I cannot allow this insult to go unpunished."

Yoshi recovered his composure. He appealed to the samurai. "Lord Chikara," he said, "before you take action consider the consequences. We have no real quarrel—"

"Quiet, fool!" Chikara hissed. "You have said enough."

Yoshi started forward. Genkai caught his sleeve. "Do not make it worse," he said. "He dare not cause you serious injury; he has enough to atone for already." He turned to Chikara. "If you harm my cousin you will not achieve Nirvana. You will be doomed for the next ten thousand years."

Chikara ignored Genkai's warning. His voice was resigned as he directed himself to Yoshi. "Before I administer a lesson, I want to remind you that you live by the grace of the *daimyos* and their soldiers,'' he said. ''If we acted differently the countryside would be in rebellion. There is unrest in the north because the *daimyos* did not act firmly. My actions set an example for the benefit of all. My family will be strong, my *shoen* secure, because I never let weakness and misguided humanity keep me from my duty.'' He took a breath and squared his shoulders. ''Enough,'' he said, ''if you do not have a sword, Kagasuke will lend you his.''

Wordlessly, Yoshi held out his hand. Kagasuke detached his sash and sword and handed them to him. Yoshi unsheathed the blade; he swished it back and forth to test its weight and balance. He had studied the sword with his uncle and in Kyoto, and though he was an amateur, he fantasied, in the foolishness of youth, that fate had given him a chance to remove Chikara honorably and declare himself to Nami.

Ietaka and Fumio were speechless. Ietaka wondered how Yoshi could remain so calm. The only sign of nervousness he saw was a beading of sweat that streaked the white makeup on Yoshi's forehead, and that might be only from the warmth of the day. Ietaka watched Chikara stalk to the portal. Chikara had not unsheathed his sword, yet something in the feral way he moved made Ietaka nervous. Would Chikara heed Genkai's warning and be merciful?

Chikara left the porch followed by Yoshi, Ietaka, Fumio, and Genkai with Kagasuke bringing up the rear. They stopped fifty yards from the castle in a flat field surrounded by thick rows of cherry trees.

Fumio's face was a mask of unease. The boy was no match for the experienced Chikara. He had to hold himself in check; years of living by the samurai code made it impossible for him to interfere. His mind scurried from thought to thought. Was there no way out? What would happen to the proposed union of the two houses? Would the wedding be completed? How could he save Yoshi from the result of his madness? As his mind darted through the implications of this duel, he realized the truth. There *was* no way out; a samurai had been struck and Yoshi would have to be punished.

Genkai stood solemnly at Yoshi's side. He was the cause of Yoshi's undoing. For the first time since he took his vows his faith was shaken. Buddha had failed to save the farmer and now Genkai could not depend on Buddha to save Yoshi. Why had he insisted on speaking to Chikara? He had been a fool. His cousins were right. There was no satisfaction to be gained and he might have destroyed his cousin by his actions. He watched Yoshi—seemingly so calm—and his vision misted with tears. This must surely end in tragedy! Chikara would not hold back and Yoshi would die because of Genkai's intransigence.

Meanwhile, Ietaka was re-evaluating Yoshi. He had accused him of being a shallow nonentity, yet Yoshi had bravely diverted Chikara's attention from Genkai while he, Ietaka, stood helplessly by. How could he help Yoshi now? Yoshi's only advantage was youth and it was not enough to withstand Chikara's strength.

Chikara turned to Yoshi. "Are you ready?" he asked. His voice was icy cold; sun glistened from his forehead and cast shadows that turned his face into a devil mask.

Yoshi faced him, sword in both hands, and nodded.

With snakelike speed Chikara slid his sword from its sheath and struck at Yoshi's midsection. Reflex saved the younger man; his blade barely deflected the attack as he gave ground. The look on Chikara's face and the savagery of the assault told Yoshi that Chikara did not intend to stop at a lesson in manners. He was trying for the kill.

The two men circled warily. Chikara came in again, and again his blade was barely parried. Two more strokes, three, and suddenly the fabric parted; blood appeared on Yoshi's shoulder.

Yoshi bit his lip, sweat beaded his forehead. Obviously Chikara was the stronger swordsman.

Ietaka considered interfering. Perhaps he could stop the duel before Yoshi was mortally wounded. As he stirred, Fumio, reading his mind, caught his sleeve and held him in place. Whatever the result, this was Yoshi's battle.

Yoshi had not made an attack, and as he fell back, each

swing of Chikara's sword came closer to maiming him. He
realized that the battle was to the death and he could not win
by continually retreating. He was losing confidence in the
face of Chikara's superior skill; he had to take the initiative
before it was too late.

He made his move.

As Chikara's blade swept past him, Yoshi slipped back
and with a shout lunged to counterattack.

Too late! He had been tricked! Chikara's first stroke was a
feint, and when Yoshi shifted, the sword reversed itself and
slit across his breast parting his robe and again drawing flecks
of blood. Yoshi jumped back holding his left hand across the
wound. He was moving more slowly now; the wounds were
taking their toll. Chikara charged. Yoshi danced heavily to
the side. He was no more than three feet from Fumio and
Ietaka. They smelled the nervous sweat that darkened the
back of Yoshi's robe and dripped from his face. Chikara
struck straight downward at the head. Yoshi managed to
block the blade but it knocked his arm down and sprayed the
watchers with blood and perspiration. Yoshi heard his own
labored breathing as he drew on hidden reserves of strength.
With an effort, he leaped forward, his sword striking again
and again, weaving a pattern of glittering steel that forced
Chikara to retreat. It seemed no defense could withstand this
attack. Yoshi's face reddened with effort as he drove his
opponent before him.

Now, Chikara's forehead was wet and his breathing rough.
He was barely able to parry the blows. But the unnatural
energy that drove Yoshi finally reached an end; he slowed
and stopped as he came abreast of Genkai. He stepped back
and lowered his sword. "Chikara," he gasped, "enough
. . ."

There was a moment of confusion. Chikara, still keyed to
parry and respond, did not hear. He blindly started a coun-
terstroke. Genkai—seeing Chikara was unaware of Yoshi's
surrender—stepped forward screaming, "Stop!" Yoshi instinctively pulled back as Chikara's sword continued toward
his midsection. In that instant, Genkai was between Yoshi

and the blade. It was too late to stop the swordstroke; the edge slit across Genkai's abdomen just under his rib cage. Red blood stained the yellow fabric. Genkai's mouth fell open as he watched his intestines spilling over his robe. He sank to his knees, his strength ebbing as he intoned the death prayer. "Oh, Amida Nyorai, who sheds the light of his presence through the ten sections of the world, gather into thy radiant heaven all who call upon Thy Name."

Yoshi flung himself at Chikara with an inarticulate scream. Ietaka, acting at last, threw his arms around Yoshi's shoulders and held him fast. Tears streaked Yoshi's powder and rouge. His long hair hung like an ugly crown around his distorted face. For the first time in his twenty-two years, Yoshi had met evil beyond his control. He prided himself on his rational mind, but in this irreversible moment of horror, he snapped under the pressure of unrecognized emotions. He trembled with rage, cursing Chikara. Consequences meant nothing as he raved wildly.

Fumio knelt by Genkai's body, too late to help; his nephew was already dead. He restrained his grief with difficulty. "Please leave at once, Lord Chikara," he said quietly.

Although he was now in better command of his emotions, Chikara was almost as disturbed as Fumio. In one terrible moment he had been changed from a samurai defending his honor to the murderer of a priest. "It was an accident . . . I had no intention of harming the priest," he explained. His voice tightened. "This is not the time to pursue it further, but I have not finished with that one." He nodded toward Yoshi who was shouting incoherently and fighting against Ietaka's restraining grasp.

Fumio ignored the struggle. He nodded coolly to Chikara and Kagasuke. "I understand . . . I must have time to think of the implications of what has happened here today," he said.

As Chikara and his brother left, Fumio turned to Yoshi. "Stop at once!" he snapped. "You have caused enough damage. If it weren't for your hot-headedness your cousin would be alive."

Yoshi subsided to the ground. His shoulders shook and tears streaked his face. Ietaka kept one arm around him, their old enmity forgotten. Yoshi looked up at him piteously and sobbed, "Chikara will pay for this. Oh, how he will pay!"

Ietaka ignored Yoshi's weeping. "Control yourself," he said. "Tears will not help. Accompany us to the castle where we can clean and dress your wounds."

Yoshi pushed him away. "Leave me," he said. "My wounds are nothing . . . I wish to remain here a while . . . ."

Ietaka shrugged. He released Yoshi and looked to Fumio for instructions. Fumio signaled him to help with Genkai's body. Together they carried the blood-smeared corpse to the castle.

When they were gone, Yoshi sat alone in the middle of the field. The cicada still called for its mate, the birds still sang, and far away the ocean still roared.

The sun was far in the west and the day had turned cold before he rose and shook his fist at the sky. "You deserted him," he cried to the invisible gods. "He dedicated his life to you and you deserted him. I will never forget. By all the gods in the firmament, I swear to avenge Genkai's death." His fist lowered to his side, his head hung dejectedly. As the sun dipped below the horizon, he shivered. His sense of loss was a cold hand gripping his heart.

Nine

Tree frogs croaked contrapuntal mating calls and evening shadows lengthened. Yoshi had not eaten since morning; the canker of hate made his belly reject the idea of food. He walked the fifty yards to the castle with leaden feet. This was not the same Yoshi who, a few hours earlier, had been called popinjay and had resented the truth of the insult. His orderly universe had been toppled by the death of his cousin. He had found that Ietaka was right: Goodness and power were not synonymous. Quite the contrary! Yoshi would never again be the innocent courtier living a gadfly existence while blind to the evil around him. Now he knew evil, and Chikara was its name. A layer of effete sophistication had been burned off by the heat of events. His hair was in disarray, his robe was stained with red, and he smelled of blood and sweat. He could not have cared less about his physical appearance as he plodded along, consumed by hatred. He had to see the family, to explain the feelings that had developed in him as a result of the tragedy in the field. His inner turmoil could destroy him or lead him to discoveries about himself. Had he caused Genkai's death? His insides shriveled at the thought. Had it been jealousy over Nami's marriage that had made him confront Chikara in so quixotic a fashion? No! No! He must not lay a burden of guilt on Nami. She was not at fault; this was between himself and Chikara. No one else.

Fumio, Ietaka, and Nami were inside the front hall. Nami was sobbing. "Poor Genkai, I cannot believe he is dead. Such a gentle soul." She raised a tear stained face to Yoshi. "Why did you have to strike my lord?"

Yoshi had no answer. His guilt at being instrumental in Genkai's death, and the additional burden of Nami's grief, overwhelmed him. Nami turned to Fumio and asked in a piteous voice, "How can I marry Chikara after what happened this afternoon?"

Yoshi sucked in his breath. How could he still dare hope that the wedding would be canceled? That Nami could still be his? His heart beat faster. The resilience of youth gave him a moment of hope and, at the same time, increased his guilt. How callous that in this time of sorrow he thought of personal advantage. Besides, it was a forlorn hope.

"Nami, the wedding will proceed as planned," Fumio said firmly. "I loved Genkai more than any of you; he was my adopted son. Nevertheless, what he did was an act of madness. Chikara could not have stopped his swordstroke. It was a ghastly accident; bad fortune, no more."

Yoshi's lip trembled. "Genkai's death was my fault," he said. "I suffer the guilt. But there is no excuse for Chikara. He goaded us into an untenable position. Nothing can justify what he did. It was murder!"

Fumio released Nami and pointed a finger at Yoshi. "Chikara is a *daimyo*. You, yourself, said he acted correctly in the matter of the farmer. He committed no wrong; it was his duty to punish the tax evaders. You, on the other hand, had no right to strike him. Buddha forgive me when I say it: you were at fault and you caused Genkai's death." Fumio considered that by the warrior's code, by the accepted laws of the land, by every applicable criterion, Chikara had done no wrong; Yoshi and Genkai had overstepped their bounds.

Ietaka fumed inwardly as Fumio spoke. Suddenly he erupted. "Chikara is beneath contempt," he snarled. He turned to Nami. "I've had misgivings about your coming marriage. I held my tongue because you seemed happy. Now I can no longer remain silent.'' He glared at Fumio. ''We were there. We know he provoked Yoshi into the battle. If Yoshi had not interceded, Chikara would have fought Genkai. The result would have been the same. He is not sorry Genkai died. This was a political act by a desperate man. The days of Taira power are nearing their end and he is fighting a losing battle against the tide of the Minamoto. He knew he would endanger his marriage, yet he coldly set out to murder an opponent because he was menaced politically.''

''Nonsense,'' said Fumio heatedly. ''You give every action a political meaning, but you are wrong in this case. This had nothing to do with politics. Yoshi struck him! There was no other reason for the duel and there was no other response possible.''

''Uncle, Yoshi was hopelessly outclassed as a swordsman.''

''Then he should not have struck Chikara. Imagine! A mere boy striking a warrior lord! I admire Yoshi's courage and at the same time deplore his stupidity.''

''He did it to save Genkai,'' said Ietaka. ''If he had not acted promptly Genkai would have been goaded into a duel. Chikara killed Genkai after Yoshi had already surrendered.''

''And you allowed him to do it without raising a hand,'' Yoshi bitterly told Fumio. ''Chikara manipulated us. While I accept the blame for my part, remember it was Chikara who killed Genkai. Will I ever be able to forgive myself for not avenging him?''

Yes, thought Yoshi, I was weak. When Genkai was struck down, I cried, I protested, and I allowed Ietaka to stop me. I did nothing. If I truly loved Genkai, I would have escaped from Ietaka's grasp and attacked Chikara. Who am I? What am I? Am I less than a man as Chikara claimed? He questioned himself as never before. The wall of complacency developed at the court cracked further in this onslaught of self-doubt.

''I should have died with him,'' Yoshi concluded sadly.

''Genkai is hardly cold and you talk of what you should

have done," Nami said to Yoshi, her voice cracking. "It does not matter any longer. If Chikara was right, he saved his honor and we will be married. If he was wrong he will commit *seppuku* tonight."

When Nami suggested that Chikara would kill himself if he was wrong, it was because *seppuku,* vulgarly called *hara-kiri,* belly slitting, was considered preferable to a life of dishonor.

The practice had begun during the Hōgen Incident in 1156. Minamoto-no-Tametomo, on the losing side of that short vicious war, disemboweled himself rather than risk the dishonor of capture. He did it in the most painful way possible, cutting through his abdomen until he severed the nerve centers of the spine. Tametomo's death brought honor to the Minamoto clan. His death was deemed the ultimate act of heroism. By the next decade, suicide by disembowelment was the only honorable choice for a samurai who was guilty of wrongdoing, or a soldier whose capture was imminent.

Nami continued, "Only Chikara, himself, knows what he will do." She hesitated, brushing a tear from her cheek. "What we say will not affect his actions." She shook her head sadly. "I am sorry, I can't bear anymore of this. Excuse me." She swept up her robe and ran from the room.

With Nami gone, Fumio turned to Yoshi, sorry for the things he had said in anger. Misery was written on Yoshi's face. After all, he was still a young man and would live the rest of his life feeling guilt for Genkai's death.

"Have the servants draw a hot bath and bring you clean clothes," he said. "Once you have dressed your wounds and changed you will see things more clearly. We will talk more over dinner."

Yoshi looked down at his filthy robe. "Yes, uncle," he said. "I'll never forget what happened. I don't need these clothes to remind me." His eyes shifted to Ietaka. "I have much to think about. I won't waste the life Genkai gave me. There are actions I will have to take," he said meaningfully. Then he turned back to his uncle. "Yes, we must talk," he said bleakly.

Ietaka took Yoshi's arm and led him off. When Fumio was alone, his head drooped and tears burned his rough cheeks, tears for Genkai and the long years ahead without the warmth and kindness of his adopted son.

The tears released a flood of memories that threatened to drown him in sorrow. Genkai as a youth, tall, straight, athletic. All the characteristics Fumio admired. And as a monk . . . the peace and serenity that had become a part of his personality. Fumio's shoulders shook. He had been jealous of his nephew's dedication to the Buddha. Instead of being pleased for Genkai's happiness, he had tried to turn him from his beliefs. Now it was too late to make amends.

He suppressed his tears; a *daimyo* could not afford to let the world see his weakness. He had to appear strong. Fumio wiped his eyes and adjusted his robe. There were practical matters to consider. He would have to act in the best interests of the living. The *shoen* and the family had to survive. He adjusted his face as he had adjusted his robe; no one would guess the true depth of his feelings.

As the family ended their meal, Yoshi asked why his mother was not at dinner.

"Lady Masaka left on a pilgrimage to Ise shortly before Chikara's arrival. She will be back in a week's time," said Fumio pushing away his empty rice bowl.

"Nami, isn't it strange that she should be absent for your wedding?" asked Yoshi.

"Not at all," Nami answered. "Your mother travels to Ise regularly. It is the only time she leaves the northern wing."

"Yet I am surprised she did not insist on being here for the final ceremony," said Yoshi.

"Your mother is not one of Lord Chikara's admirers," said Fumio. "She avoids him whenever possible. I believe her pilgrimage was a subterfuge to save her the embarrassment of being with him at the rice-cake ceremony."

The subject of Chikara had been preying on Yoshi's mind all through the meal. Now that his name had been brought into the conversation, Yoshi felt free to speak without tradi-

tional politeness. "My mother's judgment is correct. Chikara should be denied access to the castle and not allowed to
marry Nami," he said sharply.

Fumio was equally direct. He held Yoshi accountable for
the tragic events of the day and was incensed at Yoshi's tone.
No matter how much Yoshi had suffered he had no right to be
so brusque with his uncle. "Yoshi, hold your tongue! Don't
presume to tell me who my guests will be or what they will
do. Antagonizing Chikara will serve no purpose. Genkai is
dead. Rash action cannot bring him back. We have practical
matters to consider. A merger of my house and Chikara's will
give us the power and security which neither of us has alone. I
will not jeopardize that possibility because of your lack of
self-control. Show you are a man by showing respect for
others."

Yoshi responded by passionately denouncing Chikara,
while his uncle again defended Chikara's actions as the only
possible course he could have taken under the circumstances.

Ietaka, who had sat silently through the meal, interrupted.
"I agree with Yoshi," he said. "Chikara is typical of the
high-handed Taira lords."

Fumio looked at him with disdain. "I remind you," he
said, "that we owe our lives and fortunes to the Taira clan.
Whatever they do in the court is their business. Here they
have allowed us to manage our *shoen* in peace. When you
insult the Taira you insult your own kind."

"We have not descended to their level of decadence," said
Ietaka. "You are a fair and honest lord who rules by honorary
right and has earned the trust and loyalty of the people. The
Taira sit in their court circle and play empty games while the
lives of the Great Treasure—the Japanese people—grow less
bearable each year." Ietaka turned to Nami. "You sit silently, Sister, with your eyes downcast. Why have you not
leaped to the defence of your lord?" Before she could answer
he said triumphantly, "It is because you know he is not
worthy of your love. If our parents were here they would
insist on canceling your marriage plans."

Nami did not respond. Her face was sad; she refused to look up.

"Let her be," said Fumio. "She is the only one of you with intelligence. She knows Chikara will return. He has the right and the power to punish Yoshi. If he spares him, it will only be out of respect and love for Nami." He reached to Yoshi's sleeve. "She is your only hope," he warned.

Yoshi recoiled. "I don't need her help," he said. "I will leave in the morning. You will not be troubled by my embarrassing presence any longer. If Nami completes her marriage to the murderer of Genkai, it will not be for my sake."

"You cannot leave before your wounds heal," said Fumio.

"I will accompany him," said Ietaka. "I am versed in survival in the outside world and Yoshi will need my help. His wounds do not seem serious; I can take care of them. We will be gone before Chikara returns to destroy another member of our family."

Ten

At six A.M., Yoshi and Ietaka were awakened by the bells of Seiken-ji. Yoshi had spent a restless night, sleeping fitfully between alternating bouts of depression and self-abnegation. How could he have forgotten Fumio's lessons so quickly? Besides teaching him to respect the Emperor and the Imperial institutions, Fumio had taught him the qualities necessary to a samurai: to act honorably, to face adversity bravely, and to be a man among men. These values had been buried under a veneer of false sophistication, a veneer that had been stripped away by yesterday's horror. Yoshi supposed there had always been a schism between Fumio's values and those of the court; he was disgusted with himself for allowing the court's values to win out for so long.

This morning, Yoshi's face was innocent of makeup and he wore a utilitarian brown robe over a simple undercloak. He did not carry his usual fan, and without the fan, without makeup, and without soft colors, he looked like any other young man of his time. The strutting court peacock was gone forever, replaced by a slim traveler of indeterminate background. His face, no longer hidden by a white powder mask, seemed soft and vulnerable, but intelligent and alert.

Only a pain shining deep in his eyes revealed the effect of his recent experience.

The cousins ate quickly and packed a change of clothing. Yoshi hid enough gold for the trip in the *obi*, wrapped around his waist.

Mist covered Suruga Bay as they set off down the mountain, each absorbed in his own thoughts. Yoshi had been preoccupied by Genkai's death from the moment he arose. His memory of that horrid moment recurred constantly leaving him ill at ease. He tried to clear his mind by analyzing his feelings about Nami and Chikara. On the one hand, their marriage would be ideal from a political point of view. Two adjoining *shoen* united into one powerful family holding: double land, double samurai, double power in the court. Were Yoshi's selfish considerations of sufficient importance to cost Uncle Fumio the loss of the additional security a union with Chikara's house would bring? And Nami—he felt a pang as he thought of her—claimed to love the older man. Would Yoshi be causing her unwanted grief if he had his way and the marriage was not completed? Yes, he could see where, from her point of view, the union would be desirable. Hateful as he seemed, Chikara was a virile man who lived honorably by his lights, a lord to be admired for his strength of character and his determination to uphold his version of Imperial law. On the other hand, Chikara had stolen two of the most precious people in Yoshi's life and Yoshi would never accept him as a member of the family. Yoshi had vowed revenge and there could be no turning back. Time would pass. Chikara might believe all was forgotten, but Yoshi would never forget.

Lost in thought, Yoshi had not noticed the time. A half hour had passed and they were almost at the base of the mountain. The road took a last turn and the temple came into view. A short distance beyond, Yoshi could see Okitsu and the Tokaido Road winding between the mountain and the water. The black sand crescent of Miho with its cover of gnarled old pines was dimly visible through the mist that covered the bay.

The scene was breathtaking.

Below the town, at the water's edge, he saw the saltmakers already at work. A group of women, carrying heavy buckets of salt water on their stooped shoulders, moved from the sea to the sandbeds; another group raked the sand to filter out the salt. Huge metal pots of boiling concentrate sent smoke rolling along the beach and added to the thickness of the mist.

Yoshi bowed his head. Salt air left a moist film on his face and smoke filled his nostrils with a tang reminiscent of his childhood days with Genkai. A lump formed in his throat at the sense of loss that engulfed him. It was hard to realize Genkai was no more.

At the edge of town, the cousins searched for a team of bearers to start them on the way to Kyoto. They rejected an oxcart driver who offered cheap passage. The thought of returning to Kyoto at two miles an hour was unbearable. A palanquin would be faster. It would mean the difference between five days and three weeks of travel.

Their search was delayed by the entourage of a northern *daimyo* returning home from the capital. Masses of samurai in light armor blocked the road. Behind them, banners fluttered in the breeze and horses' hooves kicked up dust and streamers of morning mist. In the center of the column, the *daimyo* rode a great stallion; the horse wore chain mail with ornaments of silver and blue, while its master was in scarlet armor with a golden helmet. At the rear of the column, more samurai carried banners with calligraphic messages describing past triumphs.

To Yoshi and Ietaka, the twenty minutes until the parade cleared the road seemed interminable. When the dust settled, Yoshi called Ietaka's attention to a group of bearers by the roadside. There were six of them, alike as snow peas. Large men with stringy muscles and deformed shoulders, dressed in loin cloths that left their private parts hanging out. Each man was covered with tattoos: Dragons, warships, animals, and birds ran in profusion over their backs and chests. They shouted and laughed, opening mouths almost innocent of teeth.

Ietaka made arrangements with the leader and within minutes they were bumping down the road, two bearers in front, two in back, and two reliefs running alongside. Yoshi had to hold the ceiling strap to keep from falling out. But they were on their way.

They headed southeast on the Tokaido Road. This was the Great Eastern Road, the central artery of the outer provinces, the thin thread that held the eastern half of the empire together. From is origin in the western plains—where one day Tokyo would grow—the road ran three hundred miles to Kyoto. The palanquin had two hundred miles to travel from Okitsu to the capital.

Except for a short stop to exchange bearers at post stations every fifty miles, the palanquin moved at a steady pace all day. At night, they stopped at inns along the road and the cousins were able to spend comparably comfortable nights. On the first evening, they conversed at length before retiring. Yoshi had never heard the story of Ietaka's escape from the Taira plantation at first hand; he was enthralled by the heroic tale.

Ietaka had been only eleven years old when he was kidnapped. Separated from his parents, mercilessly beaten, underfed and overworked, there had been little hope of the previously pampered child's survival past the first weeks of captivity. But, at risk to themselves, some of the other slaves had protected him and secretly shared their rations until he grew strong enough to fend for himself.

It was a hard, cruel world he had found himself in. The slave plantation was surrounded by a high fence and was patrolled by armed guards. Even so, slaves would sometimes bolt for freedom. Few got past the fence and those that did found themselves trapped in a thick forest on a small island six miles from the mainland. None escaped.

As he grew older, Ietaka had become a source of help and comfort to his fellow slaves, ministering to their needs and

caring for the sick. The guards and the bailiff in charge were
not pleased. New slaves were cheaper than the cost of keeping old ones alive.

In the seventh month of 1164, shortly after Ietaka's seventeenth birthday, Tezuka, a friend, had died. He had been a
good man, a man who regularly shared his meager rations
with the sick, and helped those too weak to care for themselves. More important from Ietaka's point of view, it had
been Tezuka's help that was mainly responsible for keeping
Ietaka alive in the first year of his captivity. Ietaka was
punished for a minor offence by being chosen to carry the
corpse to the burial ground. To a believer in the Shinto
religion, with its celebration of the natural deities and its
abhorrence of death and decay, there was no lower form of
labor. There were no religious rites for slaves; Tezuka's body
would be unceremoniously dumped in a ravine that served as
a common grave. The gates had been opened and Ietaka—the
corpse draped over his shoulders—led the burial party along
the rocky trail toward the hills in the center of the island. As
they had approached their destination, the odor of death grew
stronger, overpowering the natural scents of the forest. The
guards had drawn back allowing Ietaka to proceed alone.

Plodding along the path, Ietaka had felt an upsurge of the
madness that had driven so many others to lose their lives in
vain efforts to escape. He could not throw Tezuka into the pit
as though he were a bundle of rags! This had been a human
being and deserved to be sent properly to the next world.
Whatever the cost, he would have a proper burial and afterward Ietaka would not return to slavery! Better to die in an
attempt at freedom.

Ietaka had buried his friend with a prayer and hid himself
in the ravine among the rotted corpses. The guards had
refused to brave the charnel stench of his hiding place. They
had been secure in the knowledge that Ietaka could not
escape.

They had been wrong. Ietaka's desire for life had given
him the strength to hide in the woods, to live on nuts, berries,

and grubs, and to build a primitive raft with his bare hands. On a moonless night near the end of the month, he had sailed for the mainland and had became the first slave to escape from the plantation.

Ietaka held the Taira responsible for their bailiff's inhumanity. His experiences left him loathing the Taira governors and their court. This made it difficult when he visited his uncle, and had been the reason for his automatic dislike of the foppish Yoshi. Since the duel, Ietaka's opinion had changed. The more time he spent with his younger cousin the more convinced he became that he had misjudged him. Foolhardy or brave, Yoshi had drawn Chikara's wrath to save Genkai. Ietaka began to see qualities that had been hidden under Yoshi's veneer of court clothing and makeup: a basic decency, a strength that allowed him to face the discomfort of his wounds without complaint, and a calm intelligence that made him an attentive listener.

There were also changes in Yoshi's attitude. For the first time in his nineteen years he reflected on the way of life of others. As he listened to Ietaka's story of heroism in the face of dehumanizing conditions, he saw that among people who had been beneath his consideration, nobility often appeared. His admiration for the strong, direct, and capable Ietaka grew and he began to develop a contempt for the parasitic courtiers who had recently been his idols. He was ashamed as he remembered his shallow life at the court. How was it that in the same family, living in the same city, two cousins could have developed in such different ways?

Ietaka's experience as a slave had taught him humility and compassion. These were concepts Yoshi had never considered and he discovered that from Ietaka's teaching, from the death of Genkai, and from his secret love for Nami, he had learned compassion too, a compassion that had been buried by court life.

While the cousins spent their evenings talking and learning about each other, their days were spent bouncing uncomfortably as they held their ceiling straps and stared at the passing scenery. The constant movement of the palanquin kept Yoshi's wounds from healing. He ignored the pain, hiding it from Ietaka. After all, he told himself, the wounds were not serious.

Ejira, Fuchu, Mariko, Okabe, Fujieda . . . the towns seemed interminable as the palanquin jounced along. The breathtaking views of mountains, valleys, ocean, and forest lost their charm and Yoshi retreated into himself, passing the hours thinking of Nami. He castigated himself for letting his hatred of Chikara make him forget her. He squeezed his eyes shut in an effort to picture her. He must not allow her image to fade from mind.

On the fifth day the palanquin crossed the Kamo River and reached the gates of Kyoto. The bearers left them just inside the city. Tired and stiff, glad to have ended their journey, they continued on foot to Suzaku-Ōji—Red Bird Street.

Suzaku-Ōji was nearly three hundred feet across, the broadest and busiest street in the world. It was lined with willow trees, a green frame around the busy life in its center. Imperial palanquins, oxcarts, and pedestrians jammed its length from the *Rashomon*—the southern gate, where thieves and beggars plied their trade—to the ninefold enclosure where the Emperor lived.

Kyoto was laid out on a series of perfect grids with Ichijō or first street in the north and Nijō, Sanjō, Shijō, Gojō, or second, third, fourth, and fifth streets continuing to Kujō or ninth street at the southern gate.

Cherry blossoms scented the air and the bustle of the great city made them feel welcome. Commercial buildings on both sides of the street were filled with people transacting business. From time to time, they passed groups of farmers who had come to the city to protest a recent raise in the Imperial tax. Many of these groups were noisy and unruly. Troops of Imperial Police rode through the streets dispersing the crowds, which simply regrouped after they passed. The street shrines were surrounded by visitors asking special favors of the Shinto gods. And the buildings themselves! Yoshi was struck, as always, by the sheer mass of architecture; many buildings towered five stories above the street. Gold, silver, red, blue: Colors ran in profusion on the lacquered eaves and gables of painted pavilions that covered entire city blocks.

Suzaku-Ōji ran three miles through the center of the capital. Yoshi and Ietaka walked side by side along the broad avenue savoring the noise and bustle of slow-moving oxcarts and jostling pedestrians. As they approached the northeast quarter, crowds grew larger and more unruly. Peasants, in wide-brimmed straw hats, rubbed shoulders with merchants who, defying the Emperor's edict reserving silk for the nobility, dressed in silken robes. Interspersed among the peasants and merchants were students from the Confucian University, offspring of lords and ladies of the court, who affected the raiment of the lower and middle class. It was a stage through which students often passed on their way to maturity.

Was it only last month that Yoshi was part of the same university? He had never understood the motivations of these politically minded students and had avoided them, preferring instead the fashionable excesses of palace society. Even so, Yoshi was aware of the two powerful families who divided Japan: the ruling Taira and their rivals, the Minamoto. Seven years earlier, the Taira had defeated the Minamoto in a series of bloody battles to gain control of Kyoto and the lands around the Inland Sea. The leader of the Taira clan, Taira Kiyomori—a distant cousin of Chikara—settled in Kyoto and joined the Imperial court where his despotic power grew more oppressive each day.

While the Taira family reveled in pomp and ceremony at the capital, Yoritomo, the new Minamoto leader, was building an army far to the east.

The feeling that social injustices would be righted if the Minamoto clan regained power—an idea carefully fostered by the Minamoto—filtered down to the students, farmers, and merchants. Yoritomo's spies constantly sowed unrest in the city by circulating through the crowd, stirring it to action against the new tax levies.

Yoshi and Ietaka were caught in a jam of shouting people.
Nijo Street was packed from the gates of the palace enclosure
for three blocks past Suzaku-Ōji. A speaker on the steps of a
corner building exhorted the people to protest the tax in-
creases, Firebrands, many in the employ of the Minamoto,
inflamed their neighbors, crying *"Hai, hai!* Down with the
Taira! They are the cause of our troubles!"

Mounted Imperial Guards, trying to disperse the trou-
blemakers, were trampling their way out of the palace enclosure. Crowds were so dense at the gate that those closest were
trapped by the horses' hooves and guards' swords. The
horsemen were merciless, slashing at the victims, who
screamed and flailed about as they tried to escape. In the
mob, Yoshi and Ietaka were carried farther away from the
palace.

Guards hacked into the crowd; blood from a headless torso
turned the street into a slippery river; a woman with her arm
chopped off at the shoulder screamed with such force that
Yoshi heard her two blocks away.

"Try to push eastward," urged Ietaka. "We have to
escape from this mob before we are trampled." He used his
weight and size to press into the current of bodies that
inexorably flowed away from the gates. Yoshi followed
holding Ietaka's sash.

An intersection was twenty feet ahead, beyond a street
lamp whose broad stone pedestal blocked the center of the
street.

Yoshi staggered and lost his grip; suddenly they were
separated, Ietaka carried by the crowd to one side of the street
lamp and Yoshi to the other.

"Ietaka!" cried Yoshi to no avail. It was all he could do to
maintain his footing as the crowd pulled him along ever
faster.

The two streams of people converged at the corner. Yoshi
searched frantically for Ietaka. Only yards away the shouts
became louder as two Imperial Guards who had ridden
around behind the crowd were slashing their way against the

tide. Yoshi spied Ietaka only a few feet ahead. He shouted to him again just as Ietaka slipped and fell almost under the hooves of the nearest horse.

The samurai raised his sword and bent toward the fallen man. Calling on his last reserves of strength, Yoshi leaped forward and caught the attacker by the arm. With an expression of surprise, the samurai slowly twisted out of his saddle and toppled into the street. His sword fell at Yoshi's feet. Without thinking, Yoshi caught it up and thrust it into the fallen samurai's body. He helped Ietaka to his feet as the screaming crowd trampled the wounded samurai underfoot.

Another samurai saw what had happened and with a shrill battle cry drove his mount toward Yoshi and Ietaka. His sword rose and fell in a crimson arc as he made a frenzied effort to cut through the hysterical crowd; he made little headway against the weight of their numbers. Realizing he might lose his victims, he signaled the other guards at the far end of the street. He pointed at Yoshi and shouted over the noise of the mob. It was doubtful if anyone heard him, but the message was clear.

Yoshi and Ietaka froze in place; in seconds the entire Imperial force would be upon them. The people nearest them milled in blind panic, some tried to push their way ahead, others tried to retreat. The guards were closing ever faster.

"Quickly! Get off this street! They're after you!" Ietaka pulled at Yoshi's robe. "Follow me. I know a way to safety."

Yoshi's stomach tightened as he realized his desperate situation. Then Ietaka was pulling him into the anonymity of the crowd and toward an opening between two buildings. They slipped unseen into a narrow alleyway and ran down the tortuous pathway away from the screaming mob.

Once away from Nijo Street, they hurried along, hugging the sides of buildings, ducking across intersections, and putting as much distance as possible between themselves and the Imperial Guards.

Ietaka led the way to a small house on the edge of town, at

the intersection of Kyōgoku and Shijō, only a few blocks from the massacre. To the east lay a loop of the Tokaido Road. Groves of cherry trees stretched to the green hills of Mount Hiei, and the sound of early evening crickets filled the air. The mob was far behind.

"This house is ours to use. The owners are friends who are away on a pilgrimage," said Ietaka. "We will be safe here."

Eleven

Ietaka went out daily and brought Yoshi word of spies searching for him. Signs had been posted offering ten pieces of gold for his capture. Yoshi had become a hero to many of the people who lived in fear of the Imperial Guard. A common man who dared kill a mounted samurai!

Ietaka's friends returned from their pilgrimage on the fourth day. When Ietaka explained the circumstances of their guest's stay, they were jubilant, congratulating Yoshi on his bravery and insisting on joining him in a celebrative cup of sake. It was not until several hours after their homecoming that they thought of their own position as the harborers of a fugitive. Though they were still sympathetic, Yoshi detected their nervousness; he sensed their fear of the consequences should he be discovered in their home. He decided to leave that evening.

Ietaka reported the search was almost over; Yoshi would be safe if he avoided street crowds and areas where guards gathered. He would disguise himself as a commercial traveler and stay a night and day at one of the large inns, then leave the city the following evening.

Yoshi waited until after dark before he made his farewells. Ietaka's best wishes and promises of support rang in his ears as he slipped into the night. He traveled by side streets, his face hidden in shadow. There were no incidents; few people were out at night. Before long, he saw the lights of the inn and hurried toward them.

The inn's central hall was lit by oil lamps that gave off a sickly sweet odor. The innkeeper told him, yes, there was one room left and it was his for two gold pieces. Rooms were scarce. So many people had come to town. So sorry for high price.

The innkeeper clapped his hands and a young girl came silently into the hall. She moved quickly, gracefully, with tiny steps, her face turned downward. "Take care of our honored guest in any way he desires," said the innkeeper with an almost imperceptible nod. "He has paid well for your services."

The girl bowed without looking up. The innkeeper smiled at Yoshi. "She will see to your every wish," he said. "If you have any complaints don't hesitate to tell me." He left with one last hard glance at the girl.

"I am sure I will have no complaints," said Yoshi. He reached for her chin and lifted her face. And gasped. Now he saw why she kept her head down; a purple bruise covered one cheek and her eye was swollen almost shut.

"Oh, I'm sorry," said Yoshi. "You've been hurt."

"I have no complaints," said the girl in a small voice.

"How did it happen? An accident?"

"No. It was one of our guests who had drunk too much sake. Please, he meant no harm. Let us say no more about it."

A week ago, Yoshi would not have given a thought to an inn-girl's problems. Fresh from his conversations with Ietaka, he was dismayed. How cruel the travelers were who thoughtlessly abused these young girls. He tried to let her know he empathized with her and understood her feelings. Yoshi's kindly tone and sympathetic smile had the opposite effect. The girl drew back and seemed uncomfortable at his interest. "Please, we cannot stand here," she said. "The innkeeper will be angry if I do not entertain you."

Yoshi felt an immediate attraction to this sweet, badly used child. A lock of hair had become disarranged making her look soft and vulnerable. Yoshi put it back in place. For a moment he saw a look of fear as his hand reached toward her head. "Please, don't be afraid of me," he said. "I will not hurt you."

She smiled wanly, tension easing. "Follow me," she said.

She led him to a room at the rear of the inn and offered him a bath, dinner, and herself, in that order. The past week had been so full of incident Yoshi had thought of no woman beyond the out-of-reach Nami. Alone with this attractive girl, he was seized by desire, and thoughts of his pursuers were abruptly forgotten. The girl giggled as his robe rose of its own volition.

"My name is Ono," she said. "My only wish is to please you." She led him to the steaming hot tub. Yoshi had never seen breasts so large. Unfashionable but exciting, they hung, swayed, and floated on the soapy surface. Ono pressed against him from behind. She soaped and massaged his shoulders, arms and back, caressing and muttering sweetly as she slid her delicate hands over his slippery skin. He grabbed her shoulders and pulled her to him; she drew back shyly. "Can we wait till we are properly in bed?" she pleaded.

Yoshi trembled with desire. Gently, gently, she handled him till he was ready to scream with the sweet agony of anticipation. She dried him and led him back to his room where she spread the quilt and lay back with her legs drawn up.

As he pressed into her, she moaned, "Please tell the innkeeper if you are happy with me."

Later, he lay on the quilt completely relaxed, pouring out his story. Softened by the act of love, he told of his childhood friendship with Genkai and the horrible accident of his death. As he spoke she stared at the half-open wounds Chikara had inflicted on his shoulder and breast. Poor boy . . . how he must be suffering from the pain.

Ono held his head close and stroked it with warmth and affection. Yoshi's voice was muffled by her breasts; she hardly understood what he was saying, but she reacted to his talking to her as a fellow creature. How different from the callous men who passed through the inn, using and discarding her as though she were less than human.

Ono had been sold to the innkeeper when she was a baby and had worked at the inn for as long as she remembered. She had no memory of her parents—poor people who had to give up their child in order to survive. Brutality and rejection were all she had ever known.

She was stirred by feelings she did not know she possessed. She tried to concentrate on what Yoshi was saying. Yes, yes, he would go home to Okitsu. She listened to his cultured accents, so different from the coarse voices to which she was accustomed. He was a gentleman, a courtier, and she had never before met anyone like him.

She stretched and purred, catlike, beginning to caress him with loving hands. Soon his voice became soft and he turned to her again. This time he stroked and stroked, longer and longer strokes, as he strained to reach deeper for satisfaction. When she gave a muted shriek of pleasure he reacted with a surge that caused an instant orgasm.

Yoshi remained in his quarters until the following afternoon. Ono had few chances to steal time from her duties. She saw him alone only once more, at five P.M., the hour of the monkey.

An hour later, Yoshi was seated at dinner with a group of pilgrims who had stopped on their way to the famous shrine at Ise. The pilgrims talked about events of the past week. They were from the south and represented a cross-section of types—farmers, merchants, and service people. Each group had its own opinion, influenced by its own interests: the farmers thought there was justice in the demands of the dissidents; the merchants and service people felt that not only was there no justice in the demands, but that anyone who resisted the Imperial Guards should be executed.

A man, not one of the pilgrims' party, took the part of the samurai. He told his dinner companions about the youth who had killed an Imperial Guard in the riot several days before. "He fought and killed one of the Emperor's samurai, then escaped into hiding. The whole city is waiting for him to reappear. I understand many good people died on the street because of this man's defiance of authority. Wasn't he wrong?" He looked around challenging someone to answer.

Yoshi put down his rice bowl. "Perhaps the Imperial Guards were wrong in attacking the crowd," he said. "And perhaps the man was only trying to save himself or to protect the life of a friend."

One of the pilgrims joined the conversation. "The guards act only with proper authority; they represent the Emperor and Taira Kiyomori, the supreme chancellor," he said. "They cannot be wrong. If people fight back, we will be living in the latter days of the law and our society will come to an end."

Another chimed in, and the conversation ran freely up and down the table. Most of the pilgrims were aghast at the idea of resisting the Emperor or the Taira government. Soon Yoshi was alone in defending the actions of the unknown rebel.

While they argued, the man who started the conversation slipped quietly out of the dining room. He left the inn and hurried toward the Imperial Palace.

Yoshi was so involved in the discussion he did not notice the man's departure. He was speaking when he became aware that Ono had entered the dining room and was pulling at his sleeve. He frowned and shook her off continuing to make what he considered a telling point. Finally, he could not ignore her. "What is it?" he asked impatiently.

"The man who just left," she whispered. "He is a spy for the Ministry of Justice."

Twelve

===

Before Yoshi left, he held Ono's hand and wished her good fortune. "Please hurry," she said nervously. "It is dangerous to tarry."

"Take care of yourself, Ono," said Yoshi, tenderly caressing her bruised cheek. "I shall return one day with a reward for the help you gave me."

She nodded dumbly, blinking away a tear as she watched him hasten across the fields. If the spy informed the Ministry of Justice he was in the city there would be no place to hide within its walls. And if the Imperial troops found him? She shuddered at the thought of Yoshi's head being paraded through the streets on a pike.

Yoshi had to escape Kyoto quickly. He had told Ono he would go to Okitsu Castle; however, it would be dangerous for Fumio if he hid there. Where else could he turn? He began to feel the panic of the fugitive. In desperation he decided to return to Ietaka's friend's house. He would borrow clothing and gold before continuing northward. Perhaps he could even convince Ietaka to accompany him.

The sun settled below the horizon as he left the grounds of the inn. Crossing under the trees he heard shouts behind him and saw lights from dozens of torches surrounding the building. A hundred or more samurai besieged the inn. His stomach felt hollow and drops of perspiration beaded his brow. He had barely escaped in time.

He quickened his steps, plunging through back alleys, open fields, and clusters of trees until he reached the forested hills north of Kyoto. After an hour of panic-stricken flight, he found a small cavern in the darkest part of the woods. He covered the entrance with branches and rocks, pulling the last branch in place as he slid inside, shaking with fear and fatigue. He had escaped the Imperial troops but the danger was not over. The woods were perilous at night; wandering bandits lived there and to be caught by them could mean death for an unwary traveler.

Nothing in his life had prepared him for this situation. As he tried to sleep he remembered a terrible story he had heard as a child. . . . A young man left his widowed father's farm to seek his fortune in the city. He was an only son so the parting was particularly poignant. An occasion for both joy and sorrow: joy that the boy, Toyo, was making his own way, and sorrow that he was leaving the father he loved behind him.

When he set forth, Toyo was young, his features still soft and unfocused by life. Despite his youth, Toyo's sincerity and ambition impressed a carpenter, who hired him. He worked hard and the passage of time changed him; he grew taller and heavier as a result of his labors.

After five years of hard work, Toyo's life came to an important turning. He was to be married within the month, and he wanted his father to share his joy and success. He decided to return home for a brief visit and to invite his father to the wedding. His fiancee had mixed emotions about his departure. Ginyo was a sensitive, high-strung young girl, daughter of Toyo's employer; she warned him to beware of danger—highwaymen lurked along the main roads awaiting unsuspecting travelers. "I love you," she told Toyo, "and I would not want to go on living if anything happened to you."

"Have no fear," Toyo reassured her. "I know the forests between here and my father's farm. I will be safe."

Though he would only be gone a short while, Toyo's friends and fellow workers insisted on celebrating his leavetaking. They met at his house where they gaily proposed toast after toast refusing to allow him to leave as planned.

"To the best friend I ever had," said one.

"I drink to a true gentleman," said another.

"To my future son-in-law," said his employer.

Since he had many friends and his fiancee had many relatives, he was unable to disengage himself until late in the afternoon.

Once on his way, Toyo made rapid progress; he avoided highways and, though the forest was dense, covered a considerable distance by nightfall almost making up the time lost by his late departure. He had planned on a two-day trip but as the sun of the second day lowered in the west, he knew he would not reach his destination before dark. He found himself tired and hungry in a small town not far from his goal.

"I will visit my aunt, Obaasen," he told himself. "Only a short distance remains to my father's house, and since I know these woods so well, I can rest and continue after dark."

Obaasen was overjoyed to see him. Toyo had changed so much she did not recognize him when he announced himself at her door. But when Toyo explained who he was, she was effusive in her greetings. Obaasen was a warmhearted, garrulous old woman. Once Toyo was in the house, she made a great fuss and insisted he stay till he had eaten a decent meal. Toyo was not difficult to convince; he had eaten little on his journey through the woods.

As Toyo wolfed down the food, Obaasen kept up a steady flow of chatter telling him of the difficulties his father had encountered in his absence. "The drought destroyed his crops. His horse and cow died from an unknown disease. The past year was terrible for him. Poor man, I can't understand how he manages to earn enough to feed himself. His old friends would help him, but he avoids them and stays in seclusion on his farm. Toyo, your visit will lift his spirits. Your homecoming is a sign that his bad fortune has changed and the gods will smile on him again.''

Obaasen cleared the bowls from the low table, and went on, ''I wish I could see his face when he recognizes you in the morning. You will of course stay the night. It has become dangerous to traverse the forest in the dark. There is a highwayman who has waylaid many travelers in this very area.''

''No,'' Toyo said. ''I am too close to home to stop now. I wish to see my father tonight. I feel he needs me.''

Toyo set out into the dark ignoring Obaasen's continued warnings of danger.

The following morning Obaasen, sleepless from worry, went to visit her brother. She was sure she would be welcome since Toyo had come home. She was surprised to see the father without the son.

''And where is Toyo?'' she asked. ''I was certain he would be here to greet me. Isn't it wonderful he has grown into such a handsome young man.''

The father was silent. He looked at her uncomprehendingly as she babbled on about Toyo and the coming wedding. With a puzzled expression, he grudgingly asked her inside and led her to the main room where the boy's robe and bag hung on the wall. ''Ah, how wonderful, your son has arrived safely,'' she said. Her brother looked at her blankly for several seconds then . . . he understood. Without warning his eyes filled with tears and he cried out, ''I made a mistake, an honest mistake. May Amida forgive me!'' With that the poor farmer who had eked out a living as a highwayman fled from the house.

When the townspeople found him, he knelt in a lake of blood and entrails at the side of his son's shallow grave. *Seppuku*. He had slit his belly from one side to the other.

Huddled under his robe, Yoshi fell into a sleep interrupted by nightmares. He awoke with his wounds swollen, his head hot and dry; the strain of the last days had taken its toll. He painfully washed in a nearby stream and changed his clothing.

Yoshi had taken only one hour of panic-stricken flight to reach his hiding place; the return trip took half a day. He had to avoid contact with other travelers, any one of whom might be an informer. Constant vigilance and the need to hide weakened him further so he had to rest frequently. He arrived at Ietaka's friend's house after midday, and knocked at the door with his last strength.

"Ietaka!" called the friend on seeing the pale apparition on his doorstep. "*Isogi!*—hurry! Yoshi needs help." Ietaka ran to the portal. "Come inside," he said hastily. "The city is full of spies looking for you." He rushed Yoshi into the house.

"You do not look well," he said.

"I am merely weak from hunger," said Yoshi. "I have not eaten since I left the inn last night."

"Well . . . we will see to your dinner, and I will examine your wounds while the food is being prepared."

When Yoshi removed his robe, Ietaka stared at his thin limbs and the transparent skin that surrounded the inflamed areas. "As I suspected," he said brusquely to hide his dismay. "The wounds have worsened. You must be patient while I wash and dress them."

Yoshi accepted Ietaka's ministrations lethargically. At dinner, despite his declaration of hunger, Yoshi ate sparingly. When he pushed away his half-eaten rice, Ietaka told him, "The entire quarter is buzzing with news of the Imperial Guards' raid. When I heard the samurai were unhappy, I knew you had escaped."

Ietaka hesitated, he toyed with his rice bowl; he was having difficulty facing his cousin with what he had to impart. Abruptly he blurted, "Yoshi, I have bad news."

"What is it?"

"The girl, Ono." Ietaka shifted on his mat. "The samurai tortured her for information of your whereabouts. I don't know how much she told them before she died.''

"Ono . . . dead?'' Yoshi's shoulders slumped and his head fell forward as though he'd been struck.

"I'm afraid so. And the search has been reinstituted, the rewards increased. The Minister of Justice announced he will not rest until you are apprehended.''

"Let them have me,'' said Yoshi in despair. "I bring pain and death wherever I go. That poor girl! Tortured and killed for helping me.'' Yoshi heavily raised his head until his eyes locked with Ietaka's. "I should not have come here. I am endangering you and your friends,'' he said dully.

"You had no choice! You cannot escape the Taira without me; you are weak from your wounds. Tomorrow we go together. With my help, you and I will reach Okitsu and seek aid from Uncle Fumio. We will rest there till you are well again. Once you have recovered, we will travel north away from Taira power. I've always wanted to leave Kyoto to join Yoritomo Minamoto. This will be my opportunity to help you and follow my original plan.'' Ietaka tried to sound confident, but a worm of doubt ate his insides. Yoshi did not look well. He was feverish and slow to react. Except for two burning spots on his cheekbones, his face was waxen and pale. Well . . . perhaps a good night's sleep . . .

In the morning Yoshi's condition had worsened. The wounds were more inflamed. Ietaka again changed the dressings before preparing breakfast. Yoshi had no appetite. Ietaka had to force him to eat; it would be a long trip to Okitsu. Afterward, Ietaka led Yoshi to the Tokaido road where they hid in a ditch, waiting for one of the groups of pilgrims who regularly marched by on their way to the great shrine at Ise. In less than an hour Ietaka spied a likely group passing and, with Yoshi in tow, hastened to join them. A small coin purchased hats and robes from one of the party. If they could blend with the rest of the group, they would be safe.

All along the way, samurai checked travelers. From time

to time, young men were taken to the roadside and held for questioning. Yoshi was sure he was the object of the search. He nervously kept his face hidden under his new pilgrim's hat. His long hair was pulled up under the straw, changing his appearance enough so that he was never stopped for interrogation. After three days, they left the pilgrims and hired an oxcart to take them to Okitsu. They had seen no samurai for twenty miles, and the cousins felt confident they had escaped the search.

Outside Hamamatsu the cart pulled to one side at the sound of an Imperial messenger's bell. The messenger pounded along on foot without looking left or right, his face set in a grimace of pain. His kimono was gathered up in a bunch over his *obi;* sweat ran down his crotch, over his legs, and left a damp trail where his straw sandals hit the road. The message dangled from a sealed packet attached to a long pole levered over his shoulder.

Yoshi watched him run by. A presentiment that the message concerned him made his throat dry. Ietaka read the concern; he leaned out and waved a gold coin at the driver. "Hurry, there are more than fifty miles to travel and the messenger must not get too far ahead."

Two days later, the cart left them on the road to Okitsu Castle. They stopped for a short while at Seiken-ji to pray for Genkai's soul. Yoshi had a foreboding. "Do you sense it too?" he asked Ietaka, who nodded glumly in reply.

The trip had taken too long. Yoshi felt he had arrived too late and didn't know why. Even the garden he loved so well had no power to calm him today. There was evil in the air.

Clouds covered the sun and late spring heat lightning flooded the landscape with light as they left the temple.

Just before the castle gates, a voice called from the shadows under the trees. "Yoshi, Ietaka, here!"

The startled cousins peered into the darkness. They saw Uncle Fumio, half-hidden behind a tree, frantically motioning them to leave. "Get off the road! Go back by way of the woods," he cried. "Stay away from the castle."

"Stay away? Why?" asked Ietaka. Before Fumio could answer he added, "We came to you because Yoshi needs a place to rest. His wounds are causing him distress. You have to help us. You cannot refuse."

"Yoshi, I am sorry. I see you are ill and I wish I could help, but there are troops waiting to capture you. I have delayed them at the castle to give you time to escape. Do not come through the gates."

"How did they know I would come here?" asked Yoshi in a dead voice. He had already guessed the answer.

"Yesterday a messenger arrived with a letter for Chikara from the Minister of Justice."

"What did the letter say? How could the Minister be so sure of my destination?"

"Chikara showed me the letter . . . a girl you knew at an inn . . ."

"She did tell them then," Yoshi said sucking in his breath. "Poor foolish girl, in the end her suffering was to no avail." Yoshi shook his head to clear it of an unpleasant vision. He was silent, scarcely listening as Fumio said, "They are offering rewards to informants and death to anyone who gives you aid, but have no fear, your life is safe; Chikara and Nami are married. He will not act against his wife's family. He has the power to stop the troops under his command. If you should be captured, I will intercede on your behalf. Chikara will listen to me."

Yoshi's feverish brain was reeling. The reminder of Ono's death by torture, the news that Nami was officially married to Chikara, the sight of Fumio hiding from samurai on his own land—it was too much to bear. "No!" he growled. "Never demean yourself for me. Chikara is a murderer. If he finds the opportunity he will kill me as he killed Genkai and no family tie will stop him." Yoshi's voice rose; Ietaka caught his sleeve to calm him. He pulled away and shouted, "I swore vengeance and I will not stop until I have it. I don't want Chikara's pardon. I want his life. Go back, tell my mother and Nami I am well. My only possessions are these rags on

my back and a few gold pieces in my sash. I will learn to live
with discomfort and fear, and I will return when I am ready to
face Chikara.'' Yoshi's voice was so loud he did not hear the
noise from the forest behind Fumio.

"What was that?" asked Ietaka in alarm.

"Horses! Troops!" exclaimed Fumio. "A sentry must
have heard us."

"Let's go. Quickly!" gasped Ietaka, pulling Yoshi's arm.

"Remember . . . one day I will return!" cried Yoshi as he
followed Ietaka into the densest part of the forest.

The heat lightning increased in intensity and the forest
grew darker between flashes. The air thickened with mois-
ture; soon it would rain. The cousins headed through the
undergrowth on Satta Mountain towards the Okitsu River.
Every mile was agony. They had to cross the river before it
rained or they would be trapped and hunted down like mountain hares.

Yoshi was feverish, his legs weak and shaky. His skin was
torn in a dozen places by the foliage. His sandals disinte-
grated as he pounded over the uneven ground. He heard the
clatter of the samurai troop racing along the road that circled
the mountain.

When the first drops fell, they were a mile from the river
crossing. Ietaka picked up the pace with Yoshi staggering
behind. The rain became heavier. At last, the river appeared
in the valley ahead; it was rising rapidly as the rain channeled
down the hills.

The bearers at the crossing were packing to leave. Yoshi
and Ietaka, apparitions covered with mud, bloody feet leaving a trail behind them, stumbled up to the bearers.

"Take us across," Ietaka gasped.

"Too late. Too dangerous. River closed till rain stop."

"There is time if we go quickly," insisted Ietaka.

"No, too late."

Yoshi pulled out his last pieces of gold. "Get us across and
these are yours."

The bearers looked at each other. One raised his eyebrows

and took the coins. "It's more than we earn in a month. We try."

Yoshi and Ietaka sat on a rough seat on a flat open platform. Each held a strap to keep himself in place as the bearers lifted the platform and stepped into the raging stream. Feeling every rock, every high spot with iron-soled feet, the bearers inched their way across. The storm worsened and the water rose.

Ten feet from the far shore one of the bearers slipped and was carried downriver, screaming and struggling against the pressure of the water. The platform lurched, righted itself and then again slowly tipped, pitching Yoshi into the darkness. Ietaka was almost torn from his strap reaching for Yoshi's robe.

Too late! Yoshi was gone. Ietaka heard one last shout that faded in the distance. "I-I-I-e-e-e-t-a-k-a-a-a-!" Then only the sound of rain and rushing water.

The three remaining bearers straightened the platform and staggered the last few feet to shore.

On solid ground, Ietaka heard faint shouts above the roar of the storm. On the far side of the river, a troop of mounted samurai waved their swords and cursed in the rain.

PART TWO

Thirteen

===

Hanzo, the blacksmith, was a giant of a man. Working the forge kept his three hundred fifty pounds in muscular condition. His upper arms measured as big around as most men's thighs, and though his tremendous stomach made him look clumsy, he moved with the deceptive swiftness of a forest bear. An eighteen-inch neck rose smoothly from his bulky shoulders to merge into a shaven skull. Bushy black eyebrows almost met over a nose that had been broken a dozen times over the years. His voice matched his appearance: When Hanzo spoke, he roared.

In his youth, Hanzo had been a Sumo wrestler; he had abandoned the profession when he was consistently beaten by men half his size because he lacked the aggression needed to win in competitive battle. Next he had become a samurai for a northern lord; this career, too, ended in disaster when his lord was captured by an enemy, and five hundred troops banded together to march on the enemy's castle. Only Hanzo remained behind, hiding to avoid his sworn duty. The five hundred samurai died to a man, most at the hands of a superior force; the rest committed *seppuku* when their lord was killed and their cause lost.

Ashamed of his cowardice, Hanzo fled the castle. After a

fruitless year of wandering as a *ronin*—unemployed samurai—he found employment at a smithy where his great size and strength made him invaluable to the master smith.

For a time, the gods smiled on him. He had found his niche, and his shame was forgotten. He loved the forge, and he worked hard learning the art of swordmaking. The master smith and his wife lived in harmony with three daughters who helped their mother at home. The smith's life was complete except for one thing: He lacked a son. Soon, Hanzo took the place of the missing son. He was accepted as part of the family, and in time, he grew to love Kimi, the oldest and most beautiful of the daughters.

The smith was overjoyed when Hanzo announced his intentions, and after three days of feasting and ceremony, the couple was married. Within a year, Kimi was with child. The family celebrated and the smith promised to make Hanzo his legal heir. Together, Hanzo and Kimi planned their future and the future of their son-to-be.

Those had been the happiest days of Hanzo's life. His past had been forgotten, and every day he had laughed as he worked.

But the gods were fickle and demanded payment for Hanzo's secret dishonor. In the space of one day his happiness turned to ashes when his wife and the baby died during childbirth, leaving him alone with his shame.

Distraught, he left his master and built his own smithy in a secluded valley near Yoshiwara. Here, he prayed and worked every day from before dawn until long after dusk, from the first fox's cry until the mournful whooo-eee of the owl.

With the ever-growing unrest between Taira and Minamoto there was more business than one swordmaker could manage. Although his smithy flourished, Hanzo was still a sad and unhappy man unable to forget the past. He tried to keep from remembering by driving himself to exhaustion. Sparks exploded from the forge, and the sound of hammer blows constantly echoed from the surrounding hills.

He desperately needed an assistant, but no one he saw satisfied him. He prayed to Buddha and to the Shinto and pagan gods until one day, in the spring of 1168, his prayers were answered.

It had been one of the worst storms of the year, earlier than usual since the heavy rains normally came in the summer. As Hanzo huddled in his dirt-floored shop with the rain running off the thatched roof, he had a vision of his dead wife and child calling to him from the forest. Despite the downpour, his vision drove him out to his shrine to Amaterasu, the sun-goddess—Hanzo's shop was surrounded by shrines to the various deities. There he knelt on the muddy ground and prayed; he asked for the courage to die, forgiveness for his weakness, and mercy for his sins.

The drum of rain on the roof of the shrine almost covered a moaning that sounded from the trees. Hanzo was terrified. Ghosts were in the forest! He bowed his head and waited for his doom.

Nothing happened. The rain continued. The moaning stopped. Hanzo's heart gradually slowed to normal; his breathing became regular.

No sound from the forest.

He rose to explore the trees around the shrine. Water ran off his bullet head down his straw cape. The rain made it difficult to see.

Then, there it was. The ghost! A shadowy figure dressed in rags, motionless behind a tree. Hanzo stood his ground, and watched the figure slowly become a muddy, half-starved boy, approximately the same age his own son would have been.

The boy turned toward him, staggered two steps, and with a moan fell face down in the mud. Hanzo hurried to his side, rolled him over, and wiped the mud from his face. The boy had neat features, a small nose, clear skin, and long almost girlish lashes. He reminded Hanzo of his beloved Kimi. Hanzo imagined his own son would have looked like this had he lived. "Who are you?" he asked in wonder.

There was no answer. The boy was unconscious. Hanzo lifted the body over his shoulder, and plodded through the rain back to his shop.

The gods had answered.

Hanzo bathed the dirt of the forest from the boy's body. He dressed the two inflamed sword cuts. Then he shaved the boy's matted hair and wrapped him in soft cotton. The boy was pitifully thin and almost feminine in his musculature, but Hanzo knew that a strong body could be developed with time and hard work.

For two weeks the boy lay in the grip of a fever. The skin of his face was drawn tight across his cheekbones and an unhealthy red bloom radiated from his flesh. Deep coughs and cries from restless dreams were the only sounds he made as he shifted back and forth between consciousness and sleep. Most people with the coughing fever died, so when the fever abated, Hanzo felt this was another sign from the gods.

As the boy recovered, he was silent about his past. Hanzo could see he was of good birth: The delicacy of his features, his lack of muscle and callous, and his cultured speech showed him to be different from the farmers and soldiers that Hanzo usually dealt with. *If he chooses to remain silent,* thought Hanzo, *so be it. I will accept him without question as the answer to my prayers.*

The boy called Yoshi would take the place of the son he had lost almost twenty years before. He would become Hanzo's assistant at the smithy and, in time, his heir.

Fourteen

The tiny shop was cut off from the main road; it was seldom that anyone passed, and though Yoshiwara was only twelve miles from Okitsu, there was no commerce between the two towns. This was ideal for Yoshi, who needed a place to hide while he recuperated from his illness.

His recollection of the night he was cast into the river was dim. His feverish mind had erased the memory of his tumbling progress down the rapids, of being tossed, bruised and shaken onto a rock in the stream, of wandering for he knew not how long until, at last, he fell unconscious at Hanzo's feet.

As his health improved, Yoshi took over the menial tasks of the smithy. He told himself he would soon leave to seek revenge, but the urgency of his mission lessened with time. As the days and weeks went by, he sometimes wondered about his family and prayed that Ietaka had escaped. By the time he fully recovered, Yoshi's daily assignments left him so exhausted he could not think of the past. Even so, his mind was alert; he watched Hanzo and tried to understand the process of swordmaking. Hanzo was pleased at his interest and taught him at every opportunity.

When Hanzo prepared to make a new sword, he fasted and prayed for days on end. "We have to be unblemished in word and deed," he told Yoshi sternly. "The duty of a swordmaker is to lead a moral life, to drive away the evil spirits, and to cleanse the body of all impurities so that nothing will interfere with the creation of a noble blade."

Hanzo showed Yoshi the process, step by step. First, the sand iron was reduced in a low-temperature oven till it became a satisfactory steel. Next, the steel was heated in a charcoal fire until it was soft enough to fold in crossed layers.

Yoshi watched in fascination as the big man, his muscles shining in the reflected light from the coals, took the strips of steel in his tongs and welded them together to make a six-by-two-inch bar about one-half inch thick. The hammer rang through the forest and Hanzo laughed with glee as he folded the layers, beat them out, refolded them, beat them out again and again and again. Eighteen times. Many bars were built up this way before they were welded into a unit. Then they were cut, folded, and reforged six more times before at last being beaten out into a blade.

One day, Hanzo noticed Yoshi watching and turned to him. "Here boy," Hanzo roared, motioning to the forge. "Take the hammer and try to fold and beat out the steel."

Yoshi barely managed to lift the hammer. He held the steel strips with the tongs, but when he raised the hammer the tongs slipped, dropping the red hot pieces of steel on the floor near his foot. He jumped away in fear.

"Try it again."

And again . . .

After these first attempts at the forge, Yoshi could hardly open or close his fingers. He marveled at Hanzo's ability to continue the constant hammering and folding day after day.

"I can't do it," Yoshi said after each failure.

"Try again!" Hanzo was implacable. The boy had to work to overcome his weakness. Strength was as much a matter of the mind as it was of the body.

A master swordsmith could make only about thirty swords

of quality a year. Yoshi wondered aloud if they could make more blades by using methods that cut the time spent on each. Hanzo was dismayed at the thought. "A noble blade is the greatest gift of the gods. Greater than land, greater than family, even greater than the Emperor. No, Yoshi, you must never think of shortening the labor, think rather of ways to improve the sharpness of the edge and the flexibility of the blade." Hanzo's sincerity made Yoshi humble.

Yoshi's next daily assignment was to bring in the coarse sand iron and fire it to release the impurities. It was hot, brutal labor; at night he could collapse on his mat, feeling pain in every muscle and joint. As the months went by, Yoshi noticed that the work was no longer as difficult, and he had the strength and desire to talk with Hanzo after his evening bowl of gruel and bit of fish.

"When can I try the forge again? I am stronger now," he said one night.

"You have changed, Yoshi," said Hanzo rising from the table to tower over him. He looked at Yoshi speculatively, then squeezed his shoulder with steely fingers. He nodded appreciatively. "I can feel it. The softness is gone. Tomorrow we start a new blade. This time, *you* will forge the steel!"

"Thank you, Hanzo." Yoshi knew how much the quality of the steel meant to the master smith and to be given this assignment was an honor. He also knew that Hanzo was right about the change in him; he had ridges of muscle across his abdomen where there had been none before; his arms were thicker and his legs more muscular from the daily lifting and moving of the iron. The labor had put him in tune with the natural rhythms of the forest. The physical pain and discomfort of his early days were gone. Yoshi was surprised to find he now welcomed physical labor.

The next morning, Hanzo put aside the blade he was tempering to help Yoshi get started at the forge.

"If it is too difficult, tell me, and you can go back to the shed," Hanzo said.

This time the tongs held; the hammer lifted easily.

"You are talented, Yoshi. You have learned well." Hanzo smiled and nodded proudly.

An exhausted Yoshi crawled to his sleeping mat after his first day at the forge. New muscles had come into play. That night was agony. His arms became insensitive as blood pumped in to repair the worn tissue. Several times he awoke unable to move and, each time, as feeling came back, a thousand pincers jangled his nerve endings. He could barely use his chopsticks at the morning meal. Hanzo noticed, but as long as Yoshi did not complain, he said nothing.

The second day was even more difficult than the first. Blisters developed and burst leaving wet marks on the haft of the hammer. Yoshi gritted his teeth and kept on.

"It is to be expected," Hanzo told him. He noted Yoshi's crestfallen look; it was time to give encouragement and sympathy. He patted Yoshi's shoulder and added, "It took me months to do as well as you did today. I think you have the ability to become a master smith. Tomorrow, instead of working the forge I want you to help me with the tempering. It's time you learned all the phases of our art."

"I am not worthy. What if I spoil the blade after all your effort?" asked Yoshi humbly.

"I won't let you." The way Hanzo said it gave Yoshi confidence.

Hanzo wrapped the core steel of the blade in the folded, hammered, and cross-welded outer surface. It had been re-heated and beaten into approximate shape—thirty-one inches long with a smooth curve from tang to tip. He showed Yoshi how to cover the body of the blade with a thick coating of a carbon-powder clay and the cutting edge with a thinner coat.

"You see, Yoshi, though the cutting edge must be hard enough to hold its sharpness, the shank must stay flexible enough to bend under pressure without snapping."

Hanzo put the clay-covered blade in the charcoal fire. "Watch how the back turns cherry red while the edge becomes white; this gives us the sharpness and flexibility we need for a noble blade.'' He took the blade from the flame and plunged it into water; there was a loud hissing noise, accompanied by great clouds of steam. ''Where the clay is thick, the blade cools slowly; but at the edge, where the clay is thin, it cools quickly for a hard, tempered finish.''

After the tempering was done, Hanzo let Yoshi remove the clay coating. The blade was an unimpressive sight, still crude, with only a hint of the beauty to come.

''We have to prepare for the most difficult stage of our task.'' Hanzo brought the sword to the side of the smithy where grinding stones and hand files were neatly arranged. ''We are ready to bring out the soul of the steel. Before we start to grind, we will purify ourselves with ice-cold water. Come let us pray at the shrine for divine guidance. Every blade is a gift from the gods.''

Yoshi had noticed that ''gift from the gods'' was an expression Hanzo used regularly. Yoshi respected Hanzo's beliefs and had come to believe in the mystical qualities of drawing beauty from the steel.

When Hanzo worked, every fiber of his being was involved in the search for a noble blade. His prayers and acts of purification were all directed to one goal: a perfect blade. Hanzo feared that if he, himself, were not pure in body, soul, and mind, the blade would be evil. ''Evil soul, evil blade,'' he would say, considering that the worst curse possible to a swordsmith. He was proud that no blade of his had ever been used for evil.

After the ritual of purification, they returned to the forge. Hanzo twisted the new blade from side to side, feeling the grain as he hand-ground the shape. Hours went by as he labored, his hamlike hands moving like butterflies, feeling, exploring, and defining the blue textures that lay hidden under the surface.

It was a work of art on the same level as a fine piece of calligraphy or a water-color painting. What beauty! And what a master craftsman was Hanzo! Yoshi felt a need to create something fine. Although he didn't have his ink stick or water-color paper, he, too, wanted to translate beauty directly into steel.

The next day, it was back to the forge. The work seemed easier. Yoshi's shoulder muscles rippled with effort as he beat happily at the folded steel strips.

After four years, Yoshi was no longer the same boy who had appeared from the woods in 1168. That soft, almost effeminate youth had been replaced by a young man with arms almost as hard as the steel they worked and with a constitution made strong and healthy from the simple life in the forest.

Yoshi worked to his full capacity during the day, not thinking beyond his immediate tasks, but late at night his thoughts often returned to the past. He would nurture the tiny flame of secret love and think in jealous agony of Nami with Chikara. "I have not forgotten," he repeatedly told the night sky. "Chikara will pay." Many of the nights he also remembered Fumio and his mother and wondered what their lives were like since he had left. And Ietaka? If Ietaka had not escaped, there would be another debt for Chikara to pay. So the nights were the times for memories as the days were the times for work.

Driven by the dream of his eventual confrontation with Chikara, he practiced swordsmanship with Hanzo in the early evenings. Hanzo was a crude swordsman, but he knew the professional tricks that were not taught in school. Yoshi had believed himself capable with the sword; hadn't he practiced with his uncle, and studied in Kyoto? He found, to his chagrin, that Hanzo beat him easily.

Hanzo was quick. Yoshi became quicker. Soon, the fights were even. Then, one evening, their positions were reversed, and Yoshi beat Hanzo by a small margin. Afterwards, Hanzo broke out the sake and they drank toasts to each other, to the shop, to the steel, and to the greatest blade of all time, one they planned to make together.

Fifteen

Five years before, in the year 1167, Taira Kiyomori had declared himself *daijo-daijin*, supreme chancellor of Japan. This consolidation of power led to a restrictive police state which tolerated no criticism of the Taira family.

In the south, where Taira power went unquestioned, the people were restless and frightened, too frightened to try to remove the iron *geta* from their necks. Farmers and merchants inwardly rebelled; outwardly, they smiled and paid excessive taxes to the collectors.

But in the north, Minamoto Yoritomo built an army to defy the Taira, and the northern lords armed their soldiers with the finest equipment available.

Hanzo's smithy was between the two centers of power on land belonging to one of the few Taira supporters north of the Okitsu River. Kichibei, the local lord, was unaware that Hanzo and Yoshi supplied weapons to the northern armies. The smithy was small, beneath his notice, and he had never interfered with it because its taxes were always paid on time. Hanzo, for his part, avoided politics. He made swords to order, and if the majority of orders were from the Minamoto, so be it.

Hanzo's swords were workmanlike, strong and flexible,

much in demand by the samurai. Only one flaw kept them from reaching the pinnacle of the swordsmith's art: a lack of fine engraving on the blade. Yoshi repaid part of his debt to Hanzo by using his skills in art and calligraphy to make designs for the blades. He experimented on scrap metal until he became proficient in handling engravers' scribes and acids.

Late at night he worked by the light of oil lamps, engraving the Sanskrit characters for the incarnations of Buddha on some blades and a dragon representing the struggle between religion and evil on others.

Yoshi's engravings increased the swords' value and brought the modest shop a certain prominence. The famous swordsman, Naonori Ichikawa, sent students from his academy in Sarashina, ninety miles to the north, to test and order blades. Hanzo was justifiably proud when Ichikawa came personally to choose a sword and later sent a letter of appreciation for the quality of steel and the artistry of engraving.

Eventually the smithy's new prosperity was brought to Lord Kichibei's attention. He was told, "They are growing rich supplying weapons to our enemies."

"They are taking advantage of my kindness and generosity," snarled Kichibei. "Raise their taxes! If that doesn't end their unwarranted prosperity, we'll find other ways to keep them in their place." He glared at his samurai retainers. "The peasants and merchants are growing fat on my largess. Raise everyone's taxes! I have been lenient too long."

On a morning in early spring, Hanzo and Yoshi were working at the forge when two of Kichibei's samurai approached.

"I am Reisuke," intoned the leader with great formality. "I stand before you descended in five generations from the great warrior, Masahira, who fought and won undying fame in the northern provinces, serving the Kiyowara lords. I follow in his illustrious path as a samurai in the service of Lord Kichibei." The samurai were dressed in black cotton robes; each carried two swords through the waistband of their *hakamas*. The long sword was worn for battle, while the short sword hung ready to decapitate a fallen enemy or, if the occasion arose, to commit *seppuku*.

"I am Hanzo, the smith, and this is my assistant," roared Hanzo, frowning in his most ferocious manner to cover his nervousness. Yoshi stayed in the background as he usually did when samurai or officials visited the shop. Although four years had passed since his escape from Chikara, he was sure Chikara still remembered. Until Yoshi was ready for his revenge he would remain silent.

"Your shop is a fine one though far from town. You should be pleased that our lord gives you protection from the many highwaymen on the roads and in the forests," said Reisuke. His manner made Hanzo uncomfortable. Reisuke was a stranger, new to Kichibei's employ; his arrival was an evil omen.

"We thank your lord for the help he has given us. We have never been bothered by highwaymen. We can take care of ourselves and are quite safe in our valley."

"Thanks to Lord Kichibei, your protector," said the samurai.

"Yes, thanks to the gods and Lord Kichibei."

Reisuke frowned impatiently. He was tiring of polite evasions; his lips tightened as he continued, "We hereby inform you that Lord Kichibei is increasing the protection in this area because of restlessness among the farmers."

Hanzo felt himself grow tense. This hard-faced samurai had not come all the way to the smithy to bring good news.

The samurai continued, "Of course, this extra protection will cost our lord more in gold and weapons. Therefore . . ." The samurai pulled out a scroll and made a show of unrolling it and reading the text. "Hanzo, the smith, and his assistant," a cool nod to Yoshi, "will henceforth deliver two blades from each four, or the equivalent in gold, to be collected by Reisuke, servant to Lord Kichibei."

Hanzo sucked in his breath. The news was worse than he had anticipated. He had always paid with one blade in four to the *daimyo*. Two out of four would be an insuperable burden.

Even at full capacity the smithy was unable to keep up with the demand for weapons. The double taxation would ruin them. But Kichibei's five thousand samurai were all-powerful. Alone, Hanzo and Yoshi had no choice.

Hanzo bowed his head. "So be it," he said bitterly.

"You are wise, Hanzo. There are those who may see fit to resist the new taxes. They will not fare well. We shall return before the end of the fifth month to collect what is our due. Till then, goodbye."

After the samurai left, Hanzo's bulky figure seemed shrunken; Yoshi saw tears running down his broad face. Pretending not to notice, Yoshi asked, "What shall we do?"

"We cannot pay it and live," answered Hanzo wiping his face with a huge fist.

"We cannot *not* pay it and live, either."

"Yoshi, the men of Yoshiwara have spoken in the past of resisting any new taxes. We could join them." Hanzo looked to Yoshi for support. He was beaten and despondent. The joy and strength that had marked his work at the forge were gone. He saw his years of effort being wiped out.

"No, Hanzo, resistance will fail. Kichibei is too strong." Yoshi looked at him sadly. "Better to pay than to die like a dog fighting Kichibei's tax collectors."

"Yoshi, I have always avoided trouble, but if the townspeople unite and we join them, perhaps Kichibei will reconsider." Hanzo was pleading, searching for a way out of his dilemma.

"Never," said Yoshi. "Kichibei will see the town destroyed before he allows himself to lose face. We will have to avoid contact with rebels. We have our shop and our peaceful valley to protect. Do not destroy what you have worked so hard to build. For the time being let us plan to give him his two swords in four, and let us continue in peace."

"You are probably right, Yoshi. I have always accepted the rule of the lords without question. Why then am I so distraught at this newest example of their power?" Hanzo hesitated; then he looked thoughtfully at Yoshi and added, "We will obey for your sake. I am responsible for your being here and will do whatever is necessary to keep you from harm.''

"Neither of us will be harmed. Together we will do what we need do to protect our smithy," said Yoshi. "As long as we can make an honest blade our lives will be full and long. Everyone needs a swordsmith. We have nothing to fear."

"You're a good boy," said Hanzo softly. "But enough discussion. We have work to do. Let us get back to our labors as soon as I offer prayers to the gods."

While Hanzo ladled water to wash his hands at the stone basin near Amaterasu's shrine, Yoshi felt himself approaching another crossroad in his life; the visit by the samurai had reminded him again of Okitsu Castle, cousin Genkai, and the vow Yoshi had made so long ago. Yoshi had told himself repeatedly a vow must be honored. Now he hesitated. . . . Life was simple and peaceful in the valley. Was there really any need to leave this idyllic existence to seek revenge for an almost forgotten action?

Though the smithy was close to Okitsu Castle, Yoshi had made no attempt to communicate with his family. From time to time, he had discreetly asked travelers for news of the south, but there had been no information about Ietaka, Fumio, Lady Masaka, or Nami. Perhaps, he thought, it would be best to leave things the way they were. Then the memory of Genkai's death returned to harden his resolve to seek revenge. No! He could no longer ignore his vows. He would have to take action or lose his self-respect.

Through Kichibei, Yoshi realized he could accomplish one small stroke against Chikara and the Taira family. He had told Hanzo it would be impossible to force Kichibei to rescind his new taxes. Yet, if enough peasants and merchants banded together . . . Could Kichibei be convinced that setting his samurai against the populace would cost him more in gold, inconvenience, and pain than it was worth?

Yoshi watched Hanzo, still washing at the basin, and felt fondness and love for the older man. Hanzo treated him like a son, and Yoshi was determined to repay him as a son should. In the years of sharing his life with the smith he had come to recognize the warmth and humanity that lay behind the ferocious appearance. He had never seen Hanzo angry, and while he did not doubt the smith's courage, he knew Hanzo would never fight if a fight could be avoided. Yoshi was certain that Hanzo would follow his suggestion and pay the new taxes.

Yoshi, however, decided to meet with the townspeople in Yoshiwara without Hanzo's knowledge. He would try to find out if there would be organized resistance to the new taxes.

Sixteen

The town of Yoshiwara was even smaller than Okitsu. As Yoshi approached it from the forest, pine trees loomed in the evening mist like silent menacing soldiers guarding the hillside. In Yoshiwara's valley, a pond supported white lotus blossoms on its surface, and tiny frogs boomed messages of love across the water.

At the smithy, Yoshi's ears were filled with the ringing of hammers and the hiss of red-hot steel being tempered. Here, in the town, he could hear a street musician plunking a plangent melody on a four-stringed *biwa*, and he saw women in long gowns, with babies strapped to their backs, moving slowly along the narrow streets while well-dressed merchants met and discussed their business on every corner. Yoshi's coarse cotton clothing, calloused hands, and vein-swollen arms made him feel like a peasant come to the big city.

Diversion in Yoshiwara was limited, so it had become Yoshi's custom to stop at the same roadside inn whenever he came to town. The two girls who worked there knew him, and they saved him from the social effort of making new acquaintances. Yoshi was shy about meeting new people. He had been alone with Hanzo too long. The habit of staying in the background combined with shame at his muscular appearance and made him taciturn. He didn't realize that, in fact, he appeared ten times the man he had been before. His muscles made him much more attractive than his former effeminate slimness. His cheeks had sunken, accentuating his cheekbones and defining his nose. His hair was modestly short and his face had developed a look of unusual strength and intelligence.

"Yoshi-san, welcome to our humble inn."

Otoki and Masa were waiting in the courtyard and were genuinely glad to see him. "Come inside, let us bathe your poor tired body and prepare dinner for you."

The girls were young. They had worked at the inn for many years, and were well versed in ways to make a traveler happy. Their skills had brought a small measure of fame to the inn and its proprietor, who was very proud of his girls' accomplishments.

Otoki took Yoshi's left arm, Masa his right. They led him directly to the bath. Otoki helped Yoshi remove his clothing while Masa disrobed behind a screen.

"There are no other guests tonight. How pleasant for us all," said Otoki.

Yoshi rolled in the hot water, savoring the incense that filled the room.

"Don't look, Yoshi. I will join you." Yoshi made a pretense of closing one eye and laughed delightedly to see the willowy figure of Masa run from behind the screen and jump into the water. Masa had delicate features that many a great lady would have envied.

As Masa scrubbed Yoshi's back, Otoki changed from her clothes and joined them. Otoki was the physical opposite of Masa. As short as Masa was, so Otoki was tall. Where Masa was slim, Otoki was voluptuous . . . too voluptuous. Her face, while not unattractive, was too strong for stylish beauty. Her nose was too prominent, her brows too thick. Her personality fit her appearance: She was the more forward of the two.

"How strong you are, Yoshi. Look, Masa, look at his

muscles. He gets stronger every time he visits." Otoki smiled in mock admiration.

Masa's response was a slight smile and an extra pressure on Yoshi's shoulders.

"And look, Masa, it's not just his shoulders that are getting bigger." Otoki's hands flew to her mouth as though she were shocked.

"I thought this was to be only a bath," said Yoshi calmly.

Masa giggled. "Of course it's only a bath. What did you think?"

"I thought I was in the court of the Emperor—the ladies are so beautiful. . . ."

"How sweet he is."

". . . and forward," said Otoki, gently stroking Yoshi with her soapy hands. The soap had a sweet herbal fragrance that left Yoshi's head spinning.

"How pleasant that you are the only guest," said Masa, soaping his back and shoulders.

"Since no one else is here perhaps you would . . . ?" Yoshi's voice trailed off into hopeful silence.

"No, no, Yoshi! Not in the bath. We would be remiss in our duties if you were not well fed and comfortable first."

Yoshi sipped his aromatic green tea and ate a luxurious meal of roast sparrow with rice cakes. In his dry cotton robe he felt clean, rested, and at ease. As he ate, the girls giggled and whispered asides from behind their fans. Yoshi made occasional polite comments as he concentrated on the food. When he finished his meal, he changed to a serious tone.

"Ladies," he began, patting his lips with a hot, damp towel, "have you heard anyone in the village discussing the new taxes?"

"Oh, Yoshi-san, we know nothing of taxes." Both girls' faces closed. They turned their heads away. It was not a subject they wished to discuss.

"Otoki, please! You hear travelers talking. They discuss their business in front of you. You are not stupid; you know what is happening.'' Yoshi ignored her distress. He forced Otoki to answer him.

"I know only that the innkeeper's taxes will be higher next year."

"And what does he say to that?"

"He will pay, though the burden is difficult."

"And what of the others?"

"Anyone who doesn't pay will be punished." Otoki paused. Her expression was unhappy as she continued in a lower voice, "True, some speak of refusing to pay. That is just talk. Lord Kichibei's spies cover the countryside; if they find people who resist, the resisters will be executed as examples to all rebels."

"Then there are rebels?"

"Not really rebels . . . only those who are unhappy with their lot."

"Who are they? Tell me their names."

"I cannot do that, Yoshi. As much as Masa and I love you, we cannot speak of such things. If you were concerned it might be different. Our townspeople's problems are not yours. You would be wise not to become involved."

"I am involved. They are raising our taxes, too."

"I'm sorry." Otoki hung her head in genuine contrition. It was obvious to Yoshi she would not say more. He thought of Ono who had paid with her life to give Yoshi time to escape. He had learned to respect the inn girls and to honor their code of silence.

"All right. Let's forget taxes." Yoshi leaned back and smiled easily. The uncomfortable subject was closed. "Since we are alone, please come to my room with your *biwa* and a bottle of sake. We'll have our own celebration."

The girls brightened. They scurried about, clearing the table and preparing for the evening.

Later, in Yoshi's room, Masa sang and played the *biwa*. Her delicate fingers were light as gossamer as they stroked the four strings. The lanterns made shifting patterns on the gold and red painted screens. A bitter-sweet incense burned in a corner, filling the room with its heady scent.

The music, the light, and the perfume made the room seem warm and intimate. Yoshi caressed Masa's thigh. She kept playing and, as he stroked, she sang an old song:

> *Though the purity*
> *Of the moonlight has silenced*
> *Both nightingale and*
> *Cricket, the cuckoo alone*
> *Sings all through the bright-lit night*

Yoshi was amused; the song was clever in that it could also be interpreted to mean that while the spirit of Buddha brings light to both peasants and priests, prostitutes worship in their own way, singing through the night.

While Masa sang, Otoki pulled up Yoshi's robe. She turned around, lifting her own robe over her naked buttocks, and wriggled backward until Yoshi had entered her.

Meanwhile, Masa's playing became ragged and uneven. She sang in a breathless voice that would lapse into soft moans as Yoshi fondled her. Finally, she put down the *biwa* and gave herself up to the pleasure. She stretched upward and writhed in ecstasy, covering Yoshi's hand with her own and guiding his fingers. She was first to finish, collapsing with a stifled cry.

Otoki reached under her robe and held Yoshi with a gentle pressure as he pressed in and out. She gave a cry, almost of pain, and shuddered violently. Her orgasm came a second before Yoshi joined her with his own climax.

Afterwards, the three young people lay together on the patterned quilt, half asleep, covered with the juices and odors of love. Too spent to move, each smiled a secret smile of sexual release and joy. In time, Yoshi fell asleep, snoring lightly. Otoki and Masa nodded to each other. They rose and silently gathered the fans, *biwa*, robes, dishes, and cups and slipped out through the painted panel.

It was late that night when a group of Kichibei's samurai arrived at the inn, tired from a long ride. They left their horses with the groom and noisily called for the innkeeper.

"You have rooms for four of Kichibei's soldiers?" demanded the leader.

"Yes, sir. We are almost empty tonight. Please come in. My girls will take care of your every need."

"We've heard of your girls. But first, we need baths, clean robes, and sake."

"Something to eat perhaps?"

"Lots of sake and then your girls." The leader laughed and winked at his followers. "Hurry up, fool. We are tired enough without having to wait for you to wake up."

"Yes, sir, right away, sir. Otoki, Masa, hurry to the front."

Otoki and Masa came in silently, their faces turned away from the bold stares of the samurai. It was going to be a long and difficult night.

Seventeen

A clear dawn. Outside, a songbird trilled, "T-o-o-o-wit, t-o-o-o-wit," on a cherry-tree branch.

Otoki ignored the signs of the fresh new day as she came into Yoshi's room to wake him. Her face was swollen from crying. A bruise darkened her cheek.

"Yoshi, wake up!" Her voice was an urgent whisper.

"What is it?" He sat up instantly alert.

"Did you hear them last night?"

"No. What? Who?" As he said it, Yoshi dimly remembered loud voices as if in a dream

"Samurai. Lord Kichibei's men! They were drunk and talking among themselves after they finished with us. They are going to make examples of people who have complained about the new taxes. You have to leave at once. I heard them mention Hanzo."

"Hanzo? That's impossible. He told me he would pay the tax. Why would they want to hurt him? They need his swords too much."

"I don't know why he was chosen. He may have complained to a spy or been indiscreet. It doesn't matter. What does matter is that the samurai are here. Please dress and leave quickly. The samurai are staying the day, so you have only until tonight.''

"Thank you, Otoki." Yoshi held her hand, feeling it tremble in his. He kissed her gently. "I won't forget your help," he whispered.

"Just remember us next time you come to the inn. Now go! Warn Hanzo while there is time for him to escape.''

She held a finger to her lips for silence while she slipped out of the room. Watching her leave, Yoshi's heart swelled with warmth for these inn girls. They were used so casually by men who never appreciated the depth of their feelings.

Yoshi dressed and, holding his straw sandals in hand, slid the panel open. He looked up and down the corridor; there was no one in sight. As he tiptoed down the hallway, he heard loud snoring from the rooms on each side.

The innkeeper was waiting on the front steps. Yoshi paid for the food and room and left some extra for the girls. The innkeeper's face was ashen, set as though in wax; his mouth was tightly compressed and his forehead glistened with sweat. He accepted the money and whispered, "Hurry. Tell Hanzo! He must hide tonight.''

Once out of the inn, Yoshi put on his sandals and walked quickly down the muddy street. A silent group of small children watched as he passed. He took a shortcut through the pine forest.

How could there be danger on so beautiful a morning?

He thought of Otoki and Masa and the pleasures of the night before. No doubt Masa was more beautiful and talented. Yet, there was something special about Otoki, an intelligence and independence that Yoshi appreciated. If she were as beautiful as Masa, she could be a great courtesan, perhaps a consort to the Emperor himself. Yoshi walked along, reflecting on how the smallest accidents of birth could influence an entire life. If Otoki had been born prettier and more delicate, or if Masa had been born smarter, how different their lives would be.

For that matter, Hanzo and Lord Fumio were not so different. If Hanzo had been in the campaign where Fumio had earned his honors, their positions might have been reversed. Further, if Lady Masaka had been a "waitress" in a country inn, what would he, Yoshi, be today? He laughed at the thought. He would probably still be a swordsmith's assistant. So much for accidents of birth.

The valley was over the next hill. Yoshi breathed deeply of the forest's heady odor. Patches of sunlight sparkled on fresh-dewed greenery. Mulberry bushes crowded in among the pines, and a profusion of berry colors and tiny flowers shone between the tall trees. The sound of Hanzo's hammer echoed from the valley, ringing counterpoint to the screech of insects and the trills of the birds.

"Ho, Hanzo, I'm back," Yoshi called.

"And about time," Hanzo said. There was no cheer in his response. "I've been waiting for you. We need more clay for the tempering."

"I thought we had enough for the next few weeks."

"No, you are mistaken. You will have to go to Mishima to get more from Matsutaro, the potter."

Yoshi's good spirits disappeared as Hanzo's abrupt tone brought him back to reality. "Hanzo, there are disturbing rumors in Yoshiwara. Trouble is brewing. We can avoid it if you come with me to Mishima. We can stay there a few days and return when the trouble is settled."

"I can't leave now. I am making the noblest blade yet." Hanzo hesitated and then, as if it were of little interest, asked, "Exactly what are these rumors?"

"Tonight, Kichibei's samurai will be sweeping the countryside, punishing tax evaders."

"Why should that affect me? I intend to pay my taxes."

"One of the inn girls heard a samurai mention your name. Have you complained to anyone who might have been a spy for Kichibei?"

"I don't remember." Hanzo was momentarily distressed. Hanzo had never lied to him, but Yoshi felt that this time he was hiding something. Hanzo shook his head as if to clear it of an unpleasant thought and said, "It never pays to listen to inn girls. They are gossips all." He paused, then added, "I maintain friendly relations with Kichibei's samurai. They buy my swords and they respect me."

"Hanzo, they are samurai. Their code gives them the right to execute non-samurai at will. Serving Kichibei kept them in check, but once their blades taste blood they become wild beasts. Respect, common sense, and friendship will all be forgotten."

Hanzo held up a hand to stop the conversation. "I have nothing to fear. I can defend myself." His voice was brave yet there was a tight furrow between his brows. He turned back to the forge and started hammering again.

"You can't defend yourself against a hundred soldiers," Yoshi shouted above the din.

Sweat ran from Hanzo's bald head, sizzling into steam as the drops hit the hot coals. He continued to hammer with deeper concentration.

"Listen to me, Hanzo. You are being foolish. You will be alone and vulnerable while I am in Mishima. Come with me. I need your help with the bags of clay."

Hanzo stopped. He wiped his brow with one meaty hand. "Don't try my patience. Remember who is the master and who is the student. If my strength won't protect me, then the gods will. I shall pray tonight at the shrines. As for helping you, you've carried the clay alone before. Hire a cart or bearers on the way back if you need them." Hanzo frowned stubbornly.

Yoshi knew that argument would be futile. He reluctantly went to the back of the smithy and changed into the rough cotton *hakama* he wore at the forge. For an hour, the two worked side by side without speaking.

"It is time for you to leave if you are to make the trip by daylight," said Hanzo during a momentary break.

"I want to complete this section," said Yoshi, holding up a blade he had recently begun.

"Nevertheless, it is time to start out." Hanzo's tone softened. "I am not angry with you, Yoshi. You are a good boy, and I love you as though you were my natural son, but sometimes you presume too much. Don't worry about me. I'll be all right. If you leave now, you will be back just after dark, and we will open a jar of spiced wine to celebrate this new blade of mine.''

Yoshi bathed at the stone basin. He dressed in a traveling robe and carried a straw raincape—clouds were gathering. He took enough money to pay the potter and some extra for the bearers. The money was tucked into his sash, hidden in a small purse. He bowed solemnly to Hanzo and set off along the path through the forest.

The weather changed rapidly. The early morning freshness disappeared and quiet settled over the valley. The air became oppressive, heavy, and leaden; rain-swollen clouds sailed overhead. By late morning, it was raining steadily; streams and rivers were rapidly becoming impassable.

Yoshi unfurled his rain cape and wrapped it around his shoulders. He was impatient to get to Mishima before the Kamo River crested and trapped him on one side. He didn't know if he could help Hanzo, but, in case of trouble, he belonged at the smithy at Hanzo's side. He alternately walked and ran eastward for nine miles, cutting through the forest to shorten his trip. He reached the bay-shore road near the small town of Hara. The streets were empty; everyone was inside avoiding the silver sheets of water that fell in undulating curtains from the sky. Less than four more miles brought him to Numazu, where bearers carried him across the rising Kano River for two pieces of copper. He increased his pace for the last three and a half miles across the neck of the Izu Peninsula that formed Suruga Bay on one side and Sagami Bay on the other. Mishima was halfway across at the base of a mountain.

At the pottery, Yoshi removed his cape and shook off the excess water. He dried himself using a rag that had been left on the covered porch for that purpose. The door swung open before he could knock. ''Ah, Yoshi, how good to see you,'' said Matsutaro, the potter. He was a shrunken little man without a hair on his head. His eyes were almost lost in a sea of fine wrinkles. His body was bent from years of toil; he moved slowly except for his hands, which danced to an unheard rhythm. They were parchment-smooth with blue serpents that coiled and twisted carrying their burden of blood beneath the skin.

"Why are you here?" Matsutaro asked. "I am sure I made arrangements with Hanzo for next week." The old man's voice was firm and deep, as incongruous as his hands in so frail a body.

"Hanzo told me he needed more tempering clay."

"Impossible. I gave him enough to last at least another ten days."

Yoshi's stomach tensed. A suspicion formed. Had Hanzo sent him on a fool's errand to get him away from the smithy? What else did Hanzo know? Had he been in touch with the rebellious townspeople? Perhaps there had been a simple misunderstanding. Yoshi could not remember if they had used extra amounts of clay during the week. "Nevertheless," he said, "I am here for a fresh supply. If you will load two bags, I will pay and leave at once."

"No, no, Yoshi. Please stay awhile. It is lonesome here; I welcome your company."

"I am sorry, Matsutaro. Hanzo is waiting at the smithy. Tonight we are celebrating his newest blade. If I don't leave at once, I won't get to the river before dark."

"Yes, I understand." The old man shook his head sadly. "Please sit while I measure out the clay."

Matsutaro climbed to the dark crossbeams under the thatched roof of his shop. He brought down two coarse brown cotton bags. While Yoshi waited impatiently, he measured an amount of clay equal to about thirty pounds into each bag. He tightened the drawstrings and slipped the bags over a pole. "Travel will be difficult till the rain ends. You would be wise to wait," he said, trying once more to persuade Yoshi to stay.

Yoshi felt compassion for the lonely potter, but his suspicion of Hanzo's motives made him anxious to return to the valley. He controlled his impatience as best he could. Forcing a smile, he said, "I must leave. On my next visit we'll have time to sit and talk." Yoshi stooped low enough to fit the pole over his shoulders. He raised the weight easily though the pole bent into an inverted U.

From Mishima to Yoshiwara was almost twenty miles along the shore road. Coming east, Yoshi had shortened the trip by crossing the hills; now his burden forced him to stay on the road. Normally he would have carried the sixty pounds slowly but without difficulty; this time, a sense of urgency made him look for bearers to speed his return. They would be able to carry Yoshi and the potter's clay at a run all the way to Yoshiwara.

As Matsutaro had predicted, the rain lightened, but still bearers were not to be found. Yoshi plodded on, his straw sandals filling with water at each step. Soon, the rain was over and the clouds broke into patterns like the *kitae-hada*, the delicate bluish sheen on the blade of a fine sword.

An hour later, Yoshi spied a group of six bearers at the side of the road. Their palanquin was tipped into a ditch and all six were shouting obscenities and waving fists at each other.

"A gold coin to take me and my load to Yoshiwara," said Yoshi.

The argument stopped as if it had never been. In seconds, the palanquin was righted. Yoshi and the sixty pounds of clay were on their way home.

"We cannot cross till the river is lower." The bearers stopped on the bank of the Kano.

Yoshi's mouth was dry as he remembered the disastrous time he tried to cross the Okitsu River with Ietaka. Desperation made him overcome his fear. He shouted at the leader, "Of course you can. I've crossed when it was higher than this."

"No, it is very dangerous. We don't dare."

To the right, Yoshi saw the sunset burning holes in the clouds around Mount Fuji. It would be dark soon, and they were miles from the smithy. "I will pay an extra piece of gold," he said grinding his teeth in frustration.

The bearers put the palanquin down by the river bank. They huddled together arguing in raucous voices; their shouts echoed back from across the river. Red light, reflecting from the clouds, spilled on their naked, tattooed backs, making them look less than human. Five minutes of altercation while the sun sank below the horizon. Finally, the spokesman came to the palanquin. "We cannot cross yet. Gold is useless to a dead man," he said sullenly.

"I'll give you two extra pieces."

"Wait."

Another five minutes! Stars were coming out in the twilight and only the red glare on Mount Fuji's snow-capped peak remained of the day.

"The river is lower now. For two extra pieces of gold, we cross."

"Hurry! The gold is yours." Every passing minute increased the feeling of fear which Yoshi tried to suppress. The darkening sky, the rushing river, the wind rustling through the mulberry bushes that lined the bank—all were ominous.

"Hurry!" he repeated.

Eighteen

Yoshi left the bearers on the road and struck off across the dark hill to the smithy. A smell of burning wood drifted through the pines. When he tried to run, the bags of clay bounced, perilously bending the neck pole until he had to stop and walk again.

Those weren't clouds over the trees—it was smoke. As he neared the top of the hill, he saw a faint orange glow in the darkness ahead. He dropped the clay and started running, thrashing awkwardly through the forest.

Yoshi topped the rise and looked down at a scene that would remain engraved forever on his consciousness: The smithy was a smoldering ruin; the crossbar over the front had collapsed carrying most of the roof with it. Flames leaped from the roof thatch, giving off acrid-smelling clouds of smoke. Around the wreckage, four mounted, fully armored men were slashing at the remaining roof supports, pulling down what was left of the shop as they searched the debris. On the damp ground, in front of where the entrance had been, lay two samurai, one dead, cut almost in half, the other dying, blood still pumping from his armless shoulder.

Yoshi hid behind a tree trunk.

The leader was shouting angrily at his three companions.

"He is here somewhere. I wounded him. Find him!"

"There is no one alive in there, Lord Kichibei," answered one of the samurai. "No one could live in those flames."

"Find the body. I won't be satisfied till I have his head on a pole."

Yoshi heard branches breaking in the thickets twenty yards below him. He pulled back further, making himself fit closer to the tree trunk. A groan . . . he recognized the gruff sound.

"*Hanzo*," he hissed. "It is Yoshi. Here, among the trees." In the light from the flames, Yoshi could see the samurai below noisily circling the wreckage while Hanzo clumsily climbed away from them. The samurai were within a few yards of Hanzo's thrashing body. Yoshi bit his lip in anxiety. How could they not see and hear him?

Hanzo was silhouetted against the fire; his head was turning from side to side searching for Yoshi among the dark trees. "I can go no further, Yoshi. Get away while you can. Leave me," Hanzo tried to whisper; to Yoshi it sounded like a shout. The samurai did not hear; they were searching the flames still unaware of Hanyo's escape.

"No, Hanzo." Yoshi ran forward and caught the huge bulk under the armpits. He pulled him farther from the firelight.

"Lie quietly. We are safe here." Yoshi's hand found the wound. Hanzo's chest had been opened by a swordstroke. In seconds, Yoshi tore away the robe and tried to stem the bleeding.

Hanzo coughed blood. "Did you see how I fought six of them to a standstill?" he gasped.

"You killed two." Yoshi watched in horror as blood continued to seep from the wound.

"I did? Good!" In spite of his pain, Hanzo smiled with satisfaction. Then the smile faded and he said, "I have atoned for my past sins. I did well, did I not, Yoshi?"

"You did well." Hot tears ran down Yoshi's cheeks. He moaned prayers to Hanzo's Shinto gods.

"Yoshi, get away at once. Lord Kichibei, himself, is

leading his men. Escape while you can, before his troops comb the forest." Hanzo coughed another gobbet. "Hurry, before they find you here."

"I can't leave you, Hanzo. I am only sorry I was not with you when they came. I will stay, whatever the consequences."

"Fool, I sent you away to save you."

"You had no right."

"Every right. You have always been more to me than an assistant. I consider you my son."

Yoshi tried to hold back further tears. What could he do? Only the noise of the fire kept the samurai from hearing Hanzo's voice. Yoshi saw them gathering around Kichibei for instructions. This might be his last chance to get Hanzo to safety. "Can you move?" whispered Yoshi.

"No. Leave me and save yourself."

"Try! Remember my first day at the forge, when you told me to try," Yoshi urged.

"No. I can't move. It's no use. I've lost too much blood."

"Let me carry you."

"Oh, Yoshi. I wanted you to be proud of me. From the first day when I found you almost dead in the woods, I hoped you would someday call me father. Now we have reversed positions. I am weak and you are strong. How fittingly the circle closes. Yoshi . . ." Hanzo's voice was fading.

"Hanzo, I *am* proud of you," said Yoshi humbly. "You fought off Kichibei and his finest troops. You killed two of them. No one could have done more. I am honored to call you father."

Hanzo coughed again; his body twisted in a spasm of pain. He grasped Yoshi's arm and with his last strength said, "Take my sword. It is a noble blade. The best I have ever made. It is for you . . . my son."

"Gladly, Father."

"I am happy then." Hanzo's body collapsed in on itself.

"Father, Father, though your gods have deserted you, I will not! I will avenge your death. I swear it!"

Yoshi pressed the dead man's eyes closed and marveled at his peaceful smile.

Hanzo had regained his honor.

Nineteen

Yoshi took the sword from Hanzo's hand, then covered the body with loose brush and pine branches. Thirty yards away, Lord Kichibei paraded his horse around the smoldering smithy, abusing his samurai. Yoshi saw that he wore expensive armor and carried the finest of weapons. Even his horse's trappings were trimmed with gold. The firelight shone on Kichibei's face, mercilessly exposing the effects of self-indulgence. His once square jaw was lax and jowly, and his eyes were hidden in unhealthy puffs of flesh. But Yoshi knew Kichibei had been a famous warrior and still practiced with the sword daily. He was a dangerous man whose troops were loyal out of fear rather than love or respect.

Kichibei was shouting, "Find him. Find him!" in a voice shrill with anger and frustration. Tonight he had ridden with his troops for sport, expecting no resistance. With two men dead and his quarry escaping, he felt a serious loss of face. He shouted again, "Find him, damn you, or you will all suffer."

Yoshi stayed in the shadows, slipping from behind one tree to another as he moved downhill toward the soldiers. Hanzo had wounded one of them. Which one? In the fading firelight, Yoshi could distinguish only Kichibei's ornate, gilt bronze armor and giant Chinese helmet. The other three, in everyday leather armor with metal trimmings, looked similar as they circled the smithy. No . . . one samurai was different; he carried the lord's crest on a lance behind his saddle.

Yoshi hid next to the clearing, close enough to one of the riders to hear his harsh breathing and an occasional muffled curse as he poked through the wreckage with his lance. The others rode off, searching the perimeter of the fire. The samurai was alone—but for how long? Yoshi had to act quickly. He scraped along the black earth until he found a heavy round stone. He gave it a shove, rolling it down between the horse's legs. The horse shied, rising on its rear legs and whinnying in fear. The rider cursed again, momentarily distracted from his search.

The stone fanned a flurry of flame. The rider spotted it and dismounted. He moved slowly toward the subsiding flare and saw the round stone. The head of Hanzo?

A hiss behind him. He turned, instinctively raising the lance. Too late! His last sight was a dim figure almost on top of him and a flash as the fire glistened on the edge of the new blade.

His head rolled into the fire with less noise than the rolling stone had made. The flame caught the forelock under his helmet and in seconds it flared up making head and helmet an unrecognizable lump of charcoal. The headless body sank to its knees, held up momentarily by the leather armor. Blood spurted upward like a Chinese firework before the body subsided into the fire. The entire episode lasted less than a minute.

Yoshi could hear Kichibei still berating the remaining two samurai on the far side of the smithy. The paper and thatch were completely burnt out. Only the wood frame still sent occasional bursts of spark and flame to light the clearing.

Yoshi led the dead man's horse to the edge of the forest. Suddenly, Kichibei's shrill voice stopped, and the only sound was the crackling of settling embers and the snuffling of the horse. Then, armor creaked and a horse whinnied; another rider was coming around to Yoshi's side of the fire.

Yoshi mounted and urged the horse forward. The

samurai's eyes bulged and his mouth dropped open when he saw the avenging angel bearing down on him with drawn sword. Too late to draw his own weapon, he threw himself off his horse away from the attacker. He landed among the fallen beams at the edge of the fire. A leg was trapped in the tangle, and flames flared up, catching the silk lining under his armor. He screamed in terror and pain as he turned into a human torch, a bright flash against the background fire.

Kichibei and the remaining samurai shouted questions from across the funeral pyre.

"Reisuke, what happened?" called the soldier.

"Where is Reisuke?" demanded Kichibei.

"I don't know, lord."

"Well, find out! And where is Yasumitsu?"

"I haven't seen him either, lord."

"Amida Nyodorai, do I have to do everything myself?" snarled Kichibei. He kicked at his horse's side, and pulled it around with a cruel tug on the reins as he motioned the samurai to ride around the fire.

"Lord Kichibei!" The samurai's voice cracked. "I've found one of them."

"Which one, fool?"

"I don't know, lord. His head is gone."

Kichibei rode over; he looked down at the headless body. His voice was cold and deadly. "The swordsmith is alive in spite of his wounds. Get off your horse and start beating the bushes."

Yoshi had pulled back deeper into the forest where he stroked and gentled the horse to keep it quiet. Kichibei rode back and forth at the edge of the clearing, shouting to the samurai who was noisily slashing his way through the bushes.

"Fifty *koku* of land if you find him for me," Kichibei shouted. "And *seppuku* if you don't."

The sky was clearing. Low scuds of cloud passed the quarter moon, leaving alternating patches of light and darkness among the trees. The smell of the burnt wood and paper had thickened with the additional smells of burning leather and flesh. Yoshi's horse rolled its eyes at the strange odors and reared in terror at the approaching soldier. In moments the man would see them. Yoshi spurred the horse forward, hoping to surprise him.

The samurai looked up, frozen in place as the armored horse bore down on him. Then, the gods saw fit to laugh. A low-hanging branch whipped across Yoshi's face, blinding him as it knocked him from his horse.

The samurai gave a cry of triumph and waddled rapidly toward the fallen figure. Yoshi rolled frantically into the shelter of a mulberry bush. His plain dark robe blended into the shadows, giving him an advantage in the darkness. The samurai was clearly visible; the metal trim on his armor and helmet shone in the patches of moonlight.

Having lost sight of his victim, the samurai moved cautiously through the undergrowth. The bulk of his armor made him clumsy as he pushed himself through the berry bushes. "I've found him. He's right here," he shouted to Kichibei.

The samurai muttered nervously to himself. He had been hurt by Hanzo; the smith had slit open his upper thigh during their first skirmish and, though the stroke had missed major arteries, the wound was painful. He respected the giant smith; wounded or not, Hanzo was a formidable opponent.

The samurai was normally afraid of nothing. Given the command to slit his own belly, he would have done so without hesitation; however, in the dark, unfamiliar forest, alone with a wraith who appeared and disappeared without a sound, he felt faint stirrings of a feeling that brought sweat to his forehead and dryness to his mouth.

There! A noise behind him.

He wheeled with incredible speed, considering his wound and the bulk of his armor.

Silence.

He moved forward, his eyes darting from side to side.

"What's happening in there? Do you have him?" It was Kichibei, beside himself with rage and frustration, screaming like an old woman.

To answer would give away his position. The samurai bit his lip and took another step into the shadow. Without warning, he was in the clasp of an arm that locked around his throat and cut off his breathing. He struggled to get leverage to fight off the hold, but his wounded leg did not give him enough support. His head was being twisted and his throat constricted at the same time. His sword fell, his fingers clawed at the arm that was inexorably tightening around him. He remembered the immense power of the blacksmith's hands. He tried to pray . . . no sound came except a dry crackling as his voice box was crushed by the pressure. His eyes rolled back in his head. Just before his neck snapped, he glimpsed his killer and died in confusion.

Yoshi let the body drop to the black earth.

Kichibei's horse was snorting and pawing the ground as Kichibei kicked its sides in a fury. Yoshi could see them silhouetted against the dying embers and could hear Kichibei threatening torture and death to his missing samurai for not answering his angry demands.

Yoshi waited till the moon was hidden behind a cloud; he stepped out from the trees and called in an eerie voice, *"Kichibeiiiiii, it is I, the ghost of Hanzoooooo. I have come to take you back with meeeeeee."*

Kichibei stopped as if hit by a crossbow. Soft living had made him unwilling to put himself in danger unnecessarily; however, it had not softened his brain. He smiled contemptuously to himself; this was a childish trick by Hanzo to throw him off his guard. So the fat old wrestler had somehow managed to kill the samurai. He would find another kind of opponent in Lord Kichibei. "Oh, ghost of Hanzo, where are you?" he called, trying to put a quaver of fear in his voice.

"In the forest."

"Come down, ghost of Hanzo, so I can see you more clearly."

"I am coming." This time the voice had shifted to another part of the forest.

Kichibei nodded in satisfaction. The fat fool was coming to meet him.

Kichibei was fully armed and armored, a fighting machine that need fear no man. His armor was not as silent as he would have liked; it gave faint clicks and metallic janglings as he walked, though—unlike the clumsier armor of his samurai—it was well made and perfectly fitted. He dismounted as silently as possible and sent the horse away with a whack across its hindquarters; then he hid among the trees and prepared his trap.

First, he removed his helmet and set it atop a berry bush near the edge of the forest. Next, he climbed uphill a few feet to hide behind a tree trunk; from there he could watch the helmet in the faint light from below. He smiled triumphantly, thinking how his reputation would grow when he single-handedly destroyed the giant who had killed his five samurai.

There was a rustling to the left. The "ghost of Hanzo" was coming through the bushes between Kichibei and the helmet. The trap had worked.

Kichibei whisked his long sword from its sheath and inched forward. Now he could see the figure dimly outlined against the embers. It was not Hanzo!

Momentarily confused, Kichibei drew back. The figure was that of a young man, much smaller than Hanzo. Were there two of the enemy? No matter. It would be better to attack and kill this young one before he was joined by the wounded swordsmith.

Kichibei, with a defiant scream, launched himself through the bushes, sweeping his sword before him. The stranger fell back. He was dressed only in a light robe over *hakama*. No armor! Kichibei's advantage. Unencumbered by armor, the man darted aside, avoiding the initial attack. Kichibei pressed forward. He was a well-trained swordsman and confident of his ability to kill this country boy quickly.

The blades rang against each other as Kichibei thrust and slashed only to be parried by the other.

Suddenly, a daring feint and reversal drew Kichibei's sword downward. First blood to the stranger. His blade bounced across Kichibei's armor and cut a deep gash through his left shoulder. Kichibei gave ground, backing uphill, deeper into the forest and away from the blade that flickered closer and closer to his uncovered head. He wished he had kept the helmet. The strength behind the stranger's blade was unnerving. At each clash of swords Kichibei retreated. He was taking an occasional sword stroke across his midsection. The armor held, but it was as though he were being hit by a hammer. His breath became shorter and his parries slower. Sweat dewed his forehead. He realized his opponent was younger and stronger and that superior skill was not enough to gain victory. For the first time in the battle, he felt fear tightening his muscles, gnawing at his confidence. A stray thought broke his concentration. Suppose Hanzo joined his young ally? All would be lost. Kichibei tasted bitter bile in his throat. He swallowed nervously, trying to think only of the battle. Parry. Retreat. Parry.

It was no use, other thoughts intruded. Where *was* Hanzo? Too badly wounded to fight? How soon would the main body of Kichibei's troops come to the smithy? Parry. Retreat. Parry. Kichibei sobbed with self-pity. He never should have gone ahead of his troops. Where were they? They were already long overdue. They would save him. No . . . He would gather his strength and destroy this country boy; then he would greet his troops in triumph. Kichibei, once more a hero!

Drawing momentary courage from the thought, Kichibei made a last effort to carry the battle to his enemy.

Slash. Stroke. Parry. Feint. Sweat covered his body under its armor. His fingers became slippery, and then it was over. The sword flew from his hand, making a silver arc in the moonlight. He backed up, frantically pulling at the short sword in his sash. His enemy, confident of victory, moved up the hill toward him, sword arm relaxed, unaware of the short sword ready to slip upward between his ribs.

"Who are you?" asked Kichibei, trying to distract the attacker.

"It is fitting that you know. I am Yoshi, son of Hanzo, the swordmaker."

Kichibei retreated another step and started the stroke that

would turn defeat into victory. Then his foot caught on something bulky, breaking his balance. He fell backward, arms flailing; the short sword flew from his hand to be lost in the brush. He twisted as he fell and saw that his foot had knocked aside the loose branches from a half-buried corpse. He fell face to face with the body. The last thing he saw before Yoshi's blade severed his head was the peaceful smile on the corpse's face. Hanzo had had his revenge.

Twenty

Unaware that a full troop of soldiers were on their way up the other side of the mountain, Yoshi made an elaborate ceremony of burying Hanzo. He put him in the ground at the foot of his favorite shrine to Amaterasu. Alongside the body, he buried the noble blade that had acted its part so well in Hanzo's revenge. He hoped that Hanzo—from his new home in the Western Paradise—would understand. The gift had been made and appreciated; now its place was at the side of its creator. Kneeling by the shrine, Yoshi renewed his vow to avenge the death of Genkai as he had that of Hanzo, and he promised himself, "I shall never again forget my vows."

The horses were milling around the clearing, trying to avoid the smoking ruins. He calmed them. Choosing the horse that had carried Kichibei's crest, he pulled the crested lance from its mounting and removed the horse's war saddle and armor. Carrying the lance, he led the horse into the woods and tied its reins to a tree near Kichibei's body.

The decapitated head was on flat ground in a bright spot between the trees. Kichibei's hair was pulled askew and his mean little mouth gaped in a surprised circle. Yoshi closed the mouth; then, almost tenderly, like a mother caring for her baby, he brushed the hair back in place. His sense of the dramatic was pleased by the result when he attached the head to the point of the lance. The Kichibei banner hung like an obscene napkin below the ghastly head.

Yoshi brought the lance down to the clearing and pressed the butt into the ground at the entrance to the burning smithy.

Horses!

Just up the road and riding rapidly. Yoshi heard the voices of many men and the jangling of armor and weapons. He didn't hesitate. The lance was in place. He picked up Kichibei's sword and without a backward look ran to the horse.

Men were in the clearing . . . any second now . . . there! Shouting, confusion, horses milling around the grisly trophy on the pole. More shouting; they had found a body, then another.

Yoshi untied the horse and led it away from the road and into the forest; the sound of his passage was covered by the uproar below.

The troops had recognized their lord's head. The troops were divided. Half felt they owed allegiance to Kichibei's family and wanted to hunt the killer; the other half now considered themselves *ronin* and wanted to disband at once. Yoshi smiled grimly as he heard them fighting among themselves. Every moment the samurai wasted brought him closer to safety.

Out of range of the firelight, the trees and shrubs frustrated Yoshi at every step. In the dark, branches tore his clothing and stung his face as he hacked a path for himself and the horse. After the tension of his battle with Kichibei, the effort left him shaking with fatigue. He could not allow himself to rest; thoughts of triumph and revenge were forgotten as he battled the undergrowth.

After the shouting became inaudible, Yoshi redoubled his efforts; his arm rose and fell again and again. Silence was no longer important. Distance! As much as possible between himself and the samurai! He was gasping for breath, a stinging pain in his side; still he pressed on.

An interminable forty-five minutes later, Yoshi burst out

of the woods onto a flat field. It took all his remaining strength to mount the horse.

Should he head northeast, away from the Taira? He could hide with Matsutaro, the potter, in Mishima. But he did not want to endanger the old man; if Kichibei's samurai decided to hunt for revenge, they would surely search as far as Mishima. It would be logical to go that way instead of deeper into the Taira domain. Of course, Yoshi thought, that is what they will expect me to do. Long ago, in Kyoto, Yoshi had learned from his teacher of military science always to do the unexpected. He turned the horse toward the south and relaxed his grip on the reins.

It was time to take stock. After four years of relative security, he was on the road again. Except for a few coins, the horse, and Kichibei's sword, he had only the clothes he wore. As the horse waded through a small stream, Yoshi regretfully threw the sword into the dark water where it disappeared below the surface. The sword had served its purpose and would only make him conspicuous; no young man in torn work clothes could wear such a sword without attracting the attention of the authorities. He sighed, feeling naked and vulnerable without it. The horse settled into a steady pace, and Yoshi realized how exhausted he was. The run to Mishima, the return carrying a sixty-pound weight, the battle, the trauma of Hanzo's death, the escape over the mountain . . . Yoshi's head nodded as he fell asleep on the horse.

His eyes snapped open. He was instantly alert. It was still night. The horse had stopped at an almost dry riverbed. Rivulets of water trickled through the jagged rocks, nudging along bits of branch and leaf that had been loosened by the previous day's rain. A quarter moon illuminated twisted trees that clung to the bank. The riverbed was filled with the dark eddies of the tide. Yoshi did not know how far he had come or how long he had slept. The river ran through the center of a vast plain. He felt it would not be a good place to be caught when day came.

Across the river, a road ran parallel to the bank and then

took off at a right angle. In the moonlight, Yoshi saw a large, deserted-looking farmhouse down the road. He was drained. There was no use going farther tonight, especially since he might be moving closer to his enemies. It was time to part company with the horse. Like the sword, it had served its purpose; if he were stopped, it might be recognized as one of Kichibei's. Wearily, he dismounted and slapped its rump, sending it back along the path.

Lifting his robe and *hakama* to keep them dry, Yoshi clambered across the jagged rocks. Twenty minutes later, he was asleep on a pile of rotten hay behind the farmhouse.

PART THREE

Twenty-one

==

High in the mountains of the interior, a cold winter gray sky
embraced the rising sun, reflecting stray beams of orange red
from the snow fields. Scattered pines bowed their deep green
branches under the weight of the heavy white powder.
Yoshi's rag-wrapped feet were sunk deep in the snow. Wind
had swept drifts so high they reached over his head. He
crouched over the corpse of a man who had lost his way and
had frozen in the night. The blue white face of the victim
seemed part of the snowbank; even his hair was stiff with
frost.

The body was that of a wealthy traveler. It was dressed in
clothing of good quality. Yoshi thought ruefully of his own
rags. The dead man would not need the heavy over-robe or
the fine warm boots. With difficulty, Yoshi stripped the icy
clothes from the rigid body and rolled them in a bale.

The crouching figure, with its long, ragged hair standing
out like a lion's mane, was unrecognizable as the urbane
Yoshi of old. His beard grew like thick black moss covering a
rock; his skin was darkened by exposure, his lips were raw
and cracked.

Yoshi had learned the art of survival. He did what was

necessary to stay alive. He had grown almost callous to the hard life of the road—almost callous, because he still had memories of a gentler time when he had written poems and practiced calligraphy and painting.

He slung the clothes over his back and started toward one of the many shrines that were used as temporary shelters by travelers. He heard a flock of geese honking overhead; they sounded like a baying pack of wild dogs. His last impression of the frozen man was of the nude body obscenely exposed to the gray sky. A scattering of snowflakes fell and stuck, like miniature cherry blossoms, to the corpse's hairy parts. The flakes gradually covered the body with a mantle of white. Soon it would sink beneath the snow and remain hidden until the following spring.

Ironically, the traveler had died almost within sight of the shelter. In minutes, the red-gabled shrine showed its roof above the vast snow field. Yoshi headed for it.

Inside, it was dark and cold; the ancient smell of incense and long-departed people filled the small room under its smoke-blackened ceiling beams. Yoshi unrolled the clothing and beat the ice and stiffness from the folds. He stripped off his own filthy rags, wincing at the smell. He went outside, took handfuls of snow, and rubbed them over his naked body, stoically cleansing himself till his flesh glowed. When he was satisfied that every bit of grime was removed, he returned to the inside of the shrine where, teeth chattering, he dressed in the new clothing.

The shrine was regularly visited by the mountain people. There was a fireplace with an iron pot hung from a crossbar over the tinder. A few vegetables rotted on a shelf. Yoshi lit a fire, filled the pot with snow and melted it. He put the vegetables in to cook. They were tasteless but they filled his belly. When he finished, he cleaned the pot and rehung it in place for the next traveler.

The snow was coming down heavily. The sky had darkened. There was no sound except the creaking of overladen pine branches. Yoshi sat staring into the flames. He fell into a reverie as he recalled some of the events that brought him to this shrine in the mountains. . . .

Nineteen months ago, Yoshi had been awakened by a flock of crows disturbing the serene morning with their raucous "caw, caw, caw." He opened his eyes slowly to look up at an azure sky with tiny wave crests of clouds. He rolled on his side to find himself lying on a haystack behind an old, earth-walled and straw-thatched shed. The hay was moldy and rotted with time and weather. The shed—once a stable—was empty and neglected. Where was he? All he knew was that he was on a deserted farm somewhere in enemy territory.

Yoshi became conscious of noise coming from the other side of the shed, a clanking of metal mixed with grunts of effort. Quickly brushing off loose straws and insects, he moved to the corner of the shed and peeked around it. He drew back with a gasp. A troop of Kichibei's samurai were prying open the boarded-up farmhouse. It was obvious they were searching for him. He sped back to his haystack and burrowed feverishly into its interior. The rotted hay clogged his nostrils, almost making him gag. With great effort he made himself lie still.

Ten minutes passed before the samurai came to the haystack. Yoshi heard them arguing. "He is not here. We are wasting our time," said one.

"The horse was found nearby. He cannot be far," another answered.

"Come, let us search in the bamboo patch across the field."

"One moment. Check this haystack first."

Yoshi cringed, flat to the ground. He heard the swish of a sword blade . . . his stomach tensed. The blade swung again . . . and again. The density of the hay kept the blade from reaching him. "Use the point. You are not striking the bottom!"

Suddenly, the curved blade thrust into the ground inches from Yoshi's head. It was withdrawn with an angry jerk. "I am ruining my blade. Use your sword if you wish," a samurai snarled.

"Never mind. The hay stinks. Ugh . . . no one could hide in it."

"Let me burn it to be sure."

"You have wasted enough time. We must leave. Come, mount your horse. I have a feeling he is far from here."

Yoshi heard the horses clattering away. He lay motionless until late afternoon when, cramped and hungry, he crept from the haystack and made his way cautiously across the fields toward the bamboo patches that spread across the plain to the north and west.

After sunset, he found a hiding place in the bamboo brakes, where he dug in and stayed the night. Armor and horses passed him several times. The moon was only a thin, sad sliver that left the bamboo in darkness, making the patrols easy to avoid. He hid all the next day and traveled that night. It was a pattern he was to follow as the days turned to weeks. The searchers forced him to give up his plan to head south. Instead, he turned to the northern mountains, where he dropped from the world more completely than if he had taken the vows and become a monk. He was now one of the *esemono:* a creature of shadows, living a marginal existence in the most primitive parts of the mountain forests. . . .

Yoshi's head nodded, breaking his reverie. He still sat in the cold mountain shrine, staring at the dying embers. "Well," he told himself with a shake of the head, "reliving the past serves no purpose." Almost two years had been wasted in hiding. No more procrastination! It was time to carry out a plan decided on long ago: Master the sword, then find Lord Chikara and exact vengeance. He had a suit of decent clothes, thanks to the frozen traveler. He would shave and trim his hair so no one would recognize him, and tomorrow he would start out to seek the master swordsman, Naonori Ichikawa, and offer himself as an apprentice. Had not Ichikawa written Hanzo of his appreciation for the workmanship on his sword? It had been Hanzo's steel and Yoshi's engraving. Yes. He would remind the master of the letter and appeal to him for employment. He would set off for Sarashina and Ichikawa's academy in the morning.

A new life would start with the dawn.

Twenty-two

Four months later, in the third month of 1174, a traveler dressed in a well-made but somewhat travel-stained blue robe approached the town of Sarashina, ninety miles north of Okitsu, in the province of Shinano. The cherry trees were in bloom. The town lay half asleep in the somnolent spring light. A few oxcarts moved cumbersomely down the main street. Venders hawked their wares in voices that blended with the soughing of the spring breeze.

Sarashina had two claims to fame: the Lady Sarashina, who had written a *nikki*—romantic diary—almost a century before, and Naonori Ichikawa, the master swordsman whose academy turned out the finest students in Japan. The master's reputation brought men from every corner of the home provinces to his *dojo* for lessons in the handling of the sword.

Yoshi was directed to an unimpressive one-story building outside the town limits; a hanging scroll identified it as Ichikawa's Academy of Martial Arts. Its roof was a patchwork of different tiles; the outer walls were wooden panels decorated with crude military scenes. Not a sound came from within.

This was the famous academy of Ichikawa?

Yoshi mounted the steps, noting the cracked well and a

broken cart that leaned against the stone foundation. Neglect and age showed in every detail. Even the cherry trees surrounding the front courtyard were stunted and unkempt compared to the splendid trees in the rest of the town. It was a disheartening sight after a four-month journey across the mountains.

"Hello, is anyone there?" Yoshi's voice intruded in the dusty quiet.

"One moment, please," someone answered. The front panel slid open. "Can I help you?" The voice was deep, booming from some deep cavern below the rib cage. It was the master swordsman himself.

Ichikawa was a small, smooth-faced man, old enough to be Yoshi's father. He had campaigned at the same time as Fumio and Chikara. When they had accepted honors and land for their heroic actions, he had refused all glory, saying he was a fighting man who would always live by the sword.

At this moment, he was as unimpressive as his *dojo*. He was barefooted, wearing only a black *hakama* and a sword sash. A coat of sweat glistened from his naked upper body. Except for thick wrists and powerful forearms he was not particularly muscular. His face was expressionless, his small mouth set in a straight line that suggested a serious nature.

"I have come a great distance through the mountains of the south to see you . . . to offer myself in your service," said Yoshi with a formal bow.

"Are you a swordsman then?" Ichikawa frowned. "Your robe and crest are those of a commercial traveler."

"No, I am not a swordsman, though I have some experience with the sword. I studied in Kyoto many years ago," Yoshi answered.

During his trek across the mountains, Yoshi had not allowed himself to consider being refused. The thought that he might be turned away left him shaken.

"Yes, I hear the accent of Kyoto in your voice. Who are you, and why should I employ you?" Ichikawa seemed cool and disinterested.

"My name is Tadamori Yoshi." There was no reaction so

Yoshi continued. "Do you remember Hanzo, the swordsmith?" he asked in desperation.

"Of course, it is his sword I wear." Still cool.

"If you look closely at the tang you will see the engraving signed by other than Hanzo."

"I know. The engraver was a true artist, an apprentice to the swordsmith."

"I was the assistant who engraved your blade."

Ichikawa's demeanor changed immediately. "You? My apologies if I was brusque. Your artistry deserves a measure of respect. Come in . . . we shouldn't be standing here on the steps. The breeze is cool; your journey was long. Let us sit, drink some tea, and discuss your situation."

Ichikawa led the way inside the *dojo*. The difference was profound. Where the outside was neglected to the point of squalor, the inside was immaculate. The polished wood floor was spotless, almost mirrorlike; it reflected the images of the practice armor, and *bokken*—wooden practice swords—lined up along one wall. Beyond the practice area was a small office, its walls covered with scrolls of appreciation from famous students. It also contained a low table set with a vase of chrysanthemums, a pot of tea, and several cups.

Ichikawa motioned Yoshi to be seated. "I am going to clean up and change. Pour tea if you wish. I will return in a few moments."

Yoshi sat on a cushion; he read the testimonial scrolls to pass the time. They were impressive. Men whose reputations had reached Yoshi even in the hinterlands credited everything to Ichikawa.

The silence in the *dojo* was almost complete; the street noises were far away. Tiny motes of dust floated in the light from an open panel. The smell of chrysanthemums mixed with that of tea and incense. It was a peaceful moment after the grueling months on the road. Yoshi thought how much he missed the niceties of civilization. Sitting in a comparatively clean robe in this quiet pleasant room brought him a feeling of inner peace. It was as though he had come home again.

Ichikawa returned, wearing a fresh white robe over a

sky-blue *hakama*. His hair was tied back, accentuating the roundness of his face. "Were you the one?" he asked, looking down without expression.

Yoshi had felt the balance of the interview turn in his favor; now he was not sure. Ichikawa already knew he had done the engraving. What else could he mean? "Excuse me, I do not understand," he said.

"The unknown one who beheaded Kichibei and killed five of his samurai." Was Ichikawa disapproving?

"Yes." There was no point in denying it, and even if he could he wouldn't. He had acted correctly. It would be an insult to Hanzo's memory to avoid accepting responsibility . . . even if it meant alienating Ichikawa.

"And you want to be my apprentice? Perhaps you should teach me." Ichikawa laughed.

Yoshi sighed with relief. Ichikawa not only approved, he was delighted. "I had the spirits on my side," said Yoshi modestly. "Hanzo guided me with his prayers and I was helped by the samurai's stupidity."

"Nevertheless, it was a mighty feat; one that is often talked about where warriors gather."

"I deserve no glory. It was what I had to do."

"Spoken like a true samurai." Ichikawa poured two cups of tea. "How can you be sure you can trust me?" he asked. "The authorities are still offering a reward for the head of Kichibei's killer."

"There is no question of trusting you. Your name and reputation for honor are known throughout the provinces."

"All right then. Tell me more about yourself: your goals . . . ambitions . . . interests. Tell me what you did before Hanzo . . . and after. Then we will discuss the possibilities of your becoming my apprentice."

Yoshi told Ichikawa about his early training with his uncle Fumio and of his six years in Kyoto. He described his homecoming and the duel that led to Genkai's death. His eyes burned with passion as he spoke of his vow to seek revenge. His voice softened when he described the friendship he had developed with Ietaka during their flight and the concern he felt when he thought of the night they had been separated. "I have always assumed he escaped," Yoshi said. "I would have difficulty facing my life if I had caused his death, too."

Yoshi continued with a description of Hanzo's final battle and his own escape from Kichibei's troops. Then his head hung in shame as he described his life as a fugitive. He spoke frankly, holding nothing back, telling of the depths he had plumbed in the name of survival.

When the tale was over, Ichikawa sat silently, holding a cup of cold tea in his hand. Yoshi seemed to hear his own heartbeat, loud in the quiet room. He knew he was being judged, and his future depended on what this man decided.

"If you work for me, there will be no pay. You will receive only food and a small hut of your own behind the academy."

"Agreed," said Yoshi quickly.

"Your engravings are beautiful, but can you write a clear letter? Can you make posters and scrolls?" Now Ichikawa was all business.

"Yes. I read and write," answered Yoshi.

"Excellent. You will do all our correspondence. Your duties will also include cleaning the school at least three times daily, and buying food and cooking meals for the staff and the students. In exchange, I will give you lessons when I feel you have earned them. When your daily duties are over, you may discreetly watch the lessons of others."

"Agreed."

"You will be my second assistant, under the command of my first assistant. His name is Kaneoki. You will obey his instructions as though they were mine."

This surprised Yoshi. Seeing the quiet building, it had not occurred to him that there would be another instructor besides Master Ichikawa.

"Kaneoki? Where is he, *Sensei*, Teacher?"

"Today is the third day of the third month. There is a Peach festival in Sarashina. Kaneoki and the students were given a holiday. They will return tonight."

"The students and Kaneoki, do they also sleep here in the *dojo*?" asked Yoshi.

"No, no. There is another building behind the cherry grove. They live there. You will, of course, also be responsible for keeping their quarters clean and in repair."

Seeing a fleeting expression of dismay on Yoshi's face, Ichikawa hid a smile. "Now," he said, "since we have time and no one is about, let us try each other on the floor. This will be your first lesson."

He led Yoshi to the rack of *bokken*. "We will use these till I have an idea of your level of skill. Choose one," he said.

He removed his white robe and swished the wooden blade overhead.

Yoshi shed his blue over-robe. He peeled the rest of his clothes down to his breechclout. Choosing the heaviest of the wooden swords, he flexed his muscles confidently. After all, he had not only studied in Kyoto, he had also practiced many an hour with a professional samurai; Hanzo had taught him well. In spite of the arduous trek through the mountains, Yoshi's tiredness fell away; he felt fresh and strong with the blade in his hand.

His confidence did not last long.

Ichikawa's sword was a blur that always managed to strike where it was least expected. Soon, Yoshi was dripping sweat and having difficulty catching his breath. His chest heaved. The harder he tried, the heavier the *bokken* became.

Ichikawa's face gave no hint of effort; his soft-looking body was relaxed and dry; he breathed easily and moved with an economy of motion that made him seem almost stationary. But the sweating, panting Yoshi knew differently. All his techniques were to no avail as Ichikawa hit him across the chest, shoulders, side, and stomach and ultimately disarmed him with an effortless flick of the wooden blade.

"*Yame*—stop," said the swordmaster. "I think we have tested enough for your first day. Actually you are better than I expected. You have spirit, though you need discipline and practice. Look at you!" His face was stern.

Indeed, Yoshi was a sad sight. His body was covered with sweat; his hair hung over his face in wet tendrils; bright red blotches appeared where the master's *bokken* had struck; his head hung down, his mouth open, gasping for air.

Yoshi shook his head in wonderment. Ichikawa might have just finished pouring tea.

"I thought . . ." Yoshi began.

"I know," said Ichikawa. "We have had young men like you before. In time you will learn, as they did, that strength is something that comes from inside. It is not a matter of big muscles. Here, if you follow my teachings, you will develop your mind and your inner strength. Skill with the sword will follow. It will be difficult for you; you have much to unlearn. Be patient. Even the most untalented student can master the art if his heart and mind are open to our teaching. Do you think you want to try?"

Yoshi answered humbly, "Yes, *Sensei*."

"Then the first lesson is over. The performance of your duties will furnish your second lesson. Start cleaning the courtyard before the other students return!"

Twenty-three

===

The yard was full of weeds. Purple-blossomed wisteria grew like morning clouds between the cherry trees. Beautiful in itself, the wisteria had no place in the courtyard. As Yoshi pulled out the weeds, it occurred to him that what he did was truly the labor of a nonperson. What would Fumio or Ietaka think if they could see him, back bent, face twisted with effort, grubbing in the ground?

As he worked he composed a poem:

> *The wisteria*
> *Sweet mauve flowers growing wild*
> *In the dark forest*
> *Unseen, unwanted, purple*
> *Weeds among the cherry trees.*

At first glance the courtyard did not appear large, but from his position, bent over the stubborn weeds, it was immense, and the second lesson turned out to be a long and tedious one. Yoshi was not sure what he had expected to learn from Ichikawa . . . some new techniques perhaps, like those learned from Hanzo? He had not expected to be shown he knew so little, and he certainly had not expected to be dismissed to perform this seemingly unending menial task.

Enough! This new life had hardly started and already he felt discontented. Perhaps the lesson to learn was that one should accept one's labors and make the most of them. He paused for breath and began to appreciate the beauty of the day. The soft spring breeze cooled him as he returned to the unaccustomed labor. It had been almost two years since he had left the forge and his hands had grown soft. Soon they were blistered and swollen, but he had the satisfaction of seeing the courtyard look more respectable. His shadow lengthened on the ground as the sun crossed overhead and lowered in the west. One section of courtyard was clean.

He went to the broken cart that leaned against the stone foundation. Yoshi's experience at the forge told him he could repair it if he had tools and a hot fire. A wheel was loose, the iron axle bent out of line. When he wiped away the grime that had covered the cart through the winter, he saw beautiful inlay and painted decoration on the sides. It was well built and worth saving. He tried to turn the cart so he could get at the axle, but it was too heavy to be managed alone.

While he struggled, Ichikawa came out on the veranda. He looked approvingly at the yard, and at Yoshi straining under the cart.

"Yoshi," he called. "You have done enough for today. It is time to eat. Wash yourself and come in to prepare our dinner."

Yoshi quickly cleaned himself in the cracked stone well and hurried inside. He was hungry. A day of working in the yard had given him the appetite of a mountain lion. Even on the days he had gone entirely without food he had not felt as hungry as this. Ichikawa showed him to the food supplies and the cooking fire and left him to work. Spurred by his appetite, Yoshi prepared one pot of vegetable soup, another of rice with small bits of fish, and more tea.

Ichikawa was served first. The master accepted the food wordlessly. When he had tasted the soup, he nodded approval and motioned Yoshi to sit opposite him.

"You cook well."

"A lesson of the road, *Sensei*. I'm afraid the fare is simple . . . my cooking skills are self-taught. In Kyoto, that part of my education was neglected."

Ichikawa allowed himself a small smile. "The cooking will be no problem and I am satisfied with your work outside. All in all, I think you will do well here, albeit there may be some lessons to be learned in dealing with people. You may, for instance, find Kaneoki difficult. Many do. But he is a fine swordsman and has been loyal to our school."

"I shall remember my place," said Yoshi.

"Yes, I'm sure you will. I think you have done well with your second lesson. Wash the pots and you may go to your sleeping quarters. The hut has been empty since last year. No doubt you will want to clean and rearrange it before you retire."

"Thank you, *Sensei*."

Twenty-four

The hut that was to be Yoshi's home was a square of dried earth walls with a thatch roof. Each wall was about three paces long, the entrance an interruption in one of the walls. The entire structure looked as though it were a natural outgrowth of the forest. It had obviously been uninhabited for a long time; there were gaping holes in the thatch roof, weeds grew over the veranda, which was on poles three feet above the ground, and thick cobwebs covered the entrance and the spaces that were the windows. When Yoshi stood on the veranda, the eaves barely cleared his head. The veranda was shaky; some of the bamboo had rotted and not been replaced. From it, Yoshi had a view of miles of cherry trees, their blossoms sparkling in the setting sun.

He brushed the webs from the door. Inside, the hut was covered with dust and a debris of old leaves, straw, and the bodies of myriad insects that had taken refuge there during the winter. The evanescence of life demonstrated again!

It was already growing dark in the hut. There was much to do before he could retire for the night. He found a broom of bamboo fronds in the corner and went to work clearing the dust and cobwebs.

The moon shone brightly through the open window when

Yoshi stopped to take stock of his new quarters. The hardpacked dirt floor was clean. A straw sleeping mat filled one corner. Next to the mat was a firebox with neatly piled brushwood for tinder. A small fire would furnish the only heat on cold nights and mornings. There was a shelf over the bed where he had found three dusty leather cases holding books of poems. These were now clean and arranged in a row. Opposite the mat, a second shelf held a flower vase and a cracked statue of Buddha. The shelf was over an old writing table. An ink stick and a carved ink holder were lined up on the table top.

Yoshi was satisfied. The hut was small and humble—even less, in a material sense, than he had had at Hanzo's forge. Nevertheless, he felt content. It was clean, comfortable, private, and his own. He realized again how tired he was. No doubt he would find more to do tomorrow. Now . . . he wanted only to sleep. He started a small fire for warmth as the night had turned cool. He stretched out wearily on the straw bed and, using the long sleeve of his gown as a pillow, he fell into a deep sleep.

Two hours later, Yoshi awoke to noise and lanterns shining in his face. It took a few moments to clear his head; he had been in a dream that mixed Ono, Masa, and Nami. Where was he?

"Look what we have here," said a coarse voice. "This is what made the fire in the deserted hut."

Yoshi focused on the speaker, a large, hairy young man who was waving a lantern in his face. The moving light reflected upward giving the man a decidedly sinister countenance. A moustache in the Chinese fashion curved around his mouth. His nose was overlong, its tip slightly off-center in his broad, flat-cheeked face. A thin scar slanted across his forehead. He wore a black lacquered *eboshi*, or headdress, and a gown with wide, starched shoulders. Two swords hung from his sash. Yoshi was reminded of the unemployed samurai who swaggered through the countryside stealing from the poor.

Behind him crowded a group of young men. It was impossible to tell how many, although it was obvious that all of them, including the sinister-faced leader, were drunk.

"A trespasser!" rasped the coarse voice. "We know how to deal with trespassers."

"Who are you?" asked the disoriented Yoshi.

"Who are *we!* You have to give this trespasser credit for having courage." The dark man drew his sword. "Before we decide on your punishment," he said, "you'd better tell us who *you* are and what you are doing here."

"I am not a trespasser. I have permission of *Sensei* Ichikawa to live here. I am his new assistant," said Yoshi quickly.

"Assistant? Assistant! I'll assistant you, you dog. There will be only one assistant at the academy of Ichikawa." He glared madly in the moving light.

"Who are you?" asked Yoshi.

"My name is Kaneoki," answered the man with the lantern.

Twenty-five

==

Cherry blossoms fell and the trees turned to a vast brocade of red and gold as spring passed and summer turned to the fall of 1174. Yoshi finished the courtyard, rebuilt the cart, patched the roof of his own hut, and fixed the cracked stone well. Daily he cleaned the *dojo*, polished the armor and weapons, cooked two daily meals, and kept the students' house in order. He accepted the hard work, but from his first unfortunate meeting with Kaneoki his life was a misery of small insults.

"Yoshi, this soup isn't fit for a pig," Kaneoki would say, spilling it on the floor.

"Yes, Kaneoki-san," Yoshi would answer, cleaning it up.

"Yoshi, do you call this floor clean? It stinks of your passage. Wash it again."

"Yes, Kaneoki-san." Yoshi hid his anger behind a face of stone.

Ichikawa, if he was aware of the tension between his first assistant and the newcomer, said nothing. He was fully occupied with the new students who flooded the academy. They were full of news from the outside, news of the imminent collision between Taira and Minamoto.

Except that more students meant more work, the political conflict hardly touched Yoshi. He listened to the discussions but made no move to join them. When the students noticed him at all, they made fun of his labors. He bore their taunts silently, learning to contain his feelings as he performed the menial tasks of the school.

On the fifteenth day of the tenth month, Yoshi rose as usual at the hour of the tiger, about four A.M., straightened out his hut, washed down the *dojo* floors, boiled water for the morning meal, and, before the sun rose, practiced for an hour, repeating the exercises he saw the students doing during the day.

Ichikawa and Kaneoki came on the floor just after dawn. They warmed up while Yoshi set up the bowls for the students' first meal. As usual, Kaneoki found something unsatisfactory in Yoshi's performance and had him reset the table.

After Kaneoki was satisfied, Yoshi worked on the accounts, handled the correspondence, and brushed in calligraphy for the school's posters while he watched the classes through the sliding door.

Before breaking their fast, the students were put through a series of exercises, including running, hopping, jumping, and kicking movements. After an hour of these strenuous calisthenics, they divided into two groups. Kaneoki took the group of eight beginners while Ichikawa took the advanced students. Another hour of concentrated practice passed before the men were released to their breakfast.

Yoshi doled out the rice, bits of octopus, shrimp, dried fish, vegetables, and the ever-present green tea. After eating, the students were given a half hour respite while Yoshi cleared the table, washed the bowls, and snatched a hasty meal of leftovers. He reset the table for the evening meal then returned to the office and the poster he was preparing. His brush moved automatically as he pondered how much patience and self-control he had learned during this long, painful second lesson. His thoughts were disturbed by a familiar voice.

"Yoshi, put down the brush. Today you will join Kaneoki's class." *Sensei* Ichikawa stood at the door while the students waited on the *tatami* floor.

"*Hai, Sensei!*" said Yoshi. He jumped to his feet and ran to the back of the class.

"You have a new student starting today," Ichikawa told Kaneoki.

Kaneoki glowered. "*Hai, Sensei,*" he said. When Ichikawa left, Kaneoki turned to Yoshi with a wolfish grin. "You will do the exercises with us," he said. "A little pain is a good thing. Keep your mind hard and don't stop till the command."

There was no doubt that Kaneoki was strong and limber. He outdid his students at every exercise. And today's exercises would be especially difficult—Kaneoki's way of putting the new student in his place.

The students groaned, their faces contorted with effort as Kaneoki drove them unmercifully. Only the newest student showed no sign of strain. He had watched the classes for six months and had practiced the exercises every morning until he was able to do them easily.

After the final exercise—one hundred fifty sit-ups—Kaneoki jumped to his feet. "Very good," he said grudgingly. "Let's start with the swords."

The courtyard flourished; another spring brought new blooms to the trees. Yoshi had terraced the front with white gravel in the style of the Imperial Palace. The inside was as neat and clean as it had ever been, and the students were happy. New scrolls proclaimed the academy of master Ichikawa to the world.

Working in the office and on the grounds had become a relief for Yoshi; he welcomed any opportunity to escape Kaneoki's attentions. In the six months Yoshi had studied under Kaneoki, he suffered innumerable physical beatings. Kaneoki was a strong swordsman, and jealous of Yoshi's progress, he took every opportunity to impress Yoshi with his superiority. Yoshi learned faster than the others, partly because of his strength, but mostly as a matter of survival. Yoshi had lost weight, and his bulky muscles had lengthened and become more supple.

Ichikawa had looked on and said nothing, but when the spring thaw brought new students, Ichikawa hired another apprentice, relieving Yoshi of household duties, and entrusted the beginners to Yoshi's tutelage.

Kaneoki felt his position threatened, and when Yoshi was taken out of his classes and was given private lessons by Ichikawa, Kaneoki's jealousy grew like a cancer.

Yoshi's life was changing, but though he was now a teacher and a favored disciple of the master, he still kept to himself, living in the little hut he had grown to love, and putting all his energies into training his students.

Kaneoki's disposition was not helped when Yoshi's new students improved rapidly. Yoshi discovered an aptitude for teaching and by midsummer his beginners had caught up with Kaneoki's intermediates. In the monthly competition, they won honors in *keiko*—free swordplay—by a small margin.

Kaneoki was furious; he drove his students harder, but to no avail. In the fall, Yoshi's beginners trounced them again. They even won some matches from the advanced students.

Kaneoki pressed even harder, until some of his students complained to the master. Ichikawa took him to the private office and slid the door shut; it was a chastened Kaneoki who came out.

From that day on, Yoshi was often aware of the first assistant watching him balefully while he practiced.

Twenty-six

Three months later, the tensions erupted during a practice session.

Winter had come again, the grounds were covered with snow, and the wind blew froths of ice crystals against the uninsulated academy. The students tried to stay far away from the cold walls; their favorite gathering place was near the office where a copper brazier cast heat into the *dojo* work area. Yoshi was defending against two of his students, holding them off while he illustrated the best method of defense against two men. He shifted quickly to his left keeping the attackers one behind the other.

"Always keep your enemies in a line. That way they will get in each other's way and only one can swing at you freely. As attackers, you must separate and come from different sides; one of you will draw the enemy's attention while the other strikes. In a military situation there is no room for niceties. Survival with honor is all that counts."

As he spoke he continuously circled to the left, effectively tying up the students. He was fully concentrated on the attackers and trusted his feet to feel his position. Suddenly, he was struck from the rear. He had circled out of his group's area and unknowingly moved into the section near the warm office; this was the area Kaneoki had reserved for himself. Yoshi reacted swiftly and involuntarily. He spun on the ball of his front foot dropping his weight low to the floor and slashing out blindly. He was rewarded with a scream of pain and anger. The wooden sword had struck across Kaneoki's shins under his practice armor.

Kaneoki attacked, his face contorted with rage. The scar across his forehead blazed red, his dark face turned even darker as he chopped at Yoshi's head. Yoshi parried. The shock of the blow almost splintered his *bokken*. He realized that Kaneoki was in the grip of a demon. Yoshi was pressed back. Even sane, Kaneoki was a stronger, more experienced swordsman; goaded now by his invisible devil he seemed unbeatable. Yoshi gave ground, again and again barely escaping defeat and injury.

As Yoshi was being forced to the outer wall, the voice of Ichikawa boomed across the *dojo*. "*Yame!* Stop!" he shouted.

The mad light faded from Kaneoki's eyes; he lowered the wooden sword.

"Classes are over for this morning," announced Ichikawa, holding in his anger. "Everyone go back to your sleeping quarters. We will meet again this afternoon." Ichikawa bowed to the class and clapped his hands in dismissal. He turned to Kaneoki and Yoshi. "You two," he said, "will stay here with me."

The students stacked their gear without the horseplay and joking that usually marked the end of a class. They donned their winter robes and filed out silently.

Ichikawa waited while Yoshi and Kaneoki stood at attention, looking straight ahead, beads of sweat forming on their foreheads.

Time passed slowly.

"All right. You are both calm now. What happened?" asked Ichikawa.

Both assistants spoke at once.

"Silence!" snapped Ichikawa. He turned to Kaneoki.

"You are senior man. You answer first."

"The second assistant overstepped his territory. He came into my area. I only struck him lightly to remind him of his position," said Kaneoki.

"Is that true?" Ichikawa asked Yoshi.

"Hai, Sensei!" answered Yoshi, inwardly seething at the injustice of his position.

"Then you are at fault in causing this unseemly disturbance in the class?"

"Hai, Sensei!" His fists were tight.

"I do not want a repetition of this behavior. You are both supposed to be examples for the students. You, Yoshi, were wrong in losing your temper on the floor. Whatever the provocation, there is no excuse for acting thoughtlessly. If this had been a real situation with real swords, you would be dead now. To attack a superior force shows a strong heart. To stay calm and act wisely shows a strong mind. Both are necessary in equal proportions. This is a lesson for you to remember. It is no less important than your lessons in the use of the sword.

"Your punishment will be a month of restriction to your living quarters when you are not on the floor teaching."

"Hai, Sensei!" Ichikawa knew that Yoshi always stayed in his hut in his spare time so the punishment was a token. The point had been made. Whatever indignity he suffered at the hands of Kaneoki, he was to maintain a hard mind and accept his lower rank.

Kaneoki realized that Yoshi had been let off easily. The scar on his forehead turned red with his effort at self-restraint. Finally he could hold himself in no longer. *"Sensei,"* he said, "if the second assistant wants the lesson driven home, I am ready to oblige him with real swords."

Yoshi stiffened. This was close to a direct challenge and no honorable man could refuse a direct challenge.

Before he could respond, Ichikawa snapped, "In my school, only I decide on the lessons. Now *you* are overstepping the bounds, first assistant. Remember who is the master here. If this minor incident should escalate into a duel without my permission, the winner will face me with live blades. I cannot spend my time training assistants so they can kill each other off. Understood?''

Both men answered in unison. *''Hai, Sensei!''*

Twenty-seven

During the rest of the winter, Yoshi spent his extra time reading and writing in his hut. He had repaired the bamboo veranda, built a sliding door, and put in windows. The firebox furnished enough heat for him to be comfortable. He sat at his writing table, filling page after page with notes during the long snowy months.

Finally, when the sunny days of the fourth month of 1176 came, he sat on the veranda gazing out over a sea of cherry blossoms almost as white as the snow they replaced. He took pleasure in watching the path of a red and black butterfly that circled from blossom to blossom. The leaves of the trees were new green, and bird songs filled the air. In the evenings, he could hear the "ho-to-to" cry of the *hototogisu*—the cuckoo—and sometimes the distant screech of a wild monkey mating under the moon.

Life was full. Yoshi rose at the hour of the tiger when the first bells sounded the hour from the temple in Sarashina. He practiced diligently before starting his classes, and when everyone rested, he practiced again in the evening. It was almost the life of a monk. He never went to the inns or joined the others in their occasional celebrations. There was talk among the students. Yoshi had won their respect by his ability as a swordsman and a teacher, but the nature of his ascetic life led the students to speculate about his background. It had not been lost on these sons and cousins of the Minamoto that Yoshi spoke with the soft accents of the Taira court.

Kaneoki had been the most persistent in his inquiries into Yoshi's background, trying many times to draw the master into conversation about Yoshi's credentials. Ichikawa was usually silent about Yoshi's past; however, on one occasion he proudly mentioned that his sword had been engraved by Yoshi. Kaneoki knew that the sword was from Hanzo's forge. He said nothing but was thoughtful and spoke little for the rest of the night. Knowing that Yoshi had worked for Hanzo might be important in the future. Kaneoki would not forget.

The fifteenth day of the seventh month of 1176 was the first day of the Festival of the Dead and the students were dismissed early in the day. They went to Sarashina to take part in a special Buddhist service; they would stay late to watch the ceremonial fires that would be lit to help the ghosts of the departed find their way home.

Yoshi and Ichikawa were left alone in the deserted *dojo*.

Twenty-one months had passed since Yoshi was put in charge of his first class. He had learned while he taught, and he had learned his lessons well.

On Yoshi's first day, Ichikawa had promised that if he followed Ichikawa's teachings, Yoshi would develop his mind and inner strength. It had not been an idle promise. With Ichikawa's guidance, Yoshi made remarkable strides. He was no longer merely an apprentice or even an assistant; he had been promoted—to Kaneoki's chagrin—to Ichikawa's second in command. Ichikawa relied on Yoshi's toughness of mind and dedication to the school, while Yoshi's respect for Ichikawa constantly grew. Despite their difference in age, they were trusted friends.

Yoshi had proved his loyalty and intelligence many times; as a result, Ichikawa was gradually relinquishing the daily management of the school to him. They were still master and disciple—that would never change—but whenever the two men were alone and freed from their *dojo* duties, they used the time to freely discuss the classes, students, and future of the academy.

As the last rays of the sun shone through the bamboo blinds and reflected bright stars from the steel of the wall-mounted weapons, Yoshi and Ichikawa finished reviewing the school's business. They sat crosslegged on scarlet cushions, a tray holding an empty teapot and two cups at their side, its upside down image reflected from the polished floor.

Yoshi took a deep breath, inhaling scents of oil, bitter tea, incense, and the faint effluvium of ten thousand practice sessions. The room was peaceful and familiar, yet despite the quiet and serenity, Yoshi was disturbed. The satisfaction he should have felt at the work he and Ichikawa had accomplished eluded him. One subject had been avoided. . . .

"*Sensei*," he said, his voice hoarse with pent-up feeling. "I have been patient. The lessons you taught me are engraved in my heart and my head. Now, it is time to accept Kaneoki's challenge. The day hardly passes that he does not press me to the wall."

"We must be understanding," said Ichikawa. "It was difficult for Kaneoki to be passed over for promotion. I hoped you would make it easier for him."

"*Sensei*, I have tried to no avail. He constantly provokes me in front of the students. For myself, I've shown I can bear it. It is the discipline of the school I am thinking of."

"Nevertheless, I ask you to bear it a while longer."

Ichikawa put a fatherly hand on Yoshi's shoulder. "A man can live by the sword just so long, and my time is past. With all my skill and knowledge, I no longer have the speed and reflexes of yesterday. I had a dream not long ago in which you were the master of this school and I was a spirit visiting from the heavenly sphere. How fitting that we should speak of this during the Festival of the Dead."

"*Sensei*, it is pointless to discuss such dreams. You are the greatest swordsman of us all and will remain master of this academy until you wish to retire." Yoshi hesitated. "As for

Kaneoki,'' he added, ''I shall respect your wishes and curb my impatience.''

Everyone had accepted Yoshi's new status except Kaneoki who still insisted on dealing with Yoshi as though Yoshi were his inferior.

Kaneoki did a minimum of work at the school and usually could be found at his favorite inn drinking with a group of new friends, three *ronin*. All three were dark, hairy, powerful men who wore black robes over black *hakama*. Their foreheads were shaved and their hair pulled back at the sides in the samurai style. The three had served together under one lord, and had wandered the countryside hiring themselves out as mercenaries after their lord was killed. They often strutted arrogantly through the streets of Sarashina, hands on their sword hilts. The townspeople avoided them.

There was usually some kind of brawl before the evening ended. The innkeeper suffered the damage in silence. He feared the cruelty that lurked so near the surface of these ruthless men. Better to accept their behavior than to speak up and goad them to greater violence.

While Yoshi and Ichikawa discussed Kaneoki, the three *ronin* sat with him on the veranda of the inn, telling stories of past military successes. With each story they drank more sake. As the oft-told stories palled, they became silent, concentrating on the *atobi*—parting fires for the spirits of the dead—so clearly visible over the low railing of the veranda. The silence could not last and after a few moments, one *ronin* loudly declared, ''I've sent so many men to hell the priests could light all those fires for my victims alone.''

The *ronin's* introspection was broken; they laughed and emptied their cups.

''Landlord, bring more wine, and let's have the girls, too.''

''I'm sorry, good sirs, so sorry. The girls have gone to the festival.''

''What? I'll kill you for this. I'll cut off your private parts and feed them to you. You let them go?'' shouted the *ronin* leader in mock ferocity.

"I am sorry, so sorry." The landlord backed off the veranda bowing frantically in his haste. "I bring wine. More wine."

Kaneoki opened his robe because of the heat. He waved a fan desultorily at his damp matted hair. Sake spilled from his cup and ran from his chin onto his bare chest. He paid no attention to his friends. "That's how I'm repaid," he mumbled. "I work for years building a school so some stranger can wander in off the road and take what should have been mine." He slobbered more drink.

"Enough!" snarled one of the *ronin*. "We are tired of hearing the same story every night. Why don't you just kill him and be done with it?"

"If I did, Ichikawa would never forgive me for hurting his pet. Look you, Higo, I am beset on all sides. There is no solution to my problems." He gulped another cup of sake.

"Wait a minute," said Higo winking at the other *ronin*. "Maybe we can lend a hand. After all, we have no debt to Ichikawa. We resent the way he sits in his academy as though he were above us. We can help you and get a little of our own back against him at the same time."

"I should do it myself," said Kaneoki.

"It won't matter who does it, as long as it's done. We haven't had any fun in months. A sword needs fresh blood from time to time to keep its edge."

"Little bastard engraver! He deserves what he gets," said Kaneoki drinking another cup.

"Engraver? I thought he was a fencing teacher," said Higo.

"Ichikawa said this Yoshi engraved his sword. Anyway, there's something strange about him. He speaks with a Kyoto accent, yet no one knows where he comes from." Kaneoki tried to straighten up and concentrate on his words, but the effort was too much. He collapsed on himself, drooling and belching simultaneously.

Higo's expression sobered. He reached out a powerful hand and clutched Kaneoki's robe. He lifted and shook him. "Tell me," he said menacingly, "what sword does Ichikawa wear?"

Kaneoki slumped forward, mumbling unintelligibly.

"Damn you. Listen to me!" Higo slapped his face back and forth until he started to struggle in the iron grasp.

"Hanzo," he sputtered. "The sword is from Hanzo."

The *ronin* released his grip and let Kaneoki slide off his cushion and onto the floor. He glared across the table at the others. All trace of drunkenness gone, his voice was deadly. "At last," he said, "our search is ended. The man who cast us to the fates, the murderer of Lord Kichibei, is in our hands."

Twenty-eight

The full moon of the fifteenth was partially obscured by drifting puffs of cloud. The day's heat had been relieved by a breeze bringing cool air from the distant ocean. Yoshi was at his desk, pensively writing in his pillowbook. The carved inkstone was full of good black ink; his brush dipped and stroked as though it had a mind of its own, effortlessly forming the calligraphic symbols.

"Ho-to-to" a cuckoo sounded from outside. Yoshi put down his brush and went to the window hoping to catch sight of the bird. The forest of cherry trees loomed thick and dark in the moonlight, the treetops outlined by the moonbeams to make an ocean of greenish black.

Yoshi started to compose a poem:

> Hototogisu
> *Swims among dark green moonlit leaves*
> *Singing mournfully*
> *A tear-stained song sent with love*
> *To the ocean of the sky.*

His poem filled him with sadness, and brought on an attack of the restlessness that had plagued him since the spring. On many lonely nights like this, he had thought of his youth, of

Nami, Fumio, Ietaka, and Lady Masaka. Now he asked himself what they were doing tonight. Did they stare at the same moon and think of him?

A rustling came from the forest. Yoshi thought it must be a deer, wandered far from its mountain haunts.

No! There was a flare of light, the moon reflecting from a piece of steel. A man was coming through the trees behind the *dojo*. Unless it was a lost traveler, no one should be there . . . and if it was a traveler, why the drawn sword? And why had he not headed for the ceremonial fires that burned in Sarashina?

Yoshi put aside the brush and book. He kicked off his sandals, strapped his swords around his waist, and covered himself with a hooded cloak that almost reached the floor. He then extinguished the lamp and positioned himself near the door. The smell of the oil lamp filled his nostrils as he waited for the moon-god, Tsukiyomi, to hide behind an approaching cloud.

When the cloud momentarily darkened the forest, Yoshi slipped out onto the veranda holding himself flat against the rough earthen wall. Now, if Tsukiyomi showed his face, Yoshi would be hidden in the shadow of the extended eaves. His toes gripped the bamboo floor; his hands pressed against the wall . . . slowly he moved toward the back corner of the house.

A noise from the front.

Then there were at least two of them. Yoshi imagined they were highwaymen out to rob and kill an unsuspecting victim. He thought for a moment of shouting for help; the quiet from the school and living quarters reminded him that everyone was in town at the Festival.

He checked the draw on his long sword. It slid silently on a thin coat of oil. He was prepared; the highwaymen would have to earn their booty. Yoshi's hooded face peered around the corner. It was dark, the moon cloaked in a cloud. He strained forward, listening to the natural forest sounds, the sighing wind, the cry of the cicada, the hoot of a distant owl. And other sounds that did not belong: a twig broken under a heavy foot, bushes being forced apart, the clink of metal on a rock.

An intruder was drawing closer. Yoshi dropped three feet from the veranda to the ground. He reached the border of trees just as the cloud passed away from the moon. He could hear heavy breathing not five paces away. The man had stopped at the edge of the trees and was on his knees mumbling a prayer. Yoshi crept closer trying to fathom the man's purpose.

The intruder's voice was unclear but occasional words were audible. "Kichibei . . . murderer . . . revenge. Amida give me strength for the task at hand."

So, after all this time, the samurai of Kichibei had found him.

There was no question of Yoshi's submitting. They would be satisfied with no less than his head.

"In a fight to the death, surprise can be a most effective weapon. The attacker with the advantage of surprise usually wins the day." Yoshi remembered these words, an early lesson from Ichikawa. If there were two samurai approaching the house, he would need every advantage he could gain.

He slipped his sword free and inched toward the kneeling figure. As he got closer, he could smell the odor of spilled sake from the man's clothing. He lifted his sword.

The man may have had too much to drink, but he was a *ronin*, one who had always lived by his strength and reflexes. He heard something—a sigh, a breath, a twig breaking under Yoshi's foot—and acted instinctively, diving away from the noise, twisting and rolling as he hit the ground. His sword was up, ready to parry an attack before the disturbed bits of earth and fallen leaf had settled to the ground.

"I think I am the one you are looking for," whispered Yoshi. "Before your friend comes, you may say one prayer to ease your path to the underworld."

The *ronin* cursed and lunged. Yoshi parried and countered with a slash to the head. He missed, but the *ronin* was already breathing heavily; Yoshi smelled sake and bile on his breath.

So far they had made little noise, which suited Yoshi's

purpose. If he won over this half-drunk samurai without warning the other, he would still have the element of surprise in his favor. However, the advantage was lost when the *ronin* lifted his blade and stepped in with a scream calculated to freeze Yoshi in place.

A childish trick. Yoshi darted toward the enemy as the sword descended. He slid into the man's line of attack and, in one step, placed himself behind his opponent's blade. He slashed at the man's hand below the wrist, and in the same motion, spun across striking at the base of his skull. The *ronin's* head, a surprised look still on its face, tumbled from his shoulders spinning lazily in the moonlight, even before his dismembered hand hit the ground.

Yoshi froze in a catlike stance ready to move in any direction. He listened for the second intruder who must have heard his companion's battle scream. There was no sound. The advantage of surprise was gone.

Yoshi stepped away from the trees into the open yard that fronted the hut.

"It is I, Tadamori Yoshi, son of Lady Masaka, righter of wrongs, avenger of the death of Hanzo the swordsmith, killer of the tyrant Kichibei," announced Yoshi in a loud voice. "Who dares to challenge me?"

His voice rang over the treetops. There was no answer. The moon shone in its fullest glory. Except that the greens of grass and tree were muted to silver and black, it might have been daylight in the open yard.

Yoshi was immobile while his eyes and ears were busy trying to locate the enemy.

The temple bells sounded the hour of the boar, ten o'clock. Soon the festival would end and the students would return. The enemy had to make his move soon.

A cloud covered Tsukiyomi's face, again plunging the field into darkness. Yoshi moved quickly to the protection of the veranda. His goal was to take a position that would protect his back, but it had another result. As Yoshi reached the veranda, he sensed someone above him. The scent of the stale rice liquor that had accompanied the first *ronin* triggered a subconscious defense mechanism. He dropped to the ground as a sword blade whistled through the air where his head had been.

The second *ronin* had reached the hut and stayed hidden, waiting for Yoshi's return. The stroke of his blade was so powerful it sank deep into one of the poles that supported the eaves. With a curse the *ronin* worked it free giving Yoshi time to recover his balance and throw off his now useless robe.

The *ronin* had the advantage of the high ground, yet he could not strike without bending awkwardly. On the other hand, Yoshi, three feet lower, could not easily reach a vital spot though he was in good position for a slashing attack at the legs. It was a stalemate. The *ronin*, realizing that time was on the side of his victim—soon the students would return—waited for the moon to appear, then leaped from the veranda chopping sideways at Yoshi's chest. The stroke was easily parried.

In straight swordplay there was no question who was superior. Though the *ronin* was a good swordsman, his dissolute life had left him no match for Yoshi's years of constant training.

"You will soon join Kichibei in Yomi. Tell me how you found me," taunted Yoshi, pressing his enemy back with a flurry of strokes.

"I am loyal to the memory of my master. You are a dog and will die like one."

"Brave words for someone who has only minutes to live. Tell me how you found me and I'll send you to Yomi painlessly."

The *ronin* shouted with rage and plunged forward with his blade flashing in the moonlight. Yoshi blocked the attack, absorbing its momentum and guiding the attacker into a vulnerable position.

"Now!" he grunted and reversed his blade to cut into the *ronin's* sword arm. A major blood vessel parted and great gouts of blood sprayed from the almost severed arm.

The *ronin* sank to his knees; his sword had fallen from

nerveless fingers. He was suffering agonizing pain but his face stayed full of hatred. "Kaneoki . . ." he said. "We found you through Kaneoki." His voice weakened. "You won't live long enough to enjoy what I told you. I am not alone."

Yoshi unsheathed his short sword and cut through the dying man's neck, severing the spinal cord. He wiped his blade on the dark robe.

There was the light of lanterns and the sound of voices on the road. The students were returning from the Festival.

Yoshi suddenly felt very tired.

Twenty-nine

So the poor dying fool did not know his companion had preceded him to the netherworld. Yoshi was depressed to think that two men, who might have led useful lives, who might have sired a dozen children, who might have accomplished great deeds, were dead. No one to miss them or mourn their passing. How many years had they wasted searching for the murderer of their Lord Kichibei? Had Kichibei deserved such loyalty?

Contemplating the heap at his feet, he thought how life was a series of cruel ironies. If the *ronin's* quest had not been successful, if he had not found Yoshi, he would still be alive.

And was Yoshi's goal of eventual revenge against Chikara any less foolish? How would it end after so many years?

He pushed the thought from his mind.

It would not be necessary to spoil the students' holiday. Tomorrow was time enough to bury the two assassins. Tired as he was, Yoshi dragged the bloody remains through the long grass until the bodies lay side by side under a cherry tree. He placed loose branches over them to keep away the night animals, then he wiped his hands and returned to his hut.

The night had turned cool. Yoshi built up the fire, relit the lantern and prepared to ink the occurrences of the night. This proved difficult. Kaneoki! Kaneoki! It was Kaneoki who had betrayed him. Tomorrow, no matter what Ichikawa said, Yoshi would settle with Kaneoki.

Yoshi lowered the inkstick and pushed the stone aside. He could not concentrate. His inner tension gave his usually graceful calligraphy a nervous, jumpy look. He fed the fire and settled down to polish his sword; it had served him well, this sword from Tomonari, the swordmaker of Bizen. It had a good blade, serviceable and honest with a keen edge and solid balance. He wiped it carefully then coated it with light oil to protect the edge design that shimmered in the firelight like clouds in a summer sky.

The voices from the road were gone, their owners asleep in their quarters. At midnight, the temple bells gonged and mournfully sounded the hour of the rat. Yoshi slipped the sword back into its red-lacquered sheath and placed it on the low table next to his sleeping mat. He said his evening prayer and rolled himself in his quilt.

Sleep would not come. Over and over, his racing mind relived the battle in the courtyard. He analyzed and reanalyzed every move. He had done well. The most important measure of success in a duel was who lived and who died. By that standard he had done everything right. He remembered the texture of the hilt in his hand and the momentary resistance as the edge bit into flesh. He could smell the stale sake odor from the *ronin's* breath.

But suddenly he realized that he was smelling it again. A sudden movement in the dark. The flash of firelight on a descending blade. All sensed in a millisecond of frozen time. He rolled from his sleeping mat in a frantic effort to get away from the dark figure that swung a sword at his head.

A third *ronin!*

Yoshi's sudden scramble threw off the man's aim. The blade hit a glancing blow on Yoshi's left shoulder. It should have ended the battle before it began, but the attacker, in his haste to finish off his victim, lurched forward only to tangle himself in Yoshi's bedclothes.

Yoshi's left arm and hand were slippery with blood. He

fumbled with his sword, managing to slip it out of its sheath before the *ronin* struck again. This time he parried from the floor, taking the shock of the blow directly on the blade. The *ronin* screamed with rage.

Yoshi was half-lying behind the low writing table, his strength seeping away with the blood from his shoulder. The *ronin* kicked the table, jamming Yoshi further into the corner. Yoshi desperately swung his sword low, almost at table level. The cutting edge hit the attacker on the shins. He fell backward kicking the firebox onto Yoshi's straw sleeping mat. The mat caught fire; flames jumped to the attacker's robe which blazed upward, turning him into a human torch. Somehow he rose on crippled legs and staggered toward Yoshi.

The *ronin* was a sight from the netherworld, his hair ablaze, his face set in a mask of pain and rage. With a superhuman effort, he chopped downward, his blade catching Yoshi across the hip. Blood gushed from the wound. Yoshi sank back to the floor, watching in horror as the fire closed around him. Flames engulfed the walls and danced up to the thatched roof. The *ronin* moaned as the flames seared his skin, blinding him. He fell to his knees and scrabbled in a circle, searching for the exit.

Yoshi's hair was smoking, his skin blistered, his lips cracked. Despite the pain he made himself move. He crawled around the *ronin*, leaving a trail of blood along the floor. He reached the doorway just as the thatched roof exploded into flames and collapsed inward.

Yoshi rolled off the veranda. He hit the earth and immediately lost consciousness.

Thirty

===

"Yoshi, do you hear me?" The words seemed to come through layers of cotton wool. At first, Yoshi could not make sense of the question.

"Ichikawa?" he asked wonderingly.

"Yes, yes. How glad I am that you can answer."

"Ichikawa, where am I?" Yoshi's voice was tremulous.

"In my rooms, Yoshi."

"What happened?"

"You don't remember?"

"Yes . . . no . . . something. A third attacker . . . why am I here?" Yoshi focused with difficulty. He lay on a raised sleeping platform. An ornamental screen was on one side, and a small stove on the other.

"You have been gravely ill. Your wounds were almost fatal." Ichikawa patted Yoshi's hand sympathetically. "Later, I will tell you everything. Now, you need food." He brought a bowl to Yoshi's lips.

Yoshi sipped the broth slowly. He felt weak, not like himself. "How long have I been here?" he asked when the bowl was empty.

"We found you outside your hut on the morning of the sixteenth day of the seventh month. Today is the tenth day of the eighth month. You have been in a coma for three weeks.''

"Three weeks!'' whispered Yoshi, shaking his head in dismay. "I am beginning to remember . . . the fire . . . the pain. Forgive me, it is difficult to talk . : . I am so weak.''

"Yoshi, if you had not been strong as a pair of oxen you would be dead.''

"So weak . . .'' Yoshi's voice trailed off, and he fell back into a restless sleep.

"Ichikawa?'' Yoshi awoke after fourteen hours of sleep. He felt heavy . . . leaden . . . confused. His voice was ragged with an edge of panic. He clutched nervously at Ichikawa's arm.

"I am here, Yoshi.'' Calmly. Softly.

"Kaneoki? Where is he?'' Yoshi tried to sit up, struggling against the bedclothes.

"Gone. He left the day we found you.''

"Kaneoki betrayed me to the *ronin*.''

"Yes, Yoshi. I fear it was my fault. I told Kaneoki you were Hanzo's engraver, and he informed the *ronin* who realized you were the one they sought.'' Ichikawa paused. "Kaneoki claims he was not responsible because he was drunk; I say it was evil jealousy that made him betray you.''

"But . . . he is gone?'' Yoshi fell back, his voice lowered, his face relaxed.

"Yoshi, I could not keep him after what he did. He begged to stay. I refused him. He left cursing and swearing revenge. We both have an enemy now.''

"How sad that the author of his own misfortune does not recognize where the fault lies,'' said Yoshi. "I am tired again. Please let me sleep.''

On the morning of the seventeenth day of the eighth month, a week after Yoshi had regained consciousness, Ichikawa gently shook him awake and announced, "I have Dr. Tanaka with me. He is here to help you.''

Yoshi turned his head listlessly. He saw a small man, completely bald. The doctor's face was old and wrinkled as the slopes of Mount Fuji, creased from decades of exposure to the sun. Only the top of his head was pale and smooth. His raisin eyes peered from deep within the folds of dark skin as he spoke in the pedantic tones of a scholar. "We will have to establish certain basic criteria before we can initiate action," he said. "It is obvious that the balance between the elements and your actions are out of concordance."

The doctor unrolled a scroll which listed the correspondences between internal organs and outside symptoms. He laid the scroll out on the floor where he could easily refer to it. Next he went over Yoshi's body, testing and palpating the six pulses to determine whether the problem was an excess of yin or yang. "I see. I see," he repeated from time to time.

Yoshi watched himself being prodded and palpated without interest. Ichikawa sat by the screen and nodded each time the doctor said, "I see."

"These late summer breezes can cause ague and fever. The first thing to do is to keep the doors and windows tight."

Ichikawa nodded.

At last the doctor was satisfied. He consulted his scrolls for the most auspicious day to begin treatment. "On the full moon, in five days, we will burn the *moe-kusa*. It is obvious the young man suffers from an excess of yin. If we can bring it into balance with the yang, he will be cured."

As promised, Dr. Tanaka returned on the first auspicious day with a supply of powdered leaf cone, the *moe-kusa*. He consulted endless charts—anatomical, mathematical, herbal, and elemental—choosing the proper sites to apply the *moe-kusa*. If he had found an excess of yang, he would have treated with acupuncture. Since his diagnosis was excess yin, he burned the leaf cone over the twelve channels of *chi* that controlled the flow of yin and yang through the body.

Although the treatment was excruciatingly painful, the patient gave no sign of his suffering as the burning herb blistered his skin. Despite the treatment, there was no improvement, and finally Dr. Tanaka conceded the failure of his modern methods of diagnosis and treatment.

"Perhaps," he suggested, "this man is in the grip of a *mono no ke*—an evil spirit or demon. Remember, he was wounded on the night of the Festival of the Dead. I can only suppose a wandering ghost, searching for his way home, saw the burning hut as a beacon and possessed the patient. If indeed this is the case, he is beyond the powers of my medicine. He needs priests and exorcists."

Ichikawa greeted this news as the worst blow of all. As a fighting man he had little belief in priests and exorcists.

"Where shall I go? To whom can I turn? You have to help me. This man is a valued friend. I cannot desert him now," Ichikawa pleaded.

"His external wounds are healed. I can do no more," said the doctor.

Ichikawa could not ignore the demands of the *dojo;* he returned to teaching a full schedule. He assigned a group of advanced students to care for Yoshi. Some tried to engage him in conversation . . . to no avail.

A new group came to the academy. They whispered among themselves about the man in Ichikawa's quarters who stared out the window and cried at the sight of the falling leaves. Everyone knew the story of Tadamori Yoshi . . . how he fought and killed three *ronin*. The story grew each time it passed from one tale-teller to another. Meanwhile, its hero sat listlessly, unheeding, and uncaring as the trees turned to red then gold, and carpeted the earth with their fallen leaves. Soon, the leaves were gone and the snows arrived.

Thirty-one

The first day of the first month of 1177, the emperor rose at four and made his obeisance to the four directions, heaven, earth, and the Imperial Mausoleums. Then he prayed to the gods for the subjugation of the evil spirits and asked his ancestors to insure a prosperous reign in the year to come.

It was a joyous time throughout the ten home provinces. But not in the Sarashina *dojo* where a saddened Ichikawa wrote a message to Tadamori-no-Fumio in his crude soldier's hand.

Outside the academy there were parades and festivities; inside, it was quiet except for the faint rustle of Ichikawa's silk sleeve as he brushed in the characters begging Fumio for help.

When he finished the letter, he tied it in a roll, inserted it in a bamboo tube, sealed the ends, and went in search of a messenger.

By the Festival of the Snake, the third day of the third month, the worst of the winter was over, and the evening was mild as the Emperor lit candles in honor of the North Star god and the Great Bear.

In the gardens of the Imperial Palace, cups of wine were floated in the streams, and guests lifted them from the water, drank from them, and recited poems with each drink. When poetry palled, a feast was held, and afterwards the nobles danced and sang all night.

While the capital celebrated, a dusty messenger arrived in Sarashina with a message roll hanging from a pole across his shoulders. He ran through the dusty streets until, just outside the town, he came to the academy. Ichikawa stopped the class. He recognized the crest of Lord Fumio on the message tube. He paid the messenger generously and opened the package with trembling fingers.

After quickly reading Lord Fumio's message, Ichikawa dismissed the students and hurried to Yoshi's quarters. "I have good news," he announced.

"What is it?" asked Yoshi unenthusiastically.

"You will be going home . . . to Lord Fumio's castle. The greatest priests in the Empire will come there to help you."

"I cannot go to Okitsu. Spies will report my presence and bring more trouble to my family."

"Nonsense! After so much time . . . your uncle writes that there will be no problem. The difficulties of the past are long forgotten," said Ichikawa.

"I am not worthy," said Yoshi.

"Lord Fumio insists. An oxcart has been sent to take you on the long trip."

"How did my uncle know I was here?"

Ichikawa rested a friendly hand on Yoshi's shoulder. "Forgive me if I overstepped the boundaries of our friendship. . . . I wrote him on the first day of the year."

"You should not have," said Yoshi without conviction.

"Yoshi, something had to be done. The doctor failed. Your problem is beyond my ability to help. You need the priests."

"Priests cannot help me."

"Let them try." Ichikawa was distressed.

Yoshi turned his face to the wall screen. "What is wrong with me? Everything I do leads to calamity. I should have died in the fire."

"Yoshi, if you only knew how much I grieve to hear you speak this way. I feel your sickness is my fault. If I had listened to you, you would have fought Kaneoki and been spared this pain," sighed Ichikawa.

"*Sensei*, do not blame yourself. No one could have done more for me. Perhaps you are right, and the priests can help. I will go willingly, if only to relieve you of the burden."

Thirty-two

The trip was hard and slow; the oxcart traveled at a steady two to three miles an hour. A well-padded pallet had been arranged in the wickerwork body of the two-wheeled vehicle for Yoshi's comfort.

Yoshi was physically recovered except for a six-inch scar on his left shoulder—near the old wound he had suffered from Chikara—and a slight limp from the tightening of the muscles where the *ronin's* sword had cut into his hip. The problem was in his mind. His melancholia refused to lift.

The weather at the end of the third month was exceptional; the rains held off, and the skies stayed clear. The oxen plodded southeast through the mountain passes. Once or twice, Yoshi saw deer standing close to the road; the signs of nature only filled his heart with ineffable sadness. He remembered when they would have made him sing with joy. Now every sign of life depressed him more.

PART FOUR

Thirty-three

==

"Uncle Fumio, he is here," Nami called. She hurried along the center hallway of the castle searching for her uncle, peering into each room as she passed, calling out the news in a breathless voice. Nami was filled with mixed emotions at the prospect of seeing Yoshi again. She still remembered the joyous summer of her fourteenth year and Yoshi's youthful professions of love. So long ago! Her cheeks flooded with warmth as she recalled how much she had admired him, the older, sophisticated cousin from Kyoto. It had been a childish infatuation that had taken her years to outgrow.

Of course, that had been a different Yoshi and, today, she was a different Nami. Their positions had been reversed. She was no longer the poor little country girl. She was the wife of a lord and he was little more than a laborer.

Still, why did she feel a tiny stirring of guilt—well hidden, deeply buried—when she remembered how she had virtually ignored him in the excitement of her wedding preparations nine long years ago? She shrugged off the feeling. She did not know how she would react when she saw him but she would do her best to make up for any pain she might have caused him in the past.

The years since her marriage to Lord Chikara had further

enhanced Nami's beauty. Her skin still had the look of fine porcelain. Her delicate features were set off by long hair hanging freely over a pale green gown lined with lightest beige at the sleeves. The silk rustled briskly as she hastened through the castle halls, calling her uncle.

Fumio was in the rear courtyard, practicing archery. "Why are you shouting?" he asked when she found him.

"Yoshi has arrived, dear Uncle. The oxcart just came through the gates. He will be at the house in seconds."

"Why didn't you say so, girl?" Fumio dropped the bow and pulled the quiver over his head with nervous fingers. He ran up the steps from the yard, almost stumbling in his excitement. He would see his nephew for the first time in nearly nine years. He forced himself to walk slowly and compose his features; it took a major effort. It would be unfitting for a samurai to show an excess of emotion, though he was overjoyed at Yoshi's return. Fumio had been lonely for so long . . . he had found no companionship with Lady Masaka, who was virtually a recluse. And Nami had been away, living at Chikara's castle until recently when rebellious farmers compelled Chikara to flee to Kyoto. Fumio's craggy face showed the unmistakable signs of the passage of time. While Nami looked as she had nine years ago, Fumio had grown visibly older. His hair was gray and thin; the only remaining traces of the younger Fumio were his honest brown eyes and a brisk way of moving that still suggested strength.

Uncle and niece hurried to the front veranda, arriving just in time to see the oxcart come to a stop.

Only the knowledge that Yoshi was sick made Fumio decide to bring him home. Yoshi was a fugitive, though the spies who had awaited his return were long gone. With Chikara in Kyoto, it was unlikely that news of Yoshi's homecoming would reach him . . . or that he would care. Yet Fumio would not have tempted the gods if he had not felt it necessary.

As the curtain of the oxcart was drawn back, uncle and niece waited, uncertain of what they would see. A boy of nineteen had left the castle. A man of twenty-eight returned. Fumio had not been sure he would recognize his nephew. He need not have worried. The months of illness had thinned Yoshi; he looked like the slim youth of long ago.

Yoshi clambered down from the oxcart. He stared up at his relatives with tears blurring his vision. All men cried when the gods turned against them, but the evil spirit that possessed Yoshi caused tears to flow at the slightest provocation.

"Poor cousin." Nami ran down the stairs, her heart filled with sympathy. Yoshi looked so forlorn. She held his arm and said, "Welcome home. We have missed you."

"Come in, my boy," said Fumio, waving off the oxcart. He turned his face away to hide the feelings he could no longer contain.

Thirty-four

==

Fumio and Nami strove to make Yoshi comfortable. They had prepared a small bright room for him. Unfortunately, the sliding door opened on the balcony where he had sat with Genkai and Ietaka on the day of Genkai's death. Yoshi knew Fumio and Nami meant well; he could not bring himself to tell them that the room only deepened his depression.

They brought him books of poetry, brushes, inksticks, parchment scrolls, and paints—everything calculated to tempt him to activity. He ignored it all and sat by the hour, staring blinding through the open screen at the sadly familiar view.

Either Fumio or Nami were always within reach of Yoshi's call. At first, they were sure that rest, fresh air, and good food would restore his health. Nami tried to engage him in conversation, asking questions, telling stories, and making up little games to amuse him. All her efforts failed. Yoshi would plead fatigue and turn away. Fumio and Nami often found themselves exchanging glances of commiseration as Yoshi retreated further inside himself. It was apparent that Yoshi's sickness was not an ordinary one.

After several fruitless days, a priest was brought to Yoshi's quarters. He heard Yoshi's story of the battle with the three *ronin* and concluded a spirit was at fault. "The spirit is the ghost of the last *ronin* who sent it to possess the man who caused his death," he said.

"Can you save him?" pleaded Nami.

"I have exorcised this kind of spirit many times. My assistants and I are specialists in cases of evil possession."

"Then we may rest assured we are in good hands," said Fumio.

It was decided that the priest and the medium would begin the exorcism ceremony on the first auspicious day. By consulting the astrological table, it was calculated to be the seventh day of the fourth month.

The room where the ceremony was to take place was open to the south. Cool breezes blew through the light-weight screens and lattice shutters, flickering the flames of incense candles that filled the room with heavy sweet scent.

The priest was an imposing figure in his long black habit, shoulders covered by a midnight blue shawl with signs of the zodiac embroidered in gold thread. He first sprinkled grains of rice to the four corners of the room to clear the atmosphere preparatory to battling the malevolent spirit that hid inside Yoshi. Then he knelt on a hassock before a painted screen and intoned his spells and incantations.

Yoshi sat cross-legged behind the screen while Fumio and Nami huddled together in a far corner to watch. Except for the flapping of the shutters and the deep singsong of the exorcist, the room was quiet. The priest droned the Magic Formula of the Thousand Hands. Candles sputtered as air currents played around their flames and smoke rose, out of proportion to their size. Yoshi felt a stirring of interest.

"Buddha, we beseech thee, deliver this innocent victim from the evil spirit which has burrowed its way into his heart," the priest chanted.

The priest's assistant walked around the room sprinkling additional handfuls of rice, while the exorcist lowered his voice to an almost inaudible drone as he recited the *kaji*, or incantations against evil. Suddenly, he rolled his eyes heavenward and called in a thunderous voice, "Bring in the *yorimashi.*"

At that, the medium, a young woman dressed in a black silk robe and full trousers, glided into the room. Her features were coarse—nose thick, eyes bulging, and mouth open over protruding teeth—but her head was crowned with a glorious fall of hair that shone with blue highlights and made her pale face seem almost attractive. She sank to her knees beside the priest and bowed her head toward the screen. The priest handed her a wand of lacquered wood, then, closing his eyes, he threw his head back and howled the sacred syllables at the ceiling.

The acrid scent of the incense bit into the nostrils of the watchers. Nami hid her face behind her fan, trembling in fear of the spirit being drawn out of Yoshi.

The medium's head snapped up; the mass of black hair undulated like the waves of Suruga Bay. Her shoulders shook and her mouth opened in a soundless shriek. Veins stood out on the smooth skin of her throat. Slowly she raised her arms, hands like claws, fingers bent unnaturally. She struggled as if battling some unseen power.

The candle smoke rose in great puffs, filling the spaces among the ceiling beams. The air was charged with currents of unseen power; mighty forces battled on some unknown plane of existence.

The *yorimashi* rose from her knees and with a piercing cry tore away her robe. Her pale breasts bobbed and swayed as if some alien thing moved inside her chest. A strange voice, deep and coarse, came from her mouth.

"I am the ghost of . . ." The voice became unclear. "I leave this earthly plane for the underworld, cursing you all . . ." again the voice became unintelligible, rising in pitch.

"I go now," it screamed, "leaving Tadamori Yoshi to the mercy of the . . ." This time the voice fell to low muttering and the medium collapsed to the floor in convulsions.

The priest had not opened his eyes; he had continued his incantation during the entire remarkable performance. He now rose to his feet and stretched out his arms; his full black sleeves made a dramatic silhouette as they draped to the floor.

"The *Goho-doji*—Guardian Demon of Buddhism—has possessed the *yorimashi*." He reached under his shawl and drew out another handful of rice which he sprinkled on the exposed breast of the writhing medium. "Thus we banish the evil spirit," he cried. "Back to the endless caverns of *yomi*."

The air cleared. The smoke disappeared into the rafters, and the incense, which moments before had been almost unbearable, sweetened and lightened until its scent suggested cloves in a field of grass.

The medium's convulsions gradually stopped. Her hair spread on the floor in disarray, framing the whiteness of her tear-washed cheeks.

Nami left Fumio's side and hurried over to adjust the girl's clothing. The medium's eyes fluttered open and her head turned from side to side searching for the priest.

The priest hurried to her side. "Are you recovered?" he asked.

"I am tired, so tired," she murmured, brushing hair from her face. "The young man . . . is he cured?"

"We were successful in exorcising the evil spirit. As we suspected, it was the ghost of the dead *ronin*. I suppose we will never know his name; he has returned to the under-world."

"How can we thank you?" Fumio asked the priest.

"No need. Your support for our temple has earned our undying gratitude. We loved your nephew, Genkai, and are aware that since his death you have made many contributions to our sect; your gifts were not as anonymous as you thought."

Fumio bowed his head in silence. Acts of generosity and kindness had been repaid.

The priest turned back to the medium and recited a final prayer over her. When the prayer was completed, she asked, "With your permission, may I go to the temple to thank the gods for helping us today?" The priest nodded his approval and the medium glided from the room.

The priest turned to Fumio while his assistant packed the candles, incense, wands, and other accoutrements of the ceremony. "Yoshi will sleep deeply till tomorrow," he said. "I believe the evil spirit is gone. Nevertheless, we must be careful. These spirits can be very tenacious. They frequently hide for years waiting for the moment to find their revenge."

"What can we do to assure his well-being?" asked Fumio.

"Make him rest, keep him amused, and don't let him dwell on the past. Have your niece read to him and take him on long walks in the fresh air. Whatever you do, keep him calm and relaxed."

"We can never thank you enough, Reverence," said Nami.

"Our house and everything in it is yours," said Fumio.

Yoshi said nothing. He had fallen into a deep, hypnotic sleep during the incantations.

Thirty-five

Yoshi's recovery seemed miraculous. He awoke the next day to feel the midday sun shining on his face and to hear birds singing in the courtyard outside. Yesterday, he would have cried at the poignancy of their song; today, he smiled.

Except for an unaccustomed weakness, he had never felt better.

"I've been here for hours, waiting for you to waken." It was Nami, watching him from the other side of his screen. She spoke rapidly. "How are you? Is the evil spirit truly gone? Why are you smiling?"

"Slowly, slowly. You are going too fast," said Yoshi, stretching languorously. "I won't be rushed today. The world is full of joy and beauty. How can I help smiling? I am reborn, returning to life from a nightmare."

"You *are* better then?"

"Yes, the sickness is gone," said Yoshi. After a bit, he shook his head wonderingly. "I didn't believe the priest could help me. I was wrong. Now I see there are forces around us that no man can understand."

Nami smiled and rose to her feet as though a weight had been·removed from her shoulders.

"Welcome back, dear Yoshi," she said. "Let me bring you tea and rice cakes."

"Where is Uncle Fumio?"

"You will see him later. First eat!"

As Yoshi nibbled his food, he studied Nami. She wore a light beige *sakura*—outer cloak—with a flame red lining. Her undercloak showed through the full sleeves and peeped from below the hem. An attractive combination. Yoshi had hardly noticed her while in the grip of the evil spirit. The truth was he had hardly noticed anyone or anything. Now he was almost overcome by a feeling of love. It was as though he had never left Okitsu, as though Chikara had never existed and Nami could be his. He shook his head to clear it of these pointless dreams.

"I have not forgotten my vow to avenge Genkai's death," he suddenly blurted. "I appreciate what you have done for me, but I can not let it influence my actions toward your husband, Lord Chikara."

"Yoshi, I am still your cousin and your friend," Nami said gently. "My husband has forgotten your very existence. He has many problems, and your vows are of no interest to him. I am sure you will eventually recognize the wisdom of conciliation. How else will we be able to live in peace under one roof?"

Yoshi shrugged. Nami did not know of the many nights he had fallen asleep racked by hatred and jealousy of Chikara. Chikara may have forgotten Yoshi, but Yoshi had not forgotten Chikara.

However, the evil spirit was gone, and Yoshi was anxious to start living again. He would settle with Chikara on another occasion. For the time being, he would try to make up for the months he had lost during his illness.

"Where is my mother?" he asked. "I am surprised she did not come to see me when I was sick."

"Lady Masaka has become more of a recluse than ever. We seldom see her in the main building. She spends her time in the north wing with the servants."

"But she is my mother! I cannot believe she did not care what happened to me," said Yoshi.

"Oh, Yoshi, of course she cared. No day went by that she did not send a handmaiden for news of your condition. She loves you deeply. You must try to understand her." Nami hesitated searching for the right words. "Our society frowns on imprudent women," she said at last. "Your mother has suffered all her adult life for the indiscretion of your birth. She has atoned for her mistake by throwing herself into the routine of managing Fumio's household. She is a dutiful woman, who feels her first obligation is to the man who gave her a home. She never leaves her wing except for an occasional pilgrimage to a temple in the countryside.

"I am sure," Nami continued, "she wanted to see you, yet did not wish to offend Fumio. A woman's lot is a difficult one. Your mother is wise. She has accepted her situation and is content with her restricted life."

"Ah, and you are not?" Yoshi looked at Nami shrewdly.

"No! I am not content to live as a chattel to a lord's castle. I want more from life." Nami took a deep breath and plunged on. "I refuse to spend my days behind a screen waiting for my husband to visit. I will confide in you: I am glad my lord is in Kyoto. Though I love and respect him, I am happier here with Uncle Fumio. I can be myself without causing gossip. No, I may have to accept my lot in the end, but as long as I can, I will resist the kind of life your mother leads."

"What of Chikara? Does he know of your views, and does he approve of your staying here without him? Why did he go to Kyoto alone?" demanded Yoshi.

"We had bad fortune this past year. The farmers rebelled; with the aid of Minamoto agents, they burned the castle and destroyed the crops. Chikara left me with Uncle Fumio and fled with what he could carry in his carts. He lives in the capital where he has ingratiated himself with the authorities. The gossips say he will soon be appointed to an important post on the Imperial Council. He has communicated with Uncle Fumio, asking him to send me to Kyoto to manage his household. I resist because I am as tenacious about my freedom as you are.''

"Me? Tenacious?" Yoshi lifted his eyebrows in surprise.

"Yes, why else would you nurture a youthful vow of vengeance for so long?"

"Honor!" answered Yoshi, stiffly.

Later in the afternoon, Yoshi was resting on the veranda when he received a pleasant surprise. A cart rolled to a stop at the main steps, and Yoshi saw a tall bulky figure alight.

"Ietaka!" he shouted.

The big man spun on his heel. His round face split in a smile of joy. "Yoshi, you are well! Let me look at you."

Ietaka came at an undignified run and clasped Yoshi by both shoulders. "You have no idea! I had given you up. I thought you were lost to the river, and then the message came that you were here . . . sick! Oh, Yoshi, I am so happy to see you."

"And I to see you," said Yoshi, beaming. "For years I worried about you. Thank the Buddha you are safe and well. How selfish of me that in my sickness I had no thought of you. We can make up for it now."

They went inside, talking as they walked. There was so much to say. Ietaka described his flight north to the tent city of Minamoto Yoritomo. "The Minamoto sent me to Kyoto as their agent. I have the advantage of speaking in the accent of the court, and though I despise most of the politicians I work with, it is the only way. I can serve my ideals. Someday things will change and . . ."

The afternoon raced by as they reminisced.

In the evening, the entire family, save for Lady Masaka, assembled to hear Yoshi retell his story. At one point, Ietaka interrupted. "I did not really know you till we went to Kyoto together," he told Yoshi. "It was there I discovered you had the strength to survive adversity, though I never dreamt you would accomplish so much. The Minamoto need men like you. Together, we could—"

Fumio interrupted brusquely. "We promised! No politics!

I don't want to spoil our first reunion in almost a decade.''

Yoshi completed his tale, answered questions, and finally excused himself to go see the only member of the family who had not been present.

Yoshi knelt on a cushion outside his mother's curtain of state. Although it was still light outside, the screens and curtains were closed, keeping the room in deep gloom.

Lady Masaka sat on a *chodai*, a curtain-dais, peering at her son through the heavy hangings. She was overjoyed at his visit. Yoshi could hear the pleasure in her voice as she asked a barrage of questions. He answered with an edited version of his adventures from the time he left for Kyoto until his return to Okitsu in the grip of the *ronin's* ghost. ''Now that the priests have exorcised the evil spirit, I have only one problem,'' he said. ''How can I continue to accept the help and friendship of Nami, knowing that I shall eventually confront her husband and exact my revenge?''

Once he spoke of Chikara, Yoshi noticed a change in his mother's attitude; she grew progressively cooler as Yoshi asked for her opinions and advice.

''I have never looked on Chikara's marriage to Nami with favor,'' she said at last. ''The man is a schemer who considers only his own selfish desires, yet I, who disliked him even before Genkai's death, have to admit he has suffered enough.'' Lady Masaka's voice wavered as she went on. ''Chikara has lost his lands and his wealth. He is no longer young, and he has no heir. We all see how Nami neglects her duties and avoids him.'' Her voice grew firm. ''Forget the past!'' she continued. ''Forget your fixation on a man who hardly remembers you exist.''

''Mother, I have sworn an oath. I can do nothing to change that.''

''You are a stubborn man. I tell you the gods will not favor your mission. Listen to me and forget Chikara! There are more important things than revenge for a half-forgotten act.''

''Not half-forgotten by me,'' said Yoshi.

Lady Masaka's thin, blue-veined hands fluttered helplessly. Her voice sounded a note of defeat. "Why can't I convince you that you are wasting the few years the gods have allotted you? Think of marriage and children of your own. I would like to run your household instead of living on my cousin Fumio's charity."

"When my mission is completed, Mother."

"My poor foolish son," cried Lady Masaka.

Thirty-six

===

Ietaka returned to Kyoto after a week's visit. He left his address and pleaded with Yoshi to visit when he could.

Yoshi practiced swordsmanship as the spring months passed. When the temple bells of Seiken-ji sounded the dawn hour, he arose to do his conditioning exercises and to practice with the sword. He repeated the formal patterns until sweat ran from his body. The flow of blood through his veins and the feeling of strength returning were like heady wine.

Spring sun shone through the trees surrounding the back courtyard. Clouds of dragonflies hovered over the grass, a moving rainbow of light and color. Breathing deeply of the pine-scented mountain air, Yoshi composed a poem.

> *The bells are sounding*
> *In Seiken-ji tower*
> *The pine trees listen*
> *As cuckoos cry golden songs*
> *To the ringing of the bells*

It was good to be fully alive again.

He spent the afternoons with Nami, listening as she read from romances.

"Life is not like that," he said one day. "The battles you read are romantic inventions. I know. Men bleed like pigs being butchered by the aborigines. There is nothing aesthetic about a man with his entrails hanging out, moaning in agony as he tries to stuff them back in his belly."

"Oh, Yoshi. You are horrible. Please don't talk that way. You are spoiling one of my few pleasures." As Nami spoke, she came to a realization that made her catch her breath and turn away to hide her reddening cheeks. Reading romances was not the real pleasure. Rather it was being able to spend the days with Yoshi. She was overwhelmed by the same emotions she had experienced when she was only fourteen years old and infatuated with her sophisticated older cousin from the city.

Spring, the afternoon sun, the scented air, the breeze whispering through the pines, and Yoshi's proximity all conspired to turn her thoughts to the unthinkable. What if they were to . . . ?

Buddha give me strength, she thought. I mustn't . . .

On the first day of the fifth month, as Nami fanned herself and read from the latest romance, Yoshi announced, "My *sensei*, Ichikawa, is coming to visit, so I will have to practice. I want him to find me ready to return to the *dojo*." He rose to his feet and bowed. "Please excuse me."

Nami closed her book. "Are you planning to leave us so soon?" she asked. And again that sensation! She hid behind her fan as a feeling of desolation engulfed her. Chikara, Fumio, the family, and her responsibilities were forgotten in the emotional maelstrom. She needed . . . she wanted . . . but she could not tell him.

He was studying a yellow flower he had plucked a few moments before. He hadn't noticed.

"You and Uncle have been very kind to me. Without your help I would still be a living corpse," he said. "Yet I cannot stay here forever."

"Why not?" she demanded. Her heartbeat was faster and a faint dew of perspiration covered her lip.

"Nami, sometimes you sound like a child rather than a married woman. You refuse to acknowledge the truth: One day soon your husband will return to claim you. I am not ready to face him. I have other responsibilities to settle first . . ." Yoshi dropped to one knee beside her. "The word from the capital is that the Emperor, Go-Shirakawa, is trying to make Taira Kiyomori enter into a truce with the Minamoto," he said earnestly. "If that happens, Taira and Minamoto swordsmen will be face to face in the same city, on the same councils. I am needed to train those men."

"You said that men do not die as they do in the romances. Yet you would send them to be butchered. It is against all common sense."

Yoshi rose to his feet again. He stared over Nami's head, his expression hard, his voice strong. "You are a woman. I cannot expect you to understand about honor and duty. It is a man's prerogative to serve his leaders and himself the best way he can. My job is to train men. I am a swordmaster, and my responsibility is to my students and my *sensei*."

"Then you are a fool." Nami snapped her fan shut and with a swish of her robe turned away, leaving Yoshi standing open-mouthed.

Lately, everyone seemed to think him a fool. Women!

Thirty-seven

The fifth day of the fifth month was the time of the Iris Festival. Okitsu Castle was hung with *kusudama*—little cotton bags filled with herbs and decorated with iris leaves. Multicolored cords were attached to shutters and eaves to ward off misfortune and sickness, and servants wore iris pinned to their sleeves.

Ichikawa arrived in Okitsu on the eve of the festival. He was hot, tired, and dusty as a result of his trip from Sarashina. Despite his fatigue, he was friendly and polite when Yoshi introduced him to Fumio and Nami. Ichikawa and Fumio exchanged a few reminiscences of their early campaigns—though they had fought in the same battles they had never met before—and Ichikawa spoke briefly to Nami. It was obvious that he was charmed by her beauty and intelligence, but Yoshi saw that he was tired and conversation was an effort for him.

Yoshi excused himself to Fumio and Nami. He took Ichikawa's arm and showed him to his quarters. When they were alone, Ichikawa expressed his delight at seeing Yoshi recovered from his illness. Nonetheless, the rigors of his trip had taken their toll, and soon Ichikawa said wearily, "Tomorrow, we will talk more. . . ."

In the morning, Yoshi convinced Ichikawa that to avoid the bustle of the Iris Festival preparations, they should walk to Okitsu. They ambled down the mountain path, breathing deeply of the pine-scented air. It had rained during the night; puddles rippled with the passage of tiny insects; the grass was heavy with dew. In the distance, Mount Fuji's majestic head broke through a crown of clouds. An arrow-tailed hawk circled lazily in the pearl sky, searching for his breakfast.

"You look well, Yoshi," Ichikawa remarked.

It was true: The color had returned to Yoshi's cheeks; the softness that had come from his long sickness had disappeared. This morning he wore a red brocaded robe over stiff white silk. The silver pommel of his sword glittered in the sun as he walked proudly, head erect and chest open to the morning air.

"Thank you, *Sensei*. I feel well and am ready to return to the *dojo*."

"That is as it should be. The school needs you. I have not been able to replace either you or Kaneoki." Ichikawa stooped to pick a red flower. He sniffed its sweetness and passed it to Yoshi. "Of late, I have had too little time to appreciate the beauty around me," he said. "I am tired. The political situation is placing a stress on me and on our school. We have more students than ever, while swordmasters are harder to find. I attribute the change to new tensions that have developed between Taira Kiyomori and the Tendai monks.

"While Kiyomori girds for the inevitable battle with Yoritomo, he is also contending with harassment by the monasteries; the warrior monks have become bandits, aggrandizing themselves by kidnapping, looting, and destroying everyone who stands in their way.

"Kiyomori is a religious man. Nevertheless, the excesses of the Tendai make him oppose them. He is hiring every swordmaster not committed to his enemies, and he constantly cries for more."

Yoshi said, "Kiyomori will be able to conquer the monks. It is the aftermath I fear. When he has swelled his armies with master swordsmen, when his troops have gained experience, and when his generals have tasted victory, what will restrain him then? Today, Yoritomo maintains a balance of power; tomorrow, Kiyomori may be invincible.''

"Tomorrow's problems will be solved tomorrow. At this moment, neither Kiyomori nor Yoritomo commands the strength necessary for a clear-cut victory. Kiyomori will have to come to a temporary understanding with Yoritomo or they will both be destroyed in a long and inconclusive battle.''

As they spoke, the two men walked toward the Seiken-ji temple. They could hear the boom of the surf breaking on the sands of Suruga Bay. The air smelled of the sea.

"Can they ever agree without losing face?" asked Yoshi.

"There is a possibility. You've heard that the cloistered Emperor, Go-Shirakawa, is trying to force Kiyomori into a peaceful accommodation with the Minamoto. If Kiyomori accepts their representatives on the Council, I believe war will be temporarily averted.''

The main street of Okitsu came in sight as they rounded the last bend past the temple. A group of six men, wearing Chikara's crest, argued in front of one of the shops. As Yoshi drew closer, a dark-faced man detached himself from the group and slunk off down the street.

Yoshi turned to Ichikawa. "These men wear the sign of my sworn enemy. I see only one possible reason for their presence. If Chikara has come with armed warriors, it is because he has discovered I am here and wishes to arrest me while he has the power.''

"He would not dare. Are we not deep in Minamoto territory?''

"He is a brave man, and this is not yet all Minamoto land. Many of the local *daimyo*, even my uncle, have strong ties to the Taira. Let us go back before they recognize me.'' Yoshi's voice was urgent.

"I do not like to retreat," said Ichikawa, loosening his sword. "There are only five of them. We needn't fear.''

As Ichikawa spoke, the man who had left the group reappeared at the end of the street. He called a question to someone behind him. Whatever the answer, the man seemed satisfied. He swaggered, hand on sword, toward Yoshi and Ichikawa.

"He wants to provoke us," said Yoshi. "I don't like this."

"If he tries to provoke me too much, he will feel my steel in his throat," whispered Ichikawa.

The dark-faced man was close and showed no sign of giving way.

"Out of my path, dogs," he snarled, pulling an inch of blade from his scabbard.

Ichikawa's mouth tightened, his eyes narrowed, and his cold stare froze the samurai in his tracks.

Yoshi saw a movement behind a shop. His pulse raced as he realized the man had arranged for reinforcements at the inn. It was a trap! While Ichikawa and Yoshi were watching the swaggering warrior, his five companions had disappeared and joined others who were, even now, surrounding the street. There was movement behind every building.

How many were there?

"*Sensei!* We are surrounded," said Yoshi, drawing his sword. Even before it was out of its sheath, Ichikawa had flowed toward his challenger, sword already in hand. Silently, he swung into the attack; the momentary advantage was Ichikawa's. The warrior fell backward under a barrage of blows. In four seconds, he had succumbed to the master's blade.

The street erupted with armed men. Black-clad warriors appeared from behind every bush and building.

Yoshi turned back-to-back with Ichikawa. Together they could stand off an army of inferior swordsmen.

The attackers got in each other's way, doing more damage to themselves than to their intended victims.

The sandy ground had dried in the morning sun. Now the dust rose in a wall, blinding attacker and defender alike. Yoshi's blade sank into flesh again and again to the accompaniment of a triumphant battle cry from Ichikawa.

A coarse voice shouted, "Fools, draw back before they escape."

The dust settled. Yoshi saw Kaneoki, red scar shining on his forehead, off-center nose wrinkled in a snarl. Kaneoki! Yoshi's lips thinned as he watched his betrayer ordering his men to retreat. Kaneoki, who had learned the same tactics and techniques as Yoshi, now sought his revenge.

"Kaneoki, come forward. Meet me alone if you dare," Yoshi shouted.

"You take me for a fool like yourself. I will see both of you dead and laugh as we carry your heads to my new master."

"Kaneoki, I tried to make you into something more than you were," said Ichikawa sadly. "I should have known that one cannot make gold from dross."

"Always the kind master," snarled Kaneoki. "You rewarded this weakling over me after I served you faithfully for all those years. You will pay with your life for underestimating me."

"You are mad," said Ichikawa. "And we are not dead yet!"

"Charge!" screamed Kaneoki waving his sword.

During the exchange between Ichikawa and Kaneoki, Yoshi had inspected the opposition. There had been fifteen including the original six. Two lay dead in the street and two more had crawled to the veranda of a merchant's shop, too badly wounded to continue. Behind them, Yoshi spied a little boy peeking through the shutters with wide open eyes. Eleven of the enemy were left, including Kaneoki, their commander. Apparently, Chikara had sent his men ahead to kill Yoshi without soiling his own hands. So . . . this was how he had forgotten Yoshi's existence! The hypocrite! He would probably apologize to Fumio and Nami and feign sorrow at Yoshi's passing.

In a fury, Yoshi took the offensive. He stepped away from Ichikawa, slashing, stabbing, and striking in a whirlwind of steel. The months of rest and the many mornings of practice gave him a strength and speed that no ordinary soldier could withstand. One samurai fell with a great gash that separated the front of his robe and cut deep into his bowels. He sank to his knees, holding himself together with one hand while the other scrabbled for support on the dirt road. Another samurai slipped in his companion's blood; his feet went out from under him. Before he hit the ground, Yoshi's thrust passed through his rib cage; the curved blade hooked upward into his heart. He was dead before the dust settled.

Ichikawa dispatched three of the enemy with brilliant swordplay, though one managed to wound him; the cut was in the meaty part of the deltoid muscle and painful, but not dangerous.

Ichikawa gritted his teeth. "Pull in closer behind me," he whispered to Yoshi as the enemy drew back in confusion. There were only six left, including Kaneoki.

Where was Kaneoki? Yoshi saw only five warriors in the street. Then, there was no time to think of Kaneoki as the five again closed into range. Yoshi felt pain in the hip where he had been wounded by Kichibei's *ronin*. He slowed down, content to fight from a defensive stance. The attackers also became more careful, but even so Ichikawa disarmed and killed another.

At a shout from the area of the shops, the four remaining soldiers retreated. Yoshi and Ichikawa were alone on the empty street. "They have had enough," said Ichikawa. His lip curled in contempt at the enemies' weakness.

"I do not trust them. Stand fast till we are sure they are gone."

Yoshi caught a movement from the corner of his eye. He wheeled to face it and recognized the glint of light reflected from the curve of a great bow. "Get down!" he shouted, throwing himself to the ground. Ichikawa was a fraction of a second behind him. Too late! The twang of the bowstring, the slapping sound of the arrow sinking into flesh, and the rustle of Ichikawa's robe as he fell, all came in one frozen moment. A puff of dust hung suspended above Ichikawa's inert form. A millisecond stretched to eternity while the bowstring vibrated in the still air.

Then the forces of hell burst loose. With a cry of agonized fury, Yoshi ran at the bowman who dropped his bow and drew his sword. It was Kaneoki, red scar blazing, brow knit in a ferocious scowl. "Come if you dare," he challenged.

Yoshi didn't hesitate. He swung with all his strength at Kaneoki's head. Kaneoki parried. The stroke made the blades vibrate as if they would break. Yoshi's face was flushed with rage at the ambush of his friend and teacher. "Monster, ingrate, animal!" he roared, the words tumbling one over the other more like the howl of a wild beast than human speech. He did not bother with subtlety, pressing his attack at full power, beating Kaneoki's blade aside, and forcing him to retreat into the alley.

Kaneoki put up a strong defense, but what he had done was cowardly and dishonorable, and sapped the margin of strength that might have turned back Yoshi's attack. Kaneoki's long sword broke under the hammering; he clawed desperately at his short sword. Too late! The end came in seconds. "*Esemono!* Back to the underworld of Yomi!" Yoshi shouted, swinging his blade. Kaneoki's head leaped from his shoulders in a frothing fountain of blood.

Yoshi did not hesitate at the corpse. Before it stopped twitching he was back at Ichikawa's side. The arrow had entered high in his chest; the older man was unable to move. He had lost a great deal of blood; the front of his robe was saturated and more poured from the wound. Yoshi knelt by Ichikawa's side, helpless as he watched the old warrior fighting the spirits of death.

The last of Chikara's men had disappeared. The street was quiet and deserted except for Yoshi, Ichikawa, and the bodies of the slain. After a while, a brown dog nosed up to one of the black-clad bodies and sniffed the blood. It barked, then ran nervously down the road. Little boys inched out of their hiding places and shuffled into the street, gaping in awe at the scene of death and destruction.

Ichikawa coughed. A thick red foam sprayed from his mouth. "Forget me," he gasped. "Go back to Sarashina. Take care of my students."

"You will come with me, *Sensei*." The words choked in Yoshi's throat.

"No, my race is run. Buddha will take me to the great

land. I have no fear. Please promise to leave me at once! There will be more of Chikara's men soon. This is not the time to fight. I see ahead to another time when you will meet''—Ichikawa coughed again—''and have your chance for revenge.''

Yoshi wiped Ichikawa's lips and saw bubbles reforming with every breath. To Yomi with revenge, he thought, and silently prayed, promising Buddha he would forego his vows if only his *sensei* lived.

The little boys circled the scene of battle. They were joined by townspeople who whispered to each other behind their hands. The brown dog returned and was joined by several others; they pulled at the corpses' bloody robes, barking and snarling at anyone that came too close.

Ichikawa gave one last sigh; his eyes closed, and his head slumped sideways against Yoshi's knee.

Yoshi knelt for a long time, remembering the strength and goodness that had guided his teacher's life. His cheeks were wet when he lifted Ichikawa in his arms for the long trip up the mountain to Okitsu Castle.

Thirty-eight

It was late summer before Yoshi returned to the Sarashina *dojo*. The cherry blossoms had fallen months before. The trees were now heavy with foliage, full of transient life that filled the summer with sound. Frogs, birds, and insects croaked, sang, and chirped from the recesses of the cherry groves. Great black birds preened themselves in the branches, greeting passersby with harsh warnings.

The school grounds were almost as disreputable as when Yoshi had first seen them; weeds once more filled the yard. Yoshi stopped at the portal, listening to the faint sounds of students practicing inside. He hesitated before entering. A lump formed in his throat as he remembered Ichikawa's funeral: the Buddhist priest intoning prayers as smoke rose from the fire to carry Ichikawa's spirit heavenward; the scent of burning flesh mixed with incense to make a perfume that would forever remind Yoshi of death.

Fumio and Nami had attended the funeral though they had met Ichikawa only the night before his death. Afterward, Fumio refused to understand that the battle had not been their fault. "The two of you," he said, "must have provoked the attack. Chikara did not know you were here. He has forgotten you exist. Your obsession about him can only end in disaster.

I know Chikara. He is an honorable man. He is not responsible for his men attacking you. It is not his way. He is probably the greatest swordsman in the ten provinces; if he wanted you dead, he would have challenged you himself.''

"Nevertheless, Uncle, they were his men. If he did not intend to kill me, why did he put Kaneoki—my sworn enemy—in charge of his soldiers?" The facts seemed clear to Yoshi. Blinded by anger and sorrow at Ichikawa's death, he was unwilling to give Chikara the benefit of doubt.

"There could be any number of reasons." Fumio threw up his hands impatiently.

"I can't believe that. The coincidence is too great. Chikara has no interests in Okitsu. His lands have been confiscated. Why would his men be here at all if not to kill me?"

Fumio would not see the logic of Yoshi's reasoning; the argument ended in bitter recriminations.

"I do not understand you. You are a grown man who is immature in these matters. You have no sense of discretion or honor," said Fumio.

"We would have been less than honorable if we had run from our attackers."

"I am not suggesting you should have run; however, discretion is sometimes as valuable as a sense of honor. You have repeated the tragedy of Genkai. Again you acted rashly and caused the death of one you love. If you had avoided the fight, Ichikawa would still be alive, and I would not have another strain on my relationship with Chikara." Fumio glared. "He is Nami's husband and closely allied with our family. We cannot afford to forget that though his lands are gone, he retains his power at the court."

"He retains his power at the court?" Yoshi echoed, his voice rising. "Therefore we must cater to him? Is that your idea of honor, Uncle?"

"You are insolent and insulting," said Fumio coldly. "You refuse to listen to reason. Everything we have we owe to our close ties with the Taira." There was a long pause as both men considered their angry words. Just as Yoshi was about to respond, Fumio opened his hands and said quickly, in a warm and sympathetic tone, "I forgive your disrespect because I know how much Ichikawa's death has distressed you."

Fumio's soft words acted like an immersion in an ice shower. Yoshi turned pale. *Buddha help me*, he thought. *Is this how I return my uncle's kindness? What have I said?* He sucked in a deep breath. "You are right, Uncle." He was again in control of himself. "I hope you will be able to forgive my careless words."

Fumio had read him correctly. A sense of helplessness at the loss of Ichikawa had caused him to speak intemperately, a luxury he could no longer afford. Ichikawa's death left Yoshi *sensei* of a sword academy, and he must grow to fill the position honorably. It would be a mark of disrespect to Ichikawa and his teachings if Yoshi fell short of his example.

With this realization and the apology that accompanied it, Yoshi passed a watershed in the course of his life. From this day forth, he *was* the swordmaster!

Nami was disconsolate when Yoshi announced his imminent departure. "You are leaving a loving family and a cousin who needs you," she said. "I am lonely, without friends in the castle. My husband is far away and, though Fumio treats me well, I feel like a stranger in his house. When you arrived, sick and helpless, my life suddenly had a purpose. I thought—"

"What did you think?" interrupted Yoshi. "Have you forgotten the conversation we had before Ichikawa arrived? You are a married woman, whose husband—my enemy—may return to claim you at any time. With his last words, Ichikawa told me he saw a future time when Chikara and I would meet. That time has not yet come. In any case, my first duty is to the academy. I am sorry to leave, but leave I must."

"Then no matter what I say," said Nami, "you will do what you want."

"I will do what I have to do," said Yoshi, raising a hand in a gesture of entreaty. But she had already turned away. Yoshi could see she was distressed. He could not understand why; it was as though he had done her an injury. Amida! Nami had been an angel of mercy when he needed help. Didn't she realize how much he loved her? He winced despairingly. Of course she would never guess—he had dissembled too well—the feelings he would always hide because of her marriage to Chikara.

That same day, Yoshi packed his belongings and left for Sarashina. . . .

Now he lingered at the *dojo* entrance, filled with remorse. Had he done Nami a disservice? Perhaps he should have confessed his love to her and agreed to stay, ignoring his responsibilities. A dishonorable thought! He would only have embarrassed her and caused her grief. He had acted properly. The only way he could tear himself away from her was the way he did: brusquely, cleanly, quickly. He had done what he thought was right and no one could be expected to do more.

No matter! *Shigata ga nai*. What was done was done and he had his duty to perform. He squared his shoulders, straightened his robe, and went through the portal.

Thirty-nine

Master Naonori Ichikawa's will named Yoshi heir to his academy. Until Yoshi's return, two assistants, Kojima and Tofushi, conducted classes and managed the school. They welcomed his return and promised to serve him as loyally as they had served his master. Though the assistants were not great swordsmen, their loyalty made up for their technical shortcomings.

Classes were full. During Yoshi's absence, many students from Taira-aligned families left due to the ever-increasing political tensions—Sarashina was deep in Minamoto territory. Their places were filled by Tendai monks from the Enryakuji monastery near Kyoto.

The Tendai had become a political power, almost a state religion, and they found themselves in constant strife with the authorities. Religion, economics, and politics were a volatile mixture that often sent bands of warrior-monks into battle against the Imperial Guards.

Though the Tendai sect acted as a balancing force between Taira and Minamoto, many Tendai leaders loathed the corrupt court and sympathized with Minamoto Yoritomo; they sent hundreds of young monks to martial-arts academies, preparing them to take advantage of any future battle between the two great families. Ichikawa's school brought many to far off Sarashina.

Yoshi was pleased with the quality of the monk-students and congratulated his assistants on their success as teachers. Accounts, correspondence, and housekeeping, however, had been neglected, and Yoshi plunged into an ocean of details. "Hire another apprentice. Put him to work in the yard," he ordered. "Repaint the *dojo* walls. Hang new posters. Replace the old equipment."

It was not until five days after his return that Yoshi completed the urgent business of the school and found time to sit to tea with the assistants. He described Ichikawa's death. Tears flowed freely as Yoshi told in lurid detail of Ichikawa's bravery in the face of overwhelming odds and of Kaneoki's treachery. When Yoshi concluded, Kojima and Tofushi cursed Kaneoki's name for ten thousand generations and wished him unending pain in the underword of Yomi.

When the leaves turned red in the cherry groves, the graduates left, and a new group of students appeared from all over the ten home provinces. The school was ready. The grounds were clean, and the living areas refurbished. While the quarters were spare, each man had his own sleeping platform, clean mat, table, lacquered cupboard, and cushion. Each room also had a charcoal brazier for warmth in the winter.

When the new session began, Yoshi taught the advanced classes. He worked from before dawn until late at night teaching swordsmanship, preparing the books, writing correspondence, and arranging schedules. Except for occasional pains in the hip, he felt good, thriving on the discipline and hard work. His hands developed massive ridges of callus as his abilities with the sword constantly improved.

On days when the students rested, Yoshi practiced with Kojima and Tofushi. He dueled with each in turn, then with both together. In the early sessions, he was able to beat either man with little effort; nonetheless, together they were too strong. At the end of two months, he won more often than not against the combination, even though his assistants also improved.

"You are now a greater swordsman than Ichikawa," said Kojima one day. He wiped his face as he looked at Yoshi with open admiration.

"You are mistaken! I shall never surpass my master," said Yoshi quietly.

"*Sensei*, you already have," interjected Tofushi. "I have trained under both of you and I mean no disrespect to his memory when I say you are the stronger swordsman. We fought well today"—he nodded to include Kojima—"yet we were unable to prevail against you."

After the workout, Kojima and Tofushi left Yoshi alone to his thoughts in the empty *dojo*. The last rays of the autumn sun sparkled from the rows of armor and swords that lined the wall. The only sound was the buzzing of a black fly trapped in a corner. Yoshi knelt on the wooden floor meditating. He still wore the leather armor he had used for the practice session. His sword and scabbard lay on the floor by his side.

The warmth of day rapidly dissipated. A light film of sweat dried on Yoshi's forehead as he considered what Kojima had said. Was it false modesty that kept him from accepting their evaluation of his abilities? Or was it an unwillingness to accept his duty, if they were correct?

When Fumio called Chikara the greatest swordsman in the ten provinces, had he realized the level of Yoshi's ability? And had the time come to face Chikara? Yoshi remembered Ichikawa's dying words: In a future time he would meet his enemy. Was this the time? No. Yoshi felt Ichikawa's presence, an almost palpable force in the silent *dojo*. Ichikawa was reminding him he was swordmaster and his primary duty was to the academy. He could not ignore his legacy and desert his students to seek selfish revenge.

Yoshi's face was calm. Inside was turmoil—questions, options, choices. How was he to choose the correct path? When he asked Ichikawa's shade for advice, the ghostly presence faded.

Yoshi would have to make his own decisions.

The *dojo* darkened further; Yoshi's thoughts went from Ichikawa to Genkai and Hanzo, also cut down in the full flood of life. How transient it seemed, how short the path between life and death. He looked through the open door as dusk encompassed the red gold forest. A cloud of butterflies was visible, hovering under the trees. How rare to see butterflies so late in the year, he thought. All life was but for a fleeting moment.

Sadly, he composed a poem as night fell:

> *The black butterfly*
> *That floats among golden leaves*
> *Leaves behind no trace*
> *As we, passing through the world,*
> *Are soon lost among shadows.*

Forty

Taira Kiyomori, the *daijo-daijin*, was a stocky man with wide shoulders and a large paunch. In spite of his sixty-two years and his girth, he was powerful both physically and mentally. True, there had been indications that he was not well, but except for private moments, when he held his midsection and grimaced in pain, he did not show signs of the disease that spread through his insides. A dozen years before, Kiyomori had suffered his first attack of his illness and had taken his vows to protect himself against the next world. He affected a simple outward appearance, wearing a cotton monk's robe with an embroidered Taira crest. He was calm in public, masking his emotions under a facade of discipline. In private, he alternated between fits of anger and depression. Those closest to him attributed his mercurial moods to the sickness he hid from the rest of the world. A merciless opponent who had few scruples in dealing with his enemies, he was completely loyal to the Fujiwara regents.

On a winter morning, late in 1179, he knelt before the cloistered Emperor, Go-Shirakawa, and held his tongue as he listened to suggestions which he felt would eventually pose grave problems. Go-Shirakawa actually ruled from behind the throne; he had ruled for over twenty years through a succession of young relatives—the present Emperor, Antoku, was only two years old. For most of these twenty years, the supreme chancellor, Kiyomori, had been at his side.

"The monks become more brazen every day," said Go-Shirakawa. "We hear them demonstrating in the streets outside the palace."

"They are under control, Your Excellency. We need not fear a group so poorly armed and so poorly trained." Kiyomori lowered his eyes to hide his anger. Despite his own monk's robes, he would squash the Tendai without mercy if the Emperor gave him a free hand.

"Still, I would sleep better if we made an arrangement for the Minamoto to cooperate with the Imperial troops in dealing with these rogues."

"Your Excellency, you will remember that recently I dealt firmly with a group of monkish plotters. They were no match for our trained troops." But they will be if we allow them time to train, he thought. We must act swiftly.

"Hmmm. Yes, I do remember. I thought you made a terrible mistake when you tortured and killed their leader. We almost had a general uprising as a result."

It had happened the year before. Kiyomori, through a spy in the Minamoto camp, had discovered a plot to assassinate him. It had been led by a monk named Saiko. The monk was captured and the plot thwarted. To Kiyomori, the most infuriating part of the affair was that the cloistered Emperor had known about the plot from the start and had not warned him.

When Kiyomori paraded the monk's head through the streets of the capital, there had been signs of mounting animosity. Using the unrest and the plot as excuses, Kiyomori removed the council members who favored the Minamoto cause and put his own relatives in their place.

"There is nothing to fear, Your Excellency. The monks are under control," Kiyomori repeated.

"Yet they are training themselves in the arts of war. I would rest easier if we cancelled out at least one group of our enemies. Because of your precipitous action last year, there is no hope of joining forces with the monasteries."

"Then, Sire, what do you suggest?" Kiyomori controlled

his voice with difficulty.

"Extend a hand to the Minamoto. Offer token seats on the Council to their most troublesome members. In that way we can keep them under observation."

Now the Emperor was trying to make him give up the political ground he had gained. "Your Excellency is most wise. It will take time to work out an equitable plan." Kiyomori smiled inwardly. It would take a long time.

As if he read Kiyomori's mind, Go-Shirakawa snapped, "No time! Tomorrow! Come to my quarters personally . . . with a proper plan!"

"As you wish, Your Excellency," Kiyomori pressed his forehead to the floor. He rose, outwardly calm, and backed out of the audience chamber.

Once in his own quarters, he smashed his fist through a carved wood panel destroying the valuable Chinese design. Then he knelt on a cushion, holding his stomach and muttering curses to the gods.

Kiyomori sat in his darkened room, ink block and brush at hand. He had been there for several hours writing a diary account of his thoughts. He concluded:

The forces of evil are destined to win out over me. Some say it is the evil spirit of the monk, Saiko. Perhaps. Yet in spite of the omens I see on every hand, I shall rule through my grandson. Even if I go, Antoku will carry the Taira name to greater glory.

I am faced with a difficult question. How can I please Go-Shirakawa, while doing the least disservice to my country and my people? Dark wings are beating in the air; the times worsen. The gods are turning against one who has tried to serve them faithfully. . . .

At length he put the brush down and called for a servant. "Bring me Minamoto Yorimasa," he ordered.

Yorimasa was the only member of the Minamoto clan who

had Kiyomori's complete confidence. Tall and cadaverous, Yorimasa had recently celebrated both his seventy-fifth birthday and his accession to the third class, high rank for a Minamoto. The rank had come too late for him to enjoy its privileges in court. It was over a year since he had retired and taken his vows. He spent his time writing poetry, for which he was famous, and preparing his affairs for the next life.

Twenty years before, Yorimasa had been a crucial factor in Kiyomori's victory during the Heiji war. By supporting Kiyomori, he had ensured the Taira victory. Since that day, Kiyomori leaned on his silence and discretion, putting his trust in this member of the enemy's family.

Yorimasa wore the ascetic robes of his monkhood; his long slim fingers held a filigreed fan, the only decorative element in his wardrobe. Pale skin stretched over his hands, accentuating thick blue veins and spatulate joints. His eyes were deep set, burning with an inner fire. If Go-Shirakawa was the power behind the child emperor, and Kiyomori the power behind Go-Shirakawa, then Yorimasa was the power behind Kiyomori. Discreetly. He never pressed his position, though his calm, well-reasoned advice strongly influenced the Taira leader.

Yorimasa entered the central chamber and waited silently until Kiyomori nodded in recognition. He bowed and closed his fan. The room was dark; shadows filled every corner. A copper brazier sputtered and cast a fitful light on Kiyomori's drawn face.

"Come in, old friend," said Kiyomori.

"How can I serve you?" asked the old man.

"I need advice, and you are the only one I can trust. Please sit by me," Kiyomori clapped his hands. Servants appeared, bringing tea and rice cakes.

As he poured the tea, Kiyomori described his meeting with Go-Shirakawa. He ended by asking, "Do I have a choice? Can I extend Council seats to my enemies without losing face? Is there a way to follow the Emperor's directive without undermining my position?"

Yorimasa considered the questions for several moments.

Then, he put down his cup and held up his fist. He opened a bony finger. "You have no choice, short of defying the cloistered Emperor." He held up another finger. "By bringing Minamoto leaders into the Council, you can keep them under your watchful eyes"—a third finger—"and separate them from Yoritomo and his northern army." The fourth finger: "With his leaders here in the capital, arrangements can be made to see that the most dangerous of them are controlled." He closed and squeezed his fist. "You can turn this to your advantage. In case of war, you can crush the Minamoto leaders without sending your armies out of the city."

Kiyomori smiled. His face suddenly looked younger. "You are a wise counsellor," he said. "I will find a way to reward you."

"Helping you is its own reward. I need nothing else. I am always at your service."

"Thank you, trusted friend."

Later that night, Yorimasa worked under a burning oil lamp. The smell of the oil filled the small stark room. Yorimasa brushed firm characters on a sheet of parchment. From time to time he rubbed his ink stick through the water to make fresh ink. When the message was completed, he folded the heavy paper carefully, affixed his seal, and called a servant.

"See to it that this is carried by messenger tonight," he said, "to the camp of Minamoto Yoritomo."

Forty-one

Heavy snows fell in the winter of 1179, and the spring of 1180 saw extensive flooding wipe out a large part of the rice crop. Continuous rainstorms finished the damage the heavy snow had started. There were other signs of anger and unrest among the gods: A great fire devastated the capital, burning sixteen mansions of the nobility and hundreds of other houses. Then whirlwinds flattened much of what remained. The earth trembled and quaked, causing avalanches to wipe out entire towns.

Signs of the gods' disfavor were on all sides. Every town had its share of beggars and homeless children cast loose to make their own way. Even well-dressed people walked the streets, begging for food in exchange for their pitiful belongings.

Meanwhile, among the Taira courtiers, almost as great an unrest was caused by two new factors: the reintroduction of Minamoto emissaries to the Imperial Council and Taira Kiyomori's decision to move the capital from Kyoto to Fukuhara, a small city on the shores of the Inland Sea.

Kiyomori had maintained a palace in Fukuhara for almost twenty years. For reasons of state, he had recently decided that the royal family and the court should move to Fukuhara, where he would be better able to control their activities. The

tragedies that had befallen Kyoto gave him the excuse he
needed to compel the Emperor to accede to his plan.

Once the announcement was made, offices were moved
from Kyoto and disgruntled courtiers began a mass exodus,
preceding the Emperor and Kiyomori to the new capital.

Yoshi rode his horse southward, through a series of
rainsqualls. Many social changes had taken place in the three
years since Yoshi's stay in Okitsu. The oxcarts of yesteryear
had fallen out of style; Yoritomo's northern samurai all rode
horses and this new mode of travel was no longer considered
barbaric. The courtiers were learning to ride; horses were
replacing oxen among every class of people, bringing the
outlying areas closer to the capital.

As Yoshi crossed the crest of Mount Hiei, he saw Kyoto at
the bottom of the valley; it was a scene of devastation. Fully a
third of the city had been leveled by the fires, whirlwinds,
and earthquakes.

Yoshi passed posters that announced the coming move.
Every part of the city had teams of men working in the rain,
dismantling homes for shipment to Fukuhara. The simplest
method of moving was to float the homes down the Yodo
River, which flowed directly from Kyoto to Fukuhara. Yoshi
rode straight to Ietaka's house, which was in one of the few
areas hardly touched by the fires and whirlwinds. The house
was quiet. Yoshi mounted the veranda and rang the gong to
announce his coming. On the third ring, a sleepy serving girl
poked her head around the corner and called out in a surly
voice, "He is not at home. Go away."

"When will he return?"

"He is at the Imperial Council. He didn't say when he'd be
back." She pushed back a mop of loose hair.

"I will wait."

"As you wish." The girl inspected the wet and dirty
traveler, then snorted and disappeared inside the house. How
typical of Ietaka, thought Yoshi, to have a surly servant who
did not know her place.

He brought his horse around to the back and tethered it to a post under the eaves. It was early, and it could be hours until Ietaka returned. Yoshi decided rather than wait idly he would leave his horse and observe the city at close range. The weather was breaking; the rain had tapered off to little more than a heavy mist.

Yoshi went directly to the central avenue; he was shocked to find that many of the famous silver willows had burned in the fire. Blackened trunks, like cemetery markers, memorialized the death of the great city. Walking along Suzaku-Ōji, south toward Gojō Street, he often saw areas cleared of buildings as far as the western wall. Dogs, ribs outlined through matted fur, ran through the wreckage, searching for food. Once, he saw a rat the size of a cat, scurrying under the veranda of a partly destroyed house. Worst of all, were the looters rummaging through the debris, looking desperately for anything of value.

At the corner, where he had lived during his years in Kyoto, the entire block was gone. There was no sign that houses had ever been there. Even the rock gardens had disappeared. The corner was covered with weeds and pools of rainwater. Only scarred willow trunks rose from the ground.

Yoshi silently contemplated the dissolution of so many of his early memories. A lump formed in his throat as he stared at the desolate corner. The storm suddenly built up again. He stood for a long time, unheeding as the rain ran off his straw cape and splashed up from the ground, making tiny water explosions.

An hour later, Yoshi was waiting on the veranda under the eaves of Ietaka's house as the big man mounted the steps from the street.

"Yoshi!" Ietaka raised his arms in welcome. "What a joyous surprise!" He drew back to inspect Yoshi. His face lit up. "You look strong. Healthy! Amida Buddha, how I've missed you."

"As I have missed you."

Ietaka shook his head and sighed. "Time passes too quickly. How can I believe I haven't seen you since your convalescence in Okitsu? Three years?" He took Yoshi's arm and drew him to the portal, exclaiming, "What kind of host am I? Forgive me for keeping you outside in this weather. Come into the house immediately. You will dry yourself and borrow one of my robes."

"I have my own things packed on my horse," protested Yoshi.

"Nonsense! I insist you use mine. You can unpack later. . . ." Ietaka led Yoshi into the house, saying, "As long as you stay in Kyoto, you will live with me."

There was much to discuss. Ietaka was horrified by the first-hand account of Yoshi's encounter with Chikara's samurai and the full story of Ichikawa's death. He had heard the bare outlines of the tale before. Now, the tragedy was graphically brought to his attention.

"What a fine man he was," he said when Yoshi finished.

"And you, Ietaka? Tell me about yourself. Then give me the news of the family."

"It is hard to know where to begin. . . . I have been in the capital, working for the Minamoto cause. You will find this hard to believe . . . I am no longer a mere agent. I have become a duly elected member of the Imperial Council. Under the influence of one of our people, Kiyomori agreed to permit a representative from each of the northeast provinces to serve under the Minister of the Right. As you know, the Taira representatives are seated under the Minister of the Left. Although they wield more power, we hold equal rank. Can you imagine? Your cousin, Ietaka, the revolutionary, is now of the sixth rank."

"We live in a strange and wonderful society, when a scoundrel like you can become a member of the court," Yoshi said, lifting a cup of sake in a mock toast.

"Yes," continued Ietaka. "Scoundrel that I am, I have a highly placed friend at court; with his help, I have been able to keep the Taira tyrants too busy to interfere with the massing of Yoritomo's armies. Yoritomo is rallying the entire northeast behind the flag of Go-Shirakawa's son, Prince Mochihito. With Mochihito at our head, we will have the legitimacy we need to replace the Taira. If we can keep Kiyomori from discovering our plans before we are ready, the next few months will show us the way to victory.''

"You make it sound too simple, friend. I am sure you will encounter problems along the way.'' Yoshi hesitated. Though he admired Ietaka's enthusiasm, he was more interested in news of the family than in politics. He cleared his throat. "Enough of Minamoto and Taira! Tell me—''

Ietaka interrupted. "I have even more surprising news for you. Did you know my brother-in-law, your old enemy, is now leader of the Council representatives of the Left? Since he was driven from his *shoen*, he has been here, charming his way to higher and higher positions.'' Ietaka looked at Yoshi shrewdly. "If you join us on the Council, I can offer you an opportunity to help thwart his rise. You may see your vows fulfilled sooner than you planned.''

Yoshi remained impassive despite a stir of emotion. "Chikara!'' he exclaimed. "I have not forgotten my vows, but I must put my other responsibilities first. He and I will meet eventually. It is not yet time.'' He paused and added thoughtfully, "I must never underestimate him. He is a ruthless and dangerous man. No. I am not ready. Though I am tempted to accept your offer, at this time only a direct challenge and a meeting with swords would satisfy me.''

"You could do him more injury through the Council,'' said Ietaka. "To a man like Chikara, a blow to his pride would mean more than a mere swordstroke.''

Yoshi shook his head. "Someday, perhaps on a day when you really need my help, you will ask again. Meanwhile, what does Chikara accomplish on the Council?''

"You have to give the devil credit. He is a clever opponent. He keeps us Minamoto councillors involved in nonsensical ceremony so we rarely get any real work done. However, we are not stupid. While he delays us here, he gives Yoritomo time to prepare for a show of arms.''

"And his personal life? How is your sister, Nami?''

"Nami seems to have accepted her responsibilities. For the past two years she has managed Chikara's Kyoto household. In truth, I've seen very little of her; her position precludes public appearances.''

"So her hope for independence was a will-o'-the-wisp. You know, we grew quite close during the time I stayed with her in Okitsu. Without her help I would not have recovered as quickly or as completely. I owe her a great deal.'' Yoshi brushed at a piece of lint on his sleeve and, with seeming casualness, asked, "Is she happy with her present circumstances? Does Chikara treat her well?''

"He treats her as well as any man of the court treats his woman. Oh, there is talk about him. We know he has more than one woman hidden away. Nevertheless, I find it strange that a man should be married for so many years without producing an heir.'' Ietaka paused. He raised his eyes to gaze directly into Yoshi's face. "They say my sister holds him at arm's length.''

Yoshi was pleased by this small crumb of gossip. "I would like to speak to her again,'' he said, "though I know that is impossible while she lives in Chikara's household.''

"Ah . . . Yoshi . . . you *can* see her. Chikara's *shinden* was destroyed by a whirlwind, and Nami temporarily resides with Uncle Fumio again.''

"With Fumio? You mean she has returned to Okitsu?''

"No, not at all. Forgive me for not making it clear sooner. Uncle is here in Kyoto.'' Ietaka shook his head and added, "I was sure you knew.''

"Knew what? Amida Buddha! Is something wrong with uncle?''

"Oh, he is well enough physically. It is just that the gods have not smiled on him. The unrest in the provinces jeopardized his *shoen*, and last year he was forced to move to the city.''

"I did send a letter to Okitsu. Now I know why it went unanswered.''

"He is a foolish man. The entire affair is unfortunate. I could extend protection if he would declare himself with us and renounce the Taira.''

"Where does he live?" Yoshi felt a momentary speeding of his heartbeat. Dared he hope that his family was within reach?

"Your mother, your uncle, and my sister are in the ninefold enclosure. The Emperor gave Fumio a small house on the Imperial grounds. For the family's safety he must remain there until they are resettled."

"I should like to see them when my business is done," said Yoshi.

"You had best hurry then, because they will be among the first to move to the new capital in Fukuhara."

Yoshi was too late.

By the time he completed his business—the purchase of practice armor, swords, and fighting gear—several days had passed. He tried repeatedly to see the family. It was impossible to get through the guards at the Imperial enclosure. Yoshi finally decided to send a message.

It was returned with a short note from the majordomo: The Lord Fumio, Lady Masaka, and their niece, Nami, had packed and left by oxcart the previous day. They were already on their way to Fukuhara.

Yoshi was bitterly disappointed. The following day he arranged for the wagonload of new equipment to be shipped to Sarashina and prepared to leave Kyoto.

"I will miss you," Ietaka said simply. "I hope to see you again soon. There are not many in the city I can trust and call friend."

"I will return when duty permits," said Yoshi, holding his horse in place with one hand.

Ietaka frowned. "Our destinies are woven together in some mysterious way," he said. "I sense I will see you again sooner than you think, and, perhaps then, you will join me on the Council to fight the Taira."

"Not too likely, old friend." Yoshi chuckled. "I wish you luck with your enemies. May Amida Buddha protect you."

Yoshi turned his horse and rode toward the city gate. He glanced back over his shoulder. Ietaka was standing alone—a small figure in spite of his bulk—in the middle of the street, waving farewell.

Yoshi gave an involuntary shudder as he felt a touch from beyond the grave.

Forty-two

==

By the fourth month of 1180, the countryside had fallen under the thrall of drought and famine. There had been no spring plowing: The crops of the five cereals had drowned in the floods.

In Kyoto, families left their homes, and vandals looted whatever was left. Former gentlepeople wandered through the rubble, shoeless and hatless, fighting for scraps. Bodies lay in the streets, torn by rats and dogs; the smell of putrefying flesh filled the city. Those houses that were left standing gradually disappeared as they were broken up and sold for fuel.

At first, the citizens prayed daily in temples surrounding the city. When the prayers went unanswered, bright red and gold panels appeared in the masses of firewood; desperate people tore apart the mountain temples for anything usable. The entire populace turned into an army of barefoot beggars, wearing rags and tatters to cover their emaciated frames.

Outside Sarashina, the academy had a comparatively plentiful store of grain. Yoshi had prudently laid in a stock on his return from Kyoto. It became necessary to patrol the storehouse with armed students; townspeople would have stripped the school of food if it were not for their fear of the swordsmen.

Before the fourth month was over, Yoshi had misgivings about the welfare of his family, caught between famine and unrest. He again mounted his horse and rode south. This time he was determined to find them in Fukuhara.

Rumor had it that Taira rule was coming to an end, that Kiyomori's move from the capital was a sign of weakness, and that more and more uncommitted nobles were ready to back Prince Mochihito and support the Minamoto. Fumio's household might need help and protection in the coming struggle.

Yoshi packed his saddle bags with as much grain as he could discreetly carry. Highwaymen were the rule not the exception as the guardians of the law pulled back from the outlying areas to protect their own enclaves. Even the greatest swordsman in the land could not prevail against a starving mob willing to die for a handful of rice.

"*Sensei*, please be careful on the road," said Kojima with a worried frown.

Tofushi echoed Kojima's sentiments.

"You are good men," said Yoshi, his voice thick with feeling. "I know I can depend on you while I am away. Knowing you are in charge, I shall rest easy as I travel southward. And never fear, I will be careful."

The two assistants presented Yoshi with a bag of delicacies saved from their own rations.

Yoshi's throat tightened as he accepted the gift, knowing how much it meant to them.

"Thank you," he murmured unable to say more without embarrassing himself.

Fukuhara was cramped between the ocean and the mountains. As Yoshi arrived in the foothills north of the new capital, he heard the roar of the Inland Sea crashing against the shore that hemmed the city on the south. The smell of salt water was strong, whipped by sea breezes and carried on a mist that rose from the frothing ocean surface.

Yoshi guided his horse past the new palace. It nestled against the hills and was impressive in a rough way. The walls were round logs chinked at the corners to fit into each other—a strange building, solid and elegant at the same time. Samurai paraded their armored mounts around the palace enclosure, horses and men sweating under their armor in the spring sun. The sea breeze gave relief from the heat, a relief paid for by the discomfort of clammy air.

Along the main street, homes were being erected using parts of buildings which had been floated down the Yodo River from Kyoto. Men in workclothes scurried back and forth in the narrow streets. Some were laborers, others courtiers who had relinquished their brocades and silks in exchange for cotton cloaks in keeping with the frontier atmosphere. Fukuhara was being prepared for the coming arrival of Kiyomori and the full court.

Yoshi reined in before an almost completed building. Workmen clambered on the roof putting the last of the red tiles in place. It was three stories high—large for Fukuhara—and obviously belonged to someone of importance.

"Are you in charge here?" he asked the most important looking of the laborers, a tall man with a stomach that protruded over his *obi*.

"Who asks?" asked the fat man as if he were condescending to an inferior.

"Tadamori Yoshi, heir to the Lord of Okitsu," snapped Yoshi.

The change was instantaneous, the fat man turned from arrogant to obsequious. "I am Kurando, foreman for the great Lord Chikara. At your service."

Chikara? Here? Yoshi caught his breath.

"Where is your lord, Kurando?" he asked.

"He stays in Kyoto on government business while we prepare his new home."

"And do you know the whereabouts of Lord Tadamori-no-Fumio?"

"Of course, sire. Lord Fumio stays at Kiyomori's palace with his family."

Yoshi nodded curtly. He turned his horse toward the log palace.

It was late afternoon before he was able to get a message to Fumio. The samurai guards proved surprisingly difficult to bribe. Gold was of no interest to them. The offer of grain finally bought a messenger who carried Yoshi's note to Fumio and returned with an answer.

An hour later, Yoshi sat in a luxuriously appointed room toasting his uncle with a cup of sake. Heavy Chinese tapestries closed out the breeze and muted the ever-present roar of the sea. Incense burning behind an ornate screen blended subtly with the odor of sea salt that penetrated the palace.

At first, Fumio was silent; he was resentful that Yoshi had never sent a message after his arrival in Sarashina. The postal service was expensive and undependable, but a message *could* have been posted. Yoshi explained that he *had* sent a letter. Apparently it had not been delivered.

Fumio was mollified by the explanation. He was also pleased Yoshi had been thoughtful enough to bring a gift of grain despite the danger of carrying it on the roads. Fumio thanked Yoshi profusely, and explained that though he appreciated the gift he did not lack for food; the tragedies that had befallen Kyoto had brushed Fukuhara lightly and the court was still able to maintain its standard of luxury.

As the level of sake lowered in its flask, Fumio asked Yoshi innumerable questions about Sarashina and the academy. While Yoshi answered, Fumio studied him carefully. His nephew certainly looked confident and strong. He noted the muscular forearms and the heavily callused hands.

"Yoshi, you have changed since your convalescence. You seem taller and heavier than when I last saw you. The life of a swordmaster agrees with you."

"Thank you, Uncle. Yes, it is true my life is pleasant. I work hard and enjoy meeting my responsibilities. My duty is its own reward."

"A very mature attitude." Fumio approved. "With so

much work, much of it physically demanding . . . aren't you troubled by your old wounds?"

"Sometimes, when I overwork, my hip aches. I have trained myself to ignore it." Yoshi refilled his cup. "Enough about me," he said after he had taken a sip. "How is my mother?"

"Lady Masaka has changed and I fear it has not been a change for the better. She has been reclusive for years. Since our departure from Okitsu she has withdrawn even further. You must spend time with her before you leave. Poor woman! She has had few pleasures in life and I believe your seeing her would lift her spirits."

"I shall not leave without visiting her. I am only sorry my visit will be a short one."

Fumio frowned. "I assumed you would be with us for some time," he said. "You made a long and dangerous trip. Surely you do not intend to depart so quickly?"

"I am afraid I have to say goodbye early enough to reach the first post stop before nightfall." Yoshi, seeing Fumio's disappointment, explained, "You have food, clothing, and shelter so you do not need my help. On the other hand, the academy needs me. Coming here took longer than I anticipated, and the return will be equally time consuming."

"I am distressed," said Fumio, "though I understand the call of duty." He filled the cups again, emptying the flask.

"Before I go," said Yoshi, "I would like to see cousin Nami. Ietaka informed me that she is staying with you."

"Nami . . . has become a problem," Fumio said after a moment of silence.

"How so?"

"She is like a nightingale released from its cage. When she is with Chikara, she is restricted to his house—he believes in the old ways. Free of his influence, she takes advantage of her freedom. She will not stay behind her screen. She has reverted to childhood, walking freely in public and even riding a horse! Frankly, I find her behavior outrageous. For her own sake, she will have to act properly before Chikara returns for her."

Though Fumio was distressed, Yoshi found the news refreshing. He always remembered Nami in the fields at Okitsu and it pained him to think of her at Chikara's beck and call, trapped behind a screen of state in the typical fashion of upper-class women. For anyone else he would have approved of absolute obedience to the head of the family, but Nami was too free a spirit. Yoshi felt a glow of pride, his secret love had not succumbed to Chikara and the pressures of society.

Yoshi hid a pleased smile and repeated his request. "I would like to see her before I go to my mother. I have not forgotten the debt I owe her for looking after me on the *shoen*."

"If Chikara were here, that would be impossible. Since he is away and she is in my charge, I will allow her to decide if she wishes to see you."

Forty-three

Yoshi was kneeling on a rich, gold-embroidered cushion in a position of prayer when Nami silently entered the room behind him. As she watched from the portal, two red spots appeared on her cheeks, she had difficulty breathing, and her hands trembled. She had thought she was prepared for this meeting, but she had underestimated the effect he would have on her. In spite of her confusion, she realized, at last, that this was the man she loved. Yes, loved! Even when she had thought she loved Chikara she had only been hiding her true feelings from herself. The time had come. She must make herself face the truth about herself and Yoshi.

If only he knew how she felt! And if only she could be free enough in her heart to tell him. She, a married woman! Contemplating the unthinkable.

Perhaps it was because he respected her marital status that Yoshi had never shown a sign that his feelings were deeper than cousinly devotion. Or—and she pushed the thought away—perhaps he did not feel the same way she did and she was being foolish . . . acting like a schoolgirl. What if he did return her love, then where would her allegiance lie?

She composed herself and cleared her throat.

''Nami!'' He was obviously delighted to see her. He leaped to his feet and came to take her hand.

"Yoshi. It has been too long since your last visit. You could, at least, have written to let us know you arrived safely in Sarashina."

"I am sorry." Yoshi was contrite; he told her about the undelivered letter and of his attempt to see her in Kyoto.

Nami said, "We seem fated to miss each other at almost every turn. You know, I had despaired of ever seeing you again . . . yet . . . now that you are here, Uncle Fumio tells me you are leaving. I demand to know why you cannot stay longer."

"Nami, dear Nami. I came because I thought you needed my help. However, I see you are well. There is no danger as long as you remain in Fukuhara. It would be self-indulgence if I stayed under these circumstances. . . . No . . . I shall leave tonight. My school needs me more than the family does."

"Yoshi! You know nothing of our needs." Nami's lips compressed. Yoshi's righteousness angered her. He acted as though they were mere acquaintances. She wanted to hurt him . . . make him aware of considerations other than his academy. "You have never been with us when we needed you. When we had to abandon Okitsu . . . you were far away. When the whirlwinds struck Kyoto . . . you were far away. And now, when we are alone in this alien city . . . you will be far away, too."

"Nami, I cannot forget that you will not be alone for along. Chikara will return to claim you. I passed his new house this morning. His foreman tells me it is almost ready. Soon you will be with your husband again."

Nami was contrite. Yoshi could not help what he was. His devotion to duty was probably one of the qualities that endeared him to her. And he did sound unhappy that she would be returning to Chikara. "I don't look forward to that day," she said. "I am happier without him. He has always been kind and thoughtful in his fashion, yet I seek more from life than his occasional visits." Nami gave a rueful sigh. "At first, our marriage was full. Chikara and I spent much time together. I entertained his guests and tried to further his career. New people, important people, came to see us regularly. They liked me, and my lord welcomed my help in dealing with them. When he fled Okitsu, his business became confined to the court; he no longer needed my help, and he spent more and more time away from me. . . .

"Oh, yes," Nami continued as she noted Yoshi's expression. "I know he has a second wife in the southeast quarter and he takes other women as lovers. We have discussed it. He says everyone does the same and he would be less than a man if he didn't. I suppose part of the fault is mine because I did not give him an heir in the first years of our marriage. However, I no longer care. To me, all that matters is that I loathe the dull life of a principal wife, and soon I shall be forced to accept it again. Perhaps, like so many others, I will take a lover to keep me from boredom."

Yoshi's pulse skipped a beat. Was she hinting . . . ? No! He could not believe she meant what she said. He embarrassedly changed the subject. "Will you stay in Fukuhara?" he asked.

"Of course. We no longer have a home in Kyoto. The houses are gone. You've seen the city. You know the destruction the gods visited on it."

"Yes, I was there after the fires and earthquakes had subsided. You must have been terrified. How did you escape death or injury?"

"Luckily for us, we were in the ninefold enclosure when the whirlwinds came. Some of our neighbors were not so fortunate and were killed by the wind. It was so sudden—the noise, the ripping up of the trees, the sound of roofs torn from houses." Nami shuddered. "Even in the palace we heard it, and looking over the Emperor's garden, I saw entire buildings flying in the black air. It was a fearsome sight."

"Poor Nami." Yoshi put a sympathetic hand on her arm. She smiled bravely. "Oh, not so poor. Even if you will not stay, I have my freedom until Chikara and Kiyomori arrive with the court." The smile faded. "After you left Okitsu, Chikara sent for me and I joined him in Kyoto. Though I was not ready to accept a life of waiting for him behind my screen

. . . I had no choice. In Fukuhara it is different. We are like country people, and—as long as Chikara is away—I can dress and appear as I please without criticism.''

"I like you this way," said Yoshi warmly.

Nami hid her face behind her fan. "That makes me very happy.''

"Yes, in the north country, all the women leave their hair loose, dress comfortably, and walk in public. I am quite accustomed to it.''

Nami frowned. "All the women? I suppose you are quite a romantic prince with the country girls.'' Nami compared Yoshi to Lady Murasaka's famous fictional hero, Prince Genji, whose romantic escapades filled the lives of the court ladies.

Yoshi caught the reference. "You misunderstand," he said. "I am so busy running an academy, I have no time for the ladies.''

"Their loss," said Nami with a smile.

Yoshi suggested a walk in the afternoon sun. He held Nami's arm firmly as he led her outside. In a small way, the grounds were a replica of Kyoto's Imperial enclosure. There was an artificial lake with a curved wooden bridge at one end. Bamboo thickets waved brush fronds on the shore while swans floated among the lily pads, disturbing the frogs and insects that variously sat, swam, or leaped from flower to flower.

As they strolled along the bank, they spoke of long-gone pleasures, and Nami laughed behind her fan at Yoshi's clever sallies. He *could* be charming. While she was with him it was easy to forget her responsibilities. She felt warm, young, languorous.

Yoshi recited a poem on the spur of the moment.

> *"The long neck'd white swans*
> *Stir the waters of the pond*
> *Disturbing blossoms*
> *And stirring up the long gone*
> *Happy memories of youth.''*

Nami was delighted. This was the romantic hero of her daydreams. "I shall compose one in return," she said.

> *"The frog is silent*
> *Sitting on her lily pad*
> *Waiting through the years*
> *For the return of the prince*
> *Who left her there so long ago."*

"Bravo, Nami, bravo. You have a quick mind."

"Are you surprised?"

"No, not really. I suppose I should stop thinking of you as a child."

Nami stopped short and turned toward Yoshi, her face level with his chest. She slowly raised her head. Her slim onyx eyes mirrored emotions she had never revealed before. Her lips were swollen . . . sensuous. She said boldly, "It *is* time to forget the child and see me as the woman I am. An emotional woman . . . a woman who feels more deeply than you have ever realized."

Yoshi was taken aback. What had happened to the light banter of a moment before? He felt Nami's heat radiating toward him and instinctively drew her closer. In a panic, she disengaged herself. What had she done? This could go no further; it was not fair to Yoshi or to herself. She had committed a grave indiscretion, allowing herself to lose control. Fortunately, she had stopped in time. Poor Yoshi! She had led him on, and now he was confused. She tried to cover the heaviness growing inside. "I think it is time to see your mother," she said.

Lady Masaka was hidden behind a screen in her gloomy room with the shutters closed against the moist air.

"Yoshi?" Her voice was thin and querulous. "How long have you been here?"

"I arrived only a few hours ago and came to see you as soon as I could." Yoshi was distressed at the change he heard in her voice. She hadn't even asked how he was! He would never understand her.

"How long will you stay?" She broke in on his thoughts.

"I shall leave tonight."

"So soon? Amida Buddha. I have not spoken to you in almost three years. A woman needs her son to talk to from time to time." There was bitterness and resignation in her tone.

"You have servants and handmaidens to talk with," Yoshi said lamely.

"They are not the same. I would like to spend time with you before I die."

"Mother, you will live for years," said Yoshi, stirrings of guilt making his heart flutter. Why was she so bitter? Was the fault his for leaving home, or was it the restrictive life imposed on women by society that made her this way?

"Where are you running now?" Her voice took a sharp edge. "Are you still wasting your life courting tragedy? Still chasing the will-o'-the-wisp, Lord Chikara?"

"I'm sorry, Mother. You don't understand."

"You are right. I am only a sick old woman, who sits alone in an empty room, dreaming of her child. What do I know of life?" Her tone was sarcastic. "All I know is that my only son deserted me years ago, and now he leaves as soon as he arrives . . . and why? Answer me! Why?"

Yoshi sighed. "If I could stay, I would," he said.

"And what prevents you?"

"You don't understand," he said hopelessly. "I love you. I want to stay. Unfortunately, it is impossible."

"I understand one thing. When I needed my son, he left me." The room was silent. Yoshi did not know what else to say. Lady Masaka paused then made a final effort to change his mind. "I ask you, I beg you to remain with me," she pleaded. When he did not answer, her voice fell to an almost inaudible murmur. "What can take precedence over a mother's love?" she asked.

"Duty and honor," Yoshi replied.

* * * *

A saddened Yoshi spurred his horse into the hills north of Fukuhara. It had turned dark; the sun's dull copper disc sank into the western sea. Gulls hooted mournfully as they circled the turbulent waters, searching for food. The night turned cold. Fishermen huddled on dozens of small boats that flocked around the harbor.

PART FIVE

Forty-four

On the evening of the fifteenth day of the fifth month of 1180, thirty-year-old Prince Mochihito, son of the cloistered Emperor, Go-Shirakawa, was alone in his room at Takakura Palace. While many of his friends were being asked to relocate in Fukuhara, Mochihito had been overlooked . . . ignored. The insult did not disturb him; Takakura Palace had escaped the fires and whirlwinds that had devastated so much of the rest of Kyoto and Mochihito was quite content to live a life of virtual exile in such exquisite surroundings. It had been a day of great beauty. Cherry trees had opened their blossoms only a few days before, and the prince—one of the finest flautists of the court—had spent his day playing his favorite flute under the fragrant blooms.

At the end of so pleasing a day, he sat by a window composing a poem. Besides being a fine musician, he was also a skillful calligrapher and poet, known for the elegance of his brushwork and the aesthetic quality of his poems.

> *The cherry blossoms*
> *Greet the coming of green spring*
> *Opening their hearts*
> *To the music of a flute*
> *That has, too long, been silent.*

He laid the brush aside and admired his own characters, so neatly written on the mulberry paper. The poem brought a certain sadness to his heart. He was so like the cherry blossoms himself, his talents hidden during this long season of his life. He smiled, pleased with the comparison, and his eyes narrowed to thin slits as he thought how the world would soon see his flowering. He stood up and walked to the portal where he could watch the azure sky bring deep shadows to the gardens.

Mochihito, second son of Go-Shirakawa, should have been next in line to inherit the Imperial crown. He was intelligent, well-read, artistic, musical, and everything a father could want for an Imperial son. However, in his youth, Mochihito won the enmity of the Empress Ken-shun-mon-in and was pushed aside from his rightful inheritance.

With all his good qualities, Mochihito was not a forceful man. His smooth, round, pudding face was unmarked by the worries that beset men of character, men who make decisions.

The sound of a temple bell ringing over the Takakura Palace garden made him recall the winter night several months earlier, when he had received a surprise visitor. . . .

Ice covered the palace grounds. The winds whined shrilly, whipping up ethereal clouds of snow crystals. Mochihito was awakened by the sound of heavy wheels crackling through the ice outside the gate just as the bells announced the hour of the ox, two A.M.

The prince stiffened with fear. Were there assassins stalking through the fields of snow? He had no sword or knife to protect himself. Only his two favorite flutes of Chinese bamboo and his brush and inkstick were at hand. Hardly useful weapons. He pulled his robe over his head.

Icicles fell from the eaves with a crystalline clatter as the stranger came up the outside stairs. The prince heard him stamping places for his feet in the snow.

The gong sounded. Mochihito trembled.

"Forgive me, sire, there is a visitor who insists on seeing

you. He will not show his face or give his name," said a
servant from the doorway.

"Tell him to go away," mumbled Mochihito.

Another voice interrupted. The stranger had silently followed the servant and stood behind him in the portal. "It is
important, Your Highness. You will find it to your advantage
to speak to me."

The voice was soft and cultured. Mochihito peered out
from the robes and saw a tall slim figure completely wrapped
in coarse cotton cloth. The cloth was draped across his face
hiding it from sight. The man did not seem dangerous; he was
not wearing a sword.

"Come inside and let me see your face," Mochihito said
nervously.

The figure nodded at the servant who left the room, sliding
the portal closed behind him.

"You?" said Mochihito in surprise as the tall man removed the drape from his face.

"Yes, Your Highness, it is I, Yorimasa, on a matter of
grave import."

Mochihito thought the old poet had gone mad, yet, as he
spoke, his ascetic face with its burning eyes and transparent
skin held Mochihito in thrall.

Yorimasa, accustomed to the diplomacy needed to deal
with the royal family, chose his words carefully. His years of
service with Kiyomori and Go-Shirakawa had trained him
well.

"How sad," he said, "that Your Highness suffers silently
in exile on the outskirts of Kyoto, while others sit in the
ninefold enclosure. You, who are the direct descendant of
Amaterasu, the sun-goddess, should be the Crown Prince in
line for the throne."

"Sad it is. . . . There are those who keep me from my
rightful position," said Mochihito with a whine of self-pity
in his voice.

"Perhaps the passage of time will bring a change.
Kiyomori grows weaker each passing day while Minamoto
Yoritomo amasses a great army in the north to wrest the

power from his weakened hands. I speak for Yoritomo when I offer you the crown if you support our cause."

"Your proposal is madness. If I accept and Kiyomori triumphs, I will lose my head," sniveled Mochihito.

"And I mine," said Yorimasa impatiently. "Our secret shall be well guarded till the time comes to strike."

"If I say no, what then?" Mochihito tried to comprehend the enormity of what was being offered.

"Then your head will roll with Kiyomori's."

Yorimasa paused, then pointed a bony finger at the prince. "Your Highness, consider this: The country is in the grip of famine. Every day more of the people, maddened by hunger, are turning against the Taira lords. Yoritomo's armies grow stronger as Kiyomori's weaken. The snows of this winter will bury the Taira hopes of recovery in the year to come. Kiyomori's soldiers will leave when he cannot feed them. The capital will lie helpless before the northern armies."

"I need time to think," said Mochihito.

"Very well. I shall return in a week. If you give the order, the Minamoto troops will pour in from every side, and the people will join them. The outcome is a foregone conclusion. You will become Emperor of Japan."

After Yorimasa left, Prince Mochihito was in turmoil. He was tempted by Yorimasa's promises, but what if the Minamoto failed? He shivered with apprehension. He prayed to Amida Buddha for guidance. Like all weak people, he wanted the security of the present and the rewards of the future without risk.

In the morning, the prince invited his foster brother, Munenobu, to join him. The fire crackled in the brazier, throwing off sparks and smoke that filled the room. Outside, it was so cold the birds neither flew nor sang. The only noise to penetrate the house was the crackling of branches under their load of snow.

Munenobu was a sad-eyed young man, less intelligent, less talented, and less handsome than Mochihito. He wore a cherry colored cloak and a white under-robe, with loose trousers of deep purple. Another under-robe of a dark red pattern showed in the sleeves of the outer cloak. The effect would have been elegant except that the robes had been worn too long. They had lost their crispness and fell in soft shapeless folds.

"Munenobu, dear Brother," began Mochihito in his most cajoling intimate voice, immediately putting Munenobu on guard. "On a day like this, we should stay beside the fire and talk. Here we share the same palace grounds, yet see so little of each other."

"You are too busy with your music and court ceremonies to spend time with one as dull as I," said Munenobu with false humility.

"Nonsense," lied Mochihito, who did indeed consider his foster brother a dullard. "I am sorry we haven't been together more. Maybe we can remedy that in the future."

In spite of himself, Munenobu was flattered. "It would be nice," he said.

"Of course it would. Tell me, Brother, do you think we will ever be accepted in the palace while Kiyomori is there?"

"You, perhaps, but I have no place there."

"Yet you think I do? How good of you to say so," Mochihito paused. He tried to look innocent as he prompted, "Do you think I have the requirements to be Emperor?"

"Certainly. You write a better hand than anyone in the Imperial Palace. You compose better poetry. I would say you are eminently qualified." Munenobu's sarcasm went unnoticed.

"Thank you, Brother," he said. "Shall we have tea?"

"They call you Physiognomy Counsellor because of your skill in the art of reading faces," said Prince Mochihito to the small, wizened man who sat beside him.

"That is true, Your Highness. By using the most modern methods—methods, I might add, that have been received with great favor in the courts of China—I can foretell the future and divine the true abilities of any man, woman, or child." The Physiognomy Counsellor spoke in a low tone, leaning close to the prince as if to give him confidential information.

"Is this true?"

"As true as my name is Shonagon Korenaga. My methods have never failed."

"I find this extremely interesting. Of course, I ask questions for no particular purpose, mere curiosity, if you will." Mochihito made an elaborate ritual of being disinterested. He succeeded in making Korenaga wonder about his true purpose.

"I understand," said the little man, as he considered ways to turn the situation to his advantage.

"Tell me, what do you read in my future?" asked Mochihito.

Korenaga rose to his feet. He walked around the prince, stooping to observe his head and face at close range. "A difficult task," he finally said. "One worthy of my greatest efforts."

"You will, of course, be rewarded," said the prince, unable to hide his eagerness.

"Of course," said Korenaga. He pulled a scroll from under his voluminous robe and spread it on the floor. Next, he made calculations and measurements from the charts inscribed on the scroll. Then he carefully measured the prince's features, head size, nose length, distance between the eyes, shape of the ears, and angle of mouth. He closed his eyes and mouthed prayers to various deities, asking for divine guidance for his scientific art. At last, he opened his eyes and rose to his feet.

"There is no question," he said. "You are eminently suited to a high position. My calculations show you are a man of great intellect, royal to the core. I foresee a shining future as leader of our people; you will become famous and live successfully for many generations."

"This is shown in your charts?"

"This is shown in my charts."

*   *   *

The temple bell rang out over the Takakura gardens. The moon was behind the cherry trees. Two hours had passed while the prince stood in his reverie; it was already four o'clock, the hour of the tiger. He gave one last thought to the joy on Yorimasa's face when he had given him his well-considered decision on that cold winter night. There was no question: Destiny would smile on the fortunes of Prince Mochihito, second son of Emperor Go-Shirakawa. He took out his favorite flute and played the melody "Was Ever Such a Day?" Outside the portal, the first pearl light of dawn began to outline the cherry trees on the eastern horizon.

When Yorimasa had returned in the dead of the winter's night for the prince's answer, he had been greeted by Munenobu, who, unable to sleep, had dismissed the servants. Even though Yorimasa's face was covered, Munenobu thought his tall spare figure looked familiar. He had led him to the prince's chamber, and silently bowed himself out. For the next half hour, he had crouched on the other side of the thin partition, listening to the conversation in the other room.

Much later, he had lain awake, huddled close to a charcoal fire, thinking about the implications of the conversation he had overheard.

Forty-five

After the beauty of the fifteenth day, Mochihito awakened on the morning of the sixteenth to gray clouds and threatening rain. From his window, the gardens were obscured by mist. He regretted missing his sleep and was irritable and surly, impatient with his music, his poetry, and all the other pleasures he usually enjoyed. The day was inauspicious in every way.

Early in the evening, he was handed an elegantly folded message that had been brushed on thick scarlet paper and sealed with wax. The messenger, who insisted on delivering the scarlet packet personally, waited for him to read it.

"Must you hover over me," snapped the prince. "I have your letter. Please leave."

"I am sorry, Your Highness, I am ordered to stay with you till you have read the message."

"What is your name? Who sent you?" The prince clutched the letter to his breast. His mouth was pinched resentfully, his voice shrill.

"My name is Ietaka. The message will explain." Ietaka looked unhappily at the prince. What a sorry sight, he thought.

"Well, please leave me till I've read it. You may wait

outside." Mochihito fluttered the hand with the letter, indicating the door.

Ietaka withdrew. His bulky figure was covered by a shapeless brown cloak unmarked by crest or decoration. His round, usually smiling face was grim. He heard a moan of anguish from the other side of the screen. The prince had read the message.

The door slid open. Mochihito's smooth unlined face was a mask of despair, eyes staring wildly from under painted brows. "Disaster," he mumbled. "Do you know what this message contains?" The letter trembled in his hands.

"Yes, I come directly from Fukuhara where Yorimasa instructed me to help you in any way I can."

"What does this mean? What can we do?" whined the prince.

"Your Highness, I am no more accustomed to this than you. I am one of the lowly Minamoto representatives on the Imperial Council. Though I am not a man of action, Yorimasa has entrusted me to help you flee at once. We must travel east to the monastery at Miidera. From there, the abbot will furnish us with an escort to Nara where seven thousand warrior-monks are waiting to ensure our safety till Yoritomo overthrows the Taira."

"How much time do I have?"

"None, I'm afraid. Lord Chikara left Fukuhara soon after I did. At present, he is in Kyoto commanding Kiyomori's Kyoto garrisons. I expect they are already on their way with instructions to take you into custody."

"My flutes! I must have my flutes." Tears streamed down the prince's soft cheeks.

"Hurry then!" Ietaka watched impatiently as Mochihito searched for his flutes. Time was being lost, critical moments if they were to escape alive. Ietaka's voice was urgent as he interrupted the search. "Who else is in this part of the palace?" he asked.

"Only my foster brother, Munenobu," said the prince over his shoulder.

"Call him. He will have to help. Our only chance of

escape is in disguise. If we pass the enemy on the road we cannot afford to be recognized."

"How can we do that?"

"You will disguise yourself as a woman. Your foster brother and I will be your attendants. Call him!"

In seconds, Munenobu was in the room. He stared aghast at Ietaka and tried to leave when he heard the plan. "It is madness," he cried. "We have to surrender."

"Impossible! Surrender would mean exile or even death for the prince and the end of Yoritomo's plans," said Ietaka.

"What do I care for his plans? I want nothing to do with this," cried Munenobu.

"Brother, it is imperative that you help me. I shall reward you generously when we are safe. Come, there is no time to waste." Prince Mochihito undid his hair as he spoke. It hung loose in a black cloud around the pale pudding of his face and changed his appearance completely. He sent his foster brother to find a woman's cloak while he added powder to his face.

Munenobu returned with a cherry colored Chinese jacket, a golden yellow under-robe and a white silk over-robe. In minutes the transformation was complete. Mochihito's spirits rose as he found himself completely transformed by these delightful garments.

"Munenobu, hold a parasol over me," Mochihito said, imitating a lady's high voice. "And you, Ietaka, take this bag of my personal articles; carry it on your head, as befits a servant." He placed a wide-brimmed straw hat over his black hair, pulling it low to cover his eyes. It was a perfect imitation of a wealthy townswoman traveling with her personal retainer and a servant.

The three fugitives escaped from the rear of the palace just as a troop of Imperial Guards noisily arrived at the gate. Like three shadows they slipped silently down the street toward the eastern wall. They could still hear the uproar as they hurried across the Kamo River bridge. Even on the other side they did not feel safe. Ghosts of other fugitives drove them onward, away from the roads and into the hills surrounding Kyoto.

It was a long and tortuous route. The prince and his foster brother wore light sandals, suitable for a stroll on the palace grounds; here, in the rocky foothills, with rain beginning to fall, the sandals were almost worthless. The prince cried in pain and frustration as he cut his tender feet on the sharp rocks and twigs that littered the way. He left a trail of dark stains soaking into the moist earth as he struggled onward. Their cloaks were torn by the underbrush and saturated by the rain, but the three travelers held them together for the little protection they afforded against the chill spring air.

The sky was lightening over Lake Biwa when they staggered down the final track to the monastery. From a distance, it seemed a small unpretentious place. As they drew closer, they realized it was actually a mighty, moat-encircled fortress.

The rain stopped, and the sun broke through the clouds. Ietaka, followed by a tearful Mochihito and a sullen Munenobu, staggered across the bridge to Miidera's inner courtyard. They were quickly surrounded by warrior-monks and escorted into the monastery, where the abbot awaited them.

Forty-six

The fugitives were given baths and clothing—the prince insisted on a fresh white silk robe—before being brought to the central dining hall. There, dry and clean, at last, they drank cups of green tea and told the abbot of their escape from Takakura Palace.

The abbot listened intently. When they concluded, he nodded and pursed his lips. "We expected you," he said. "Yorimasa was wise to send you east to us. You never would have escaped by going straight to Nara. The south is now an inauspicious direction and will remain so for several days."

The custom of directional taboos guided much of the travel among the nobility. It was because southerly travel was taboo during the week of the fifteenth that Yorimasa had planned the flight eastward and had sent a messenger ahead to prepare the abbot for Mochihito's arrival. The abbot paused as he noticed the expression on Mochihito's soft face. "Have no fear," he reassured him. "We can hide you till my chart shows it safe to march south." He hesitated again. "Then we will have to face the problem of an escort for your party. Unfortunately, the monastery cannot furnish enough troops to ensure your safety once you are on the road."

"Without the protection of your monks, how will we get to Nara? The roads will be filled with Taira spies," said Ietaka.

"I am sorry," said the abbot. "I can provide you with thirty of my warriors as guards, no more. Our mutual friend, Yorimasa, will be here before nightfall. He comes with his sons and a troop of Minamoto warriors. Perhaps he will know a way."

"We are undone," whimpered Mochihito, wiping his cheek with his silken sleeve. He was disconsolate and spent the afternoon with Munenobu crying and complaining of the fates which had treated him so harshly.

In the evening, Yorimasa appeared. In place of his usual monk's robe, he wore warrior's armor over a long-sleeved court cloak. He was accompanied by his two sons. Nakatsuna, the older, was a tall, burly man with the sloping shoulders of a wrestler. His legs were tree-trunk thick and bowed from a life on horseback. He wore black armor over red brocade, in contrast to his younger brother, Kanetsuna, who dressed in orange Chinese silk over royal blue. Kanetsuna was a younger version of his father—tall and wiry, with Yorimasa's deep-set eyes and a hard, hatchet-thin face. Behind them rode only one company of mounted soldiers—less than fifty men!

Yorimasa was furious at the abbot's inability to mount sufficient troops from among the warrior-monks. He had expected several hundred monks to join him. Yorimasa accused the abbot of betraying him and warned of Yoritomo's wrath.

The abbot hung his head in shame. "I am sorry, Lord Yorimasa. We do not have the authority to levy monks from other monasteries, and here we have barely enough men to protect ourselves against the marauders from the forest." He looked up gravely, his eyes pleading for understanding. "I said I could spare thirty men. . . . Perhaps I could let you have a dozen more. That is all I can do."

"Will you protect us till I can arrange for more troops?"

"With our lives, my lord," promised the abbot.

Yorimasa settled beside Ietaka. He evoked the image of a caged tiger as he stared balefully across the monastery courtyard. "I have seven thousand warrior-monks waiting for us in Nara," he growled. "All useless if we cannot reach them." He banged a fist on the low table. "Sooner or later, Chikara will discover where we have taken sanctuary. Meanwhile, we are trapped until travel south becomes auspicious. And, even then, we dare not brave the roads without sufficient escort. Even another handful of soldiers would help—"

"Sire, I have a thought," interrupted Ietaka.

The old man turned to him. "Any thought is worth considering," he said.

"I have a cousin in Sarashina who owns a martial arts academy. He has, among his students, many well-trained monks. If I ride north through the mountains and ask for his help, he might be willing to aid us."

"If he has enough men, and if we can convince him to help. What is the name of your cousin's academy?"

"Ichikawa was the original owner. My cousin, Tadamori Yoshi, is now the master."

"A fine school. I know of it." Yorimasa rubbed his bony fingers along his jaw. His eyes narrowed thoughtfully. "What can we offer this Yoshi to induce him to come to our aid? He is a Tadamori, and except for you, the family is among the most loyal supporters of Kiyomori."

"Sire, this Tadamori does not support the Taira. True, he has never taken an active part against them, but he has always hoped for a chance to avenge a wrong done him by Lord Chikara. When I tell him Chikara is in charge of the enemy, he will leave everything to join our cause."

"Sarashina? It is a difficult journey. Perhaps I should send one of my sons." Yorimasa studied Ietaka's unathletic figure. It would be disastrous if this slim chance failed because Ietaka did not return before the Taira discovered the prince's whereabouts.

"Yoshi will listen to no one else. We have not seen each other often these past years, but I know I can count on his friendship."

"We shall reward him with gold!"

"No! He is not motivated by wealth. . . . However, your influence could get him appointed to the Council; that would be enough." Ietaka felt that this time he could convince Yoshi that the Council would give him an opportunity for revenge. If Yorimasa could arrange it, Yoshi would become a valuable ally of the Minamoto, and Ietaka would be reunited with his cousin. It would be a good bargain.

"Done! You know that once my part in this adventure becomes known, I will no longer have influence at the court, but there are others who will carry on our cause. Tonight, I will send a message to a friend in the capital who will start the preparations, so on your return you will be able to arrange for Tadamori Yoshi's admittance to the Council.

"Now, take our finest horse and set out for Sarashina. May Amida Buddha travel with you, for all our sakes."

A horse was saddled. It was chosen for its dark brown color to make it hard to see in the forest. Ietaka pulled a black cloak over his other clothing and strapped a sword at his side. The ride would be dangerous. He would avoid trouble, if he could; he would face it, if necessary.

The spirited animal snorted, daintily lifted its legs, and broke into a brisk trot. Ietaka took one last look behind him to the courtyard where the monks were chanting sutras in unison. Smoke from dinner fires filled the air; Ietaka smelled the odor of damp wood burning as he rode through the ornate wooden gate, over the bridge, and through a field of purple thistle flowers. Once on the mountain track, he spurred his horse into a full gallop under the menacing pine trees.

Forty-seven

"Hold the sword in line with your body. It has to become part of your arm. When you move, a combination of the blade and your *chi*, inner power, is guided in the direction of the enemy. This technique is called the dragon fly. Notice how my sword moves in a circular pattern, while my body acts in concert with the movement." Yoshi stepped through the action, the glittering steel making a pattern around him, a phantom pattern that covered every direction. The class stood at attention, watching the details of his performance, trying to absorb the subtleties of his movements.

As he finished the demonstration, he became aware of Tofushi, at the edge of the practice area, politely trying to catch his attention. He frowned. During class only the most extraordinary of emergencies were permitted to interfere with the routine.

"What is it, Tofushi?" he asked brusquely.

"A dusty stranger insists on speaking to you immediately! He says he is a friend."

"Where is he?"

"He awaits your attention in the office."

"Please take my place." Yoshi bowed to Tofushi and to the class before leaving the floor.

"Ietaka!" he exclaimed on seeing the haggard rider.

"What are you doing here? Sit down, please. Have some tea. Let me call a servant."

"No. No. Yoshi, listen! There is no time. I need you to help me as I once helped you." Ietaka's voice was urgent. He clutched at Yoshi's arm, pulling him toward the door. Yoshi could see a vein throbbing in his pale forehead; Ietaka was close to collapse.

"Anything you ask," said Yoshi. "If it is in my power, consider it done. However, you ought to rest first. Look at you—you are exhausted. When did you sleep last?"

"That's unimportant. I have been on the road for two nights without sleep or food. Nonetheless we must leave at once."

"Not till you rest. You will be serving us both best if you relax before you speak." Yoshi led Ietaka to a small table where he made him sit. He ordered the young man who managed the household chores to bring tea while Ietaka fidgeted in an agony of impatience.

They sipped the bitter brew as Ietaka described the situation in Miidera. He concluded by asking Yoshi to ride with a party of his advanced students to help escort Mochihito from Miidera to Nara. "If we can protect him on this thirty-mile trip, the warrior-monks of Nara will see that he is safe. The entire Yoritomo cause is at stake. I will ride with you as far as the Kamo River, then slip back into Kyoto to protect my position on the council."

"Who is our opposition?"

Ietaka's head hung wearily. "Your old enemy, Chikara . . . at the head of twenty-eight thousand troops."

"And you want me to escort the prince with thirty students, a handful of monks, and one company of Yorimasa's soldiers?" Yoshi asked softly.

Ietaka nodded. "I wouldn't ask if you weren't our last hope. I will understand if you say no. After all, this is not your battle."

"A chance to thwart Chikara?" Yoshi stopped for a moment, studying his cousin's face. "I will call for volunteers from among those who have mounts. I cannot speak for my students, but you can count on me . . . even if I have to face the twenty-eight thousand alone.''

Ietaka brightened. The mask of fatigue that swelled his eyes and made his round face haggard lifted, and for a moment he smiled. "You are a true friend," he said.

That afternoon, under a blazing spring sun, thirty armored warrior-monk students rode from the *dojo* on their way south. Yoshi and Ietaka were in the vanguard. Yoshi wore black armor laced with Chinese leather over a robe of scarlet brocade. His gray horse was lightly armored and ornamented with powdered gold lacquer. Next to him, black-cloaked Ietaka presented a stark picture on his dark brown horse.

Behind them rode the leader of the student group, a warrior in his own right who had come from the Miidera monastery to take advanced training with Yoshi. He was Tsutsui-no-Jomyo-Meishu. Meishu had a flat, broad-cheeked face that bespoke physical strength. He wore his own armor laced with black over a patterned robe. On his head was a five-plated helmet, and on his back, a black-lacquered bow with twenty-four arrows. A white handled *naginata*, its five-foot-long hardwood shaft tipped by a nine-inch crescent of sharp steel was in his hand, and two swords hung at his side. He rode proudly on a jet black horse, followed by the troop of warrior-monks.

Yoshi was in high spirits. The thought of facing Chikara and overwhelming odds, instead of inspiring fear, gave him a feeling of exultation. He tried to engage Ietaka in conversation until he saw that Ietaka preferred silence. Yoshi attributed Ietaka's taciturnity to fatigue and spurred a few feet ahead where he absorbed himself in his surroundings, feasting his eyes on the greenery and sniffing the crisp country air.

As they reached the foothills of the first mountain range, Ietaka caught up. "Yoshi. Forgive me. I have been lost in my own thoughts." Overhead, three birds circled aimlessly on the warm currents that rose from the mountain side. Maple leaves spotted the ground and moist red berries were crushed by the horses' hooves as they rode under the trees.

"That's all right, old friend. It is a glorious day, and I was enjoying the scenery and thinking of our mission."

"Yoshi, before this unfortunate affair, I had already determined to seek you out in Sarashina." The movement of the horse caused Ietaka's head to bob tiredly up and down; a fine coating of perspiration covered his forehead. The fatigue that had built up during the ride to Sarashina had taken its toll; his resources were at a low ebb and he spoke in disjointed sentences, blurting disordered words and thoughts. "I know you hold yourself away from joining our struggles against the Taira. The time is coming when you will have to choose sides. Kiyomori's popularity is at a new low. He is sick and floundering. You know the cloistered Emperor compelled him to accept some of us into the Imperial Council. Now he has taken a new tack. Chikara, under Kiyomori's instructions, has killed two of our Council members. He insults them; then, when they respond, he challenges them to a duel. Our men are not warriors; they are politicians. If we could convince you to join us, Chikara's councillors would have to stop their murderous tactics. Yoshi, we need you on our side."

Ietaka's sincerity was apparent in his words. Yet Yoshi felt the request was unreasonable. He said, "I am sorry, Ietaka, my responsibility is to my academy. Though I sympathize with you, I have no interest in politics. I am tempted when you tell me Chikara is at the heart of this, but I am not prepared to live as a court politician. Anyway," he continued, "I would be an outsider at the court. There would be no legal way for me to help you."

Ietaka shifted in his saddle. He hesitated for a few moments then spoke rapidly, urgently. "I have a confession to make—with Yorimasa's help, I have started the process of appointing you to the Council."

"Impossible!" said Yoshi, vehemently.

They rode in silence except for the hoofbeats of the horses and the jingle of arms and armor. Ietaka's head nodded wearily on his chest. His haggard eyes were fixed on the road.

The warrior-monk, Meishu, spurred his horse abreast of Yoshi's. "The crossroad is coming soon," he said. "The messenger will leave us there. It is the last turn-off before Miidera."

It had been a long, hard ride. Yoshi reflected that in his youth the trip would have taken three weeks by oxcart. Now it took only a day and a night. He turned to Ietaka. "Up ahead, at the crossroads, we will separate." Yoshi's tone was cool. He was annoyed with his cousin for having presumed too much and angry with himself for having refused. It was not fair to be put in this position, the business of the Taira council was not his affair.

Ietaka nodded numbly. "Thank you for what you are doing," he said. "Please take care of the prince and yourself. If all goes well, I still hope to see you in Fukuhara . . . if you are not too late. . . ."

"Too late? Too late for what?" asked Yoshi, filled with sudden apprehension. There was desperation in Ietaka's expression.

"Nothing. I am tired and don't know what I am saying."

"Tell me! Too late for what?"

"You have enough to think about with Yorimasa and the prince. I don't want to burden you further." Ietaka turned his face away.

"Nonsense. Speak up before we separate."

"If you fail in this mission, it will not matter. . . ." Ietaka's voice trailed off.

"I do not understand."

"Oh, Yoshi," Ietaka said with a hopeless sigh. "I am next in line for Chikara's sword. Though he is my brother-in-law and Nami has tried to intervene on my behalf, he is determined to remove me from the Council. He insults me daily. How long can I turn the other cheek and ignore the insults? How long can I accept this demeaning conduct?" Ietaka paused. "You see, my cause is hopeless. Even if you joined me tomorrow, it would probably be too late to help me." He held up a hand to keep Yoshi from interrupting. "Because of me, you are risking your life for the Minamoto cause. I cannot ask you to do more. Forget what I said. . . . I must solve my own problems."

Yoshi rode, oblivious to the beauty of the scene that spread before him. It was near the hour of the dog, eight o'clock, and the setting sun reflected golden lights from the deep blue surface of Lake Biwa. Purple flowering bushes far below made a dark carpet leading to Miidera's high gate and curved bridge. The monastery towers pierced the azure sky in serrated rows. On the temple grounds, groups of monks walked and gathered like black-feathered crows, unaware of the approaching warriors.

Meishu rode at Yoshi's side. From time to time he glanced at his *sensei* and wondered what had happened to make him so pensive.

Yoshi's heart and mind were with Ietaka. Once he had told Ietaka to ask for his help when it was needed. Now Ietaka needed him, and Yoshi could not refuse. He could not allow another member of his family—and one of his few friends—to perish at the hands of his nemesis. The longer his life continued, the more he found it inextricably interwoven with the life of Chikara. He saw himself continuously dancing to Chikara's tune. Chikara, Chikara! The name ran like a refrain in his mind. Always hiding and running from Chikara. Since Genkai's death, he had made two lives for himself, and each time his nemesis had made him a fugitive.

No more! No more running. He had promised Ietaka he would accept the Council post. When they had parted at the crossroads, he had spoken with misgivings, unhappy at the choice imposed upon him. Now he knew it had been the right choice. If he lived to deliver Mochihito to Nara, he would become a Council member, and the time predicted by Ichikawa would be at hand. He would meet Chikara face to face.

He was suddenly brought back to the moment by the shouts of a sentry.

"We have arrived," said Meishu.

Forty-eight

"Tonight! We must leave tonight." The thin old man repeated the words forcefully.

"My men are tired. They need rest, and they need time to feed their horses. We will have to curb our impatience; in the end, we will accomplish more if we act with restraint now," said Yoshi.

"Every hour the enemy draws closer. Nevertheless, you are right. I bow to your wisdom and welcome you to our cause." Yorimasa nodded his approval. "We will leave before midnight. When the bells ring the hour, we shall be in the forest on the way to Nara."

"Agreed, sire."

Yoshi had the horses tethered and fed; then he ordered his men to rest. He returned to Yorimasa and his sons, burly Nakatsuna and wiry Kanetsuna. "You are Tademori-no-Fumio's godson?" asked the old man. When Yoshi bowed in assent he continued. "Why have you allied yourself with us on this hopeless mission?"

"A chance to repay my cousin for a favor and a chance to avenge myself on an enemy," answered Yoshi. He asked in turn, "You are a minister of high rank in the court and a trusted friend of the regent—why do you risk your life in this cause?"

"My life is behind me," replied the old man. "I have many regrets for past deeds but none for what I do now. Once my inaction lost the Hōgen War for my Minamoto family. How often my sleeve has been wet since that day!

"Now I will redeem myself. For years, I turned a false face of friendship to Kiyomori, while I secretly supported Yoritomo. The irony and pathos of it is that the old poet, Yorimasa, will die in this adventure, a Minamoto soldier to the last." He smiled mirthlessly.

Yorimasa's eldest son, the thick-necked Nakatsuna, said in a quiet, firm voice, "No need to speak of dying, Father. We shall prevail and return to Kyoto in triumph at the head of Yoritomo's armies."

The prince and his foster brother were pacing the main room while Yorimasa and his sons conferred with Yoshi.

"I am very nervous about all this. I can't rest even for a moment," whined the prince.

"Nor I," said Munenobu. "I find the company of these crude warriors appalling. We should give ourselves up. Kiyomori would never dare do us harm. Exile would be better than this."

"Do you think so? All would have been perfect if Kiyomori hadn't discovered our plans. I wonder who could have told him. So few people knew—"

Munenobu quickly interrupted. "Why don't you play your flute?" he suggested. "It would cheer us on this dreary day."

The prince immediately brightened, all thought of betrayal forgotten. He played softly, starting with light happy dances of the rice festivals. Gradually the music slowed and became sad until Munenobu begged him to stop. "Rather than lighten my spirits, your music makes me grieve for our past happiness," said Munenobu. "I find its beauty unbearably poignant. Please . . . for my sake . . . no more."

The prince acquiesced. He carefully placed the flute inside his white under-robe while his sad-eyed foster brother watched him.

Shortly before the temple bells signaled midnight, Yoshi

and Yorimasa woke Meishu; together they went to waken the sleeping warriors.

Except for the swish of cotton cloaks and the faint tinkling of metal as armor and swords were girded in place, it was silent in the monastery. The monks had long before finished their evening sutras and retired to their dormitory quarters.

"Did you rest well, Your Highness?" Yoshi asked the prince.

"I couldn't rest. Not a bit. I am too anxious to finish with this entire nasty business," was the prince's surly answer.

Yorimasa and his sons led the band of warriors. Mochihito and Munenobu rode in the center of the group, on the gentlest horses available—the prince was an inexperienced rider and feared the great war mounts. Yoshi and Meishu were advanced scouts, ranging back and forth, checking for signs of danger. All the riders, except Mochihito, wore dark, soft cloaks over their armor to cut the reflections of the crescent moon and to muffle the sound of metal on metal. Mochihito insisted on wearing his white silk robe as a sign of his divine status. Yorimasa conferred with Yoshi as to the advisability of insisting the prince cover himself like the others. They decided that the value to morale of the prince's apparent bravery, even though it was motivated by vanity, was worth the risk of discovery. Dark-cloaked riders would surround the prince to keep the white robe from betraying them to enemy eyes.

The band followed the rocky shore of Lake Biwa toward the town of Otsu. They skirted the town, then quietly crossed the Tokaido Road and disappeared into the midnight darkness of the mountain forests.

The second time the prince fell from his mount, it became obvious to Yorimasa that it was impossible to continue on the mountain route. He conferred with Yoshi and Meishu. Meishu suggested following the banks of the Uji River. The river was deep and rough with many tributaries branching off to the south and east; by staying on the northwest bank, the prince and his escort would have a comparatively smooth trip.

Although the route was not as direct, it would lead them to the town of Uji, almost halfway to Nara. From there, the last leg was only fifteen miles long and offered safe passage in the level fields that stretched from the road to the surrounding mountains. They would be able to ride quickly and safely, while avoiding the main highway.

"Let us go that way then," decided Yorimasa. "Chikara and his troops are well on their way to Miidera by now. We need to reach the garrisons of Nara before they cut us off."

Pressing their mounts as much as they dared in the dim moonlight, the men eventually reached Uji. The prince fell several more times, and rather than risk serious injury to him, Yorimasa decided that despite the danger of being overtaken the party would stop to rest at the Byōdō-in on the far side of the Uji bridge.

The Byōdō-in was a residence built over a century earlier for a cloistered Fujiwara Emperor. For many years it had been used as a chapel by the Miidera monks. Its graceful roofs rose in ornate splendor from the shores of the Uji River. The grounds were surrounded by tall, straight birch trees that reared white trunks like guardians in the moonlight. In front of the chapel, blossoming cherry trees covered the river with fallen white petals that rushed like lost souls on the current.

As a precaution against a surprise attack by their pursuers, Yorimasa ordered the monks to dismantle all except the approach and the framework of the Uji bridge. The river beneath was wide enough and the current strong enough to discourage anyone but a madman from trying to ford it.

The moon disappeared and a rainstorm developed as they worked. Thunder rumbled and lightning flared. Heavy rain flooded the already engorged Uji River.

Forty-nine

===

Lord Chikara was resplendent in full battle armor. His dark, hawk face glared out from under a horned helmet. His white, lamellar armor was laced with maroon leather; a white twill cape painted with a scene of two dragons battling in a sea of clouds covered his back. Two swords hung from his waist, and a lacquered bow was fastened to his maroon and gold saddle.

Chikara held his white horse firmly in position while he signaled the troops to hasten. His mouth was a thin, hard line, his jaw clenched to hide his impatience as the cumbersome ranks of warriors slowly reversed direction. Because spies had informed him that the prince was at Miidera, he had led an army of twenty-eight thousand men on a hard, fast night march, only to find their victim had escaped.

He would have burned Miidera to the ground if he had had his way, but Kiyomori had ordered him to move carefully in dealing with the monks. It would be a race to Nara. If Mochihito and his escort arrived there first, all would be lost.

"Faster, captains! Get those men moving!" It took a supreme effort of will to stop the muscle in his cheek from twitching.

"Yes, sire." The captains rode back and forth shouting at the troops to move faster. Even so, the noise of twenty-eight thousand men and fifteen thousand horses, tightly packed on a dark and narrow road, made it difficult to hear the commands. Horses snorted and scraped, armor and weapons jangled, and men cursed and called for instructions.

The army was a hastily gathered, ill-disciplined mass of three thousand foot soldiers, fifteen thousand mounted samurai—many disgruntled at having been routed out of their warm futons and forced to march with little prospect of reward—and almost ten thousand grooms and retainers, who followed behind their masters' horses and added to the confusion by running between the horses, at their masters' command, in an attempt to discover why some troops were turning while others held fast.

Over an hour passed before the mile-long column reversed itself. The noise and confusion, the billowing dust from the horses' hooves, and the darkness of the night made it impossible to maneuver quickly. The moon, which earlier had been shining brightly, now took to hiding its crescent face behind thick low clouds. The column had come five miles from Kyoto in under an hour and now had to retrace their steps—in absolute darkness—almost back to the capital. No matter how hard the captains pushed the troops, it took two more hours before they reached the fork in the road that turned south toward Nara. Here the route was older, and the troops made even slower time.

Chikara was in an agony of frustration, cursing and goading his captains to greater effort. "I will reward the first man to reach the prince," he promised, spurring his horse up and down the column.

The clouds suddenly burst, driving rain onto the men and horses. They were soon covered with mud, stirred and splashed by thousands of hooves. The foot soldiers muttered unhappily while the mounted samurai cursed aloud—many had been on horseback in full armor for five hours.

With the first streaks of morning light, the rain stopped, and the advance scouts reached the Uji River. They spied the encampment of Yorimasa and Prince Mochihito and, immediately taking the initiative, shouted their war cry three times—the customary warning before joining battle.

The prince's men, resting in front of the soaring facade of Byōdō-in, leaped to their feet to answer the challenge.

Chikara heard the shouts from his position at the side of the leading company of horsemen. "Charge!" he shouted, digging his spurs into his horse's flank and pulling his sword from its scabbard. "Gold to the first man to reach them!"

The order to charge was enthusiastically echoed by the company commanders as the vast army surged forward to greet the handful of the enemy. The troops blindly galloped in the semidarkness, ignoring the road, churning up mud and dew-heavy grass. The first group arrived at the bank; they saw the dismantled bridge and the Uji River below with its current carrying bits of twig, cherry blossoms, and the detritus of the long, spring flood season. They turned back to scream a warning. "Stop!" they shouted. "The bridge is gone. The river is in flood. Stop before it is too late!"

A few of the riders in the next ranks heard their warnings over the rush of the river and the thunder of the hooves, but they were unable to turn or stop, so powerful was the onrush of riders pressing from the rear.

"Lord Chikara!" cried one of his captains. "The horsemen are being driven into the river!"

If Chikara heard, he gave no sign. His mouth was distorted in a scream of triumph. "Charge!" he shouted again and again. "I want their heads." He heard the screams of the men in the vanguard and assumed they were the cries of battle.

"Take them! Take them!" he ordered, waving the troops on with his sword.

In the forward companies, horses and riders tumbled into the swollen Uji and were carried off as though they were no heavier than the cherry blossoms that floated on the surface.

Fifty men, a hundred, a hundred fifty, kicked, struggled, and screamed as they were pushed into the rushing waters. Chikara finally reached the bank and took in the scene of devastation. He spun his horse around to order the troops to stop. Those who heard him, reined in their mounts; horses with all four hooves planted in the earth were still inexorably driven off the bank.

Twenty-five more, then fifty. More than two hundred horses and riders were lost to the Uji before Chikara's order to stop was obeyed.

The sun moved higher; bright beams shone through the broken clouds on the blossom-speckled black waters. No sign remained of the horsemen who had been swept away.

Chikara was filled with rage. The enemy was almost in his hands, yet still beyond his reach.

Horsemen milled about on the riverbank, cursing and waving their fists at the handful of monks standing just beyond arrow range.

Fifty

===

The waters of the Uji were an apparently impassible barrier. Chikara and his captains rode up and down the ranks of horsemen, shouting orders to the forward companies.

"Dismount! Move the horses back. Bring the strongest archers to the front!" Chikara's voice was almost lost between the noise of the horsemen and of the Uji. Order was finally restored, and the company captain carried out his commands.

Two hundred archers took up positions on the east bank. Their leader, Kazusa-no-Kami Tadakiyo, sent off the formal humming arrow that announced the challenge. It was answered by the humming arrow of Meishu. The battle was joined. The width of the Uji prevented the Taira bowmen from taking their full toll. Their arrows were spent by the time they reached the far bank and were easily turned by the warrior-monks' armor.

Each samurai in Chikara's force carried twenty-four arrows; as each man shot his last, he was replaced by another. Throughout the long morning, Chikara's archers kept the prince and his escort pinned down near the Byodo-in.

Yorimasa called Yoshi to him. Yoshi hastened to where Yorimasa, helmet in hand, stood with his white hair waving like a pennant of defiance in the river breeze. "They will not be stupid enough to continue this through the day," said Yorimasa. "Even their great army will eventually exhaust their supply of arrows. Soon they will seek methods to ford the river. We must keep them angry and off balance as long as we can. Given time, the monks of Nara will come to our aid of their own volition. Meanwhile, I am considering another plan whereby the prince can escape to freedom."

Yoshi bowed respectfully. "How can we do more?" he asked.

The old man scratched his jaw. "Send a challenger to face their champion in single combat."

"I shall challenge him myself," said Yoshi.

"No. No. I prefer you to stay at my side. Do we have anyone else strong enough to fight their champion to a standstill?"

"My best is Meishu. He is the equal of any Taira." Yoshi pointed proudly to where Meishu, at the head of the warrior-monks, exchanged arrows with the Taira. Yorimasa saw that Meishu pulled a bow over fifteen handbreadths, where the Taira archers only pulled thirteen. The power of his arrows was having an effect on the enemy. Meishu's body armor was only dented where enemy arrows struck, while his arrows were piercing armor and mortally wounding those they hit. Yorimasa nodded approval at Meishu's strength and bravery. "Call him," he told Yoshi. Yoshi bowed and, unmindful of the arrows that fell around him, hurried to Meishu's side.

"Meishu, will you challenge their best man to single combat?" asked Yoshi.

"Gladly, *Sensei*. No one can equal me today. I feel supernatural power in my arm. Give me the chance and I will prove myself," replied Meishu with a tight-lipped smile.

"Very well. You shall have your chance. Fight hard and keep their man engaged as long as possible. We need to gain time in the hope that the relief force will arrive from Nara."

"I shall fight long and hard. When I have killed their greatest champion, I will challenge the next. I cannot tell how many thousand there are, but if necessary, I will fight every one in turn.''

Yoshi clasped Meishu's shoulder. ''Spoken like a brave soldier,'' he said. He stepped back and bowed solemnly. ''Go now, and give the challenge.''

Meishu ordered his band of monks to put their arrows in their quivers and stand back. He removed his helmet, walked to the edge of the bridge with his arms outstretched, and shouted to be heard over the sound of the river. He easily avoided the few arrows that flew around him. Gradually the archers stopped and waited to hear him speak.

Meishu was silent for one minute . . . two. . . . The enemy forces shifted nervously, an empty bowstring twanged to fend off evil spirits. ''My name is Tsutsui-no-Jomyo Meishu. Some of you see me standing here alone. Those who cannot see will hear my voice,'' he roared at last. ''I am a priest of Miidera, descendant in ten generations of the great warrior, Hidesato, who defeated Taira Masakado in Shimosa to win fame throughout the ten provinces. Is there one among you who has not heard of Meishu, the warrior-monk who is worth a thousand samurai? Is there one among you foolhardy enough to challenge me in single combat?''

Meishu folded his arms across his breastplate and stared haughtily at the enemy.

He did not have to wait long.

A dappled grey warhorse pulled out of the ranks and daintily stepped onto what was left of the bridge approach. The horse was in full armor, its saddle painted sky blue with a gold-leaf sun. The rider sat tall and straight in his red armor with black lacings. He wore a helmet with two metal horns and was armed with two swords, a *naginata*, and a red-lacquered bow.

''My name is Motozane. I am nineteen years old. My family comes from the great Omuro, who defeated the pirate, Sumitomo, and won land and riches for our family twelve generations ago. I fear no man. Since my family still owes much to Taira Kiyomori, I stand ready to meet any warrior of the Minamoto who dares face me.''

With this pronouncement, young Motozane dismounted and, five-foot *naginata* in hand, walked to the edge of the bridge platform. There he stood above the torrential waters, only a wood beam between him and his enemy.

Meishu donned his helmet, adjusted the neck plates and strode to his side of the bridge. He removed his foot-gear and leaped to the bridge support. With his bare feet holding the narrow beam he walked over the boiling river as if he were strolling down Suzaku-Ōji in Kyoto.

His young opponent, seeing this act of bravery and not to be outdone, immediately removed his own foot-gear. He jumped on the beam and hurried to meet Meishu at the middle.

As a courtesy, Meishu waited, his own *naginata*, its crescent tip gleaming wickedly, held crosswise in front of his body. He allowed Motozane the first attack, a lightning sweep of the long shaft toward Meishu's legs. Normally a move calculated only to disconcert an opponent and throw him off balance, it was a deadly technique on the narrow beam, since it was too low to be effectively blocked. Only one course of action was open to Meishu. He took it. As the shaft swept at his feet he leaped high in the air with his knees tucked upward toward his chest. The shaft passed under him with a swishing sound audible even over the roar of the deadly water.

Meishu landed like a cat; his bare toes clung to the old wood. His own *naginata* was already in motion. With blinding speed he drove the blade-end downward using his left hand on the haft as a fulcrum, his right hand pushing the shaft down as though it were a lever. Motozane blocked upward, and Meishu's strike broke through his *naginata* at its center. Motozane faltered, then recovered quickly enough to draw his long sword. He could have avoided the next cross-strike by stepping backwards, but to do so would have been an admission of defeat. He held his position, trying to block Meishu's whistling *naginata* with his sword.

Too late!

The nine-inch blade at the end of the weapon, traveling at tremendous speed, smashed into his helmet. The armor held, though one of the horns flew off to turn end over end on its way into the river. Motozane's toes closed convulsively on the beam in an attempt to regain his balance. Even as he fell, Motozane tried to strike at Meishu with his long sword. He spun outward—the red armor a drop of blood that hung in midair for the space of a heartbeat—then splashed and disappeared beneath the surface of the Uji.

Chikara, who had watched his champion from the shore, was furious. "Ten pieces of gold," he shouted, "to the man who kills the monk!"

Half a hundred samurai simultaneously leaped from their horses and kicked off their footgear. They raced to the bridge, some with swords, some with *naginatas*, according to their preference. Where the bridge ended, the beam allowed only one combatant at a time. All discipline forgotten, the samurai fought among themselves for the honor and the promised reward.

Meishu waited on the span, his mind alert to every nuance of his surroundings. The sky had turned cerulean blue, and the sun was already past its zenith. A vee of wild geese flew overhead, honking like lost souls. The thousands of horses that crowded the approach to the bridge stamped and snuffed nervously on the far shore.

The first samurai reached the center. In his eagerness he lost his footing before he finished his first stroke. His place was immediately taken by a second, who suffered the same fate. The third man was more cautious. He moved out carefully, sword extended. He was met by a furious attack. Meishu seemed as comfortable on the six-inch beam as if he were practicing in the *dojo*. The *naginata* struck once, twice, three times before the careful samurai was able to counter. He spun downward to join his comrades.

The fourth attacker came in a flurry of sword play. He lashed out in a frenzy, with no regard for his own life. Meishu easily avoided the first assault saving his strength and stalling for time. This madman would surely slip and fall to the river.

Meishu was right, but before the fourth man fell, a lucky stroke of his blade cut through Meishu's *naginata*, removing the blade end. He threw away the useless shaft and drew his sword in time to meet the next attacker.

The next eight men were met by a dizzying display of sword technique. Meishu used the zigzag style, the cross, the waterwheel, the figure-eight, the interlacing, and the reversed dragonfly to dispatch them, one by one, into the river.

The thirteenth man came in quickly with his head down. Meishu struck a two-handed blow aimed at the center of the helmet bowl. The helmet gave way and the blade split the samurai's skull, spraying brains and blood into the clear air; the blade continued downward into his breastbone where it caught fast. As the victim fell from the bridge, Meishu's blade, trapped in the chest cavity, was twisted and broken off at the hilt.

Meishu drew back, wiping sweat from his face. He had fought well and defeated thirteen opponents. Live or die, his reputation as a warrior would be assured for future generations. For a long, silent moment no one approached the bridge. Then, with a battle cry, men sprang to the beam to challenge Meishu once more. He drew his short sword and, even with this great disadvantage, managed to defeat the next five men by fighting with berserker fury.

Wounded in several places, Meishu still held the bridge when Yoshi came up on the beam and ordered him back. "Just give me another long sword, and I will destroy their entire army, *Sensei*," said the monk. "I don't need help." His face glowed with the excitement of battle.

"Nevertheless, you are to rest, change your armor, and get fresh weapons. Don't argue! Go before the next man comes. You will have another chance if you hurry!" Yoshi's urgent tone brought Meishu back to his senses. He saw the wisdom of his *sensei's* orders. He flattened himself, maintaining a precarious balance while Yoshi exchanged places with him.

"I will return as quickly as I can," said Meishu. Yoshi was already engaged with his first opponent and didn't answer.

Meishu trudged wearily to the Byōdō-in, where he was

warmly greeted and congratulated by Yorimasa and the prince. He removed his armor; there were sixty-three dents, five of which had cut through causing him minor wounds. He treated himself, cleaning the wounds, then started to dress in the armor again. Yorimasa stopped him with strong fingers.

"No," said Yorimasa. He held Meishu's arm tightly. "You have done enough here. I have a more important mission for you." He shook his head as Meishu tried to object. "Our fate depends on you. I had hoped the monks of Nara would march north when we did not appear on the first auspicious day. Apparently they are holding fast, awaiting my orders. They will not arrive in time to save us. Our only chance is for you to leave secretly with a message to the Nara commander. Tell him we are under siege, and bring him back with you. If the Taira recognize you, they will grasp our plan; so hide your face, and go with Buddha . . . quickly!"

Meishu was loath to leave, though he realized the importance of his mission. Without the warrior-monks of Nara, all would be lost. "What of my *sensei*?" he asked, as he quickly donned a hooded floor-length robe.

"We will relieve him when you are gone. He is too valuable to risk. There is an important place in our plans for him too," answered Yorimasa.

"Look at him," said Meishu, pointing to where Yoshi's sword flashed on the bridge. "He is the greatest warrior in all Japan."

"I know," said Yorimasa, "and you are surely the second."

Meishu bowed humbly and, without further words, started the long trek to Nara.

Fifty-one

Chikara glowered at the battle on the bridge. His entire army was held at bay while they played the enemy's game. Yet treachery in the face of a challenge would be dishonorable and an unbearable loss of face. As he sullenly pondered his dilemma, a scout delivered a message. Chikara read it quickly. His face turned gray. "Call the captains. Bring them immediately!" he ordered his aide.

In minutes, more than two dozen samurai captains clustered around Chikara's white horse.

The sun was already near the horizon, and long purple clouds sailed in the darkening sky like fishing boats sailing across Suruga Bay. At the bridge, Yoshi had relinquished his spot to another warrior-monk, who fought valiantly, inspired by his and Meishu's example.

Chikara described the situation to the captains. "If we kill the man on the bridge, another will take his place. Their delaying tactics have held us here too long. We have to get to the other side . . . and quickly. A message from my spies informs me an army of warrior-monks is ready to march from Nara: They may leave at any moment. You all understand how important our mission is. For us it can mean death if we fail, rewards if we succeed." He stared at each captain in turn, until they stirred uneasily in their saddles. None wanted to break the silence that fell over the group. Who would presume to suggest a course of action to Chikara?

Finally, one of the older captains said, "We can ford the river by going either east or west." Everyone looked at him as though he were mad until he added, "There are places that can be crossed by the Yodo, Moarai, or Kawachiji. Everywhere else the rains have made the Uji impassible."

Chikara digested this opinion sourly. "If we move any great distance we lose time and give the Nara monks an opportunity to reinforce the prince's escort. Their arrival will mean the loss of our quarry," he said, scowling at the older man.

A younger captain, perhaps foolhardy because of his youth, interjected, "Leave the chicken-hearted to go to Yodo. That is not the way of the samurai. History tells us that in the past brave warriors forded the Tonegawa River after their boats were destroyed. They used their horses as rafts, and we can do the same. If we do not cross the river, we disgrace ourselves as samurai. Remember, to drown is only to die."

The other young captains agreed.

Chikara silenced those older and more experienced men who advocated caution. "Let the young men lead us, then. There is no choice. We must stop the prince or suffer the consequences."

The young captain who made the suggestion said, "We can cross the river if we leave the bank quickly and keep our horses facing upstream. The water is no deeper or swifter than the Tonegawa. It was my own great-grandfather who led the Ashikaga forces across the river to earn eternal honor, and I, Ashikaga Matataro Tadatsuna, shall lead our troops to destroy the traitor prince."

Chikara studied the young man. He saw a tall youth, not more than twenty years old, clad in gold-trimmed red armor that set off his ivory pale skin. "Your bravery will be rewarded," he said. "But first, take five captains and their samurai. . . . If enough of you live to cross the river, the rest will follow."

"Gladly, Lord Chikara. Some of us will die, others will reach the far bank to show the way for all."

Tadatsuna chose five among the dozen young men who volunteered. He mounted his horse and spurred it toward the river. "Come, all of brave heart, come with me to win fame and fortune!" Behind him, the five captains, carried along on a tide of enthusiasm, raced to the bank. Yamakami, Fukasu, Ogo, Sanuki, and Hirotsuna, followed by three hundred men, drove their horses from the bank shouting war cries as the horses plunged into the water.

The golden orb of the sun was half obscured behind the Byōdō-in. The shadows lengthened minute by minute. The samurai held their horses firmly, facing them toward the deep shadows of the far bank. Tadatsuna's horse led the way, while its master stood high in his stirrups, shouting encouragement and advice to the others. "Stay together! If the enemy shoots, ignore their arrows. Don't take your hands off your horse. Don't shoot back. Keep your heads down. That's the way, feet firm in the stirrups. Aim across diagonally upstream."

He moved back and forth freely as though he were riding through the pond at the ninefold enclosure. When some of the horses seemed ready to lose their footing Tadatsuna in his red and gold armor appeared miraculously at their side to help their riders steady them against the rush of the stream.

"Sit tight in the saddle. Keep your horse's head up. Move along. Let them walk where they touch the ground. Quickly. Quickly!"

Tadatsuna reached the steep slope of the far bank and announced his challenge to the defending monks. "I am Ashikaga Matatoro Tadatsuna, son of Ashikaga Taro Tochitsuna of Shimotsuke, descended from the great warrior, Tawara Toda Hidesato. I risk divine anger by drawing my weapons against the prince, yet I owe the Taira my life and fortune; I challenge all who dare face me." He spurred his horse over the rise and charged at the monks who stood, with bows drawn, ready to defend the gate to Byōdō-in.

On the other bank, Chikara, seeing Tadatsuna top the rise,

ordered the army to ford the river. Two hundred abreast, they pushed into the powerful current. As the first group started across, the samurai who were downstream stayed almost dry; the great mass of horses upstream momentarily dammed the raging waters. At the halfway mark, clumps of horses and riders were pulled out of line and started a chain reaction as they smashed into their neighbors. The terrified whinnying of horses and the clanging of armor made a hideous din as hundreds were swept away by the current. Red, green, blue, white, gold—armor of every color was washed away, to disappear like the leaves of autumn. Six hundred were lost before the army reached the opposite bank.

At the gate to the Byōdō-in, the warrior-monks of Miidera, the soldiers of Yorimasa, and the student monks from Sarashina fought valiantly. Chikara's samurai dismounted; horses were a disadvantage in the confined area. The noise of horses running wild and men shouting filled the air as the superior numbers of the Taira army were held at bay by a relative handful of Mochihito's protectors.

Yorimasa, Yoshi, and Yorimasa's two sons barred the gate, fighting off their enemies with swords and *naginatas*. The narrow gateway allowed no more than six men to attack at a time, and after the first onslaught, the melee of bodies and armor made it impossible to shoot arrows effectively.

Time after time, Yorimasa dispatched enemies some fifty years his junior. Yoshi fought alongside him proudly. To die next to the great poet and leader would be an honor . . . though none were ready to die yet.

Yoshi used the eight-sided attack, his blade flashing and cutting into the enemy armor. First to fall was the handsome young man in red armor who had delivered the challenge. As he reeled backward holding his face, Yoshi's sword caught him directly under the neckplates, severing his head in a burst of red that matched his armor. Another samurai took his place, and another, and another . . .

Yoshi lost track of how many men he fought. He became aware that Yorimasa had fallen back from the gate. A quick glance told Yoshi that Yorimasa would fight no more; a great

war arrow had found its mark, piercing his sword arm and
breaking the elbow joint.

The enemy redoubled their attack in an effort to reach the
wounded poet. The gate was jammed with warriors crushed
breast to breast, slashing and hacking at close quarters. Men
went down from minor wounds only to be trampled by the
battlers. Yorimasa's second son, Kanetsuna, his hatchet-face
twisted into a grimace of concern, spurred his horse to the
gate and bent forward to lift his father to safety. Just as he
succeeded in lifting Yorimasa onto his saddle, Kanetsuna
was pulled from his mount. He fell heavily to his knees and
struggled to regain his footing. In the fast fading twilight,
Yoshi saw a samurai leap on his back before he could rise.
The two figures disappeared into the general melee. When
Yoshi next saw him, Kanetsuna had the head of his enemy in
his hand but was surrounded by fifteen samurai who separated him from his father. Even in the semidark and from a
distance, Yoshi made out his deep-set eyes glowing with the
heat of battle. Though Kanetsuna could not reach his father,
he was determined to die in the attempt. With a strength born
of desperation he wielded his two swords in the windmill
style, wreaking havoc among the overwhelming enemy.

The conclusion was inevitable. Kanetsuna was lost.

Yoshi left his place at the gate to two monks and rushed to
Yorimasa's assistance; the old man was in great pain, and
Yoshi saw he would be unable to control the horse, which
reared and circled, nostrils flared in fear. Yoshi caught the
reins and led the wounded Yorimasa to the villa. Looking
back, he saw an enemy samurai holding Kanetsuna's head
aloft. Yorimasa's youngest son was dead after a brave fight.
Yoshi cursed under his breath. He wanted to avenge Kanetsuna's death, but he realized the importance of bringing
Yorimasa to safety. With regret, Yoshi turned away from the
enemy. Tenderly, he helped the old man from the horse and
carried him into the Byōdō-in.

Meanwhile, Yorimasa's older son, Nakatsuna, seeing his
brother's head hanging from the samurai's grasp, went into a
killing rage. He used his great size and powerful shoulders to

chop his way through the Taira ranks, ignoring a dozen mortal wounds, and killed the man who had beheaded his brother. He removed his brother's head from the samurai's grasp and, withdrawing from the battle, brought it to the villa where he buried it under the veranda. The Taira would be denied the triumph of exhibiting the head of Minamoto Kanetsuna!

Nakatsuna, weakened by wounds so severe he could not continue and with death or capture imminent, fell to his knees and ordered one of his retainers to help him commit *seppuku*.

As Yoshi and the old man came into the hall they saw Nakatsuna press his sword into his abdomen while the retainer stood by to remove and hide his head.

Yorimasa gasped with pain as Yoshi set him down. He had seen both his sons die bravely and now he felt the black wings of death fluttering over him and his—almost lost—cause. Better to have ended this way than to have suffered any longer under the Taira rule. The cause was not lost yet; no, there was still hope. The young swordmaster would succeed, though the rest of his warriors would fall.

Yorimasa clutched Yoshi's sleeve with his good hand. "You must carry out the final part of my plan," he said. "When I am dead, dress yourself in the prince's white robe and ride out from the rear of the villa. Be sure the Taira see you. In the dark, they will be convinced you are Mochihito. Lead them away from Byōdō-in to give the prince time to escape. Do not fail me, Yoshi. I depend on you to make our deaths worthwhile. The prince has been instructed to hide when you are gone. Remember, the Minamoto need Mochihito to legitimize their cause."

"Yes, sire, I shall do as you command."

"Good! Now, kill me and hide my head. Chikara shall not have it to display in the public square."

"I cannot kill you, sire," said Yoshi.

Yorimasa frowned. "Then give me your short-sword. When I am dead, remove my head and hide it." He regarded Yoshi with a silent plea. "This you must promise to do."

"I promise, sire." Yoshi tightened his jaw to help control

the feelings that threatened to engulf him.

Yoshi handed the old man his nine-and-a-half-inch killing sword. Yorimasa accepted the blade with a nod of his head. Outside, the battle raged. Defenders of the gate were dying, one by one. In spite of the shouting and confusion of the battle, Yorimasa was calm. Ignoring the pain of his shattered elbow, he removed his armor and pulled down his long-sleeved robe so he was naked to the waist.

Yoshi could hardly bear to look at Yorimasa's poor frail form. The old man's skin was almost transparent, and every rib showed clearly through the flesh. Blood pulsed lazily from the smashed elbow joint, running down his forearm and staining the knife. Yoshi's throat tightened. His mouth was dry. He wanted to say something to reassure the old man. Your sons' deaths were worthwhile. . . . You will live. . . . Your cause will prevail. . . . Your life was not wasted. . . . We will escape. The thoughts echoed through his mind—the things he wanted to say, yet no words came from his lips.

Yorimasa turned to the west and intoned the *Namu Amida Butsu* prayer ten times. Then he knelt and carefully tucked his sleeves under his legs so he would not fall forward in death. With both hands he raised the knife to his forehead.

"I have spent my life as wisely and as well as I could. I am saddened to see my sons die before me. Now my own time has come. Before I die, I make one last request of Amida Buddha. Grant safety to Crown Prince Mochihito and victory to the Minamoto cause. All my life I have been a poet and in this last moment I compose this stanza in the hope of immortality."

He bowed his head and recited in a firm voice:

> *"Like a fossil tree*
> *On which no flower grows*
> *Ever so am I.*
> *My life ends in sadness*
> *Without hope of fruit."*

He held the sword with a steady hand and pressed the blade into his left side drawing it slowly across to the right. Blood poured from the wound; he leaned forward and cried, "Now!"

Yoshi's vision was blurred by tears as he ended Yorimasa's agony with one stroke.

Under the spell of the old man's last words, Yoshi had forgotten the battle outside. He became aware that the defenders were losing the gate and were retreating into the front hall of the villa. He quickly wrapped Yorimasa's head in a sash and ran from the room. He came to Prince Mochihito and Munenobu cowering in a corner. "Give me your white robe," he demanded. He grasped the prince's shoulders, half lifting him to his feet. "For Yorimasa's sake, if not your own, hurry! Before he died, Yorimasa told me you know what to do when I leave. I will lead the Taira away to give you your chance. Hide well! Lord Chikara must not find you. If you are discovered, we shall all have died in vain."

The prince, despite having been prepared by Yorimasa, was terrified by the intensity of this blood-spattered monster. He handed Yoshi the robe, afraid to raise the questions and doubts that made him shiver with fear. Yoshi tore off his own armor and covered himself with the white robe. Carrying Yorimasa's head under his arm, he ran from the prince and out the rear of the villa to where his horse was tethered. He leaped to its back, spun it around, and charged through the milling fighters at the gate. The white robe fluttering behind him, he galloped along the Uji's bank until he was momentarily out of sight of the Taira. "Amida Buddha, I consign this brave man's soul to your custody," he gasped as he flung Yorimasa's head into the stream.

An outcry arose behind him. The white robe had been recognized. Among the shouts, he heard, "Prince Mochihito is escaping! After him! Kill the traitor prince! Gold to the man who brings back his head!"

Yoshi raced south across the plain to the mountains and safety. It was five miles through mostly open terrain. The night was dark, the moon blessedly hidden by clouds. Somewhere in the distance, an owl hooted its lonely call. Yoshi felt the surge of his horse and heard his own harsh breathing. Far behind him the earth seemed to move as thousands of horsemen pounded in pursuit.

The promise of reward drove the samurai troops wild. Like a giant pack of hounds with the blood scent hot in their nostrils, the horsemen stampeded across the plain, chasing the white will-o'-the-wisp. Two things gave Yoshi an advantage in the race for the foothills: He was a lighter burden for his horse, and the armored samurai were disorganized and ill-disciplined, fighting each other for the front positions in their eagerness to win the reward. Gradually Yoshi pulled farther ahead. The foothills were almost within reach. The moon appeared fitfully between the clouds. The labored breathing of Yoshi's horse and the beating of its hooves were the only sounds. The pursuers had fallen back out of earshot.

The night was peaceful after the carnage and din of the battle at Byōdō-in. Able to catch his breath, Yoshi reflected on the tragic contrast of the bloody battle played out in front of the graceful pillars and airy architecture of the old villa. How transient were the lives and works of men!

The moon again disappeared as Yoshi's horse reached the edge of the pine forest that led into the dark reaches of the mountains. Safety seemed at hand. Once Yoshi was in the mountains, no horseman would ever find him. Then his horse stepped into a hidden gully and, with the sound of a breaking branch, snapped a leg bone. Yoshi flew over the horse's head, rolling over and over as he hit the ground.

Fifty-two

At Byōdō-in, the few remaining defenders continued to battle overwhelming odds. They had been driven back, and back again, their numbers diminishing as they died heroically.

Chikara guided his white horse around the periphery of the battle, coordinating his troops against the defenders. His first temptation had been to ride with the huge army in pursuit of the white-robed rider, but . . . it was too easy . . . the white rider appearing so conveniently, so obviously. Also, the man rode too well; Chikara knew the prince was a poor horseman. The sixth sense that made Chikara a leader told him the prince was still in his grasp.

In the darkness, some of the defenders could have escaped, but honor was more important than life. Swords and *naginatas* flashed and spun in a smaller and smaller circle, until only one man was left—a giant monk, who wielded his sword like a man possessed. A circle of steel surrounded him, and those who came too close found their armor cut through as though it were paper. Five hundred men crowded in from all sides as the giant's blade flew in the eight-sides-at-once pattern.

It was only a matter of time. The clank of sword on sword, the grunts, shouts, and hard breathing were suddenly swallowed in a great roar as the monk slipped in a puddle of his enemies' blood. He went down fighting under an avalanche of weapons and armor. There was a victorious roar from the massed troops. The last defender was dead.

Chikara was not satisfied. "Fan out around the villa," he ordered. "The prince may be hidden there. Search every inch of the courtyard from the gate to the steps. There will be a special reward for the man who finds him."

Chikara went into the main hall to start the interior search. On every side, he saw beautiful screens and tapestries smashed and torn into useless junk. The fighting had demolished the thin walls and latticework shutters. Chikara was momentarily depressed at the havoc. He regretted the loss of these priceless art objects more than the loss of the two thousand men who had died in the battle. Soldiers were made to fight and die. They could be replaced. The screens and paintings could not.

Chikara almost fell across the headless body of Yorimasa. He recognized the armor and the age and frailty of the poet. He nodded approvingly. The man had died well and, by denying Chikara the satisfaction of having his head, had won a small triumph.

There was no one alive in the villa. Chikara strode to the back veranda, where he paused to inspect the gardens and artificial lake and to oversee the troops who were searching the grove of trees and the clusters of feathery bamboo shoots, shouting and cursing to flush out any fugitives.

Chikara's eyes flicked to one side. He saw a movement under the curved bridge, a lighter spot that pulled back into the shadows. It was the moon reflected from a pale round face. He leaped from the veranda and followed the artificial stream to the bridge. The moon, having done its damage by exposing the fugitive, hid its face in shame behind the clouds. Chikara dimly saw pale lotus blossoms on the water. Frogs croaked as he passed, disturbed by the invasion of their privacy. The battle had not extended to these rear gardens, and it might have been any peaceful spring night undisturbed by warring men.

A lone cherry tree spread its branches over one side of the

old bridge. As Chikara reached it, the prince scrambled from behind it, crawling on his knees and babbling entreaties for mercy.

How disgusting! Chikara never questioned the divinity of the royal family, descended in so many generations from Amaterasu, the sun goddess, but this was no god; this was less than a man. If the prince had been less craven, Chikara would have spared his life out of respect for the royal family; the sight of this soft womanish figure begging for its life was intolerable.

With one stroke, he ended the revolting display. Prince Mochihito's head rolled down to the water's edge. The gurgle of blood bubbling from his severed carotid artery blended with the soft sound of the water lapping against the grassy shore.

Chikara picked up the head and shouted to the men who were beating the bamboo stand at the far side of the garden. "Over here!" he called. "Our search is over. You will all be properly rewarded."

When they came to him, he ordered them to bring a shutter to carry the body. He wrapped the head in a cloth and gave it to one of the samurai to carry; it would be presented to Kiyomori on their return to Kyoto.

Shivering in the pond, among the waterweeds, lay the prince's foster brother, Munenobu. He had hidden in the water, urging the prince to join him. When Mochihito refused, Munenobu dug himself deep into the mud at the edge of the pond. The waterweeds covered his face, allowing him to breathe without betraying his hiding place. Though the soldiers, brandishing their swords and cutting randomly into bush and bamboo grove terrified him, he maintained his position.

He heard Chikara's shout and saw the men laughing coarsely as they marched by within five feet of him. He shrank deeper into the water and watched with revulsion as the samurai heaved the headless body on a shutter and carried it off.

In the dark, Munenobu was not sure at first that it was the prince. The soldiers passed . . . something fell from the corpse's robe and rolled toward him. The moon, which had betrayed the prince, shone shamefacedly at the scene. Munenobu recognized the prince's favorite flute inches from his nose. The flute Mochihito had played so beautifully . . . the flute he had loved. A wave of horror swept over him. There was no doubt then: The headless corpse was the prince.

Munenobu wanted to run out and throw himself on the body to beg forgiveness for what he had done. Jealousy had caused him to betray his foster brother, fear kept him frozen in place. His legs trembled, he could scarcely breathe, no amount of shame could make him leave the pond.

All night he lay in the black waters, listening to the soldiers repairing the bridge. At dawn, he heard them shouting orders as they left for Kyoto. He rose from the pond, aching in every joint and muscle. Moving like a puppet, he plucked the flute from the ground and studied it with mounting pain and regret. He was wracked by a sudden convulsion of shame and with a spasm he flung the flute far out in the pond as though it were contaminated by some horrible disease.

Then, wet and dismal, he sat for hours in the formal garden of Byōdō-in and cried for the prince, a gentle soul, interested only in music and calligraphy, who lost his head to foolish ambition. And he cried for himself, a coward, too weak to die like a man, with the defenders of Byōdō-in.

Fifty-three

===

Dawn found Yoshi scrambling up the mountain with an entire army in pursuit. Foxes, hares, deer, and birds fled before the soldiers who thrashed their way upward. The armored horses could not climb the steep inclines, so the samurai were on foot, cursing at the inhospitable slope. A few wisely removed their armor; most were still encumbered by leather and steel. Regardless of their difficulties, the samurai gained ground. Yoshi's old hip wound throbbed as he climbed. The fall from the horse and the full day and night of battle and flight had taken their toll. He moved slower with each passing minute.

The morning sun moved upward. It was a hot day for spring; dew evaporated from the leaves, and the temperature rose. Yoshi heard his pursuers closing in around him. Ahead was a waterfall, part of a tributary of the Kizu-Gama River. In desperation, he scrambled toward it along the river bank. Deep crimson berries shone against the dark loam of the bank, and the welcome shade of pine groves made the morning heat more bearable. The waterfall spilled over a twenty-foot drop. Yoshi could go no further; he worked his body into a niche in the rocky wall behind the water, where he hoped he could escape unseen.

Shouts of the enemy were audible over the roar of the falling water; gradually, the cries became fainter. Yoshi held his position, pressed to the rock face until late afternoon, when the forest had been silent for several hours. He was not aware that the troops had been recalled shortly before noon. When Yoshi finally emerged, he collapsed on the river edge and allowed the sun to dry and warm him as he rested.

The next day, Yoshi—hobbling slowly down the road to Nara—was overtaken by Meishu with the advance riders of the Nara forces. They had found Munenobu and heard the story of the prince's death. There was nothing left to do but return to their headquarters. Meishu helped Yoshi onto the saddle behind him.

Their arrival at the ancient city was a sad one: Their mission had failed. The prince was dead, Chikara triumphant.

PART SIX

Fifty-four

In the twelfth month of 1180, during the winter period of the General Confession, there was widespread rejoicing among the members of the court. The Kiyomori experiment—the move of the capital to Fukuhara—had failed. The court was once more officially established in Kyoto and had enthusiastically taken up its ceremonial duties. The twelfth month was a busy one; the General Confession was scheduled from the nineteenth day to the twenty-first. Priests would hold services each night of the three-day period for the cleansing of sins committed during the year. A party of monks was busy transporting a bronze statue of the Goddess of Mercy to the Dais of the Imperial Palace. The statue would be surrounded by painted screens showing the varied punishments of Hell to remind the unrepentant of their eventual fate.

Most of the courtiers would be too busy to worry about repentance during the coming winter; despite their satisfaction on returning to Kyoto, there were many duties to perform. Supervising the reconstruction of their homes kept the majority occupied. In the time between the opening of the Fukuhara Palace in the sixth month and the return of the courtiers to Kyoto in the twelfth, the Imperial City had deteriorated further. Fires, whirlwinds, and earthquakes had decimated it. After six months of complete neglect, the city outside the Imperial Enclosure was in ruin. Animals, birds, and insects lived in the undergrowth that covered once proud streets. Gates of formerly imposing homes lay broken and scattered in clumps of mugwort, while entire gardens were buried in wild rushes.

Those courtiers fortunate enough to live in the ninefold enclosure—where workmen had been busy for months, patching and painting to prepare for the return of Kiyomori and the Emperor—were buried in an avalanche of bureaucratic paperwork. The business of government continued behind the scenes of penitence and repair. Typical of the orders of the day was a paper describing the standby appointment to the Imperial Council of Tadamori Yoshi, which was being routed through the Imperial Bureaus.

Ietaka, as a member of the council, had drafted the appointment while still in Fukuhara. It had, in due course, reached the Emperor's secretaries, who carefully rewrote it in Chinese to prepare it for the Emperor's eyes. Several weeks after Ietaka's first draft was submitted, the Chinese version, beautifully calligraphed on heavy mulberry paper, reached the Emperor's writing table; he formally entered the date in the indicated place, signifying his approval.

A secretary removed the completed document and forwarded it to the minister of central affairs from where a completed "Report of Acknowledgement" was sent to the Emperor.

The minister of central affairs carefully examined the document—though his approval was automatic. When sufficient time passed to show that the minister was a careful and prudent man, he signed it under his title and sent the form to the senior assistant minister.

The senior assistant minister, after several weeks of delay, wrote "Received" and sent it to the junior assistant minister, who signed it with the character for "Perform." The entire document having been perused and copied by the Emperor's secretaries, signed by the Emperor, noted by the minister of central affairs, checked by the senior assistant minister, and signed by the junior assistant minister, was transmitted to the scribe's office, where it was recopied and shuttled to the major councillor of the Great Council of State, who signed another Report of Acknowledgement. Once again to the Emperor for his formal approval, and back to the scribe's office for multiple hand-calligraphed copies. Each copy was then signed by the prime minister and by every official concerned with the appointment.

In Lord Chikara's new Kyoto home—one of the newly completed buildings within the Imperial Enclosure—there was much discussion on the day the document arrived for his signature. "This Tadamori Yoshi has been a constant source of irritation. He is a devil brought to earth to punish me for crimes committed in a previous existence," said Chikara angrily.

His younger brother, Kagasuke, who acted as his buffer on the Council and his sounding board in political decisions, commented, "If he is so much of a problem, why not turn him over to me. I will see that you are no longer bothered."

Chikara knitted his brow. "It is not so simple a matter," he said. "He has been in my grasp before . . ." Chikara shook his head—"and escaped."

"Then we should refuse to sign. We can arrange to misplace the papers among the various bureaus." Kagasuke sat back smug in the conviction that he had solved the problem.

Chikara pursed his lips, considering the suggestion. Finally he said, "No! I think it would be better if he were here where he can be watched." So saying, Chikara signed the appointment and called for a messenger to return it to the palace for the Imperial Seal that would make Yoshi the legal representative from Okitsu.

After the messenger left, Chikara thoughtfully sipped a cup of sake. When he spoke, there was weariness in his voice that made him seem older than his fifty-six years. He spoke so softly Kagasuke had to lean forward to hear.

"I have a feeling," Lord Chikara said, "that soon we shall resolve the problem of this evil spirit."

Fifty-five

At the end of the year, a weary stranger rode his horse through the empty main street of Sarashina, looking for the martial arts academy of *Sensei* Tadamori Yoshi. The town lay under a clean white blanket. Smoke drifted lazily skyward from the quiet buildings; no one ventured out when it was so cold. Two-foot drifts of snow crackled sharply under the horse's hooves. The air was clear and the icy blasts of wind reddened the nose of the rider.

A short distance out of town, he heard the sign at the gate of the academy creaking mournfully as the gusts of wind pushed it against its chains. He pulled up to peer through rime-crusted brows at the calligraphy that announced the school. He nodded to himself and guided his horse through the gate.

"My name is Hiromi." The rider was seated comfortably in Yoshi's office, munching bits of octopus and washing them down with gulps of hot tea. The blue color gradually left his face as he warmed himself inside and out.

Yoshi had been studying him for several minutes, this stranger who had appeared from the cold claiming to be a messenger from Ietaka. He was a slightly built man distinguished only by intelligent eyes, prominent teeth, and a thin face that showed evidence of a sense of humor. While he was not a prepossessing figure—no one could mistake him for a warrior—Yoshi liked the thin man on sight and felt he could trust him.

"So, Hiromi-san, you have come a long way over cold and dangerous roads to bring me this message from Ietaka. Let us speak frankly. Do not let ceremony stand in your way. This is not the capital; we do not waste time with polite evasions; we speak our minds directly. I promised Ietaka I would help him one day, and I suppose you are here to ask my help."

"*Hai*, Yoshi, indeed I am here at Ietaka's bequest, and I *am* going to ask your help." Hiromi's knuckles whitened where they squeezed his cup. His voice was grave. "Not for Ietaka. We are too late for that."

Yoshi felt a pang. All was not well, else why a stranger in Ietaka's place? "Tell me quickly. What of Ietaka?"

"Three weeks ago," said Hiromi, "Ietaka responded to an insult by striking another councillor in the face. They dueled. Ietaka—foolish man—died. That is the whole story."

Yoshi leaned forward and held Hiromi's arm. "Not the whole story," he said. "Who killed him?"

"It doesn't matter. It was part of a plot fostered by Kiyomori to rid the Council of Minamoto sympathizers. Ietaka was not the first." Hiromi lowered his tea cup. His hand was trembling. The strain of his journey and the weight of the bad news he carried suddenly showed in his face.

"It matters greatly to me." Yoshi ignored Hiromi's distress and demanded, "Who killed him? Chikara?"

"No. It was not Chikara; it was his brother, Kagasuke."

"Kagasuke follows Chikara's orders. I hold Chikara responsible, though I am surprised he sent another to do his killing."

"Chikara is above taking direct action against his enemies. Two months ago, he won a great victory at Ishibashiyama in the Hakone mountains. This, coupled with his destruction of Prince Mochihito, gave the Taira their only two victories this year. Chikara's star now stands high in the Taira heavens; he is their only leader able to best the Minamoto, and many consider him next in line for Kiyomori's chancellorship."

"Chikara as *daijo-daijin* would be a disaster for Japan. Thank Buddha, his accession is unlikely."

"But not impossible! Kiyomori is fatally ill. Knowing he will soon die, he placed his son, Munemori, in charge of the Council and appointed Chikara Minister of the Left with instructions to rid the court of Minamoto councillors. He tries to accomplish two purposes: his son Munemori, entrenched in the Council and Chikara at odds with the cloistered Emperor. Thus far, he has failed with Munemori, who is an ineffectual fool and will never be accepted by his peers. He is partially successful with his plan to neutralize Chikara. Chikara is a national hero. He and Kagasuke are always careful to be the challenged rather than the challenger. Though Go-Shirakawa is angry at the flouting of his edict to allow Minamoto on the Council, he is powerless to act against samurai defending their honor. However . . . he respects Chikara and would still prefer him to Munemori."

As he listened, Yoshi nodded from time to time. Now he knew what he would have to do. When Hiromi's tale ended, Yoshi said, "I have given much thought to the proposal Ietaka made me. I am not an ordinary samurai, merciless and unfeeling. I am a swordmaster and live by a higher morality. Until today I believed it immoral to take advantage of my training to kill unsuspecting political enemies. The death of Ietaka changes that; it makes me realize that Chikara must be stopped. If I had the power to stop him and did not, I would dishonor Ietaka's memory.

"I will take Ietaka's place on the Council, and I will do what I can to avenge his death. Ietaka shall not have died in vain. Tadamori Yoshi or Taira-no-Chikara . . . one of us will die."

When Hiromi realized that Yoshi was accepting the council appointment, his scholarly face broke into a broad smile. "I speak for all of us when I welcome you to the Council. Ietaka prepared a place for you in his home. The building is being restored, and you will be comfortable there."

"Thank you, Hiromi."

"There is no reason for you to thank me. Before he died Ietaka said you would come only after his death. He faced death more easily, knowing it would help accomplish his goal. He was confident your abilities would change the course of events and save the remaining Minamoto councillors."

"Do the other council members know my profession?"

"No! We will announce you as the councillor from Okitsu, then let the enemy discover your background for themselves."

"I will not provoke them," warned Yoshi.

"It will not be necessary. They will surely approach you with their insults. Chikara and Kiyomori are furious that deceased councillors are being replaced. Their goal is to strike fear in our ranks so no Minamoto will be willing to accept a council position."

"Tonight I will pray to Amida Buddha for the eternal rest and peace of Ietaka's soul. It is a wild, degenerate age when a man of goodwill and gentle spirit dies so senselessly. Nevertheless, in his way, Ietaka did his part to bring about the change that will surely come."

"*Namu Amida Butsu,*" said Hiromi.

On the last day of the last month of the year 1180, the Ministry of Central Affairs in Kyoto prepared to join the Yin-Yang masters in a special Service of Expulsion. An Imperial Attendant was trying on the red shirt and golden mask he would wear that night when he acted as Devil Chaser and marched through the palace shooting arrows at the sky, twanging his bow, and banging on his shield to exorcise the evil spirits of the old year. Private homes throughout the capital would perform similar rites.

Several hundred miles away, two horsemen, unrecognizable in bulky robes and cowls, set off through the snowy fields of Sarashina on their way south. They had no interest in the kind of ceremonies being performed at their destination. They plodded along, specks on a vast plain of unbroken white snow.

The cold sun glowed in the southern skies—Amaterasu was far from her people. The landscape was silent, barren, unrelieved by warmth or color. If the world came to an end—as many in the capital predicted—it would be on just such a day as this.

Snow hawks soared overhead looking for white rabbits concealed in their holes. A hawk saw an almost invisible movement; it dropped with heart-stopping velocity to snatch up a small furry body in its predatory claws. The horsemen continued breaking through the snow crust, unaware of the tiny drama that had just been played out behind them.

Fifty-six

On entering the gate of the Palace of Administration, the meeting hall that hosted the Great Council meetings, Yoshi beheld a scene of formal beauty. Snow covered the gardens. An artificial stream and lake broke blackly through the white powder, making faint lapping sounds in the quiet morning. Small wooden bridges carried undisturbed puffs of snow on their shoulders. The brisk air brought a pinch of red to the noses and cheeks of the councillors, who moved like great dark birds across the courtyard. They marched in a single file to their meeting hall, a building whose massive stone base supported red-lacquered pillars that soared upward to elaborate green tile roofs.

Yoshi walked solemnly behind Hiromi. Somewhere on the grounds a temple bell proclaimed the hour of the hare, six A.M., the time all good public servants reported for duty. Yoshi wore clothing carefully chosen for his first public appearance. Under his cloak, the outer robe was a fresh lime green that contrasted vividly with the deep blue violet of his under-robe. He had not tucked in the bottom of the under-robe and flashes of color showed beneath his cloak as he walked the path.

The Great Council meetings were impressive ceremonies. Today each of the forty-four councillors wore his full court costume, a black-lacquered *koburi* on his head, a gray cloak, a patterned over-robe, silk *hakama*, thick padded shoes, a baton signifying rank and power, and a decorative ribbon attached to his sword belt. Each councillor went wordlessly to his place. The great hall extended into the dark corners of the Palace of Administration. Black columns of highly polished wood stretched in mathematical precision down the two sides. The ceiling was twice as high as any normal ceiling, with ornate beams crisscrossing into the upper reaches of the roof. Along the walls, round copper braziers emitted a haze of burning charcoal and incense. A few oil lamps gave flickering light. The Great Council room was empty of other furnishings except for a long, V-shaped dais where an embroidered brocade cushion was prepared for each councillor's comfort. At the far end of this impressive room, opposite the councillors' dais, was a gigantic screen decorated with an allegorical painting of the creation of Japan by the god Izanage and the goddess Izanami.

Behind it was the cloistered Emperor, Go-Shirakawa.

Facing down the length of the hall toward the Emperor's screen, Kiyomori sat in the center of the dais on a square platform which set him six inches above the others. As *daijō-daijin* he was head of the council.

Lord Chikara was on his left. Where Kiyomori was dressed in the sober brown tones that befitted a Buddhist Monk, Chikara wore a combination called red plum blossom. His outer cloak was a vivid scarlet; his under-robe of deep blue violet showed through his sleeves.

Chikara's counterpart, the Minister of the Right, was on Kiyomori's other side. The councillors of the Left and the councillors of the Right were seated—twenty-two on each arm of the V—according to their rank; beyond the ministers were the major and middle councillors, the minor councillors, the middle and minor controllers, the senior scribes, and at the ends, the junior scribes.

Yoshi was seated next to Hiromi about two-thirds of the way down the right-hand side. His appointment as a minor councillor automatically awarded him the fifth rank.

Kiyomori opened the meeting with a quiet prayer to Amida Buddha, then turned to Lord Chikara, "My son, Lord Munemori, is indisposed today, so the Minister of the Left will conduct today's Council meeting in his place," he said.

Chikara nodded gravely before raising his wand of office to announce the official opening of the meeting. After completing the ritual formalities, he read a list of the items to be discussed. The first item was the welcoming of a new member.

"I introduce Tadamori Yoshi, duly appointed representative from Okitsu. He replaces a gentleman who recently suffered an unfortunate accident." Chikara turned the floor over to Yoshi with a nod.

"I appreciate the opportunity to make my voice heard in this august Council," said Yoshi. "I am not sure it will be as wise or as well-measured a voice as that of the man I replace.

"It is said that we are living in a wretched and degenerate age . . . an age that many take to signify the coming end of the world. I do not believe the end is near, in spite of the problems laid at our feet by grim nature. Plague, fire, and famine have brought us pain and discomfort; however, even worse is the political enmity that has turned brother against brother and weakened our Empire when we needed our strength. I believe that good men with the well-being of our royal family at heart can save us from disaster if they speak up, and if the listeners take heed of their words.

"I come in peace with my hands extended in friendship. I offer the hope that if Taira and Minamoto cooperate, the end will be averted. If they do not, the future will indeed be bleak and hopeless.

"On this, my first day as a councillor, I offer my heart and soul to the service of our Divine Emperor, to preserve him from the cruel machinations of those selfish few who draw power hiding behind his Imperial robe and thus serve him falsely."

A buzz of protest arose from the ministers of the Left. A sardonic voice cut through the hubbub to hiss, "His first day may be his last." The Emperor's advisor, Yuritaka, scurried across the floor to deliver Yoshi's speech to the Emperor.

Kiyomori remained impassive as he beckoned Chikara closer and whispered instructions in his ear. Chikara nodded and turned back to the Council. He held up his wand for silence.

"Our newest representative speaks harsh words. Perhaps he does not understand the implications of his speech. To insult fellow councillors is hardly the path to the cooperation he demands, but we appreciate his zeal and understand the impetuosity of a newcomer in our ranks. Perhaps he will learn restraint and live long enough to prove himself in the service of the Emperor many times in the years to come."

Chikara voiced the subtle threat with outward calm. Only his brother, Kagasuke, sitting next to him, saw the pulse jumping in the corner of his jaw. Chikara continued as though nothing untoward had occurred. "The second order of business will be a discussion on the disposition of the traitorous monks of Miidera. The Council has vacillated for many months; shall we confiscate their property or merely punish their leaders? We must decide before the week is out. Junior officials will state their opinions first."

Fifty-seven

Chikara and Kagasuke were alone; the others had left the council chambers. The huge hall was draughty and cold; the braziers gave little heat, and the few oil lamps left much of the area in gloom. Alongside the black brocade of his brother, Chikara's bright scarlet cloak was a drop of blood in the vast reaches of the hall.

Kagasuke's expression combined anger and confusion. "I don't understand," he said. "He insulted us, yet you allowed him to leave with hardly a reprimand. We should have—"

Chikara interrupted. "Kiyomori ordered me not to act, to ignore the insults. Believe me, Brother, it was a difficult course for me to follow. I taste bile when I think of it."

"Despite his orders, Kiyomori would be relieved if we solved the problem without his knowledge. It is not too late to allow me to deal with Yoshi." Kagasuke was a powerful man, who was proud of his physical strength and took every opportunity to display it. While the ladies and gentlemen of the court accepted Chikara and his warrior background, they found Kagasuke a comic figure and nicknamed him "The Butcher Boy." Since Chikara had appointed him Captain of the Inner Palace Guards—automatically giving him a seat on the council—Kagasuke had been earning his nickname in a way the court ladies had never imagined.

"Never fear," said Chikara. "Kiyomori is wise; though his body is failing, his brain is working. He realizes that if the Minamoto are represented on the council that orders the destruction of Miidera, the warrior-monks will hate them as much as they hate us. By keeping the Minamoto tied to our council we share the blame and keep the monks neutral. In time, we will conquer the monks, reap the rewards, and be more than repaid for the loss of our *shoen* in Okitsu. After the confiscation of the Miidera lands is ordered by the entire council, we will attend to Tadamori Yoshi.''

"I hope you will allow me the honor of personally disposing of him,'' said Kagasuke grimly.

"I am not sure. He is no ordinary man. For years, he has haunted me like an evil spirit. I have a presentiment that fate will intervene, and I shall face Yoshi alone.''

Kiyomori's health had been failing long before the court's abortive move to Fukuhara. Once back in Kyoto, he found it more and more difficult to keep up with the daily meetings and ceremonies that his position as prime minister demanded. There were mornings when he awoke retching blood from a stomach that flared with the fires of hell. He was absent from the Great Council more frequently each passing week.

Chikara—strong enough to control the council in spite of Kiyomori's absence—was thwarted by Kiyomori's appointment of his son, Munemori, to head the council. Chikara pleaded with Kiyomori to give him control of the council, but since Yorimasa's treason, the sick old monk trusted no one except his own flesh and blood. As he weakened physically, he developed a paranoid distrust of those not in his immediate family. Unfortunately, his choice of Munemori was a disaster: besides being incompetent and more than a little stupid, Munemori was loathed by Go-Shirakawa, who went out of his way to embarrass him. In order to avoid losing face, Munemori skipped council meetings, pleading poor health. His grasp of the intricacies of council politics, tenuous at best, suffered from his absences. The Minamoto took advantage of the situation, cleverly playing stupid Munemori against wily Go-Shirakawa.

Munemori's frequent "indispositions" and his inability to control his allies led to disorganization and resulted in a stunning defeat for Lord Chikara. During Yoshi's first week as a councillor, Chikara had campaigned for the confiscation of the Miidera monastery and lands. Though the Taira councillors would have normally supported him in a bloc, some—confused by the vacillation of Munemori—decided to take no action. Instead, they agreed to reinvestigate the charges against the monastery and render another report. There would be an indefinite delay, and the Miidera lands would not be redistributed.

Chikara had gained stature as a result of his capture and execution of Prince Mochihito; now he found himself reduced from a hero awaiting his reward to just another landless council member.

On the eighteenth day of the first month, the day after the vote on Miidera, the council meeting ended early so the councillors could attend the archery contests that marked the official end of the New Year celebrations.

The annual event was held in the courtyard fronting a block-long pavilion in the ninefold enclosure. The Imperial Pavilion's red wall panels were trimmed in black and gold. A six-foot wide veranda ran the length of the building; it was guarded by a black-lacquered handrail and was approached by ten broad steps in its center. The Emperor sat behind a private screen in a warmed area at the head of the steps. Overhead, golden eaves carved with animal heads protected the veranda from snow. Braziers warmed the inside of the pavilion and gave enough heat to make the open parts of the veranda bearable for warmly dressed spectators.

Councillors of the fifth rank and above were there with their wives, mistresses, and concubines. Of the highest ranking members of the court, only Lord Chikara was absent; he was angry and disappointed at his defeat in the council and refused to give his opponents a chance to gloat at his discomfiture. The archery contest was between teams representing the Inner and Middle Palace Guard. As Captain of the Inner Palace Guard, Kagasuke could not avoid being present. Not to appear would mean default to the Middle Guard, and default in the annual competition would be an unbearable loss of face.

Traditionally, each guard captain chose four men from his command to complete the archery teams. Kagasuke, hiding his resentment behind a mask of indifference, chose quickly.

A ten-foot-wide strip of snow had been cleared for a distance of a half *cho*—about sixty yards—and gaily decorated targets were set up at one end.

The guard officers were dressed in their brightest armor: the Middle Palace Guards in pale green with white lacings, the Inner Palace Guards in blue violet with black leather. Each officer wore a quiver with arrows lacquered the same color as his armor.

The Emperor signaled the contest to start. Lots were drawn; the Inner Guards, under Kagasuke, drew first shot. Yoshi, at one end of the veranda, among a group of Minamoto councillors, noted that the contestants were all excellent bowmen. Each drew a bow of at least fifteen spans, and each breathed easily, releasing a tiny puff of vapor in the cold air, when he drew back the bowstring and released his arrow. The score seesawed back and forth as each team took its turn at the target. Yoshi was amused to see that many of the court ladies, who professed great disdain for these crude martial exhibitions, were nonetheless peeping through the shutters and shouting encouragement to the contestants.

The Middle Guards were slightly ahead as the two captains prepared their final arrows. Kagasuke shot first. Seemingly without strain, he drew a bow of seventeen handbreadths. His shoulders and arms looked enormous in the bright painted armor. The string came back to his cheek, rested for a few moments, and released. The arrow, as if of its own volition, flew to almost the exact center of the target; it quivered in the cold air as Kagasuke smiled and lowered his bow.

Yoshi, though he loathed Kagasuke, was among the first to

applaud the splendid shot. It would be almost impossible to beat.

The other captain pulled back his bowstring; his face was calm and concentrated. Kagasuke, confident of victory, was already walking up the stairs to the victory celebration that would be held in the pavilion behind the Emperor's screen.

The arrow left the bow.

The audience gasped in unison as it struck dead center, pushing Kagasuke's arrow out of the way.

A loud cheer sounded from the spectators. Kagasuke froze on the stairway. His neck turned red as he realized what had happened. He turned to stare at his opponent's arrow deep in the exact center of the target. Victory had been snatched from his grasp. He glared up at the wildly applauding spectators. Directly in front of him was the new representative, Tadamori Yoshi, leading the applause. Kagasuke had shot well. He deserved to win the rewards and prizes that went with victory. Somehow, the upstart on the veranda had had something to do with his loss. It didn't make sense, yet he knew it was so. Chikara had called Yoshi an evil spirit, a curse; it was true. At that moment, he decided, no matter what Kiyomori or Chikara said, he would have satisfaction.

Fifty-eight

In the pavilion, after the archery competition, Yoshi allowed himself to be carried along by the colorful tide of guests. This was his first experience with social life since coming to the capital a week earlier. He had been so occupied by the bureaucratic demands of his position that he had seen no one outside of the council meetings except Hiromi. Here, he was surrounded by male guests garbed in embroidered Chinese jackets, elegant riding outfits, ornately painted capes, and outer-robes of royal blue, Chinese red, and apple green. The bright-hued courtiers mixed with the softer colors of the ladies: young dianthus-leaf green, peach, plum blossom, and the softest of yellow rose.

Yoshi had forgotten the standards of court entertainment: the opulence, and the careless expenditure of wealth. The Emperor had provided delicacies for the palate from the farthest provinces of Japan, Korea, and China. For the ear, complete ensembles of musicians: flutes, drums, bells, lutes, and zithers. For the eye, dancers from Korea and India, acrobats from China. Sake flowed liberally, and the crowds laughed and jostled as they eddied from one lavish entertainment to the next. Yoshi drifted from group to group . . . from five musicians playing a nostalgic version of "Was

Ever Such a Day?'' to Indian dancers accompanying themselves with finger cymbals.

As the afternoon progressed, older guests departed, and
the entertainment grew more informal: young men borrowed
instruments from musicians and sang for groups of their
friends; others vied with each other in impromptu dance
competitions. At one point, a bemused Yoshi was drawn into
a poetry-reading contest, where he was easily bested by the
other contestants.

With the arrival of evening, flares and lanterns were lit on
the veranda and in the courtyard. The temperature had risen
and warmly clad guests were able to stroll in the snow-
cleared yard to admire the moon.

Yoshi was ready to depart when there was a flurry of
excitement at the entrance; the old Empress, Ken-shun-mon-
in, had arrived with a party of ladies-in-waiting. In the light
of the lanterns, colorful costumes swirled around the royal
party as guests jockeyed for a position near the Empress.

Yoshi was near the entrance when the entourage passed.
He saw Nami among the Empress's ladies-in-waiting. *Nami!*
His mouth went dry, and his pulse quickened. He tried to
catch her eye to no avail. She disappeared into the center of
the group, without a sign of recognition.

He could not leave. He had to speak to her, had to let her
know he was nearby.

The Empress had joined Go-Shirakawa in a private room
sectioned off from the rest of the pavilion by movable screens
. . . and everyone seemed to gravitate toward that spot.

Behind the screen, the Emperor gave a private party for the
Inner and Middle Palace Guard archery teams. The winners
were to be publicly honored at the end of the festivities. Until
then, Go-Shirakawa had provided them with special foods
and wines. Seven of the eight contestants enjoyed themselves
hugely, basking in the attention of the Emperor. The eighth,
Kagasuke, drank steadily, paying no attention to the others.
Kagasuke's face was mottled red, his full lips slack from the
effects of the sake.

When Nami entered with Ken-shun-mon-in, Kagasuke

nodded sullenly in greeting. His sister-in-law's bright smile only depressed him more. Why was she here without her husband? And thinking of Chikara . . . why had he deserted his own brother when he was needed for support? No, that was unfair. Kagasuke knew why Chikara had avoided the celebration. Would that he had been able to avoid it too. He frowned drunkenly . . . Nami should not have come without her husband, even if the Empress requested her attendance. She should have claimed to be indisposed. What was happening to the fabric of society? Was there no respect due a lord from his wife?

The hour was late when Go-Shirakawa finally ordered the screens removed and called on the archery teams to stand before the assemblage for the twin toasts of victory and defeat. Kagasuke, half-drunk, lurched to his feet and tried to stand erect before the Emperor. It was no use. He staggered and would have fallen if his second-in-command had not caught his elbow. His eyes had difficulty focusing. He became aware that the front of his robe was sodden with spilled liquor. His face grew redder with embarrassment.

The audience clustered close to the participants. They applauded the slim handsome Middle Guard Captain and laughed behind their fans when Kagasuke sipped the bitter wine of defeat. Kagasuke tasted bile mixed with the flavor of the wine; it was a bitter moment. He belched and to his horror the wine made a rivulet that ran out of control from the corner of his mouth. As he tried to choke it back, he looked up to see his sister-in-law smiling radiantly at someone in the crowd. Her lips formed the words "Come see me when you can" and sketched a kiss in the air.

Kagasuke's bloodshot eyes searched for the recipient of the message. Tadamori Yoshi, the nemesis! Was it possible that Nami and Yoshi were lovers? That look on her face! It was not the controlled liking of one cousin for another. He knew with dreadful certainty that he had seen a message of love being passed in a public place. Who else had seen it?

He could never tell his brother of this perfidy; he would have to act alone to save the family honor. After the archery contest, he had decided to seek Yoshi's death to satisfy his own needs. Now it was a matter of family honor. Yoshi had to die, and after his death, Kagasuke would see that his faithless sister-in-law was punished.

Yoshi had received the message. He was unaware of the connotations Kagasuke had read into it. He was pleased to see Nami looking well and holding an important position in the Empress's entourage. He knew it would be impossible to approach her while she was with the Empress. Enough . . . he was well satisfied. He would send a message at the first opportunity and arrange to see her privately.

It was time to leave. Yoshi donned his over-robe and stepped out onto the veranda. The evening was pleasant, not cold at all. Braziers and lanterns added their glow to the light of the winter moon. He inhaled the incense filled air and blew out a faint plume of vapor.

"Here is another worthy contestant," said a jovial voice in his ear.

"A fresh talent, I'll wager," said another.

Yoshi found himself at the head of the stairs, in the center of a group of courtiers and ladies, who insisted he join their poetry improvisation contest. Ghostly white-powdered faces and blackened teeth bobbed up and down in the shadows of the eaves; the courtiers laughed immoderately at their own jokes and waved their fans at Yoshi's protestations.

"You cannot depart until you have contributed a verse," said the leader unsteadily. Yoshi smiled with amusement . . . why . . . they were all quite drunk. He wrinkled his brow in an exaggerated pose of thought. If the price of departure was a poem, he would pay it with good grace.

The courtiers chuckled with anticipation. "This will be a good one," said a pale-faced lady. "I feel it."

No one noticed Kagasuke coming through the portal and striding purposefully through the deepest shadows. The distance was short, and Kagasuke cut through the courtiers as though they did not exist. One moment, Yoshi was preparing to recite a poem, the next he was reeling out of balance at the head of the stairs, clutching at the cold railing to save himself from tumbling to the snowy ground below.

"Clumsy, crippled bastard," Kagasuke snarled. "You will have to learn to get out of the way of your superiors."

Yoshi managed to regain his footing. The courtiers and ladies looked on in horror as he brushed his robe and calmly recited a poem for the occasion:

> *"There are forest beasts*
> *That hide in the darkest gloom.*
> *Closed mouths help them hide*
> *The angry light that reflects*
> *From their sharp and shining teeth."*

Someone laughed nervously. Another applauded, and in seconds the entire group was chattering as though nothing had occurred.

Kagasuke, excluded, stood outside the crowd, a giant frog of a man. "Maybe I cannot compose verse," he snarled at Yoshi. "Nonetheless I am a man who does not have to hide among the robes of women."

Yoshi raised his head slowly, a hint of sadness and regret in the look he gave Kagasuke. The courtiers and ladies were suddenly silent. At a motion of Yoshi's hand, they shrank out of the way, leaving an empty space between the two men.

"Kagasuke," said Yoshi quietly. "You do not understand what you are doing. Drink and the disappointment of losing today's contest have confused you. You would be wise to apologize and retreat while you are able."

The onlookers held their breaths as Kagasuke swelled in anger; cords on his neck bulged in fierce relief. With a roar, he took three heavy strides toward Yoshi and swung a meaty fist at his head. Almost negligently, Yoshi ducked under the blow, slid behind Kagasuke, and gave him what appeared to be a slight shove. The move was calculated to take advantage of the force of Kagasuke's own swinging arm. To the horrified audience, the motion seemed to slowly continue outward as Kagasuke tripped over Yoshi's foot, spun into the low railing, and disappeared over the side.

Those nearest the railing saw Kagasuke fall into a snow drift and sink almost out of sight.

For ten seconds there was silence. The moon shone on a tableau of pale faces and dark open mouths.

Kagasuke rose from the snowbank—a prehistoric monster—and climbed back over the railing. His hair was in disarray, and clumps of sticky snow dripped slowly from his face. No one laughed. Kagasuke's hand was on his half-drawn sword; his body vibrated with suppressed fury.

"I am Taira Kagasuke. Son of eleven generations of Taira warriors. My father served under Kiyomori in the battle of Hogen. His father earned land and riches in the wars against the Emishi. I fear no man and will defend my honor to the death. I challenge this upstart to meet me in hand-to-hand combat tomorrow at the hour of the hare."

"So be it," said Yoshi, bowing resignedly.

Fifty-nine

Kagasuke was alone in his quarters. The effects of the wine had dissipated. He was sober and physically recovered except for a stomach that growled nervously and felt like torn gauze. A single oil lamp flickered on the wall above him, casting fitful shadows on his scowling face. He stared into the charcoal brazier worrying a thought that hovered at the edge of consciousness. Something was wrong. Yoshi should have been afraid. Instead he had seemed maddeningly confident. Kagasuke had accomplished what he had set out to do: Yoshi had accepted his challenge. Why was there no feeling of satisfaction?

The problem was more than the liquor and the evil taste it had left in his mouth. He had wanted to be a hero and instead had been a fool.

Kagasuke did not consider himself an evil man. He lived honorably by his own lights, yet many of the court people thought him insensitive and brutish. Oh, yes, he knew the nickname they had given him. The Butcher Boy! Like turned wine, it had a bitter taste. They thought themselves superior to him with their poetry and perfume smelling. Perhaps he did not write a beautiful hand or excel in other womanish pursuits; he was a man's man, versed in the arts of war. They said he was his brother's lackey. In truth, he was, and wasn't

that an honorable position for one who respected the authority of a higher rank? He was proud of the Taira name and tried
to live up to it in every way. Yes, he was jealous of his brother
and the easy way he traveled between the disparate worlds of
the court and the warriors. And, yes, he wished he could do
the same. How surprised the court would be if they knew that
the Butcher Boy lay awake many nights, hating himself
because he could not compete with the courtiers in wit and
charm.

Tomorrow at the hour of the hare, he would regain the
family's honor by killing Yoshi. How he hated the self-
contained representative of Okitsu! Chikara called Yoshi an
evil spirit put on earth to hound them. Well, tomorrow that
spirit would be sent back to Yomi. Let it wander the underworld for ten-thousand years, waiting to be reborn.

Kagasuke had no fear of the morrow. He had won too
many battles to doubt his own prowess. Few were his equal
with the sword, *naginata*, arrow, or bare hands. He brightened when he thought of the physical aspects of the coming
encounter; he was confident of his abilities. Yoshi would
need the powers of the underworld to escape with his life.
Kagasuke lay back on his sleeping platform, pulled the quilt
to his chin and in a few seconds was snoring noisily with his
mouth relaxed in a confident smile.

Yoshi was surrounded by Minamoto representatives. Only
Hiromi remained silent, as the four others chattered nervous
advice.

"You should not have accepted his challenge. He is one of
the Taira's most formidable warriors. Your only hope is to
abandon Kyoto. Leave while you can . . . hide," said one.

"Perhaps an apology would persuade him to cancel the
duel," said another without conviction. "Otherwise, you
will meet the same fate as Ietaka."

"We are not warriors; we are lawyers and politicians.
Yoritomo should send samurai to be his representatives."

"It isn't fair to ask us to die at the hands of the Taira
butchers."

Yoshi listened calmly, serving tea and rice wafers to his guests, who—unaware of his background—were sincere in their efforts to save him. They saw Yoshi as a quiet modest man, who would have been content to stay in the background. They heard his cultured conversation, admired his calligraphy, and enjoyed his sensitive poetry. Yoshi was obviously a man of peace, not of action, and would be committing suicide if he faced Kagasuke in the darkness of the morning.

"I will do what I must," said Yoshi in answer to their well-meaning entreaties.

One by one, the councillors' objections were exhausted in the face of their doomed associate's stubborn calm. Soon, there was nothing left to say, and shaking their heads unhappily, the guests bid Yoshi goodnight.

Hiromi was last to leave. He clasped his arms around Yoshi for a heartbeat of time, then he stepped back and bowed. "Amida be with you in the morning," he said before he turned and hurried after the others.

The moon shone coldly on the crisp white snow. Its harsh light created an eerie world of black and white. Here and there, a snow-crowned tree pressed upward, adrift in the billowing seas of white powder. The hooting of owls in the northern hills sounded a weird counterpoint to the soughing of the wind.

Temple bells rang the hour of the hare as the first pearly signs of dawn tinged the horizon. Other bells joined in from the farthest reaches of Mount Hiei. The wind brought a faint sprinkling of wet snowflakes, which stuck like stars to the hair and clothing of the two men who moved toward each other . . . figures on a dream landscape.

Yoshi wore a soft woolen cloak over a loose under-robe. His clothing gave no protection, but allowed him to move freely and quickly in the snow. He reached the center of the field first and, like an avenging angel, watched Kagasuke approach.

Kagasuke was a fearsome sight; he had prepared himself in

full battle dress: blue-violet armor, dead gray in the moonlight. His helmet was embossed with a twin-horned devil face. A riveted plate protected his neck, a cuirass and hanging laminated skirt—attached with decorative toggles and leather lacings—guarded his chest and groin. His right side was covered by iron, laminated between sheets of leather, while another sheet of iron, padded with rawhide, covered his back. A leather apron was tied below shoulder guards and draped to where his shins were protected by three black-lacquered iron plates, tied over bearskin boots. From head to toe he was an armored juggernaut, hardly human, an almost invulnerable fighting machine.

The wind and snow increased, silently laying a coat of white over the waiting combatants. Kagasuke drew his long sword with a flick of his wrist. The armor hardly affected his speed or strength. Yoshi met the blade with a lightning parry and an immediate counterthrust that rang from the iron breastplate.

The gray-streaked horizon lightened with the first touches of a cold, yellow sun as the figures struggled back and forth on the snowfield. The advantage of Yoshi's speed was partly offset by the snow blanket, which made intricate footwork dangerous. The best coordinated move could be thwarted by a slippery ice patch under the surface. Conversely, Kagasuke's armor had the disadvantage of holding wet snow in its interstices, snow that clung to his underpads, making movement more difficult.

Time after time, Yoshi's blade rang against leather and steel plates. Time after time, Kagasuke swung at the wraith who melted soundlessly out of range. The duel would have continued until one or the other fell of exhaustion, if a combination of Yoshi's weak hip and a patch of ice had not thrown him off balance. One foot slid out from under him, and he fell on his side, already rolling as he hit the ground.

With a roar of triumph, Kagasuke sprang—only to meet the same disaster. Both legs skidded forward on the ice. The weight of armor helped speed his fall. He hit the icy surface with a bone-shattering crash and lay there like a gigantic upturned turtle. His sword had flown from his hand, and—stunned—he feebly waved his arms.

Yoshi was up instantly. He pounced on Kagasuke's supine figure and put a knee to his chest, a blade to his throat. For a moment, Yoshi hesitated and the point wavered. Then, as Kagasuke, eyes bulging with hate, pressed upward, Yoshi gritted his teeth and whispered, "For Genkai! For Ietaka!" and slipped the steel under the throatguard. Kagasuke's body convulsed in one terrible spasm then fell back in the snow.

The sun was just high enough to light the growing patch of red that spread thickly in the snow around the head of the dead man.

The council meeting had been in session for almost an hour when the newest representative came in and took his place on the dais. The cushion next to the Minister of the Left remained vacant. The Minamoto representatives, seeing Yoshi alive, supposed that he had wisely avoided the suicidal confrontation with Kagasuke—all except Hiromi, who smiled a discreet smile, and pressed a hand on Yoshi's shoulder.

Lord Chikara, Minister of the Left, tightened his lips in the middle of a speech and cut himself short. Where was Kagasuke? He was always on time, except when he dueled with the Minamoto. Chikara had not heard of the incident of the previous night, but he observed Hiromi's smile, the touch to Yoshi's shoulder, and the slight nod of acknowledgement. A gut feeling told him he would never again see his brother alive. He shivered involuntarily. A ghost from the past had cast its long shadow in his path. Would it never end?

Sixty

When the Captain of the Inner Guards was found, his normally red face drained of blood, the Taira camp buzzed with the story of Kagasuke's challenge. Taira men gathered by twos and threes in a dozen palaces to speculate on how their champion had been bested. How could the man from Okitsu, a nobody, a nameless turncoat, have beaten the mighty Kagasuke in fair combat? Although Kagasuke had never been popular even among his own clan, everyone acknowledged his skill with sword and arrow; except for Lord Chikara, he was their best.

In contrast, the Minamoto councillors were jubilant. They questioned Hiromi about Yoshi's background, and reluctantly, he told them the full story. Minamoto walked the halls of the Palace unafraid for the first time since they had been accepted in the Great Council.

Yoshi stayed in his rooms, deeply troubled. Hanzo had taught him the sword was a mirror reflecting the soul of its bearer. An evil blade meant an evil soul. Before Ietaka's death, Yoshi had refused to use his swordmaster skills against his enemies. Yes, ordinary samurai could duel and kill men of inferior strength or ability—accepted behavior for mere warriors. However, Yoshi was more, a teacher who owed society a higher standard of conduct.

Ietaka was avenged. Yoshi told himself this innumerable times and derived no satisfaction from the thought. Kagasuke spread-eagled on the snow, his throat open for butchering, was not a pretty sight to remember.

Yoshi took up his brush and a sheet of mulberry paper:

> *A strange furry beast*
> *Roots deep inside my bowels,*
> *Snout turned away*
> *From the death that soon will come*
> *Enfolding me in darkness.*

He shivered as he finished the last strokes of his morbid poem. He pushed aside the inkstone and washed his brush. This fruitless introspection had lasted too long. He prepared himself for sleep. It was no use; sleep was far away. He watched the dancing flame of the oil lamp, and his thoughts drifted to Uncle Fumio, his mother, and Nami. Especially Nami. On dozens of cold and lonely nights just like this he had thought about their last conversation in Fukuhara. Often, before falling asleep, he remembered her saying, "It is time to forget the child and see me as the woman I am." And, "Perhaps, like so many others, I will take a lover to keep me from boredom." Tonight, she appeared to Yoshi as she had during the victory celebration in the Emperor's pavilion. How lovely her lips when she sent him a kiss and her message. *Come see me when you can.* How sparkling her eyes, delicate her nose, soft her chin, fine her hair. Yoshi longed for the seemingly unattainable and, in that moment, recognized what he should have seen long before. Despite her marriage to Chikara, Nami returned his love. Lying alone in his cold bed, he knew that she had declared her feelings, and he groaned at how stupid he had been not to understand her meaning. He had to go to her . . . no matter what the consequences, he had to see Nami and tell her he loved her. The life of a swordmaster suddenly seemed hollow compared to the life he could lead if Nami were his. The richness of daily love, the warmth and closeness that she could furnish—those were what made life worthwhile, and neither honor nor duty could take their place.

He extinguished the lamp and turned on his side, pulling the quilt over his head. Tomorrow, he told himself, I will go to her.

He fell asleep unaware that in another part of Kyoto a group of Taira councillors were discussing an action that would change his life.

On the morning of the twentieth day, the willows that lined the main street of Suzaku-Ōji were stooped under a heavy load of new snow. Black birds circled ominously over the southwest quarter, where more of the poor and hungry had succumbed to the cold of night. Monks marched through the snow, looking for the bodies of the winter victims and marking their foreheads with a calligraphic ''A'' to call them to the attention of Amida Buddha. In the palace courtyard, chattering groups of servants beat the willows, pines, and cherry trees to dislodge snow, while others walked along the verandas, knocking down icicles with long sticks.

Yoshi came to the Council Hall with Hiromi and several of their friends.

A group of Taira councillors waited.

One stepped forward and loudly announced that Minamoto were cowards and Tadamori Yoshi was most cowardly of all. He then delivered a standard challenge, ending: ''. . . and, I, unworthy of the task, do therefore offer my poor sword in the service of the Lords of Taira and challenge all comers to mortal combat.'' The tall young challenger was dressed in a plum over-robe, the Taira crest embroidered at his breast and back. Yoshi had seen him at meetings and admired his calm behavior and intelligent comments.

''I have no quarrel with you, Shigei,'' said Yoshi. ''I am not wearing a sword. With Buddha's mercy, leave us in peace.'' Yoshi's words were delivered with calm sincerity. To no avail.

''Then it is true. You are a cowardly upstart who murdered Captain Kagasuke by trickery.''

"If my confession to cowardice will avoid an unnecessary battle, I confess to being a coward and an upstart, although I am not a murderer."

The Minamoto councillors looked at Yoshi in dismay. They expected their champion to be a firebrand who would leap at the chance to defend his good name. This apparent cowardice on their hero's part left them shaken.

Young Shigei was also dumbfounded. He hesitated, unnerved by the situation. His companions glared at him, angry at his silence. He spoke haltingly at first, "We Taira cannot accept the death of Kagasuke as anything other than deception and murder." Shigei stopped and looked to his friends for encouragement. Then he stiffened and his voice rose. "Would you have us believe you defeated Kagasuke in fair combat? No! I do not believe your confession. If you will not accept my challenge, I will see you punished as an ordinary criminal."

"So be it," said Yoshi with a shrug of regret. "Since you allow me no choice, I accept your challenge. You may choose the time and place."

"North of the Palace, in the cemetery field atop Mount Hiei, in one hour," snapped Shigei.

Yoshi bowed his head in submission.

It was midafternoon. Yoshi descended from Mount Hiei with a heavy heart. High, gusty winds picked up powdered snow and blew it in a spray that penetrated the back of his robe with wet needles. The snow fields had melted and refrozen throughout the winter; polished by the winds, they glowed unpleasantly in the bleak sunlight. The scenery matched Yoshi's mood. Behind him lay the cemetery with its hundreds of snow-topped ancient stone markers, each marking a soul returned to the eternal cycle of life and death.

Only one body lay unmarked in the cemetery. Young Shigei.

Yoshi's sword slapped against his side, reproaching him for what he had done—*evil blade, evil soul*. This time it was murder. Shigei was young, strong, and aggressive . . . and no more skilled than the students at the Sarashina *dojo*.

The battle had lasted less than ten seconds. Shigei was waiting, both hands on the haft of his sword, blade upward at a forty-five degree angle. He seemed confident as Yoshi drew his own sword, letting it hang downward to the snowy ground. With a tremendous *kiya*—an explosion of breath which focused his inner power—Shigei lunged point first at Yoshi, who stepped lightly to his left and cleaved Shigei's chest with one stroke. Shigei's own forward momentum, adding to the speed and strength behind Yoshi's blade, drove the keen edge through his robe, deep into his ribs and inner organs. He froze in place, his sword still pointed to where his target had been, then he slowly folded over, collapsing face down in the snow.

Yoshi rolled the body over. He knelt by its side and sadly recited a prayer commending the young man's soul to Buddha. He arranged the bloody robe to cover Shigei's gaping wound and turned away for his long, lonely walk down the mountain.

Yoshi's background became common knowledge; suddenly, there were no more challengers, and he was able to concentrate on the bureaucratic paperwork that kept him constantly occupied. At his first opportunity he sent a message to Nami, asking permission to visit. He included a poem to remind her of the time he had composed a poem as they walked on the grounds of Kiyomori's Fukuhara palace. Using the same reference he wrote:

> *The swans still swimming*
> *Among the lily blossoms*
> *Have not forgotten*
> *That once they brought memory*
> *Of joy to a poor traveler.*

He received an answer the following afternoon. It came in a scroll sealed with a silken bow. He tore the ribbon with trembling fingers. Inside was a poem, brushed on heavy red paper, in graceful calligraphy:

Drifting lily pad
A small weight on its surface
The patient green frog
Still floating on blue water
Waiting for her handsome Prince.

What a clever, beautiful, talented girl. He truly loved her! He would go to her this very evening.

While Yoshi read Nami's message, six men met at a local inn in the northeast quarter. The meeting room, hung on four sides with bamboo curtains, was empty except for two candles set in tall holders, a few scattered cushions, and a brazier that sputtered and crackled in a fruitless attempt to heat the cold room.

"He has to die," said the leader of the six.

"No question of that. We are agreed. When and how shall we do it?"

"I hope we are not making a mistake. We are overstepping our authority, making this decision without Chikara's knowledge," said one man who was considerably older than the others.

"Chikara has grown too cautious. We can no longer wait for him to act." The leader was a soft-faced courtier whose breath hissed through a space between his front teeth. He spoke earnestly, and his young companions nodded agreement.

Only the one older man hesitated. "Still, we will be defying our leaders," he said. He took a deep breath and looked at the others speculatively. "And if we fail?"

"We are six and he is one. We will not fail! A spy tells me he sent a message to Chikara's wife. It is our duty to kill the man and save the minister from scandal. Yoshi will visit the woman in the Imperial enclosure. Probably tonight. When he comes out, we will be waiting."

"Count on me."

"And me."

"And me."

"What if . . . ?"

"Silence! We all go together. You are either with us or against us. Which is it?" demanded the leader.

"I am with you . . . of course." Under the pressure of his more aggressive peers, the older man acquiesced, beads of sweat appearing on his forehead despite the cold.

"Then it will be tonight. We will meet at the eastern gate of the palace. He passes there on his way home. Everyone who doesn't live in the enclosure has to leave before dawn. Be prepared to wait the long night. When you are cold and uncomfortable think how our friends will cheer us tomorrow. We will have done what other men lacked the courage to do and we will be well rewarded."

Sixty-one

Yoshi reached Chikara's gate at the hour of the bird. The sun was already below the western horizon. The grounds of the Imperial enclosure were quiet under thick snow. Palace business had finished hours before; no one moved in the white streets. A servant opened the gate and discreetly brought him to the center room, where Nami waited behind her curtain-screen.

Yoshi knelt on a cushion in front of the *chodai*.

"We have grown formal again," he said, as he adjusted his robe around his knees.

"It is necessary in Kyoto. My behavior has caused much embarrassment in the past. I am only trying to conform to the court standards." Nami's voice was muffled by the screen. It was cool and distant. Not what Yoshi had hoped it would be after the enthusiasm of her greeting at the Emperor's pavilion.

"I am disappointed. After months apart, I had hoped for a warmer welcome." Yoshi leaned closer. "Remember the time we spent together in Fukukara?" He tried to see through the curtain.

She stayed back, avoiding his gaze. "We are not in Fuku-hara," she said. "We are in the capital, and my behavior is different. I am obliged to please my husband and follow his dictates.''

"I hate this formality between us. It isn't necessary. I've known you too long to find you hidden behind a screen. I want to speak freely. The screen inhibits me.''

"Yoshi, dear cousin, I cannot afford the independence I once had. I always enjoyed my freedom, and I resent the need to hide myself this way, but Chikara insists. It is his right, and I choose to obey.''

Did he hear a faint sob as she spoke? "And so you sit behind a screen . . . ?''

"Yes! Please understand, I am not happy. Once, I hoped for a different kind of life . . . it was not to be.'' Nami sighed.

"Perhaps it is not too late to find happiness. I have thought a great deal in the past few days . . . disturbing thoughts. I questioned the lonely life I lead as a swordmaster.'' Yoshi cleared his throat and continued in an almost inaudible voice. "I am proud of my abilities, and I live honorably by the swordmaster's code—yet pride and honor are not enough. There is an important factor missing: My life is incomplete.'' Again Yoshi paused. Then: "I have thought much, and my thoughts concern you.''

"How can your thoughts concern me?''

"Nami, I love you. I have loved you for years. I was blind, never seeing that you loved me, too. How could I have been so stupid? Because of your marriage, I hid my feelings even from myself. Now, I have no more time to waste. If you love me as I love you, I want you to leave Chikara. Marry me. Have my children. Live in my house. I want you with me always.''

"Yoshi!'' Nami's voice was shocked. "You never gave me reason to believe you loved me. Without warning you raise questions I cannot answer. Leave Chikara? You know I cannot do that. He would never forgive me and would retaliate by destroying Uncle Fumio and our family. Marry you? Children? Yoshi, dearest, what you suggest is impossible, though I am gladdened to hear you say it. I thought it was obvious that I love you, too. When you were ill, in the grip of the demon in Okitsu . . . when you visited in Fukuhara . . . I thought you recognized my love and rejected it.'' Nami's voice became so soft Yoshi had to lean forward to hear her say, ''Though I love you more than life itself, what you suggest is impossible.''

''Impossible? Don't say impossible. We have a lifetime ahead of us.''

''No. No. It *is* impossible,'' said Nami. Yoshi heard her crying. ''I am heartbroken. Nevertheless, I shall respect Chikara's wishes. You must never come to this house again. If my husband knew you were with me, it would mean death for both of us. Because Chikara is away, I took the risk of inviting you here this one time. We can never meet this way again.''

''Risk be damned to Yomi! You just said you love me. Can I forget that?''

''It shall remain our secret.''

''No!'' said Yoshi. ''I have learned about myself these past days. I need you to make my life complete. Now that I know you return my love, I will be jealous of every moment you spend with him. Need I add jealousy to my reasons for hating him?''

Yoshi bowed his head. There was a lump in his throat that swallowing did not remove.

''All those years . . .'' whispered Nami.

Yoshi reached through the curtain and took her hand in his. ''In spite of your marriage, I cannot give you up.''

Nami pulled aside the curtain with her free hand. Her eyes, shining with unshed tears, gleamed deep and black in the shadows. She drew Yoshi toward her. ''We can do nothing about tomorrow; we have only tonight. Let us be together while we can. Let's not allow the curtain to come between us.''

Yoshi parted the curtain the rest of the way and slipped into the gloomy recess behind it. Nami held her arms out and enfolded him, pressing his face to her breast.

''How I longed for your touch as a man,'' she said.

"Through the years when you treated me like a child, 'the patient green frog.' Though tonight may end everything, suddenly I don't care. We will have it always . . . to remember."

"No, dear Nami, Chikara notwithstanding, this is the beginning not the end. The world will never separate us again."

"If only it could be so. How I tremble at the thought. Yoshi, place your hand on my breast; feel how my heart beats." Yoshi found her breast and caressed her gently until she moaned in pleasure.

"This is all I ever dreamed and more," she said tenderly.

Nami awoke with a start. "Yoshi, please rise," she said. "It is almost morning." She nestled close, her face to his throat. "To be so close . . . to be part of you . . ." She pulled back in sudden panic. "Please don't let me wake and find this only a dream. I never want you to go. I don't want to forget tonight. Hold me, Yoshi . . . tighter! I don't want tomorrow to ever come."

He pulled her face deeper into the curve of his throat. "Nor I," he said, his happiness tinged with a premonition of evil.

The first arrivals, underclerks and junior scribes, at the ninefold enclosure shuffled through the narrow streets, kicking up puffs of snow and leaving wispy vapor trails with their breath. Many wore swords under their cloaks, armed against the dangers of darkness. The bells had just signaled the hour of the tiger, and outside the enclosure footpads, robbers, and highwaymen moved freely through the night, stopping anyone foolish enough to appear unarmed.

At the Taiken-Mon gate, an armed man waited in the shadows shuffling his feet and blowing on his hands for warmth. He peered from under a monk's cowl at everyone who passed. There was no crest or insignia on his clothing. Those who noticed gave him a wide berth. An armed monk standing in a doorway before dawn was someone to be avoided.

A cock crowed in the distance, as faint streaks of light touched the eastern sky. The wind had lessened, and except for the crowing, the streets were silent.

With dawn, a trickle of courtiers left the Imperial compound; it was the hour of leavetaking for lovers. Those who had spent the night with their paramours were on their way home.

A single figure came through the Taiken-Mon gate. A man who walked with a slight limp, his face hidden under a wide straw hat that fitted over his eyes like a helmet. He strode lightly, watching the road, a smile on his face.

The man in the monk's cloak stepped out of the doorway and followed stealthily behind his intended victim. He drew his sword and waved a signal to five other men hidden in dark doorways farther down the street. They slipped like shadows from their hiding places to form a wall across the narrow street. All were wrapped in hooded black cloaks that covered their faces and draped almost to the snowy ground. The rising sun glinted from drawn steel.

Yoshi became aware of them at the same time he sensed a man rushing at him from behind. Instinctively, he stepped sideways, drawing his long sword. With one rapid movement, he sliced backward at his attacker. The blade struck with the full force of Yoshi's spinning body. The man fell wordlessly to the ground, his mouth open for the shout of triumph that never came.

Yoshi held his blade downward in front of him and walked slowly toward the wall of assassins. "I have no gold," he announced. "Part! And I shall go in peace. I have no quarrel with you. Let me pass."

The leader of the cowled men stepped forward, his sword at the ready. "You do have a quarrel with us. Murderer! We are here to avenge the deaths of Kagasuke and Shigei. This will be your last morning on earth!"

Yoshi kept walking. "Please, step aside and allow me to go my way," he said quietly.

The challenger faltered trying to see Yoshi's face beneath the broad hat. Then, with a shout of rage, he raised his sword and leaped forward. Yoshi faded to the left and swung at the attacker's back as he passed. The blade sliced through layers of cloth, cutting flesh and muscle until it severed the spinal column. The man took three more mindless steps before falling in the snow.

With a scream, two more attacked, clumsily getting in each other's way, in the narrow street. Neither finished a stroke as Yoshi slit the throat of the first and plunged his point into the midsection of the second.

The two remaining men hesitated in the center of the street. Yoshi continued to march toward them, his red sword blade extended. "There is still time," he said as he drew nearer. "Withdraw!" They backed off nervously. Yoshi followed. At the corner, a stone night lamp still burned. He stamped his foot and shouted a piercing battle cry. The two would-be assassins scattered around the lamp, running in opposite directions.

Yoshi wiped his sword blade and sheathed it before he returned to the scene of the short battle. One of the men was still alive. Yoshi pulled back the man's hood and recognized him as a friend of Shigei. These were not samurai. How foolish they were to attack a trained swordsman.

Yoshi knelt by the side of his victim. "Who sent you?" he asked.

"It was the plan of . . ." The man coughed blood and muttered unintelligibly. "I was against it . . . I told them . . ." He shuddered again.

"Who planned it? Was it Chikara?" Yoshi became more urgent.

"Chikara . . . plan . . . Chikara . . ." The voice trailed off.

Yoshi rose to his feet, his jaw clenched, his eyes blazing. So it *was* Chikara! He drew his blade and held it up before his face. "I swear again, by Amida Buddha, by the gods of war, by Hachiman, Chikara's head will be mine." Yoshi slipped the blade back in the sheath with an angry thrust. It clicked loudly in place.

On the ground, the dying man was trying to talk. "Chikara

. . .'' he mumbled. "He doesn't know . . . our idea . . .
not Chikara . . . doesn't know.''

Yoshi was already far down the street and didn't hear.

Soon the voice faded, and the oldest and wisest of the
assassins gave a last convulsive cough and turned his face to
the snow-covered ground.

Sixty-two

At the next meeting of the Great Council there were several empty cushions on Chikara's side of the dais. He had arrived late, hastily taking his place and not seeming to notice the missing men. Yoshi watched him closely, expecting signs of disappointment when he discovered his intended victim alive and the would-be assassins missing. However, Chikara remained impassive, even nodding coolly to Yoshi when their eyes met.

Kiyomori intoned the opening announcement—Munemori was absent with one of his frequent indispositions—then bowed to Chikara and handed him the wand of office indicating he wished Chikara to preside over the meeting. Kiyomori was pale with dark smudges under his eyes. From time to time he covered a thick croupy cough with his fan. Yoshi switched his attention from Chikara to the *daijo-daijin*: Kiyomori was a very sick man, and it was obvious that his wealth and power would not keep him alive much longer.

Listening to the drone of the councillors' speeches, Yoshi's thoughts wandered far from the routine considerations of the day. How was it possible to be elevated so high one moment and cast so low the next? Was it some evil spirit in himself? Had his blade, which had always served good, turned evil? Did a man change because of the power he possessed? Did Yoshi's ability make him something more—or less—than other men? And when he used his swordmaster skills to kill Chikara, would Nami understand? Questions on questions, replacing each other before he found answers. Though he was outwardly calm, inside was chaos. There was no choice, Chikara must be challenged! If Yoshi did not act promptly, Chikara would send more assassins, and next time they would not be soft politicians; they would be professional samurai.

The challenge had to be given . . . without delay!

During the recess, Kiyomori left, and the councillors split up to discuss the morning's business and to comment on the unexpected absence of so many Taira. Yoshi was talking to a group of Minamoto when he spied Chikara in the midst of a handful of his colleagues. Yoshi bowed and excused himself; then, with the surprised Minamoto trailing behind him, he approached the Taira.

"Lord Chikara," Yoshi announced in a loud voice. "You are a jackal." There was an instant cessation of the conversation which had filled the high-ceilinged hall. Braziers seemed to crackle more loudly as charcoal turned to ash. Yoshi's voice echoed and re-echoed in the dark spaces between the upper beams. "No," Yoshi continued, "less than a jackal. Jackals stay together, loyal to their pack. You send your jackals to attack a tiger, then look away when the tiger strikes back."

The Taira councillors drew back, leaving a wide space between Yoshi and Chikara. Some looked horrified, others wore satisfied smiles; their champion would be compelled to take action against this young upstart. Chikara's mouth was a thin, hard gash, his eyes almost closed. He held himself in check with great effort. Several seconds passed before he spoke. Though the words were polite, there was menace in his voice. "Excuse me young man," he said. "Are you a tiger?"

"Indeed, sire, I am. And are you a jackal?"

The oppressive silence was broken by a nervous giggle

from one of the councillors, and a gasp of outrage from another.

"I think you have gone too far, young man. My relationship with your family will not protect you from my sword. Apologize at once!"

"I have no apology to offer. If you are not a jackal, we can ignore family relationships and deal with our problem like honorable men."

The two groups of councillors clustered behind their champions, tensely glaring at each other. There were no smiles on the faces of Minamoto or Taira. Yoshi and Chikara were committed before their peers.

"Very well," Chikara bowed politely, his face chiseled in granite. "Let us finish this afternoon's business without involving the prime minister. He is not well. Tomorrow, after I have done with you I will explain what transpired between us. Now, if you agree, we will meet at midnight, the hour of the rat, with swords."

"In the cemetery field, north of the palace," said Yoshi, returning a bow fully as cool as the one Chikara had given him.

"Agreed."

Chikara turned on his heel and marched back to the dais for the final ceremonies of the day. Evil fate, he thought. No good can come of this. Yet it had to be done. The nemesis had to be faced and destroyed once and for all. Chikara did not fear the enounter. Fencing masters had fallen before him, and though he was no longer a young man, he knew he had the power, speed, and ability to win. Damn the fates that put a man in so difficult a position! He would kill Yoshi at midnight, then try to salvage his relationship with his wife and with Fumio.

By the time the council meeting was over, Chikara had changed his mind. Nami was spending the night at Fumio's home. Before he faced Yoshi, Chikara would explain his position to her and her guardian. The old man, despite his gruff manner, loved his nephew. Nevertheless, he had been a soldier, so he would understand the code of honor that made anything less than Yoshi's death unacceptable.

Chikara arrived at Fumio's house in the early evening. With unaccustomed humility, he asked Fumio to see him on a matter of grave importance. Once they were comfortably seated, he solemnly explained the situation. He concluded: "Your nephew is causing the Taira more trouble than an entire company of Minamoto archers. Shortly after we returned from Fukuhara, he killed my brother, Kagasuke. Then, he killed Shigei, another of our loyal councillors. If this continues he will singlehandedly tip the balance of power in the Imperial Council. Go-Shirakawa gloats at our discomfiture," he paused. "I ignored your nephew's actions because of my connections to you and your family. This time, I cannot ignore them. He challenged me directly, and I accepted. I am sorry; no other course is open."

"Unhappily, I agree." Fumio sighed. "Would that it were different, but Yoshi has changed too much since he left Okitsu. You will understand him better when you consider what he has suffered. First, Genkai died at your hand . . ." Fumio raised a palm to halt Chikara's objections. "Yes, I know it was accidental, but Yoshi was young and impressionable. Remember, it was his life that almost ended that day, and he was driven into exile. Since then . . . Kagasuke killed his cousin, Ietaka, and your samurai killed his beloved *sensei*, Ichikawa. Is it any wonder he has turned against us? Though I am pained at the prospect of what will come, I know no way to avoid it." Fumio used his fan vigorously; the room was oppressively warm. Heavy tapestries closed out the cold, and the center firebox sent hot tongues of flame upward.

The two men sat over a low tea table. Fumio rested one arm on a hand-carved elbow rest covered in deep red embroidery. Suspended lamps competed with the firebox in giving light.

Chikara spoke quietly. "Fumio, I respect you deeply. Perhaps it is the passage of years . . ." He hesitated. "Your friendship has become more important to me than Yoshi's death."

"You are confident of victory?" Only a nervous toying with an empty teacup gave away Fumio's feelings.

"Of course. My dear Fumio, he is a fencing master—of a well-known but small country school in Sarashina—and has triumphed in two duels. But Shigei was an amateur and while Kagasuke had some ability with the sword, my skills are of a different order. Your nephew will die at my hand." Chikara lowered his gaze.

"Our lives are so short. How sad it should come to this," said Fumio softly.

"I am here, old friend, because I want to avoid enmity between us. I hope you will not feel it necessary to declare a vendetta when this is over."

"Lord Chikara, your actions have been entirely honorable. How can we blame you? We heard how Yoshi provoked you. I wish he had stayed a courtier. Years ago, when he returned from his stay at the court, I was heartsick at what he had become. I prayed he would grow more manly and lose his foppish ways. Such is the payment for trying to interfere with fate. Would that we could start again." Fumio was overwhelmed with nostalgia and regret for lost opportunities. Chikara's appeal to his friendship threatened to burst the dam of his reserve. He cleared his throat to cover his discomfort.

Chikara did not notice. He was wrapped in his own world of unrealized ambitions. "To start again . . . yes . . . if it were possible. Sometimes I think how our lives would have been different, if only . . ." His voice faded as he stared in his cup. "Tell me, is my wife with you this evening?"

"Yes. She is with Lady Masaka, in the north wing. Lady Masaka has been ill since our return from Fukuhara."

"Does the lady know of my impending meeting with Yoshi?"

Chikara seemed anxious. Fumio read this as a desire to save the family additional grief.

"We thought it best not to tell her. It would disturb her even more."

"I am saddened that I cause her more pain. Once, long ago . . ." Chikara again sank into his own thoughts, rambling on about the past. "How strange is fate," he said. "I fear I will lose my wife because of this duel. Will she forgive me for killing her favorite cousin? How Yoshi haunts me! I believe that in some other cycle of existence I did him great injury. Our paths are so intertwined. . . . Can it be ghosts and spirits interfering?" Chikara's chin sank to his breast; he gazed sadly into his cup. The overhead lamps and the flames cast deep shadows in the curves and hollows of his face, making him seem older and more vulnerable.

A door to the room slid open, bringing in a draft of cool air which stirred the fire.

"Oh, excuse me . . . I did not know . . ." It was Nami, standing in the doorway, her face hidden behind her fan.

"Come in, niece," said Fumio rising to his feet. "Your husband is here."

"I hasten to change my robe. I am scarcely dressed for this occasion." Nami was flustered. She had not expected to see Chikara and, taken by surprise, was sure her face would give away her clandestine meeting the night before.

"Nonsense! Your lord will not be offended by your informality. Why this sudden modesty? It ill becomes you," said Fumio.

"Your own instructions, Uncle. I shall leave at once." She hid the redness that came to her cheeks and tried to flee.

"Come, Nami. Since our marriage night, you have asked to be treated as an equal. Why do you run from me, now?" asked the unsuspecting Chikara.

"Perhaps I have learned my place," answered Nami with a hint of sarcasm. She watched Chikara warily from behind her fan.

Chikara smiled without humor. "Enough small talk. I have important matters to discuss."

Nami yielded; she nodded obediently and went to the farthest corner of the room where she could remain in shadow.

Chikara told her of his coming duel with Yoshi, preparing her for what he felt was the inevitable outcome. As he spoke of Yoshi's imminent demise, Nami dropped her fan in shock, and her face betrayed her feelings. Buddha! Chikara thought, are they secretly lovers? He suddenly realized Nami's feeling for Yoshi was far more than cousinly love and, whatever the outcome of the duel, he would not emerge the winner. Though Nami would remain his wife, he could never trust her again.

The cruelty and unpredictability of fate stopped him in the middle of his speech. He felt old and tired. He stared dully at Nami, finding it difficult to concentrate. Her grief-stricken expression mocked his ambitions. "Yoshi . . . Yoshi!" he thought, "You have done this to me." He lowered his eyes. "Why does he hound me?" he asked in a hopeless voice.

Nami's chin trembled. "He believes he has many reasons. He is young and headstrong compared to you, a mature man of good sense. What can I say to make you spare him?"

"Nothing! I go unhappily to my duty. I am a samurai lord. I cannot turn my back on his insults." Chikara, whose voice had risen on his last words, continued in a lower tone. "Unfortunately, I am driven to this position. I cannot forgive Yoshi's actions, though I understand his grievances. Grievances caused by a fate over which I had no control. You know Genkai's death was an accident, and as for the incident with the swordmaster . . . How could I be held responsible? I came to Okitsu only to see you. Then your brother, Ietaka . . . Despite what everyone believes, Kagasuke acted against my orders. The list goes on, although I was never at fault."

"Perhaps not your fault. Nevertheless, you can atone for all that has happened. As your wife, I beg you to spare my cousin." Nami burst into tears.

Chikara regarded her bitterly. "I see that your feeling is deeper than cousinly love," he said.

Fumio, not understanding the direction the conversation had taken, interrupted. "I won't have this," he said holding up a hand to silence Chikara. "Much as I love my nephew, I will not allow you to dishonor yourself to save him. You will fight, no matter how much pain it causes. Your honor is our honor."

"No, Uncle," Nami sobbed. "You misunderstand me. I would not have my lord avoid his duty. I ask only that he spare the life of your poor foolish nephew. Let him win the duel, and let Yoshi live."

Chikara inspected her for the time of six heart beats. Then he went to her, cupped a hand under her chin, and lifted her face to his. He wiped a tear from her cheek. "You must love him very much," he said and dropped his hand to his side. Before Nami could answer, Chikara turned away and walked to the portal. "Though you are my wife, you are lost to me forever. I will save what small honor remains to me. Tonight, we will fight to the death!" he said.

Sixty-three

At eight P.M., the hour of the dog, Chikara received a delegation of Taira councillors. They told him of the morning's episode. Because of his preoccupation with the council meeting, his confrontation with Yoshi, and his visit with Fumio and Nami, Chikara was the only member of the Imperial court who had not heard of the assassination attempt and its failure. Outwardly expressionless, inwardly, he raged. Now he understood what had precipitated Yoshi's behavior. How could Yoshi not believe Chikara was behind the ambush?

Chikara's voice was steady. He told his visitors, "Tomorrow, I will dispense justice to the two who were foolish enough to survive. Besides the insubordination of their action, to run from an enemy is cowardice. They should have fought and died for their honor." He paused. "What can I expect from the weaklings who surround me? Sometimes I think it would be better for the world if the Minamoto succeeded in destroying us."

After dismissing the delegation, Chikara knelt before a small Buddha and prayed for guidance. His robe blended into the darkness of the room, which almost swallowed the light of the single candle. His sword lay across the mat at his knees. He stared at the dull reflections on the blade. There was another way. . . . He could give Yoshi the gift of life and Nami the gift of happiness.

Chikara drew his second sword. He held the nine-inch blade to his forehead. The cool smoothness of the steel seemed to calm his fevered thoughts. *No!* Suicide would be a coward's way. He shuddered with self-revulsion. How could he even consider it? *Seppuku* would be a dishonorable death under these circumstances. He slid the short sword back in its scabbard and determinedly rose to his feet. Yoshi must die!

While Chikara prayed to Buddha, a heavily draped palanquin was carried across the city. It stopped in front of Yoshi's residence; two passengers alit, paid the bearers, and trudged along the snow-covered path to his door. The visitors were heavily dressed in cloaks and hoods that covered them completely.

The taller figure knocked until a servant answered.

"Who are you?" the servant asked warily. The hour was late and inauspicious.

"Our names are unimportant. We come to see your master. Please call him at once." The smaller of the two handed a coin to the servant, who bowed and backed away, letting them inside. They brushed snow from their cloaks while the servant hastened to announce them. They did not hear Yoshi enter behind them. He watched silently to be sure they were unarmed. When he was satisfied they did not pose a threat, he cleared his throat. The visitors turned toward him, faces still hidden in the shadows of their hoods. "Welcome to my small home," said Yoshi. "How can I help you?"

"Yoshi, it is I," answered the taller visitor, showing her face.

"Nami!" Yoshi exclaimed. He wanted to rush to her and hug her to his breast. The presence of the other cloaked figure made him hold back. "You and your friend should not have ventured out on such a cold night."

"Friend? Friend?" said the second visitor opening her cloak. "Surely I am more than just a friend!"

"Mother! Forgive me. I did not recognize you," Yoshi

said in surprise. "You are both being so mysterious—hidden in cloaks and hoods, not giving your names. When my servant announced you, I did not know what to think. Please remove your cloaks and come inside where we can be more comfortable. Of course, you will join me for tea."

On seeing his mother, Yoshi immediately perceived the reason for the women's visit, and while he invited them in his mind raced ahead to determine the best way to handle the situation.

Once settled with cups of aromatic green tea, Yoshi studied his mother. She had grown so small and old! Her hair was white, fine wrinkles laced her cheeks and brow, and her hands trembled. How sad that she, a famous beauty in her youth, should have changed so drastically with time.

As if she read his mind, Lady Masaka said, "Yes. The years have left their mark."

"Mother, you are beautiful to me, and I am honored that you have come. Seeing you fills me with joy," said Yoshi.

"Except for my pilgrimages, this is the first time I have voluntarily left my northern wing in many years. I had to come to speak to you on a matter of importance."

"Yes, Mother. I have guessed why you are here," said Yoshi paying an inordinate amount of attention to his teacup.

"Son, I have appealed to you in the past to forget your quarrel with Lord Chikara." Lady Masaka's voice quivered. "Perhaps the pleas of an old woman have no meaning for you. So, this time, I ask for Nami. She told me of your feelings for each other. We agreed that if you will avoid tonight's encounter she will divorce Chikara and come to you. I will be able to spend my last years in your house with my daughter-in-law. We will work together to make your life a full and happy one." Lady Masaka turned to Nami and added, "Nami will tell you how much we need you."

Yoshi raised a hand to silence the women. "Mother, Nami," he said. "You are too late. I cannot turn back. In a few hours I will meet Chikara and the matter will be settled."

With a sinking heart, Nami cried, "Yoshi, I love you. I don't question your bravery or your sense of honor. I will not respect you less if you refuse to battle Chikara. It is *not* too late! You can come with me. We will leave Kyoto tonight and start a new life.''

"I am sorry. Honor demands that I meet Chikara tonight.''

Without warning, Lady Masaka started weeping. Nami wrapped an arm around her thin shoulders and comforted her until, at last, she slumped forward, spent, a look of unutterable sorrow on her lined face. ''Yoshi, Son . . .'' she moaned. ''In a few hours you will face one of Japan's greatest swordsmen. Nami and I will lose you when we need you most.''

"You will not lose me. I do not fear Chikara. I am a swordmaster,'' said Yoshi simply.

"Chikara is not a country bumpkin,'' cried Lady Masaka. "Yes, we know of your fencing academy in Sarashina. Nonetheless, Chikara has bested many of the most famous masters in the land. He is cunning and experienced.'' She paused then continued despairingly. "Compared to him, you are a boy.''

"Yoshi,'' interjected Nami. "Your mother is right. Avoid this battle! I come to you at the eleventh hour to beg you to listen. I will divorce Chikara and build a new life with you. Leave Kyoto to Chikara. We can go north to Kamakura where Yoritomo builds his armies and be happy there.''

"Nami, why won't you understand? My life, my honor, my future rest with this duel. Wait for tomorrow. I will return to you.''

"You will not return. There is a curse that hangs over us all,'' said Lady Masaka before Nami could reply. She held up one frail hand in a dramatic gesture and continued, "I can only explain by telling a story I have never told before. Listen, and understand why you cannot battle Lord Chikara.'' She took a deep breath to steel herself. "Many years ago, before you were born, I was a proud lady of the court. The other ladies were envious because I was the favorite of the Empress and received privileges usually reserved for those of higher rank. The envy of my peers made them avoid me; I was friendless, unhappy, and alone.

"There was one man, however, who paid me attention and treated me with respect. He was young and strong, and I was soon in love with him. Love or infatuation, I could not sleep for dreaming of my handsome warrior. During the day, I concocted elaborate fantasies about us and—as I imagined it—our mutual love.

"And I was jealous! Yes, I, who had been taught from childhood to believe jealousy the worst of sins, was eaten by jealousy every time he spoke to another.

"Picture me, then, dreaming about a great love that existed only in my mind. Oh, yes, I made quite a fool of myself. I was young and inexperienced, and my supposedly secret feelings were visible to all.

"Imagine my distress when I was told that my love was showing an interest in another of the Empress's attendants. Distress? It was more than that. I could not eat or sleep. The Empress, herself, remarked how poorly I looked. In my sleepless hours I devised a plan. I would use my beauty as women have always done.

"Men are clay in the hands of a determined woman. My hero was no different. I enticed him into my *chodai*. It was the first time a man had ever been invited behind my curtains, and despite my lack of experience, we spent a night of ecstasy. I was confident he would be mine. He left—a satisfied lover—at the hour the cock crows, and I spent the entire day waiting for his next-morning poem and letter. They never came. Instead, I heard he was seeing my rival again.

"I was young and proud—too young and too proud to face the snide smiles and secret laughter of the ladies. I hired a cart and left Kyoto for a temple on Mount Hiei. I intended to shave my head and become a nun. The abbot recognized my confusion and distress and bade me wait.

"Soon it became obvious I would not take my vows. . . . I was with child. I prayed for guidance. None was forthcoming, till the abbot—seeing my term coming close—sent me home to Okitsu."

Lady Masaka's voice had grown progressively lower as she spoke. She reached for Yoshi with one blue-veined hand

and sobbed, "Yoshi, you were born on the night I arrived, born during a storm that raged because the gods were angry with me. In terror and shame, I refused to name your father, and he never knew you were the result of our night together."

"Poor Mother!" exclaimed Yoshi placing his hand over hers. "Why didn't you tell me before? I would have understood. You have suffered far too long for a youthful indiscretion. At last, the story is out and you can tell me the truth: Who is my father?"

Lady Masaka had to repeat it twice before Yoshi understood. "Lord Chikara," she said. "Lord Chikara!"

Sixty-four

After Nami and his mother left, Yoshi slumped before the
firebox, staring into the flames; his world had been turned
upside down by his mother's words. His first reaction had
been disbelief. Then as the truth penetrated, a mixture of
horror and despair. He had been cast, rudderless, into an
ocean of surging emotions. Chikara, the lodestar of a
thirteen-year search for vengeance . . . the devil figure that
had driven Yoshi since Genkai's death. . . . Chikara was
revealed as his father, and in one stroke the motivation of his
entire adult life was removed. How could he grapple with this
twist of fate that threatened to topple the structure of his
universe? It was unbearable! The years of misunderstanding!
If either one had known the truth, how different their lives
would have been. Lady Masaka had had no right to hide the
truth from them; it was unnatural to allow a father and son to
live their lives as enemies, unaware of their relationship.

As the initial shock of the revelation began to wear off,
Yoshi tried to analyze his feelings. Had he missed knowing
his father? In his early years, Fumio had taken his father's
place and had been moderately successful. Yoshi's childhood had lacked for nothing—except the security and love of
a normal family relationship. In retrospect, he saw that his
life had gone in two directions at once: the search for ven-

geance against Chikara and the simultaneous, though unconscious, pursuit of a father through Fumio, Hanzo, and Ichikawa. Hanzo had given him love, a sense of place, and had
guided him physically. Ichikawa had been more than a mere
teacher of the martial arts; he had molded the steel, formed by
Hanzo, into the fine-edged sword that was Yoshi. Yet no
matter how important they had been to him and no matter
how he had wanted to accept them as a substitute for his real
father, neither the swordmaker nor the swordmaster had
furnished the complete answer. Yoshi saw that all his life he
had unknowingly sought the filial love his childhood had
lacked. He had thought he had found it for a while with
Hanzo and again with Ichikawa. But now he was a swordmaster and no longer needed a father—real or substitute.
With this understanding, he would find the strength to face
Chikara in the cemetery field.

So, where lay the truth of their relationship? Was there
some residual core of love? Some connection hitherto unrecognized? Though Chikara had never given him anything
but pain, he was Yoshi's own blood, and there had to be some
emotional tie buried in Yoshi's heart. Search deep. Could it
be found? As he stared into the glowing coals Yoshi felt
nothing but a gut-wrenching disorientation.

He had to ask himself if it was not futile to hope for a
reconciliation. His mother's tale was final proof that the spirit
world had malignantly conspired to intertwine his fortunes
with those of his father. What misery they had caused each
other!

He held his hands over the firebox, feeling the warmth on
his cold fingers; his hands trembled as with palsy. He recalled
the story that had haunted his childhood—of the father who
unknowingly killed his son and then committed *seppuku*.
Was that how his life would end?—or would he live the
tragedy in reverse, the son murdering the father? He looked
longingly at his blade and wished he could accept the easy
release it offered. He, Tadamori Yoshi, who had long dreamt
of a father he had never known, who had conjured heroic

images, built elaborate fantasies, would soon face his real father at swordpoint.

No! He was the flower of his father's seed. He could not do it. He would go to Chikara, throw himself at his feet, and tell him the truth. Father! he would cry, I am the son you never knew.

These dreams were only the hypnotic effect of staring into the flames. Yoshi wrenched himself back into the present. Thoughts of reconciliation and forgiveness were fruitless. It was too late.

Faintly, through the thin walls, he heard a distant temple bell marking the hour of ten. Two hours left. Little enough time to pray for guidance to Amida Buddha and for strength to Hachiman, the god of war.

When he finished his prayers, Yoshi chose his clothing with great care: comfortable robes and a loose *hakama* for quick movement, bearskin boots for warmth and traction in the snow. He checked his swords one last time, polishing both already spotless blades; he slipped them through his waist sash, one over the other.

It was time to start for the cemetery.

The moon was reduced to one quarter; the month was coming to a close. The sky was clear; the Shinto gods would have an unobstructed view of the battle. Tall pine trees, laden with snow, bowed their upper branches as if supplicating the moon and stars. Feathery bamboo groves rose above the undulating sea of snow and whispered softly in the north wind.

The roadway was rocky and steep. From the north gate of Kyoto, it led up the mountain to the old cemetery yard. Yoshi walked slowly, deliberately measuring each step, feeling the rocks beneath his boots. His timing was perfect. As he passed through the cemetery gate, he heard the bells from the thousand temples of Mount Hiei. They rang clearly in all their voices—some deep, some light—across the rows of stone. Wisps of low clouds trailed through the ancient rock sculptures, graves of twenty generations of warriors, courtiers, and noblemen, each with its crest of nacreous snow.

Chikara was waiting.

One moment the road was clear, the next moment he had stepped lightly from behind a monument, barring Yoshi's way. Yoshi stopped. In a blur of motion, his blade was out and ready, held at a forty-five degree angle, point directed at Chikara's throat. The years of academy training had taken over. Yoshi's mind was clear as a mountain lake, its surface waiting to react to movement. The man who barred the path was not his father; he was an opponent, nothing more.

Chikara's legs were comfortably bent, holding the ground firmly without unnecessary tension. He held both arms overhead, his sword pointing behind him ready to slice forward in either a body or head attack. Yoshi moved his foot, feeling for the ground with his toes. His opponent shifted weight slightly, then leaped forward with incredible energy in a double attack, body then head. Yoshi instinctively parried; his blade range with the power of the strokes. He was holding the haft of his sword, his left hand at the bottom pommel, right hand directly behind the *tsuba*, or guard. His fingers were tight, his arms relaxed, a slight sweat—cold and slippery—under his palms. Yoshi's sword whipped back to the ready position, again pointed at his opponent's throat. Summoning every ounce of speed and power at his command, he lunged in under Chikara's guard. This tactic had undone many opponents before; this time it was not even close. As though he could read Yoshi's mind, Chikara took a step to the left, avoided the lunge, and counterattacked with a cross-strike to the midsection. Yoshi felt the blade cut through his over-robe, missing flesh by hundredths of an inch. He twisted to the side, countering desperately. He thought his blade missed, for he felt no resistance. He was momentarily helpless; his stomach contracted in anticipation of the death blow which should have fallen. But Chikara had retreated a step, giving Yoshi a chance to recover—and there was a streak of red near the tip of Yoshi's sword. His uncontrolled defense had cut into Chikara's left hand, severing the ring and little fingers.

Within less than half a minute Yoshi had drawn first blood. Both men were breathing heavily from the strain. Chikara shifted his sword to his good hand and, alert to Yoshi's possible counterattack, wrapped a cloth around his wound, pulling it tight with his teeth. The wind whistled among the gravestones, freezing the sweat that formed on both men's foreheads.

Yoshi set his feet again, holding a strong defensive position. He made himself relax; the slightest tension in his shoulders could prove his undoing. Chikara drew his short sword with his wounded left hand. His face gave no hint of the pain he was undergoing.

Yoshi advanced; he struck with catlike precision, downward, crosswise, crosswise, downward. A blindingly fast series of strikes, each blocked by Chikara's swords. The cloth around Chikara's hand was saturated with blood; every time he used his short sword to parry, a mist of blood was released by the impact. The spray froze instantly in the frigid air and settled around the fighters like fine red snow glistening in the light of the quarter moon. The two men circled cautiously, searching for an opening. Yoshi had never before met anyone with Chikara's speed of reflex. The older man blocked Yoshi's finest techniques—and this with a badly wounded hand!

Yoshi was having difficulty swallowing; his mouth was filled with cotton wool. Icy air rasped into his lungs, making him short of breath. For the first time, his concentration faltered as he realized he might have met his master. Then, he forgot his nervousness as Chikara charged. Yoshi gave ground. Chikara could not be held in a close block because of the short sword in his left hand. Even though Chikara used a one-handed grip, Yoshi's blade quivered with the power of each stroke.

It was almost a stalemate, each offense negated by defensive parries, each counterattack avoided or blocked with split-second precision. As they battled over the icy field, the advantage of youth worked in Yoshi's favor. Chikara's assaults became less frequent, then slowed down and lost their power. The great difference in age was finally taking its toll. Chikara retreated, and Yoshi, smelling victory, pressed harder. Another step . . . and another. Suddenly, they were among the gravestones, and Chikara, who had cunningly planned every move, shifted between two gravestones, using their bulk to protect his sides and give him a momentary respite.

Yoshi drew back and lowered his sword to entice Chikara out of his sanctuary. The older man held fast; he was gasping for air, trying to regain his strength.

Yoshi felt the bite of the wind and knew this pause was to his disadvantage. Chikara rested in his haven while Yoshi's hands grew numb. Yoshi drew back and for a fraction of a second relaxed his vigilance.

With a blood-curdling war cry, Chikara leaped over the gravestone. Yoshi had the impression of giant bat wings blocking the moonlight—Chikara's robe blown wide by the wind—and the dull glint of steel. Then he reeled backward, his robe parted across his hip, and a thick pulse of blood stained the fabric in an expanding circle. He slipped to one knee. With a burst of demonic energy, Chikara reversed direction and drove forward with a classic head attack. The blade would have split Yoshi's head in two, but it didn't land. From the wet ground, Yoshi thrust upward into the midsection of . . . his father!

Chikara dropped his weapons and clutched at his middle. With a cry of grief, Yoshi scrambled to his aid. The older man collapsed into Yoshi's arms. Yoshi's hip could not support the additional weight and face-to-face, chest-to-chest, they sank to their knees. Chikara's blood spurted over his hands mixing with Yoshi's to make a spreading dark patch at their feet. The amount of blood and the location of the wound—Chikara's stomach was completely exposed—made it obvious he was beyond hope.

Yoshi shifted Chikara to one side, straightened his legs, and eased him onto his back; he placed a hand behind his head. The old man's eyes were already glazing; he felt light, as though the weight and power that had driven him were leaving with his spirit. Yoshi looked down at the face of his enemy—his father—and was shocked to see the face of an old man.

"Buddha, what have I done?" Yoshi cried aloud.

The old man moaned in pain. Bubbles of blood formed on his lips. "Please," he begged. "Finish me . . . you have won. . . . Honor me with the final stroke." He motioned toward his throat with one bloody hand.

"I cannot," murmured Yoshi, looking away in horror.

"Devil! You must!" commanded the old man with a last burst of strength. "Has fate sent you to . . . cause me even this last indignity . . . ? What have I done, Amida Buddha forgive me, to deserve this . . . ?"

Yoshi felt his insides shrivel. He wanted desperately to say, "Father, forgive me. I am your son." Yet how could he? How could he cause greater pain and confusion for one whose life would be measured in minutes?

"Please," begged his father.

Yoshi put down the tired head, wiped the lips with his headband. Then, without allowing himself time to think, lifted his blade and with one lightning stroke cut through the spinal cord ending Chikara's pain forever.

"Evil blade . . . evil soul," he moaned. Yoshi was simultaneously nauseous and light-headed. The price of victory was too high. He pulled apart his robe and inspected his hip; blood seeped forth with every heartbeat. A strip from the robe helped stop the bleeding.

Yoshi's enemy, his father, was gone, dead at the hands of his own son. His father! Nami and the family—how would they react to him after what he had done? What had been the purpose of his life? Had it been evil? Why did Buddha bring people into this cycle to suffer such tortures and pain?

As he knelt in the red snow beside the corpse the almost closed eye of Tsukiyomi, the moon god, stared coldly down on him. Yoshi knew what he would do.

He removed his *obi* and placed his swords on the ground with ceremonial dignity, then he peeled back his cloak and robes, baring his torso to the north wind. He raised his short

sword to the heavens. "Amida Nyorai, who sheds the light of
his presence through the ten sections of the world, gather to
thy heaven one who calls upon thy name," he chanted, his
voice blending with the moan of the wind through the cemetery. "Grant me eternal peace. Forgive me for what I have
done," he concluded.

The silence seemed to fill with ghostly voices. Yoshi,
weakened by the loss of blood, his system in shock from the
encounter with Chikara, fell into a semihypnotic trance. A
single plangent note from the lowest scale of the *biwa* rang in
his ears. Though he was motionless, the earth reeled around
him. He became aware of a voice resonating in his skull; it
was filled with malevolence, hissing, spitting, and growling
curses. In some way beyond knowledge, Yoshi recognized
it. He had never known the man, but he knew the voice.
Higo! The *ronin* ghost banished to Yomi by the exorcist of
Okitsu.

Higo's ghost spewed forth a stream of invective. Yoshi
barely made out the words, such was the intensity of the
voice. "Bastard. You think . . . you are the better man?
You, a swordmaster? Swine! Filth! Soon you will be with me.
Then we will see how you fare. You murdered your own
father, as you murdered my master long ago. Whatever my
sins, at least I never committed patricide. I was an honorable
samurai yet you doomed me to ten thousand years in the
underworld. If I had to wait twice ten thousand I would wait
for you. Nothing will save you. Soon you will belong to
me!"

Yoshi tried to shut out the terrible sounds but the voice
continued undiminished, and another voice joined it: the
malicious, fawning tones of Kaneoki. "He killed his
father," whispered Kaneoki. "What more can you expect
from a bastard engraver?"

Yoshi had to stop the ghostly voices. His hand tightened on
the hilt of the killing sword and he pressed the point against
the bare flesh under his left ribs. His fingers were almost
nerveless, refusing to obey his commands. Now! he thought,
increasing the pressure and feeling the tip of the blade pierc-

ing his side. He was disoriented and his breathing became faster and more shallow with every passing moment. As the blood oozed from his wound, he grew weaker. The cold attacked the inside of his nose and seared his lungs. The echoes in his head grew louder and more confusing. Now he heard other voices and felt the presence of other shades swirling around him. Gradually the blur of shapes and sounds cleared and he saw them. There . . . Genkai. And there . . . Hanzo, Ichikawa, Ietaka! Tears squeezed from under his lids and his heart lifted. His friends had returned from the heavenly land. But would they help him after the events of this terrible night? Hadn't Higo and Kaneoki spoken for the spirit world? How could he blame his former friends if they turned against him? He had committed the most shameful crime of all.

Yoshi strained to drive the blade deeper into his side. His arm lacked the strength and his fingers merely slipped on the sword hilt.

But wait . . . what did he see? Whirling planets, stars, suns, and Tsukiyomi glaring down; and silhouetted against them was the figure of Genkai, hand clenched above his head, sprinkling rice at the ghosts of Higo and Kaneoki, damning them and driving their souls back to the underworld. "Amida Nyorai, come to the aid of one who needs and deserves it," Genkai's shade intoned as Higo and Kaneoki faded into the darkest reaches of the night. The last Yoshi saw of them was the red scar on Kaneoki's forehead as he faded into nothingness.

They had come from the Western Paradise to help him, Genkai and Yoshi's other friends of the past. Genkai's shade swirled upward, his yellow robes temporarily breaking into facets of light, and in his place the bulky figure of Hanzo loomed. Hanzo, bullet head limned against the moon god's face, spoke in his gruffest tone: "Yoshi, you are a good boy despite what happened tonight on this bleak ice field. You have fought evil at every turn and you have never refused those who called on you for help. To me, you were a gift from the gods, a favored son of Buddha. Your blade and heart are pure, and I am still proud to call you son."

Behind Hanzo, Ichikawa nodded in understanding. The vision was so solid that Yoshi could hardly discern the stars shining through Ichikawa's body as he said, "*Seppuku* is not the answer. Tonight you fought bravely and well. Now, face life and learn to live without hate. To die now would be to surrender to the evil ones of Yomi. Deny them their satisfaction. Live!"

In Yoshi's delirious state he had almost forgotten his wounded hip. Now he was transported to another level of experience and the pain in his hip receded until it had completely disappeared; the voices around him grew stronger. Ichikawa melted backward, the apparent solidity of his patterned blue robe losing cohesion and separating into myriad pieces only to change color and reassemble in new form. This time as Ietaka. Ietaka was dressed in a burnt umber robe with tan geometric figures. He was saying, "Beloved cousin, you did what had to be done. Nobody can blame you. The ten provinces will be better because of you. The future of our country is more important than any one man's life."

"But he was my father," moaned Yoshi, trying to tighten his grip on the cold haft of his killing sword.

The ghosts glided between the gravestones—a shifting blend of yellow, blue, and brown—and chanted in unison, a chant that harmonized with the repeated note of the *biwa*. "You must carry on, Yoshi. Your life must continue. Atone to Nami and your mother for the pain you and your father caused." And over the other voices, came Genkai's words: "Amida Buddha bless you, Yoshi. What you did you did for us. We beg you . . . live! Forget the past. Look to tomorrow and let the gods be with you." The voices faded and disappeared.

Hours passed as Yoshi knelt on his robe, partially protected from the wind by his father's body. He was slumped forward with the short killing sword still in his icy palm. He drifted in and out of consciousness; inchoate images like wisps of night fog left faint traces on the sere landscape of his mind. The clear visions of the ghosts of the past had broken and diffracted into random shards of light and dark, but the advice the ghosts had given echoed and re-echoed in the vault of Yoshi's skull. "Face life. Face life. Face life. Forget the past. Forget . . . Carry on . . . on." Each time Yoshi sank into darkness he was brought back to the surface by the repeated admonitions to live. Yet life was too heavy a burden! It would be so much easier to surrender to the powers of the night . . . to avoid facing the shame and dishonor of what he had done.

Yoshi was more grievously wounded in mind than in body. His confused brain struggled to sift right from wrong. Hadn't Genkai blessed him? Hadn't Hanzo absolved him from evil? Hadn't Ichikawa and Ietaka assured him he had done no wrong? Then where was the point of honor or dishonor? Yoshi had vowed to avenge his friends' deaths. Vows taken on so many sad occasions, taken before he knew who Chikara really was. He had kept his vows, avenged injustice. And his father? Chikara had lived fully, a ruthless but honorable life. And he had died while still at the height of his physical powers. He would have chosen this way to die. Honor and duty to the last. A death in heroic battle.

The bells signaling the hour of the tiger rang bringing Yoshi gradually into longer periods of lucidity. He grew aware of the world around him: the slow fall of flakes that had started their earthward drift while he knelt in semi-oblivion. He stared at his father's corpse, already partly covered with white crystals, and was reminded of the blue white corpse of the commercial traveler whose robe had once given him a new start, and he knew he did not want to die as the traveler had died, stiff and cold on a lonely bed of ice.

An elemental force swelled upward from his abdomen, from the central core of *ki,* the life force that burned like a miniature sun two inches below the navel. His arms and legs tingled as adrenaline made his heart race and his blood circulate faster. He had to live to carry out the mandate of the spirit world, to atone for past sins. The path opened before him. The more difficult path: the path of life!

The blood coursing through his veins made Yoshi conscious of the cold that raised ridges of gooseflesh on his naked back; he shuddered and pulled the top of his robe across his shoulders, then wrapped the *obi* around his waist, sheathed the *seppuku* sword, and placed it with the long sword at his side. Now he reinspected his hip; the bleeding had stopped. The wound would not hinder him if he moved carefully. He rose to his feet and turned his head slowly, straining his eyes and ears in all directions; the ghosts were gone. The night was silent except for the whisper of the wind and the far-off creak of settling ice. Yoshi raised his face to Tsukiyomi, opened his mouth, and tasted the wetness of snowflakes on his lips and tongue. How many times had he raised his face heavenward, making vows to the gods—vows of hatred and vengeance? He saw things more clearly now. He was no longer blinded by the lust for revenge. He recognized that his father had been an honorable man within his limitations. Chikara had caused grief by his unswerving dedication to duty, but whatever his faults, he had died an honorable death and deserved an honorable burial. Yoshi—as his son—would see that he received it.

Yoshi brushed the accumulation of snow from Chikara's robe. He closed the staring eyes and covered the dead face. Then he sheathed Chikara's swords and placed them in his *obi* one over the other as befit a samurai.

Yoshi's mind had achieved the stillness of clear water. He had made the difficult choice and would no longer court death. His debts were paid. Yoshi shifted his own swords out of the way so he could lift his father's body, lighter than a feather, and together they started down the mountain.

In the east, Amaterasu stirred beneath the horizon and sent the palest streak of gold to tinge the edge of the world. A new day had begun.